HARD CHOICES

Blood Brothers #6

MANDA MELLETT

Published 2018 by Trish Haill Associates
Copyright © 2018 by Manda Mellett

Edited by Brian Tedesco
(www.pubsolvers.com)

Book and Cover Design by Lia Rees at Free Your Words
(www.freeyourwords.com)

www.mandamellett.com

Disclaimer

This is a work of fiction. Names, characters, businesses, places, events and incidents are either the products of the author's imagination or used in a fictitious manner. Any resemblance to actual persons, living or dead, or actual events is purely coincidental.

Warning

This book is dark in places and contains content of a sexual, abusive and violent nature. It is not suitable for persons under the age of 18.

ISBN: 978-1-912288-15-1

CONTENTS

CHAPTER 1
Aiza

Gritting my teeth as I eye the stairs, I already regret the promise I'd made to myself, that I'd start to exercise by walking up the four flights of stairs rather than be lazy and use the lift. As though to taunt me, the sound of the doors temptingly sliding open almost make me change my mind. Knowing that would do nothing to help me keep fit, I hoist my bag firmly over my shoulder and take the first step, and then the next, and continue methodically upwards, pleased that I'm only just breathing a little heavier than normal by the time I reach the fourth floor. Checking my pulse rate on my iWatch, I see it's hardly risen at all. *I'm not as out of shape as I thought.*

Wearily, I pause with my fingers gripping the handrail on the last step knowing the hard bit's behind me and smile. *I survived.* I glance along the corridor, where my flat is the third one along. Then freeze. My door is open and not locked shut as it had been when I left it this morning.

My heart beat speeds up, my brain taking only a split second to conclude that it would be madness to proceed further and investigate by myself. *Is there a burglar inside? Someone waiting for me?* I look sideways, seeing the indicators on the lift showing it's currently on the twelfth floor, far away from my level. Deciding discretion is the better option at this point, I turn and quietly start descending back down the stairwell, my pace increasing the lower I get. My eyes are open wide, scanning for any danger as I make my way to the ground floor, my panic only subsiding when I reach the lobby and exit, almost at a run, onto the busy street.

Knowing I may not yet be safe, I spy the coffee shop opposite my building. Quickly dodging the London traffic, I cross the road and slip inside, taking an empty table at the back and out of view of anyone who might be passing by on the pavement.

My phone is immediately in my hand, and while part of me is screaming that I don't want to place this call, I know I have no other choice, even though dialling just one number will end the months of anonymity I've been enjoying. I'll lose my freedom. With danger literally at my door, I'd be crazy if I didn't summon help. Some things can't be handled alone.

I'm not an ordinary citizen. Even if I did call the police like anyone else would to report a break-in if, hopefully, that's all it turns out to be, it would call up the same shit-storm, even if it was by a more circuitous route. Whatever I do will alert the authorities to my presence in the UK. I'd do better to take the bull by the horns, pull up my big girl pants, cut out the middle man, and place myself directly in the line of fire. *Damn. I thought I'd been clever.*

A waitress approaches. To avert any suspicion, I quickly plump for their special offer that's advertised in huge letters over the counter—a cup of coffee and a toasted teacake. While she disappears to get my order, I take a deep breath to prepare myself, summon up contacts, and dial. The phone rings twice before it's answered.

"Ben Carter."

"Aiza Kassis." I introduce myself quickly.

"That's why I answered so fast, Princess," an amused voice tells me. "I do have number recognition, you know."

"I need your help," I break in. This is no time for a general chit chat, as my quickened breathing and sweating palms remind me. "My flat's been broken into. Someone might still be there, Ben."

"Why not ring a local contact?" I hear the curiosity in his voice.

The time of reckoning approaching me with the speed of a runaway train, I inhale deeply again before admitting, "Because I'm in London."

Stunned silence. Then, "What the fuck, Aiza?" Ben's voice takes on a deeper, angry tone. But fast getting to business, he ignores, for now at least, that as far as everyone is concerned, I'm supposed to be safely ensconced in Switzerland living in a secure compound. "What's your location? Are you somewhere safe?"

I confirm, relatively speaking, I am. My education guided me to a crowded place and a position out of the direct line of sight. I offer up the name of the coffee shop and the address where I've been living. After I hear his muffled conversation, which sounds like he's got his hand over the mouthpiece, and I've got his attention again, I explain, "I got off work early. I saw my front door was open and decided to get out of there fast."

"Thank bloody goodness for small mercies," Ben snarls, then sounds like he is trying to control his temper as his voice is calmer when he resumes. "Stay right where you are. I'll have someone there as quickly as I can." His clipped tones sound exasperated, so I do the only thing I can and meekly agree. I might have enjoyed my independence, however, now trouble's quite literally come to my door, I'm not stupid enough to investigate or even show myself on the street.

My coffee arrives, and despite that I feel keyed up and my hands are still shaking, the hot toasted teacake looks surprisingly inviting. Checking around, reassured no one's taking any particular interest in me, believing I'm as safe as I can be, my stomach growls, suggesting it wouldn't be averse to some food. I'd worked through lunch, so I'm hungry. While hoping the meal for one I thought I'd be shoving into the microwave is still going to be in my not so distant future once my flat has been made secure, I slather both halves of the bun with butter—well, I'll work it off on the stairs later—and take a bite. It's as good as it looks and disappears fast. While I look in surprise at the few crumbs left on my plate, there's a squeal of brakes outside and blue flashing lights have a kaleidoscope effect as they shine through the coffee shop's windows. Peering around the other customers, I'm able to see a car door being flung open and a man in uniform stepping out.

The police officer wastes no time entering the café, phone in hand, studying something on the screen and looks from it to the faces of the bemused customers wearing expressions ranging from simply curious to almost guilty. He scans the shop until his eyes alight on me seated in the back. Pushing through the inquisitive, and now relieved throng, he makes an obvious beeline to me. The release of tension around me is almost palpable and the suspicious glares now being thrown my way make me want to slide under the table.

"Prin…"

"Aiza Kassis," I correct him before he can get my title out of his mouth. "Call me Aiza, please. I presume Ben Carter sent you?"

Belatedly realising how much interest he's drawing, he indicates the empty seat opposite. "May I?"

I shrug. "Be my guest."

He pulls out the chair and squeezes his large frame into it, his eyes wide. Well, I suppose it's not every day he comes face to face with royalty in a backstreet coffee shop in not the best part of town. Patiently I wait for him to begin to speak, which he does, leaning forwards conspiratorially and keeping his voice low.

"Grade A Security called us in to keep you safe until they can get here."

I can't help sniping. "I was hiding out of sight and hoping not to draw attention to myself."

His eyes widen further, and his brow creases. "Ah."

Ah, indeed. By approaching me so carelessly he might as well have painted a flashing arrow above my head. I sigh. Since arriving in England I've been successful in keeping under the radar. Now I have to accept I won't be able to hide any longer. It's not his fault, Ben Carter was only looking out for my safety. Grade A Security is based on the other side of the city, and it will take time for their operatives to get through the start of the rush hour traffic. By calling in the local boys in blue, Ben had made sure I had someone with me as soon as possible. Anyway, I reason, my game's already up. I've already given myself, and my location, away when I placed that call to Ben.

The waitress appears again, and the police officer declines any refreshment. While the coffee and cake were pleasant enough, I want nothing else, so simply ask for the bill. I pay in cash, adding in a decent enough tip. Having scooped up the money, she hovers, her face going from the policeman to me and then back again, then eventually realising we're not going to drop any juicy details in her hearing, steps away to deal with her other tables.

"Constable…?"

"Crowther," he supplies.

And that's the end of our conversation.

We sit in awkward silence until a motorbike draws up outside, parking illegally on yellow lines right in front of the police car. Although it won't get ticketed. Not today. I peer over the heads of the seated customers between me and the door, and watch with mixed feelings as the Grade A operative I have no problem recognising enters.

He comes straight over, nodding dismissively at the police officer, and addresses me directly without resorting to formality. "You alright?"

"I'm fine, Hunter. I turned tail and ran as soon as I saw something suspicious."

A sharp nod, then, "I can take it from here, Officer."

Constable Crowther stands. "You're expecting back up?"

Once again Hunter's head dips and rises. "Yeah. I came on the bike to get here quicker. My colleagues aren't far behind."

"We'll be going in first."

Hunter's face twists, he can't argue a crime has been committed, and while Grade A might be security specialists, they have no authority over the police. He gives in gracefully, but shows they're not going to be left out. "We'll be right behind."

The tall, tousle-haired man waits until we're alone, and then takes the seat Crowther had vacated. Unconsciously mimicking the action of the police officer moments earlier, he leans forwards over the table. There any similarity ends, as instead of being respectful and polite, he hisses, "What the fuck are you doing, Aiza?"

Immediately bristling, not feeling any necessity to explain myself to him, I shake my head and give him all he needs to know. "I've been working in the UK for the past few months. I took a flat in the building opposite. I finished up quicker than expected today, came home earlier than usual, and found my door wide open. I didn't wait to find out why."

"Working? What the fuck do you mean you're working?" Hunter glares at me. I answer him with a shrug. I know what he, and everyone who doesn't really know me, thinks of me. To them I'm just a spoiled princess, my life nothing more than living a pampered lifestyle, spending money from a huge allowance earned simply by being the younger sister of the emir of Amahad, a small but rich Arab state.

As I stare into the eyes of the undeniably attractive man sitting opposite me, I don't attempt to disavow him of his belief in the worthlessness of my existence. Refusing to justify myself, deigning not to explain how I spent all my hours not out partying as he probably expects, but instead studying, earning myself a degree in social sciences, and henceforth putting my energies into working for a charity that tries to bring much needed medical aid to children who need it to survive. Using my contacts and wealth not to entertain myself, but to link world-renowned surgeons with deserving cases who would die without their skills. A heart surgery here, a lung transplant there. My large allowance paying for air ambulances and, in many cases, hefty bribes—loosely called donations—to get around visa restrictions to get the child out of the country where they reside, then to the location where their treatment would take place.

As the fourth child of the late emir, and being a girl at that, I was of no immediate use to my country. Coupled with my sex, the fact that my birth caused the of death of my mother meant I'd been shipped off abroad to boarding school at the earliest age possible. Out of sight and mind. After an education in England, I was sent not to university, but to a prestigious finishing school in Switzerland. There, to learn how to be a lady and to become perfect wife material to eventually make a marriage which would, at last, prove my worth to Amahad. It hadn't been difficult to hide my rebellion over the years, as no one really cared what happened in that interim period before I would receive that expected call back home to do my duty. To become a bride purely to foster some diplomatic alliance. A future I'm determined to avoid.

My relationship with my older brothers is cordial, though awkward, with a lack of understanding on all our parts, a result of spending hardly any time in each other's company. The one positive being all three have ended up marrying English wives who've helped bring them into the twenty-first century. I've hopes I can enlist the English-women onto my side when the question of my future marriage does eventually arise.

Hunter stares at me, and I steadily meet his gaze, refusing to be intimidated. Our mutual contemplation allows me take in his all-American-boy appearance. Though he's lived in England since his teenage years, he still retains that clean-cut look. Sharp blue-green eyes in a rounded face, reddish-brown hair which keeps adorably flopping over his forehead, and impressive muscles in his arms flexing as he raises a hand to push it back; in all, he's wrapped in a good-looking package, making me wish we were meeting under different circumstances.

He's itching to question me further, the vibes I'm giving off informing him I'm not willing to talk. Before the silence becomes awkward, another vehicle draws up behind the police car and two men step out. Men I remember seeing around the palace when I've made my rare visits home to attend my brothers' marriages. As they enter the coffee shop, Hunter rises to his feet to greet them.

"Aiza, this is Ryan and Seth." Then without pause asks, "Which apartment is yours?"

I give a small smile. Even though Hunter's spent half his life in England, his American origins shine through in the accent he hasn't quite lost, and the American terms he hangs onto. "I live in Flat 403." I impart the information to Ryan, another tall, striking, muscular man. Not for the first time, I wonder if Grade A uses looks as part of their operatives' selection procedure. Seth, standing slightly behind, wouldn't score badly on an attraction register either.

As I go to stand, Hunter waves me back down. "Let the boys go over there first. We need to know what we're dealing with here."

"Um, excuse me, we're closing up now," the waitress manages to stammer out, even though her jaw has almost dropped to the floor. I don't blame her for her reaction. Hunter, Ryan, and Seth make quite a striking trio.

Hunter flashes her a grin filled with boyish charm. "Another five minutes, please, ma'am?"

Her face flushing, she looks like she needs to fan herself as she answers with a jerk of her head and slowly backs away and disappears out the back. I wouldn't be surprised if she's gone to find a fresh pair of underwear.

It's actually ten minutes before Seth and Ryan reappear and the police car takes off. Hunter pushes away from the counter where he's been leaning and raises an eyebrow. I stand. This is my business, and I want to know anything and everything they've found.

"Door was shut. Locked. Nothing inside looked disturbed," Ryan updates, his brow furrowed.

Quickly I fill in the blanks. If the door was no longer open, someone had to have closed it, and that means… "He was there when I went up."

"He, she, they. Yeah, Aiza. If you weren't mistaken about the door, that would be the conclusion I'd have to come to as well." Ryan's mouth turns down. I interpret his expression as sympathy.

"I wasn't mistaken," I confirm. "The door was definitely open when I got home." The knowledge my home's been invaded is chilling. I'm just relieved I had followed my instinct and not gone to investigate myself. *Someone would still have been there.* Then something else Ryan had said filters through, and my eyes narrow, remembering that having expected the door to be open, I hadn't handed over my keys. "How did *you* get in? Did you break the lock?" That would be one more thing for me to deal with.

"Skeleton key. It wasn't difficult. Your security is crap, Aiza."

Well, damn. I'm no locksmith, and a lock is a lock is a lock to me. I thought it was safe enough. I shrug off the implied criticism just as Hunter speaks.

"Princess, you better come over and check, see what's missing."

Yeah. I suppose I had. Though I don't want to see what state my home's in, and what has been taken—imagining it's hard enough. Despite Ryan saying it had looked undisturbed, someone had been in there for a reason.

Moments later, accompanied by the three men from Grade A, I'm in the lift. Soon I'm gingerly entering my flat with the sensation of being violated, knowing that a stranger had been here. I hadn't been imagining seeing that door open. However, as I walk in I can see why Ryan had questioned my memory. The place looks untouched. *I know* someone was definitely here. *Who were they? What did they want?* Nervous, I follow Hunter inside. With Seth' and Ryan at my rear, I go from room to room, mentally cataloguing the contents. It doesn't take long—why waste my money on rooms I have no use for when it could be used for a much more beneficial purpose?

The small lounge is untampered with, likewise the one bedroom. The small kitchenette and bathroom are just how I left them.

"Christ, Aiza. You live in a dump."

I bristle at Hunter's implied criticism and bite my tongue to stop myself pointlessly blurting out that though there's mould on the walls and the carpets are worn, I do keep it tidy and as clean as I can. He can see that for himself.

After inviting me to take a seat on my own couch, Hunter takes the chair opposite. He clasps his hands between his knees and looks at me with a serious expression. "You've not said anything. Is there anything missing?"

I shrug. As far as I can tell, no. "Nothing seems disturbed at all, Hunter. No one's rifled through my drawers or taken anything." My brow creases as I wonder what the hell whoever it was had been doing. If I'd come home at my usual time I wouldn't even have known anyone had been here. The thought is chilling.

Hunter's blue eyes gaze at me a little accusingly. "Think back carefully to when you left this morning. Are you one hundred percent certain you closed the door? Were you in any particular hurry? Late perhaps? Is it possible that you didn't shut it, and in the meantime one of your neighbours noticed and closed it for you?"

"I know how to lock up behind me," I snap, not even having to think. Even a princess trying to keep out of sight has basic security measures ingrained in her. "The door was locked when I left it." I can see the doubt in his eyes.

Seth and Ryan are continuing to look around. What for, I don't know. I suppose any sign that someone's been in here. When they don't come up with anything I start wondering whether they believe my story. While I wouldn't admit it to Hunter, I'm starting to question myself. *Did I forget to shut the door?* Bloody hell. *Have I exposed myself when there was no need?*

"Well, some good's come out of it at least. We know where you are now and can sort out proper protection." Hunter looks pleased at that pronouncement. It's the very opposite of my expression as he adds, "We'll be able to get you into decent accommodation. And of course, Kadar will be happy when we tell him we've got it all under control."

Kadar, my oldest brother and emir of Amahad, is likely to throw a fit that I'm not on the secure compound in Switzerland—and haven't been for the last six months. In his anger he'll probably call me straight home. I'm starting to formulate a plan of how I can avoid that scenario when Ryan suddenly exclaims and calls Hunter over to look at something. Turning, I see he's taken the air vent off the wall.

"What...?"

Moving fast for such a big man, Hunter's quickly by my side with one hand over my mouth and holding up the index finger of his other. "You must have been mistaken, Aiza," he says forcefully. "No one's been here." His eyes fixed on mine seem to implore me to go along with everything he says. There's no longer any judgement there. He looks worried instead.

"You're right, Hunter. I must have been careless."

Nodding his approval, he again speaks, his voice at odds with his expression. "It's been ages since we last got together, Aiza. Why don't I take you out for dinner?" We've never 'got together' in any shape or form, so he's not extending a friendly invitation. I take it that it's an instruction. When I eye the air vent and at the same time analyse his behaviour, I realise my flat's been bugged.

Nodding as comprehension dawns, ruefully I look down at my jeans and jumper I'd worn to work today. "I'll just go and change."

A dismissive shake of his head. "You're fine as you are, Aiza." He leans forwards so his lips are against my ear. To anyone else it would look like a lover's caress. "Just go with it, pet." Then he raises his voice. "Pack an overnight bag. You know where we'll end up. You'll be staying with me tonight, just like old times." Before I can protest he's intimating a relationship that never existed, his arms surround me, and he pulls me so quickly I stumble into his hold. I've no time to take evasive action as his lips crash onto mine.

15

Stunned, his action totally unexpected, I gasp. My mouth inadvertently opening gives him an advantage he doesn't miss, his tongue quickly gaining entrance.

I've known Hunter for years and am well aware of his reputation as a womaniser. My youngest brother, Nijad, hates him for flirting with Cara, his wife. Apart from admiring his good looks from afar—a woman would have to be dead not to appreciate those—I've never thought of taking any attraction further.

When his lips move over mine he incites reactions I don't expect. Boy, can this man kiss. His flavour mingling with the residual taste of coffee remaining in my mouth, his tongue toying so dominantly with mine, the intoxicating scent of whatever aftershave or soap he uses inflames me, sending signals straight to my core. Annoyed he's taken the upper hand, I lift my arm and place my hand around the back of his neck, roughly pulling him down to me, and attempt to take over the kiss.

Our mouths mate together, fight together. A duel that goes on and on, with neither coming out the victor.

What the fuck am I doing? I drop my hand and push him away. My eyes are glazed, my lungs heave as I stare vacantly up at him, bemused.

He's smirks then leans down and murmurs, into my ear, "Convincing, pet. Very convincing."

CHAPTER 2
Rami

This is far from my first visit to the Palace of Amahad in the country's capital, Al Qur'ah, although it is the first time I've been sat around the boardroom table with Emir Kadar and his two brothers, officially representing Alair, my country. We're in discussion about how to celebrate the first barrels of oil which have successfully been extracted from the oil field that lies underneath the three countries of Amahad, Alair and Ezirad, the latter our joint landlocked neighbour to the south. For once it's a joyful meeting, congratulatory slaps on the back all around, even if none of us, personally, got our hands dirty digging in the ground.

The pipeline, constructed at great expense, crosses Amahad and goes to the port just outside Al Qur'ah. Knowing it was uneconomical to carry oil over our country, my father, King Asad, agreed to terms by which we would provide funds for the venture in return for our share of the profits. Ezirad, completely landlocked, was a willing partner as well. Thus, we've coming together to form a joint project between our countries.

Over the past two years a variety of terrorist attacks have tried to prevent the oil field development and, more recently, to cause damage to the pipeline. Cleverly Amahad had persuaded their desert tribes to invest heavily in the scheme, with the result that they're tied into protecting their venture, providing fierce manpower in the process. It was a stroke of genius on the part of the country whose palace I'm now sitting in.

Alair has always maintained a friendly relationship with Amahad, and Ezirad is hanging onto the coattails of our more advanced economies and socially developed countries, hoping to reap the benefit and become more akin to its richer neighbours. Tellingly, the representative of Ezirad, Sultan Qudamah, is reserved and quiet in the exalted company he finds himself in today.

Also quiet is Sheikh Rais, leader of the desert sheikhs, and a man who looks like he could protect the pipeline all by himself. Like the other nine desert sheikhs, he's perfected a fierce countenance that shields his thoughts and emotions and, unlike the rest of us, currently he's not giving the slightest hint of a smile or wearing any other suggestion of pleasure on his face. That he, too, must be over the moon with the success of the oil travelling from the extraction point to port is unquestionable. Looking across the table I decide it would be wise never to chance a game of poker with him.

My eyes flick to Nijad, Emir Kadar's youngest brother, and then to the Jasim, only eighteen months older. They're both raising glasses of fruit juice in celebration. I smirk behind my hand, expecting they'll be commemorating with something stronger when they return to their private quarters after this official meeting. As indeed I will be doing myself. Although our countries are technically dry, having been educated in the West, it was difficult for us not to pick up certain habits.

The agenda completed, Kadar bangs on the table for quiet. "Thank you, Prince, sheikhs, gentlemen, for attending today. Please, stay, talk, and partake of the hospitality. If you will excuse myself and my brothers, we have another meeting to attend." He pushes back from the table and stands. If I hadn't been watching them I might have missed the bemused glances that flick over his brothers faces momentarily before they also get to their feet to follow the emir out of the room.

To my astonishment, as he passes me he places his hand on my shoulder. "Prince Rami, if you will be so kind?" Then, before I have a chance to reply, he nods over to Rais. "And you, too, Sheikh Rais?"

An invitation from the powerful emir cannot be refused. Neither of us waste time following the Kassis brothers out through the door, leaving behind the clinking of glasses, and, for once, conversations voicing satisfaction.

A short walk down the corridor has us entering Kadar's office, a pleasant room, one end dominated by a large and antique desk, the other by a conference table. Floor to ceiling windows look out onto a colourful garden. After waving us to take seats, Kadar stands for a moment with his back to us, gazing out onto the view. Even with his back turned towards us he looks stiff and tense.

"I received an email during the meeting," he starts without turning, taking out his phone and glancing at the screen. No one interrupts his train of thought as he's clearly rereading something. After a moment he swings around, his robes billowing with the sudden movement.

"Aiza." The one word, managing to carry both concern and resignation, has me sitting up straight.

"What's she done now?" Jasim sounds weary. "And why was it so important to pull us away? Couldn't it have waited? I wanted to speak to Qudamah's representative."

Nijad nods at his brother. "I too. It would have been useful to see how he's proposing to strengthen the borders."

A subject that interests me too. Jihadists and terrorists have often found it all too easy to use the underdeveloped Ezirad to cross over into the southern boundaries of both our countries.

"As long as he doesn't bring up the suggestion of building a wall again," Rais sneers, raising a smile on my face and causing short laughs from the others. I've always hoped that suggestion was made in jest, the impracticalities of building a solid construction across hundreds of miles of uninhabitable desert, and some of it mountainous, was surely not a serious one. Not that it would have stopped anyone anyway, walls can be climbed or flown over. Where there's a will, there's a way.

Kadar waves his hand dismissively. "I'm afraid this takes precedence, brothers." Nodding at myself and Rais, he includes us in that familial definition. No one speaks as the emir takes a seat at the head of the table. We wait, hoping for him to enlighten us without further prompting. I'd like to get back to the celebration myself. Not that I'd want to miss hearing the latest about Aiza. I frown slightly, wondering whether the information which I believed only myself was party to is going to become general knowledge.

The emir's eyes flick to the phone that's still in his hand, and he shakes his head as though he can't quite believe what he's reading. Then, after taking a breath, he starts. "Someone broke into Aiza's flat."

"What?" Nijad exclaims. "The Swiss compound is fully protected. Security is top notch."

Kadar throws a stern look at his brother and gestures with his hand. "Let me finish." His authoritative voice thunders, and a look of rage crosses his face. "She isn't in fucking Switzerland. She's in England, and has been for the last six months."

Jasim's face drops and he leans forwards. "What. The. Fuck? How come no one reported her missing?"

Kadar's head's still moving side to side in disbelief. "Because no one noticed she was. She apparently always kept to herself. It wasn't unusual for her not to be seen around the campus, so no one thought anything of it."

Nijad's head moves back and forth as though mimicking his older brother's actions. "Hang on, she's a party girl…"

"If you'll let me finish?" When Nijad nods and Jasim sits back again, Kadar continues. "Seems she's not been doing anything we expected. She's been studying with the British Open University for the past three years. Head down, working all hours, and managed to get herself a first-class honours degree. With that, she's been doing charity work."

As his brothers exchange surprised looks, I smile to myself. *Good on you, Aiza.* I'm not surprised no one knew. Probably in her view, if her brothers didn't give a damn enough to ask what she was doing, she didn't think it was up to her to let them know. Then again, I frown. *I had no idea she'd gone to England. Reckless, foolish girl.*

Rais is the only one whose face remains expressionless. "Tell us the rest, Kadar. You haven't called us here to update us on Aiza's education and employment."

Kadar's eyes swing to meet those of the desert sheikh's. "You're right, Rais, I haven't. You all seem to have forgotten that I've already told you, her flat was broken into."

The reminder pulls us all up short. "Robbery?" Nijad suggests.

"Nothing was taken. Rather, things were left." He waits until he knows he's got all our attention. "Bugs. Girl was at least smart enough to call Ben Carter when she noticed someone was in there. He got some Grade A operatives around as soon as he could, and they found the stuff that had been planted."

"Which Grade A operatives?" Nijad growls.

Kadar doesn't even have to consult the email. "Hunter," he says succinctly.

Nijad growls and Jasim laughs, earning him a punch on his arm from his younger brother.

"Ryan and Seth," Kadar adds belatedly, ignoring their reaction.

"Who placed the equipment? And why?" Rais gets directly to what I agree is the most important point.

Kadar raises his shoulders. "They don't know. There's no clue. Russian-made kit, but that could mean anything."

"She's got to come home." Nijad sums up exactly what I was thinking. Someone like Aiza is at risk of kidnapping and being held hostage every minute of her life. A very good reason why she should be on a secure compound. If she's baulked at security, moved without anyone knowing and seems to have no idea about keeping herself safe, well, I agree with her brother. She needs to be somewhere where her protection can be guaranteed. Here in Amahad, or…

Her brothers clearly regard her as a nuisance. To my mind, it seems it's excellent timing for me to step things up. Aiza's a beautiful woman I certainly wouldn't object to having in my bed, and her personality would complement mine. Clearing my throat, I look straight at Kadar. "I'd like to remind you, Kadar, your father, the late Emir Rushdi, proposed a union by marriage…"

"No." Nijad interrupts me, slashing his hand through the air. "Our father's dead, and so are the old ways. Arranged marriages are in the past for this family."

Kadar cocks his eyebrow at his younger brother. "Really? And yours turned out so badly, did it?" He pauses, waiting for Nijad to deny his marriage was the best thing that ever happened to him. Which he can't possibly do. When no refute comes, he carries on. "And my own marriage was arranged. As," he breaks off to point at Jasim, "was yours, Brother. You hadn't really a choice when you wanted to save the English woman."

Nijad and Jasim look at each other, twin expressions of dismay on their faces. Unexpectedly, it's Rais who's next to speak. "Your fate, Emir, could have been very different. Don't forget, I saw the devastation on your woman's face when she thought you were destined to marry another, and it was I who used my influence with the desert sheikhs to prevent that from happening. That you and your brothers have ended up happy is due to chance, not design. And certainly not process. Even in the desert we've moved on from your father's time. I agree, Aiza shouldn't be pushed into anything she doesn't want."

I shift in my seat, sending him a sharp look. Now I've settled on the notion I don't like anyone challenging it. "Who say's Aiza wouldn't want it? What's to say Aiza and I wouldn't have a happy marriage? We've both been brought up to accept it was always on the cards. I'm willing to do my best to make it work." I certainly wouldn't look on it as a chore. Aiza's just, well... I've never seen another woman I wanted more, and always thinking one day she'd be mine for the taking, I've been looking forward to it.

Kadar clears his throat and throws me a look that manages to appear both sympathetic and awkward. "The thing is, Rami, Rais is correct. Circumstances have changed since my father put forward the original proposal." He coughs as he clears his throat.

Now it's my turn to interrupt. He won't be telling me anything I don't already know, and it certainly doesn't matter to me. I chuckle slightly, realising he thinks I've made my offer in ignorance. "It doesn't matter to me, Kadar, I assure you. I'm very well aware she wouldn't be a virgin bride."

Several things happen immediately when the words are out of my mouth. Nijad and Jasim cover their mouths in shock, Kadar jumps to his feet, knocking his chair over in the process, and Rais leaps across the table and proves the scimitar in his belt is not ornamental as he presses it into my neck.

"Rais!" Kadar shouts to prevent blood being shed, for which I'm heartedly grateful. While Rais doesn't push the blade in any further, he doesn't withdraw it either. Kadar looms over me, spit flying from his mouth as he roars, "Seems you've pre-empted the wedding. Which, of course, must now go ahead."

"Or I kill him instead." Rais's softly spoken words are worse than Kadar's bark.

I go to shake my head, then remember the threat of death, which I'm quite certain at this point Rais wants to deliver. Thinking rapidly, I realise that while leaving them to assume I've personal knowledge of Aiza's, in their eyes, tainted state, might push me into a marriage I wouldn't be averse to, it could alternatively end up with me returning to my country in a coffin. Grasping letting them know the truth might be best course of action, I swallow rapidly, then, in a voice an octave higher than normal, squeak out, "I assure you, I've not touched her myself. I've seen her playing in clubs around Europe." As silence falls I can't help making it worse. "And once in the States."

"*Clubs?*"

I hadn't known it was possible for Kadar's voice to get any louder. As Jasim sniggers, Kadar rounds on him. "What the fuck do you know about this?"

Nijad puts his hand on his brother's arm, as though for moral support, and answers on his behalf, kicking off with one of his customary shrugs. "I've known she's been playing in BDSM clubs for a while. I told Jasim…"

"And you didn't think to inform *me?*" Kadar retakes his seat and puts his head into his hands. Begrudgingly, Rais withdraws his scimitar and retakes his seat while we all give the emir some space to re-evaluate his thoughts about his young sister. After a while he wipes his hands across his face, then looks up. "Well, there's no doubt about it. She's got to come home now. *And* we need to find someone to take her off our hands pretty damn quick."

"You're old fashioned, Kadar. This is the twenty-first century. I know it's hard for Amahad to accept, but Aiza's not going to sit back and wait to be traded for a herd of camels," Nijad scorns.

Jasim's staring at his brother open-mouthed. "We're not going to force any marriage on Aiza, camels or no camels."

"My father's got a good stable," I drop in now the threat of imminent death has been removed. I can't hold back a grin. If Kadar wants someone to take her on, I'm more than willing. Unwittingly, Aiza's played right into my hands. It's the thoughts of my hands on her that has me adjusting myself under the table.

There's a growl from the man opposite, and after a quick glare in my direction, Rais turns to Kadar. "I agree with you, Kadar. Aiza's been enjoying too much freedom for a woman her age."

Jasim's hand bangs down on the table. "Aiza needs to come home so we can protect her. But I refuse to accept that protection means curtailing her freedom or coercing her into a marriage she doesn't want. She's twenty-four years old, a woman, a *person* in her own right, and should be able to make her own choices. Don't forget it was for this very reason I myself stayed away from Amahad and was reluctant to return home. The country still has archaic views on such matters. I won't allow you to use ancient laws against my sister. She will not be forced into a marriage she doesn't want if I have anything to do with it." His eyes catch mine. "Even with you, Prince Rami. No offence."

I raise my chin to show none has been taken. I don't want her to be forced either. I'm sure enough of myself and what I can offer, to think that she'd come to me willingly. There had been signs our attraction had been mutual.

Kadar seems to have aged in the last few minutes. He studies Jasim, then slowly nods his head, his hands rising in a gesture of defeat before pronouncing, "Aiza comes home and stays until we can analyse any threat against her and negate it. As a member of the royal family she's in the public eye, her every action examined and discussed. Any free-living lifestyle she's taken advantage of while abroad will be denied to her here. Prince, I will discuss your proposed marriage with her, nevertheless I will take her views into account. If she refuses yourself, or any suitable partner that I put forwards, then once it is safe she can resume her activities in the country of her choice. If she does, she will have bodyguards at all times. Fuck knows how she managed to get away without protection for so long." He turns his tired eyes towards me. "Prince, Aiza is headstrong, and if she accepts your proposal I can't vouch that you will have the subservient wife that perhaps you were looking forward to."

I nod, letting him know I was serious about my offer. I don't say it, but I wasn't joking. My father *has* got an excellent stable of camels, and I reckon I know quite a bit about headstrong females.

CHAPTER 3
Aiza

Hunter's kiss had been something else, unexpected and rendering me nigh on speechless. Unnerved, I ignore his comment and offer no protest as I obediently trot off into my bedroom and start throwing clothes into a small bag. It isn't until I open my underwear drawer and begin choosing which pants and bra combination I'm going to take that I pause with my hand in mid-air. *What the fuck am I doing?* Hunter told me to go pack, and I just obeyed him. Without any discussion or argument. Okay, so I couldn't very well talk back without the risk of being overheard, though I could have pulled him outside and told him exactly where he should put his overbearing attitude and demands.

Then the memory of why I couldn't speak openly to him hits me with full force. Rather than worrying about Hunter's audaciousness, I should be more concerned that someone's gone to the bother of placing bugs in my flat. The thought sends a shiver down my spine and spurs me to get moving again. I have no idea where Hunter's planning to take me. But I don't want to stay here. I'm not stupid. Being who I am means I'm at risk of being abducted and used against my country. I'm a princess of Amahad, and while that personally does me no favours, only curtailing my freedom to live as I wish, I bear the country no ill will, as it provides me with funds to do with what I want. For Amahad's sake and my brothers' sanity, I really have no option other than to throw in my lot with Hunter and trust he, and his colleagues from Grade A, can get me out of the predicament I find myself in.

Who would want to listen in on me? I'm boring, not interesting. I have no state secrets to give away. I barely know my family or what goes on in my country.

That question unanswerable, my mind turns to the next and more immediate one. *Why did Hunter kiss me?* Was it just an act for whoever is listening and watching? Or was it something he wanted to do and seized the opportunity? If the latter, how does that make me feel? The stickiness between my legs reminds me I wasn't entirely unaffected. Hunter's an undeniably good kisser, and a fine looking and fit specimen of a man. No doubt about that. *Would I turn down a chance to know him better?*

Before I can summon up an answer, the man invading my thoughts appears at the door, nodding towards my half-packed bag. He jerks his head to show he's getting impatient. Under his scrutiny I toss the last few items in and then look around to see if I've missed anything. *My phone charger.* I go to unplug it and slide it in with the rest of the contents. *My e-reader and tablet.* I take those too. Hunter comes over and takes my bag, zipping it up with a grin and a shake of his head preventing me putting anything else in. The look on his face suggests he was expecting me to pack the kitchen sink next.

"An overnight bag," he stresses, something innocuous for any listening ears.

Certain I've left something vital behind, I follow him out. Seth and Ryan are waiting in the corridor as Hunter shuts the door behind me, another shake of his head when his eyes fall on what has proved to be an inadequate lock.

I don't protest the lift, simply get in alongside the men, feeling cramped and claustrophobic being surrounded by three tall, masculine bodies which take up all the space, glad to get away from my flat, which had felt so safe, but now so violated. *Who'd want to spy on me? And why?* The notion that someone's been listening and watching me in my private space is alarming.

Outside, Hunter leads me to the SUV Ryan and Seth had arrived in, then my eyes fall on his bike, a Ducati if I'm not mistaken. The slick Italian machine looking fast and mean. "Can I go with you?" I'd ridden with my brother, Nijad, before when I'd visited him in Paris many years ago now, and had always loved the feel of the wind in my face and freedom of the road passing underneath. The chance to blow the cobwebs away with the edge of excitement is oh so tempting. I bite my lip, hoping Hunter will agree.

He gives me an amused smile. "You want to ride on the back of my bike?"

"Why not?"

"You'll be too exposed." Ryan steps up, using a tone that brooks no argument. "Safer to come with us." He cocks his head at Hunter, who seemed to be considering it.

I know I'm pouting, believing they're being over cautious, but after a silent conversation over my head it's clear I'm not going to get my way. With a heartfelt sigh, I obediently step alongside Ryan and get into the back seat without further objection when he opens the door. Ryan goes back to talk to Seth and Hunter, presumably to agree where they're taking me now we're out of range of the bugs. Unfortunately, they're out of ear shot. When at last they return, Seth gets into the front passenger seat and Ryan starts the engine.

There's silence in the car as we drive away. Finding the quiet unnerving, I break it by asking, "Where are we going then?"

The men in the front exchange glances. "To a hotel," Ryan informs me.

"Which one?" I start to ask.

Ryan deliberately catches my eyes in the rearview mirror. As he gives a violent shake of his head, I interpret what he's telling me, and then it falls into place. *They think I could be bugged.*

Now I understand the need to stay mute. I keep my mouth shut as Ryan drives through the streets, looking around at people going about their business as though they haven't a care in the world. While I'm being targeted. The question is, by whom, and why?

That's when the revelation hits me, making me shudder. *If I hadn't come home early and seen the door open, I'd never have found out someone was watching and listening to my every move.* It's a sobering thought. I've already discounted they were after information, as I've got none to give away. The only thing of value is my body. The sole conclusion I can come up with is that this was a prelude to kidnapping me. How close I'd come to remaining ignorant about the unknown person or persons' preparation scares me. *I'd been careless, thinking I had no enemies.* Of course I have. However much I try to forget it, I am a princess.

Having battled through the traffic at the very worst time of day to be driving through London, we at last draw up outside a modern hotel, all glass and chrome in the renovated docklands area. It must be near to the head office of Grade A Security which I know is around here somewhere. It makes sense they brought me somewhere close by.

Hunter has predictably arrived before us, the bike managing the evening rush hour easier than the car. I no longer need the finger he's holding to his lips to keep my mouth shut as the men surround me, and once again I'm in a lift, this time heading up to one of the top floors. Watching the numbers of the floors increase as we pass, pointlessly I think to myself. *If I'm staying here long I don't think I'll be attempting those stairs.*

Hunter opens the door to a room which must be the penthouse suite, and after a look up and down the corridor, ushers me quickly inside where I find another man already there and waiting. I haven't met him before, but as he approaches holding out his hand for my carry-on bag, I find I'm giving it to him automatically. My handbag I hand over a little more reluctantly.

As the unidentified man passes some sort of wand over my possessions, an audible bleeping sounds, which for a moment I don't know is good or bad. I glance at Hunter, his face impassive. Then I frown and want to protest as he starts taking out my carefully packed clothing. Soon there's a pile of everything I'd brought with me on the floor. I blush as he passes the wand over everything, including my flimsy underwear.

The wand stays silent until it produces another bleep when he scans the bag's lining. Nodding in satisfaction, he puts the bag to one side. My eyes widen as he places my tablet next to it. Then he turns to my handbag and empties the contents out next to my clothes on the carpet. My cheeks redden once more as loose tampons fall out of the pocket. However, a glance at the men show their faces are focused on their job, seemingly disinterested in what I carry around in my bag. *They're professionals. They've seen sanitary products before.* Even so, the inspection of my personal possessions seems overly intrusive.

My handbag and purse, having provoked the handheld machine into life, join my other bag and tablet. Hunter takes the carrier bag, which the stranger had thoughtfully come prepared with, and starts to scoop up the scattered contents, which seem to have passed their test. The pile thankfully including my phone which the man had examined very carefully. Embarrassed, I fall to my knees and push him aside, collecting up everything myself. Him touching my tampons seems far too personal.

Now the man is waving his wand over me. It bleeps. He indicates I should remove my jacket, which I do. That, thankfully, is the only offending object. For a moment I'd worried I was going to have to strip down in front of them.

With a satisfied grin and a lift of his chin towards Hunter, at last the unknown man gathers up everything that's made the machine leap into action and takes it out of the door. I stand stunned, looking at Hunter, then Ryan, then Seth, not knowing what I'm supposed to do next.

Hunter moves in front of me. His hands rest on my arms, and his intense eyes stare down into mine. "You okay?" He breaks the eerie silence at last.

"I don't know," I answer quickly and truthfully. "They've been watching, listening to me for a while now, haven't they?" They couldn't have planted everything today—I'd been wearing my jacket and my bag had been over my shoulder. Once again I shiver, wondering how long someone's been eavesdropping, and how much they now know about me. Hunter moves closer, his arms wrapping around me, pulling me into him. I'm a strong woman and don't normally rely on the strength of a man to hold me up, but right now I need the physical contact, and tonight welcome the comfort he's giving me. "What happens next?" I mumble into his chest.

"We meet with Ben Carter. Try and get some answers."

"With the bugs removed, they'll know I've found out about them."

Hunter chuckles. It's an ominous sound, and one that makes me immediately suspicious when he says innocently, "Mason, the tech who was just here, he'll sort it out." His tone doesn't give the reassurance it should have done.

My eyes narrow as I glance up. "What do you mean?"

Now he gives a deep laugh, this one full of amusement. "You really want to know, darling?" At my nod, he continues, the sides of his mouth turning up. "Right now they're listening to a sex tape. They'll think it's you and me."

I raise my hand and put my fist to his arm. "Hunter! How could you?" I'd thought it was impossible to feel more embarrassed than the tampon incident. It appears I was wrong.

He's unrepentant. "Easiest way to buy us some time and decide what to do." He pulls away from me and rummages in a bag that I hadn't noticed before, and that the strange Mason must have left. He returns with a sweatshirt, which he hands over. It's about five sizes too big. Hunter shrugs apologetically. "You haven't got a jacket, and it's cold out there. Mason must have grabbed some of his own stuff, sorry. We didn't have much time to get anything organised."

I take the offered item, pulling it on over my head, having difficulty finding the arm holes in the ocean of material. As I do, I realise I was probably lucky I hadn't had to take all my clothes off, suspecting I'd have ended up wearing a pair of Mason's boxers if I had.

Dressed in the sweatshirt that reaches almost to my knees, I leave the swanky hotel and get into the car with Ryan and Seth for the short journey to the main offices of Grade A Security. We park in the underground garage alongside Hunter's bike, then take the lift to the third floor.

As I follow in Hunter's wake it dawns on me that since discovering my open door all I've done is exactly what I've been told, without question or protest. It's not like me at all. Normally I'm the one in the driving seat. As I enter a conference room and eye the men already seated around the table, I decide to start speaking up for myself, taking back the control that, for me, is as necessary as breathing.

Discarding my oversized coverup, I smooth down my long hair and pull back my shoulders. As I walk to a vacant chair I give a nod worthy of that of my oldest brother to the men and the woman around the table. Ben rises and comes over, pulling out the seat for me. As one, all the men stand, only sitting back down when I do so myself.

After giving me a moment to get settled, Ben begins. "Welcome to Grade A Security, Princess. I think you know most of the people here?"

Finding my title unfamiliar—I haven't used it in months—for a moment I'm put off my stride. Then, pulling myself together, I glance around again, this time taking note of those assembled, and jerk my chin in agreement as I put names to faces. There's Jon Tharpe, who, along with Ben and the elusive Jason Deville, own the company. Jon spent years as my youngest brother, Nijad's, bodyguard until they had a falling out. Next to him there's Ryan, then Seth, then Harry, who'd taken over from Jon for a while when Jon had refused to work with Nijad anymore. I quirk my brow at the woman who I can't identify, and she introduces herself.

"Nafisa," she says, giving a little wave. "I've taken over from Vanessa." Ah yes, Nessa, who's now the wife of Sean, another Grade A operative, who is off doing some secretive work with Jason Deville. I seem to remember hearing that Nessa is pregnant, although now's not the time for idle chit-chat to catch up.

There's a knock on the door, and the tech who I'd last seen taking my stuff away appears. Remembering the sex tape Hunter said they'd been playing, half thinking, hoping, it had been a joke, before anyone else can talk I speak up. "What am I doing now, Mason?"

He smirks. "Resting quietly. From what they heard, you need it."

Chuckles go around the table. *Hunter hadn't been joking.* I feel my cheeks flush.

"Which brings us to the first question." Ben gives me a sharp look and takes over. "Do we let them know we're on to them, or keep up the pretence?"

"I've been thinking about that," Jon answers him. "We've already agreed we need to get the princess out of the country, and any misdirection we can offer will help. I propose we keep feeding them false info until she's safely away. That way they, whoever they are, won't be on the lookout for her at airports." My eyes widen. Just how much appetite for sex does he think I have? Surely they won't play that tape over and over.

"Kadar's sending the family jet." Nafisa's voice gets my attention to her. She's consulting her tablet. "It will be ready to leave Heathrow tomorrow morning. She only needs cover for tonight."

"*She's* sitting right here," I snap. Hating they're talking about me, not to me, and making plans without any consultation. "I don't want to go back to Amahad. My work's too important here. I can't leave." The last place I want to return to is my homeland. I shake my head. "You'll have to come up with something else."

"Work remotely." Ben has no sympathy as he addresses me directly. "I shouldn't have to spell out, Princess, that you've put yourself in danger by entering the UK alone, let alone taking an unsecured residence." His eyes examine me accusingly. "I almost hate to ask… How did you get to and from work? You had no driver assigned to you."

I raise and lower my shoulders and admit, "Using public transport, of course." I came to escape, to live as a normal person.

There's a collective groan around the table. "Fuck it, Princess." Hunter looks apoplectic, his face a dark shade of red. "Have you no fucking brains in your head?"

That makes me bristle. "I've been careful to keep off the grid." I shoot him a glance, showing I'm not happy with his criticism.

Hunter just shakes his head and casts a weary look towards Ben. "Not careful enough, obviously."

Given the events of today, I suppose I can't argue with him. Instead, I ask a question of my own. "Why am I being targeted? And by whom? Have you found out anything yet?" Know thy enemy. That's what they say, isn't it? It's my view there's no point discussing what's gone on in the past, it's how to move forwards that's more important.

"And that's the six-million-dollar question." Ben's nodding. He passes his hands over his cheeks as he pulls his thoughts together. "Let's see where we're up to. Amahad has recently been in the headlines, as the first oil has been extracted and pushed through the pipeline. Once it starts flowing, Amahad and the neighbouring countries are going to reap dividends, and the West gets more fuel for consumption. That's something Amir al-Farhi worked hard to prevent. We can't rule out the international terrorist being at the bottom of this."

"Or it could be someone wanting to kidnap you for ransom," Jon puts in. "Anything's only conjecture at this stage."

"My money's on al-Fahri," Ben almost rebukes his partner. "That's the worst threat. Once he's got his sights on something, he doesn't give up."

Both proposals put forward come down to one thing. Kidnap. I shudder, imagining myself in the hands of unknown men, in their power, my life or death under their control.

I run through my options. Obviously I have to do what I can to avoid being taken for whatever reason and by whom. I can't make it easy for any would-be kidnapper. On the other hand, neither do I want to deliver myself into the hands of my autocratic brother. A man and family I barely know. Thinking fast, I tap my fingers on the table top. "Why can't you protect me in England?" The last thing I want to do is to go home. "I could drop out of sight, work remotely as you suggest, Ben. Or we could find some way to make whoever it is show their hand. Surely that's better than not knowing?" If we don't know the direction the threat's coming from, who knows how long I'll be in Amahad. *I might never get away.*

"Kadar would never agree to you being used as bait, Princess. Wherever we try to hide you, if you're working, your IP address can be traced."

Not if I speak to Cara, Nijad's wife. She's an expert at that sort of thing. "There will be ways around that. Bounce the signal around…"

"Princess," Ben drawls. "You don't have a choice in this. Kadar has tasked me with getting you home, and that's what I'm going to do. You can speak to him while you're there about making other arrangements. Tomorrow morning you *will* be getting on that plane."

My temper flares and I push back my chair. "In that case, Ben, there's no point in this sham of a meeting. Your minds are already made up. This is no discussion, you've told me what I'm supposed to do." The sooner I can leave here, the sooner I can think of an alternative myself.

Jon rises opposite me. "Please sit back down, Princess. We need to try to figure out who we're up against, and for that we need your help."

My outburst stops at that. If they can identify who it is and negate the threat, I'll be able to get back to my life. If we can do that tonight, maybe I won't be getting on that plane in the morning. Briefly I close my eyes and take a deep breath. "What do you need from me?" As instructed, I sit.

Hunter leans forwards. "Have you seen anyone following you? Has anything happened that's made you concerned?" He ruffles his hands through his hair, pushing back the lock that's fallen over his forehead. "Tell us anything at all, however insignificant you thought it at the time. It might help."

I cast my mind back over the past few weeks. "There's been nothing, Hunter. Nothing to raise my suspicions." Okay, flirtatious looks on the tube, I'm used to those. And the underground trains are usually so crowded it's hard to distinguish one person from another. "I haven't noticed anything, but then again, I didn't know I was supposed to be looking." I break off, seeing Hunter's giving me a strange look. "What?"

Again he shakes his head, his features tight. "You should be aware of your surroundings at all times. Weren't you taught about that? Or did you just not fucking listen?"

It's a combination of all of that. Of course I was lectured about safety, but at the time it didn't seem relevant. I couldn't live my life constantly looking over my shoulder. Though I'm not completely daft. "I try to be careful, Hunter. I avoid dark alleys and keep to populated areas…"

Swiping his tousled hair back from his forehead, Hunter glares. "What you were doing was clearly not enough. They've tagged your stuff, bugged you, and have obviously been watching you for a while. Someone's been in your flat, Princess. And today wasn't the first time."

I have nothing to say at the reminder.

CHAPTER 4
Hunter

I want to pick Aiza up and shake her. No, spank her until her little ass turns red and she's begging me for forgiveness. I can't believe she's been so naïve, coming to the UK without anyone knowing she's here, or even giving Grade A a heads-up. If she'd been upfront with us she'd have been living in a secure apartment with top-notch security, and we would have regularly swept it to check no one was keeping tabs on her the way that they have.

I glance at Ben, immediately seeing he's also angry and irritated. Although we weren't responsible for providing the security arrangements in Switzerland, by not knowing his young sister's whereabouts he'll be feeling like he's failed our most important customer, Emir Kadar al Kassis. Grade A should have had their ears to the ground, and it shouldn't have slipped by us that Aiza had entered the country. In some respects, she's been clever, staying as hidden as she has.

I push back my chair and get comfortable, crossing one leg over the other, my right ankle resting on the opposite knee, and turn my attention back to the woman sitting opposite. I'd first officially met her when my dearest friend,

Cara, married Nijad. She'd appeared, walking alongside her new sister-in-law, looking like the first glimpse of sun on a cloudy day, her beauty immediately overshadowing everyone around her. It was clear she didn't know it. Had no idea that every man was entranced by her, that no male past puberty could keep their eyes off her. As women looked on with envy, Aiza remained oblivious. Her love for life, her vivaciousness captivating us all.

Cara glowed on her wedding day, Aiza's presence somehow serving to enhance her radiance. Instead of diminishing others in her proximity, they basked in her reflected glory. Simply by being there she made everyone feel alive. The women wanted to be her. The men, well, it probably wasn't right to think what I—and every man there —was envisioning doing to her.

I'd stood, supposedly watching the ceremony, unable to take my eyes off the young beauty until I realised having a rock-hard cock was perhaps inappropriate under the circumstances, and forced myself to look elsewhere.

The Kassis brothers were overprotective when it came to Aiza, although their protection was given from afar. They were content to live in a bubble, believing at that time, at her age of twenty-two, meant she'd barely grown out of playing with dolls. Two years on, and she's only become more beautiful.

I know something they don't. She certainly was playing with toys, just not the one's they envisioned. Even then she wasn't the innocent virgin they thought she was. They lived in blissful ignorance while I, though I hadn't then known who she was, had seen her playing in clubs, and not the kind where you risk losing money at cards. No, she likes to frequent BDSM clubs, picking the ones that can guarantee her anonymity so she could conduct her illicit activities discreetly. The same clubs I go to for a similar reason, preferring to avoid those which any of our clients might visit.

Affording her the privacy she'd clearly been seeking, when I'd realised who she was, I'd always kept out of sight, watching from a hidden vantage point. I'd been successful, and she'd never caught a glimpse of me. Whenever I saw her I was unable to take my eyes off her. *Perhaps I'm as bad as the stalker we're now trying to identify?*

The memory of her playing has a predictable reaction, and I sit forwards again, pulling my chair into the table to hide the swelling in my jeans. Now that she's got herself into trouble, I'm determined it's going to be me who takes charge of her. *Yes, I'll jump at the chance to get to know Aiza Kassis a whole lot better.* For once in my life it goes beyond sex. I want her in my life, as well as my bed.

Kadar doesn't like me, wouldn't want me for his sister. Maybe I can get into his good books if I'm the one who now keeps her out of trouble and protected. Raising my hand, I hide my grin, keeping the eagerness off my face and trying to look professional. It won't be easy, nonetheless I'm determined to tie this independent woman to me. Get permission from her older brother to make her mine.

I've watched you for years, Aiza. And now I'm going after what I want.

"Yeah, Hunter. You'll be going with Aiza to Amahad."

Hearing my name, I come back to my senses and suppress a smile as Ben's unknowingly played straight into my hands.

I'm not even deterred when Aiza snorts, "No way. There must be some other option. I am not going home."

"Think you are, darlin'," I drawl, my American accent coming to the fore. "Your brother has spoken."

She huffs, and as she folds her arms pulls her ridiculously tight t-shirt around her. Her action serving to make her nipples more apparent, and there I go, having to fight with my libido again.

"Be sensible, Princess." The way he snaps shows Jon's losing patience with her. Yeah, she's a brat. One that needs a firm hand. *My hand.* "Until we identify who's interested in you, and for what reason, it's makes sense for you to go home." Jon glares at her as she goes to speak. "If it is the terrorist organisation that's had eyes and ears on you, we'd have to put every man we've got onto keeping you safe if you were to stay in England. If it's an opportunist kidnapper, maybe we could have a lighter touch. At the moment we've fuck all idea who these pricks are who are watching you. I, for one, would prefer out of the country, and somewhere it's easy to ensure your safety."

Aiza bites her lip, again making me adjust myself in my pants. *That mouth...* "Can't you trace the bugs or something?"

"Of course we'll be doing that," Ben assures her. "However, tracing where they came from is going to take time. Go back to Amahad, Aiza. If we can remove the threat quickly it might not be too long before you can come back."

She shoots me a worried look. "Kadar might not want me to leave."

Fuck. She's her brother all over again. "I doubt Kadar will use pressure to keep you there." I glance at Ben, who gives me a slight nod. "I promise to make sure you're not kept in Amahad against your will. If there's any sign that's your brother's intention, I'll get you out of there before you can blink."

Opposite me Ryan huffs a laugh, and I recall it was he who'd once made a similar undertaking to Jasim, Aiza's middle brother. Against all odds, Jasim, in the end, hadn't wanted to come back, had made Amahad his home, giving up all his assets in the UK. *Jasim.* An idea clicks in my head.

Ben bangs his hands on the table. "Until Mason's analysed the equipment that was in your flat and we've got something concrete to go on, there's no point discussing anything further tonight. Princess, you *will* be on that plane in the morning. Hunter, you make sure of it." The way he's looking at me shows he doesn't expect me to fail.

"Okay. So everyone knows what they've got to do. The last thing to decide is where Hunter and the princess will be staying tonight."

Aiza looks beaten. I hate to see the life go out of those gorgeous eyes as she slumps, resigned, and says, "I presume you'll be taking me to the embassy."

"I was thinking a safe house," Ben contradicts. "The embassy could be under surveillance. If Mason's tapes don't fool them, it's the first place they'd go looking."

There's a suggestion in my head. Dare I voice it? I'll out her if I do. Almost everyone sitting around the table is already a member, or even an owner. I glance at Harry — he's the only one who didn't want to join — but he's clued in to what we all do. The words come out of my mouth before I can stop them. "Club Tiacapan."

Ben snorts. Aiza's eyes open so wide they seem to take up all of her face. Jon's burying his head in his hands, Seth and Ryan are chuckling.

It's Aiza who's the first to speak, her eyes now narrowing and focused on me. "That's Jasim's club. I can't go there."

Jon's recovered quickly. "Actually, Princess, you're wrong. You're out of date. Jasim sold his shares when he got married. The club belongs to me and Devil now. Hunter has made a good suggestion. It's one place where you can be guaranteed privacy. No one can get onto the grounds, and Jasim's old apartment is still there and unused. Perfect for you to stay in tonight. Good call, man."

I don't bother acknowledging Jon's nod. I'm too busy watching Aiza's face. A myriad of expressions cross over it, finally settling on a flicker of interest. She thinks for a moment longer, then grins and shrugs, looking down the table at Jon. "Can I get temporary membership for tonight?"

Now there's an audible gasp around the table. Not from me. I just smirk.

With a bemused expression on his face, Jon leans forwards. "You know what kind of club this is, Princess? It's not the place for a girl like you."

Suddenly Aiza's on her feet, her eyes blazing as she brings her fist down. "It's a BDSM club. The most exclusive in the UK. Don't presume that you know anything about me." The others are shocked, me not so much. Except I didn't expect her to come clean.

Silence. Then Ryan laughs. "You a sub, Princess?"

Ben looks like he wants to kill him, but can't keep his eyes from going to the woman who's looking incensed. But it's not for the reason we're thinking when she informs us in a haughty tone, "I'm a Domme."

I very much doubt that. Oh, I've seen her playing the part, but I think there's something she'd prefer better. However, I'll go along with it for now.

Taking pity on her, I crane my head so I can address him directly. "Jon, the princess has got experience. I've seen her in a couple of clubs on the continent, and one in the States. I can vouch for her if necessary."

Her eyes widening again, Aiza retakes her seat and throws me a look which somehow combines thanks and also concern that I've seen her play, when she hasn't seen me.

Ben leans his head towards Jon and they have a murmured conversation. No one else speaks. Well, it's not every day a princess is outed for enjoying kink. I hope Jon agrees, selfishly on my part, though also for her. Give her this last night of freedom. It might make my job tomorrow easier when I have to get her on that plane.

Finally, Jon shakes his head. "Not what I was expecting from tonight. If Hunter vouches for you, explains the rules to you *and* you stay out of the private rooms, I'll make a call and get a temporary membership sorted." As Aiza's eyes light up, he continues, raising his hand and pointing it at her, then at me. "On condition you make no further objection to returning to Amahad tomorrow and give Hunter no trouble."

I'm a Dom. She might think she's in the same league, but she's so far away it's laughable. If she gives me trouble she'll be paying for it, and in a way I'll make sure we would both enjoy.

She looks at me, then at the two men at the head of the table. Her breath comes out on a sigh. "I agree to your terms."

Ben closes the meeting. As the room starts to empty and she stands, I watch her carefully, thinking how well everything has fallen into place. It couldn't have turned out better if I'd planned it.

Yes, Aiza. You might not know it yet, but you're going to be mine. As I stand aside for her to precede me out of the conference room, I hide my smile behind her back while allowing my eyes to feast on her delicious ass as she walks away. *Mine.*

Grade A owns a number of identical black SUVs, and we bring these into play tonight. Although it's highly unlikely she's been traced here, we're taking no unnecessary chances, so employ subterfuge to get her away. Soon there are three vehicles, all with darkened windows, leaving one after the other. I'm driving Aiza in the final one. Even before we leave the underground garage I can feel her simmering with excitement despite the events of this afternoon. Club Tiacapan has a well-earned reputation for being one of the best clubs in Europe, and I can understand that she's eager to find out why for herself. She's fidgeting, and her hands are clasping and unclasping in her lap. As I pull out onto the now almost empty street, populated only with the occasional black cab, she speaks to me.

"I don't know what to say to you," she admits, making me glance at her quickly in the mirror before turning my attention back to the road. "I've always wanted to see Club Tiacapan. Apart from my brother being responsible for starting it, it's got an amazing rep across the globe."

"But?" I prompt, hearing the but in the words she's not voiced yet.

"I'm angry, as you gave me away." She speaks a little sadly, as though what she gets up to is a secret she wants to keep for herself.

It's true I hadn't cared whether I did or didn't. It's not true I betrayed her. "It was you who asked for temporary membership, Princess. If you hadn't had said anything they'd have assumed you just agreed that it would be an unlikely place for anyone to think of looking for you."

She's quiet for a moment, then says, "I hate that someone's been listening and possibly watching me. And, Hunter, you're not much better. If you've seen me in clubs, why didn't you let me know you were there?"

I sigh. "Because I didn't think you'd want to know you'd been seen. I get your need for privacy."

"Do my brothers know?" Another look in the mirror, and I see she's biting her lip.

"They haven't heard it from me," I'm quick to reassure her. I'd never do that. It's not anyone's business what she gets up to, she's an adult.

Clever as she is, she reads between the lines and sighs. "However, they know."

There's no point hiding the truth from her. "Yeah, Princess. Well I'm pretty sure Nijad and Jasim do. I don't think they've dared tell Kadar yet."

She swears. "Bloody hell."

Knowing she'll have to face her brothers tomorrow, tonight I'll try to take her mind off what lies ahead. She'll have a lot of explaining to do to the Kassis Sheikhs once she's back on Amahadian soil, and will be receiving several lectures if I'm not mistaken. As she goes quiet while we make our way from East London to the Hampstead Heath in the south, I peruse my options. Sneaking a glance at the woman by my side, I decide to wait until we arrive at the club and go with my gut when I see her reactions.

"Hunter?" Her voice breaks in to my thoughts. I look over at her. "Can we please dispense with you calling me by a title I never use? Please call me Aiza."

I nod. I'll try to give her that. What she doesn't understand is that I'm using 'Princess' not so much in recognition of her position, but as a form of endearment.

Having kept a careful check on what's going on around us I'm confident we haven't been followed, so I don't bother making a detour to make sure, just take the turn into the sweeping driveway that leads up to the mansion that houses Club Tiacapan. Located well off the road and hidden by trees, the grounds are patrolled, and the gates opened only by the remote identifiers located in all authorised vehicles. As practically all the top team at Grade A are members, most of the company cars we use are equipped with such devices for our convenience. As I park up behind the mansion I'm as happy as I can be that we've managed to keep Aiza's location quiet tonight.

The car park is about half full, what I would have expected for a weekday. Aiza's out of the car and standing, looking up at the floodlit building before I can come around to open her door.

"It's amazing, isn't it?" Her mouth has dropped open.

I look at the sixteenth-century building now converted for a twenty-first century use, seeing it as though through her eyes, then I look down and grin. "Inside's better. You want to go around the back way and straight up to the apartment first?"

She looks down at herself and ruefully tugs at the over-sized sweatshirt she'd put back on to ward off the cool evening air when leaving Grade A. "I think I'd better. I'm hardly dressed the part."

My damn cock twitches at the thought of how she'd look if she were properly attired. Making an effort to get myself under control, I lead her around to a door at the side and select a key from the bunch Jon had given to me. She follows me up the back staircase which would have been used by servants in centuries past, and finally to the third floor where Jasim had kitted out a small apartment for himself. Another key selected, and the door opens. As she steps in, I'm curious myself, never having been here before. It's not large, just designed as a place for her brother to crash. The door opens into a small, pleasantly furnished living room with a bedroom off to one side with an ensuite bathroom attached.

Aiza's nodding as though she's satisfied with the arrangements, while I frown. Unless I can get into her bed tonight, and that would be moving too fast, I can see I'll be having an uncomfortable night lying on the sofa that's far too small for my large frame. Just as I'm cataloguing the practicality, or lack thereof, of apartment's furniture, a knock sounds on the door.

Always cautious, I wave Aiza into the bedroom and go to look through the peephole, opening the door as I recognise the person outside. I usher her in, my body only moving enough to just give her room to pass while remaining prepared in case anyone's followed her, using her to get access to the private apartment.

Behind her the hallway's clear. Closing the door, I pull Mia in for a hug. As she's Jon's wife, I've met her on numerous previous occasions. It's then I notice the bag that she's brought with her.

"Is it safe to come out?" Aiza calls petulantly from the bedroom.

"Yeah, all clear. Come and meet Mia."

She appears immediately, coming to an abrupt halt, her face splitting into a wide grin. "Dexie Sanders. I've read all your books. It's amazing to meet you." I'd forgotten for a minute that Mia writes what's essentially porn in my eyes. I've read a couple myself. Even I have to admit they're good. Then, she would get the BDSM details correct, she's married to a Master Dom.

Mia grins, and not for the first time I see what attracted Jon to his wife. She's stunning, and a natural submissive. I watch, interested in seeing their interaction. If Mia was talking to me it would be more likely she wouldn't meet my eye. Addressing Aiza, she's staring her straight in the face.

"I love to meet fans." Her smile widens. "And I understand you're having some trouble. Anything interesting?"

I place my hand on Mia's arm and give a small growl. "Mia takes every opportunity to get ideas for her books," I warn Aiza.

Aiza's smiling. "I've no clue what's going on. Just someone seems to be interested in me. Tell you what, if it turns out to be something juicy I'll let you know."

"Deal." Mia holds out her hand, and Aiza shakes it. "Jon told me you had no clothes and that you were the same size as me." She eyes the Arab girl and bites her lip. "Though sometimes I wonder if he needs glasses."

Which draws my attention to both women. To me they look similar in height and weight. Mia's clearly seeing something I'm not.

Aiza laughs and supports her ample boobs with her hands. "I think I've got a bit more up top."

Which makes me look, and I find I'm looking at my boss's wife for comparison. Oh shit, Jon would kill me. I wave them into the bedroom to get them out of my sight. "Go with Mia, Aiza. See if she's brought something you can wear."

The girls disappear, and as I hear giggling coming from behind the closed door I'm thankful for Jon's foresight. At least Mia's presence is cheering Aiza up, and hopefully taking her mind off the journey she'll be making tomorrow.

When the girls reappear I change my mind and want to curse Jon instead. Aiza's dressed as no client of mine should ever be. She's wearing a corset which, yes, definitely emphasises her boobs are bigger than Mia's, barely constrained behind the tight laces. Boy shorts complete the ensemble, showcasing long, lean legs which go on for miles. The red satin material makes her olive skin glow, and as for those boots...

Fuck.

Keeping my hands off her is going to be hard. Here I was, planning to take things slow. Just using tonight to plant the idea of us fitting together in her mind. My cock presses against the zip of my jeans. Letting things progress gradually is going to be difficult when all I want to do is throw her down and thrust my swollen cock into her.

CHAPTER 5
Aiza

I'm so happy Mia arrived, and slightly in awe of her. She's a renowned erotic fiction writer, and I hadn't lied when I'd said I'd read every one for of her books. I wouldn't admit it, but it was Dexie Sanders who got me intrigued in the lifestyle. It was after reading about her Doms and Dommes that I started to get involved in BDSM myself. I wish I could repay her by giving her the juicy details of what's happened to me today. However, while unnerving, it's too boring to put it into words. Sure, someone unknown has been spying on me, I doubt that's much of a plot.

I have to stop thinking about her books. The latest was a menage, and seeing the author brought the story back into my mind, with the result my nipples are hardening and my tiny boy shorts are dampening. I really don't want to start my night in the club downstairs with a very visible wet spot.

"Mia, I can't thank you enough." I indicate the fet wear I'm wearing. Hunter makes a strangled sound, and looking up quickly I now see him staring at me. Being caught out, he quickly turns away. I continue to address myself to Mia.

"Thank you so much for the change of clothes. Hopefully Kadar will still have my stuff on the plane, so I shouldn't need anything else." While I don't often fly in the family jet, I do keep a basic wardrobe there.

"You're welcome." Mia smiles her engaging smile. "Are you coming downstairs now?"

"Yes…"

Hunter interrupts me, and I notice he's widened his stance, drawing my attention to a bulge in his jeans. The confirmation I must look good in what I'm wearing makes me suppress a grin. "Mia, when we go into the club I've got to go to the locker room to get changed. Can you wait with Aiza by the bar? Is Master Ralph on duty tonight?"

"I've got to go change myself," Mia replies. Hunter frowns, obviously so engrossed in what I'd put on, he hadn't noticed she was still in street clothes.

"Hunter," I snap. "I'm no sub that needs to be watched out for." I hope he knows that from the times he apparently spied on me. I've gone to the clubs on my own, after checking their reputation thoroughly, of course. I'm no stranger to being unaccompanied. "If you can fix me up with someone to talk to about seeing limits lists and the club rules, I'd be grateful."

His brows come down to meet in the middle, and as he gives me another look I see I've surprised him. Confirmed when he goes to speak, then looks like he is, for once, at a loss for words.

I link my arm through Mia's and start taking charge. "Come on then, show me the club. I can't wait to see it, I've heard so much about it..." As we walk through the door I hear an exclamation which makes me smile, and then running feet as my bodyguard comes to his senses and catches up. *Hmm. Toying with Hunter is fun.*

"Wait up." Hunter's annoyed voice makes us pause, and he brushes past, throwing a look at me as he does. Taking point, he leads us down the stairs and pauses at the bottom before opening a door that leads into the back of the club. The door is obviously soundproofed. As soon as he pushes it open familiar sounds come to me like music to my ears —actual music of course, the rhythm punctuated by cries of satisfaction and screams. The air throbs with the cacophony of sound and is tinged with odours of sweat and arousal. I pause for a moment, taking it in. Since coming to the UK I haven't indulged in playing, too worried about being recognised. As a princess of Amahad, I do have a reputation to maintain. While this club is exclusive and my identity would be hidden, not having realised Jasim's giving up his stake in it, I'd assumed it was off bounds. Although I probably wouldn't join anyway. I'd baulk at the sky-high membership fees. There's far better things I can spend my allowance on, my charity projects being one.

Mia takes my hand and leads me to the bar. There, sitting on a stool, is Jon Tharpe, who I'd left not that long before in the headquarters of Grade A.

"Jon." I greet him with a nod of my head while noticing his wife is standing before him with lowered eyes.

"Go change," he tells her softly, then turns to me, examining me head to toe, his eyes landing pointedly at my thigh-high boots.

I say nothing. I'm no sub, I don't need to go barefoot or totter around on six-inch heels. *Others* do that for my satisfaction. When his eyes again meet mine, he's got a smirk on his face.

"Take these." He hands me two wristbands. "If you intend to play tonight, there's a two-drink limit." That's fairly standard. In some places I've been in the consumption of any alcohol is prohibited.

A bartender's been watching me carefully, and seeing Jon's action, comes across. "What can I get for you, pet?"

I meet his eyes and raise a brow but answer politely enough. "I'll take a scotch."

"On the rocks?"

"Neat."

Within moments I've swapped a wristband for a measure of the amber liquid I've developed a taste for.

Without waiting for an invitation I slide onto the bar stool next to Jon, and after taking a sip of my drink place the glass back on the bar. "You're my babysitter for now, I take it?" I spend a moment examining him. He's wearing tight jeans and a leather waistcoat which hangs open, revealing a very fit body underneath. *Mia's one lucky woman.*

"Have you been trained?"

"Yeah. I trained as a Domme at a place in the States." I give him the name as I nod my head towards a seating area where I can see a few women and a couple of men lounging, seemingly unattached and looking up hopefully as Doms and Dommes walk past. "Subs area?"

"It is, though don't get your hopes up."

My eyes snap to his. "You going to censor me here, Jon?"

There's a twinkle in his eye as he nods his head in the direction behind me. "I'm not, but I'm pretty sure *he* is."

As I swing around I see Hunter sauntering up. He's changed into leather jeans that mould to his legs and a leather waistcoat which, like Jon's, hangs open. I have to stop myself from licking my lips as a six pack comes into view. If I was in the market for a man for the night, Hunter wouldn't be far from the top of the list. His tousled reddish hair flops forwards, and it's hard to resist stretching out my hand to sweep it back.

"Jon." He greets his boss with a chin lift.

"Hunter."

Having exchanged their manly greetings, Hunter holds out his hand towards me. "Allow me to give you a tour?"

Still wondering about Jon's cryptic comment, I finish my whisky then slide off the stool. It would be interesting to see the place which I've heard so much about, from friends in the lifestyle as well as what I managed to eavesdrop on those rare occasions I was home in the palace of Amahad.

Hunter starts to lead me around the enormous room which must have been constructed by taking down original internal walls, replacing them with steel supports instead. Stages are set up along the sides, equipped with a variety of apparatus. One wall is set up with rigging, and I watch as a Shibari expert gives a demonstration. He's just completed binding his sub and is now hoisting her into the air. I pause to appreciate the look of bliss on her face, and wish it was me who had put it there.

"Will you let me tie you up, Hunter?" I ask, half turning so I can see his face. His eyes also have been captured by the scene in front of us. While his attention is elsewhere, I imagine wrapping rope around his naked body, tracing patterns as I bind him both physically and metaphorically, gradually bringing him under my spell, taking his trust, seeing him swollen with arousal…

"No fucking way." His curt dismissal breaks the thrall the scene had placed me in.

Hmm.

A gentle tug on my hand, and we're moving forwards again. Now pausing in front of a scene where role play is taking place. A female teacher castigating a female student for some infraction, the latter leant over the desk having a ruler applied to her bare arse, her punishment obviously having gone on for a while, as her fair skin is a lovely shade of pink. The pair are exhibitionists for certain, the pupil conveniently placed so anyone passing can see her arousal glistening in the spotlight.

Another stage where there's a spanking bench, and the next two have tables—one where someone's using a violet wand, and the other dripping wax, the sub's body already a colourful canvass.

"What takes your fancy?" asks the man by my side.

I turn around and look over to the unclaimed subs, and a hand comes under my chin, moving my head back so I'm facing him.

"I meant you and me. And I ain't no sub, baby."

My face creases in confusion. "Neither am I, Hunter. You know that."

He's shaking his head as if he knows nothing of the sort, then his eyes soften. "Come."

With his hand to the small of my back, he leads me over to a roped-off area and points to a comfortable couch. He scans the room behind him, then waves his hand. A beautiful sub in a baby doll dress comes over and folds to her knees, head bowed, hands palms up. A perfect and practiced pose.

"Diamond," he says softly, "could you bring us some drinks, please? Master Ralph will know what we want. And can you tell him neither of us will be playing tonight?"

"Yes, sir." With that the sub gracefully gets to her feet and goes off to perform her task.

I'm bristling. As Hunter sits beside me, I can't keep quiet. "That was a bit presumptuous. I haven't made that decision."

"I decided for you."

"What gives you that right?" My cheeks are burning.

He sighs. "If you're not playing with me, I can't very well let you go off with anyone else." As I raise my eyebrow he continues. "There's someone spying on you, Princess. Unless you can think of any names, we've no idea who he, she, or they could be." He lifts his hand and circles it, drawing my attention back to the room behind. "I can't trust anyone, even in this club."

I don't believe him. "The people here will all have been vetted. I don't see there's any risk."

"I don't think you're in a position to say that, Aiza. You've clearly not got any sense of self-preservation. Fuck, you've been jetting all over the world, coming to the UK, without any regard for your safety." As I go to speak he puts a finger to my mouth. "No, Aiza. Let me finish. You're a princess of Amahad. *The* princess."

"My sisters-in-law are also princesses," I correct him.

"But not by birth. If you were taken, kidnapped…" Hunter doesn't need to complete his sentence. Much as they seem like strangers to me, I know my brothers would do *anything* to get me back. Start a war, damage their new oil industry.

As Diamond returns carrying a tray and puts two glasses of amber liquid in front of us, I think about what he's said.

Perhaps he does have a point. When I'd come to England I thought I'd been careful and that no one knew who or where I was. I'd been wrong. While I doubt anyone in this exclusive club would be my enemy, perhaps I should start looking over my shoulder a little bit more.

Reaching for the glass, I notice it's a double. It's good stuff, and there's a slight burn to my throat as I swallow it down.

Hunter lets out a breath and relaxes seeing I've given in. I won't be playing tonight, as there's no way in hell I'll be playing with him. Not two Dominants together. He picks up his own glass and agitates it, making the ice cubes which he prefers tinkle. "So, Aiza. Why a Domme?"

"For the same reasons you're a Dom, I expect." It seems an odd question. I go on to explain. "All my life I've been controlled, as you know, Hunter. I was sent to the right schools. I lived away from Amahad, but all the time my father, and after his death my older brother, Kadar, have been pulling the strings." I gaze at the area he's brought me too. It's quieter here than in the middle of the club, though the sounds of the music and people having fun still penetrate. "I could never escape who I am, and the restrictions that imposed on me. I could only rebel internally."

As I go quiet, he prompts, "And you knew you were a Domme...?"

I raise my shoulders. "When I first started playing." I look down at my drink, hearing the sounds from the play area behind me, the snap of a whip, the groans, the screams, even able to make out floggers hitting their target in time to the music. It makes me smile. "You should know what it's like. How fulfilling it can be when a sub gives over their control. When I get them out of their heads and into subspace, it does something to me. It's something I've done, have been responsible for. The giddy feeling of headspace... I've never found that anywhere else in my life." I huff. "You see me as a sub, Hunter, because that's what everyone thinks I ought to be. Someone weak who needs to be directed. You're wrong. It's because I have little power in the rest of my life, that I take it here."

"But you do, don't you? That's why you came to the UK. You took back control over your own life."

"And look where that's got me." I sip the splendid single malt again. "My rebellion has ended with me being called back to my homeland." There's a hitch to my voice as I tell him my fears. "And this time I'm frightened I won't be able to escape."

Hunter raises his hand and cups my chin, turning me to face him. He waits until my eyes meet his, then, "Princess, I won't let that happen to you. I promise. I'll be there with you as your close protection officer, and if that means protecting you from your family, that's what I'll do." There's a pause before he adds, "And I'll be there as your friend."

I give a small nod to satisfy him, while thinking he doesn't understand. Kadar's got absolute power in Amahad, and if he's got other plans for me, Hunter will be unable to stop him carrying them out.

CHAPTER 6
Rais

"Your Excellency." I bow my head as I greet the emir.

Kadar waves his hand as he takes off his headdress and throws it down on a chair. "No formality, Rais. I get enough of that crap. Here, we're just two old friends." He sits and waves to the refreshment on the table. As I nod he pours two glasses of fruit juice. He pushes one across his desk, and I take the seat in front of it. "What can I do for you?"

"Aiza."

He sighs. "Can't say I'm surprised. Stupid girl is all I can think about." He consults his expensive Rolex. "Shouldn't be long before the plane lands. I'll breathe easier once she's on Amahadian soil."

So will I. I'd had to wait until my rage was controllable before coming to see Kadar when I'd heard how she'd exposed herself to danger. Luckily I'm able to control my expressions, which is why he probably didn't see my anger in yesterday's meeting. "She needs a strong hand."

Kadar barks a laugh. "You'll get no disagreement from me. We've been too lax with her, have clearly allowed her far too much freedom."

I keep quiet. In my view they'd given her none at all. Kadar and his brothers, as his father before them, had been quite content to keep Aiza contained in the protected compound in Switzerland. I'm not surprised she escaped, and admire her for the way she evaded exposure for as long as she had. I only wish she'd been more sensible about it, remembered she was royalty, and had made sure she had proper protection. I frown, realising if she'd asked for help Kadar might have forced her back to Switzerland. Or home, to Amahad. No, in reality, she hasn't had much freedom at all.

"Not that I don't always enjoy your company, Rais, but why this meeting?"

Sitting forwards, I place my palms flat on his desk, determined just to come out and say what I'm thinking. I'd have kept quiet, spoken to her first, but with that bugger Rami making a play, I've been forced to accelerate my game. "I won't beat around the bush, Kadar. I'd be happy to take responsibility for Aiza. She needs a strong man and a firm hand."

"You?" Kadar sits back in his chair, his eyes wide, staring at me for a few seconds as he digests my words. Then, with a shake of his head he states, "I didn't see that coming, Sheikh." His hand wipes over his brow before smoothing his short beard. "While I'm grateful for the offer, and do see some merit in it, I couldn't ask you to do that."

"You didn't ask." Annoyed that he thinks of it as little more than a tiresome duty, I continue to plead my case. "Aiza's in danger, and you can depend on me to protect her."

"Have I misunderstood you, Rais? I thought you were suggesting something more." He chuckles at what he thinks is his mistake.

"You weren't mistaken." I inhale then let it out in a way there can be no misapprehension. "I would like to take Aiza for my wife." I can't put it any plainer than that.

He looks stunned. "Rais, my old friend. You know what esteem I hold you in. I see the merit of your suggestion, although I do have some objections. Your age for a start."

I'm not surprised he thinks I'm older, the way I carry myself and act. I have to maintain a certain persona to lead the other desert sheikhs. I put him right and draw a valid comparison. "I'm only ten years older, there's a similar gap between yourself and your wife, Emira Zoe, I believe?"

His eyes widen. "Fuck. I'd forgotten that. You married young, didn't you?"

I raise my chin. Yes, I had an arranged marriage to a girl from another tribe when I was sixteen. No emotion involved, and we did what we had to. She got pregnant fast and died giving birth to a boy who hadn't survived. I'd been devastated. What man wouldn't be? Having done my duty once, I evaded ensuing pressure to take another woman as my wife, and two years later, when I inherited the leadership of my tribe on the death of my father, no one could persuade me to do anything I didn't want to again. I'd taken my nephew under my wing, and have been grooming him to be my heir.

My prowess in battle and my leadership skills came to the fore early, and I earned my place as the sheikh speaking for all the ten desert tribes. I'm not surprised Kadar forgot the number of years that I've walked this earth. I'd aged early. I had to.

"I'm thirty-four, Kadar. Young enough to take Aiza as my wife, and old enough to be the man that she needs."

He laughs again. "I don't think anyone can control her, Rais. And I'm not sure I'd wish her on any man. Even my enemy. And particularly not someone I call a friend."

Imperceptibly, I stiffen. Kadar's brothers might be able to admonish him, but though I hold a respected position in Amahad, any friendship between myself and the emir has boundaries, and I need to be careful not to cross them. I've known the princess all of her life, and she has intrigued me since she grew into a woman. It's true since then I've not met her often, only on her rare visits home, recently to attend the weddings of her brothers. It annoys me that he's talking about her as though she's a problem to be resolved, a dilemma to be passed onto someone else to deal with. She's his sister for fucks sake.

There's not a lot that gets past the emir. He looks at me sharply. "You think I'm wrong, don't you?" Both hands go up and his fingers rake across his short hair. "I don't know her, Rais, and that's the problem. That's in part due to her age. When she was born, my brothers and I were already learning to be men. Being groomed for our future roles." His brow furrows, and I suspect he's remembering his harsh father and exactly what that exacting training had involved. "Aiza was brought up by a nanny. Even when she was here our paths rarely crossed. When my father died I tried to get her to come home, but she said she was happy where she was." Now a rueful grin appears. "Or where I *thought* she was. And as you witnessed yourself, Rami has made his case for her."

"Rami couldn't handle her." He's a nice enough man, well-educated, intelligent, affable. He could probably give a good account of himself if challenged, however his skills lie in diplomacy. For such a man to be married to such a strong-willed woman? I shake my head as I dismiss it.

"He wants her," Kadar says conversationally. "There would be merits in the union."

"Aiza wouldn't be happy." I'm certain of that.

He starts as if he hadn't looked at it that way before. That, to my mind, is the problem. Brought up by the late Emir Rushdi, happiness was not something to be taken into account. While Kadar has tried to shake off the shackles of his upbringing, groomed as he was to follow in his father's autocratic footsteps, there are times he settles back into the old ways.

I play my trump card. "Zoe seems fond of Aiza."

Another sharp look. Then he chuckles. "You're a bastard, Rais. You know my wife would have my balls if I didn't put Aiza's wants and wishes first. Trust you to go straight to the heart of the matter." He thinks as he finishes his drink. "If you can persuade Aiza, I'll not stand in your way. There'd be worse men to have as a brother-in-law." He consults his watch again and then stands. "We're running out of time. She should be landing shortly. You want to come to the airfield to meet the plane? Give Aiza a welcome?"

If that puts me ahead of my rival, nothing will stop me. Oh, I'll play dirty to get what I want. Impatient now to see her again, I wait, my fingers drumming against my thighs as Kadar puts on his ghutra, fastening it in place with his golden egal of office. Once his headdress is in place, I follow him out of the room and through the winding corridors of the palace.

I take my place alongside him in the back of the armoured limousine that's waiting to take us to meet Aiza. As the transport of the emir warrants, armed outriders surround the car, with black SUVs in front and behind, each carrying armed guards, all ready to lay down their lives for their emir. I, myself, am equipped with weapons and have the same intention. Anywhere Emir Kadar goes, he must be fully protected.

We drive away from the palace, through the modern business district, a wide boulevard lined with palm trees, and then out through the more meagre housing. I note, with approval, some of the shacks have been demolished, and new housing estates going up instead, part of the modernization that Kadar has brought to the country.

The emir's been silent, lost in his own thoughts. Now he speaks, and the snap in his voice indicates he's come to a decision. "Sheikh Rais. My desire is to see Aiza married. Nevertheless, it must be her choice. Pursue her if you wish. I do need to warn you, I will, of course, be having the same conversation with Prince Rami."

That, for now, is the probably the best I can hope for. My mouth purses as I begin to put my plans together. I hadn't been joking when I said Aiza needed a strong man beside her. I'm going to prove to her that should be me. I need a strong woman to be my wife.

An explosion, and the limousine spins sideways. Dust swirls around us as we slide off the road, the vehicle now diagonal and at a stop on the hard shoulder. I've thrown myself automatically over my emir, but peer up to look out of the window, appreciating that the driver's quick thinking had expertly avoided the hole in the road that's appeared in front of us. Without pause he now puts the car into reverse and turns it around.

"Aiza." The word escapes from my lips.

Kadar's voice sounds muffled, making me realise I'm still covering him. "She'll be alright. The airport's well protected. They can't get her there. No, this must have been an attack on me."

Something in my gut tells me he's wrong. "Stop the car," I shout to the driver, then tell the emir, "Kadar, get back to the palace." I'm already reaching for the door handle as I speak, waving to a guard whose SUV wasn't so lucky and is undrivable. He comes running and only needs a brief instruction to take my place.

"What are you doing, Rais?" Kadar tries to sit up, the soldier pushes him back down.

"Going to the airport," I tell him, my eyes taking in the scene as I work out my plan. *It could be an attack on the emir, or it could be a diversion to stop us from getting to the plane.* With Aiza's safety at stake, I'm not taking any chances.

"Rais..."

"I'll see you later, Kadar."

The limousine's already moving as I slam shut the door. Running to one of the outriders, I shout at him. *"Aetani dirajat nariat alkhasi bik."* I'm used to it only taking one look at my face before any man does what I ask, so it doesn't surprise me when he immediately leaps off his motorbike, and I strip off my robes, revealing the jeans and t-shirt I'm wearing underneath. Leaving them and my headdress by the side of the road, I'm on the bike and away before anyone can stop me.

Aiza. I could be wrong. This might be someone trying to kill the emir. I can't discount this feeling in my gut though. It seems too much like coincidence.

Twisting the throttle, I push the bike to its limits, feeling my stomach drop as a boom sounds, followed quickly by a billowing cloud of smoke rising in the air ahead of me. *The airport terminal.* I try to go faster, the front wheel coming off the ground. Reluctantly I ease off my right hand, my aim to get to her, not kill myself.

A few more minutes and I'm laying the bike down. Giving no thought to my own safety, I run towards the blazing terminal. One of my tribal members who's joined the palace guard is outside helping with an evacuation. I grab his arm. "The royal jet?"

He nods at his radio. "Been diverted to runway two. They'll have to hold it there until we're clear here. First thing we need to do is get everybody out."

Loud reports of gunfire start.

Ignoring the screams of the people inside, I rush back to the bike. "Help me," I yell at the guard. It's quicker with two people to pick up the heavy BMW. Once it's upright I'm back on and again revving the throttle, riding down the runway and crossing the grass. An eerie silence has now descended, broken only by the thwacking sound of a helicopter's rotors as it rises up into the air, shortly followed by a second.

With dire thoughts in my mind I race to the second runway and head for the royal jet, quickly assessing the people lying injured or dead, seeing no sign of the woman I'm looking for. I do see Hunter, holding his hand to his arm and staring up into the sky.

It's him I make a beeline for, knowing at once from the expression on his face that Aiza's been taken away in one of the helicopters. "What the fuck happened? You were supposed to fucking protect her!" I scream into his face. Some fuck-up of a bodyguard he turned out to be.

Not retaliating or trying to defend himself, he stands, bemused, stunned, and shakes his head as if to clear it. "I don't know what fucking happened, Sheikh. It went down so fast. One minute we were coming into land, next we were told to circle as there was a fire at the terminal building. The plane landed on a different runway."

Where security wasn't waiting for them. Or at least, not all of them. No, they'd been diverted to help the civilians. A decision someone would suffer for.

"Why the fuck didn't you wait until security changed position?" I'll give Hunter this, he knows how to do his job. He's been working down in the southern desert for months overseeing the security on the oil pipeline while it was being constructed. I've never seen him at such a loss, and never before today have known him to make a mistake.

His eyes narrow. "I'll tell you one thing, Sheikh Rais, this wasn't a couple of people snatching her for a ransom. This was a well-oiled machine. It would have taken some planning. They diverted half the waiting guard, must have overpowered the others. Two helicopters came down, one taking her, the other taking their men who weren't injured or killed." He pauses and looks at me. "And their injured men who couldn't walk had headshots put in them, and only then were they left behind."

Like a light bulb going on, things start falling into place. I elucidate them aloud. "That was the plan all along. They wanted to drive her back here." I spit on the ground in my disgust. "They wanted to laugh in Kadar's face. Taking her off a street in the UK was too easy. This sends a message about how powerful they are."

Hunter nods. "It was well orchestrated, that's for sure. Amir al-Farhi has the organisation and the manpower for something like this. And he'd delight in thumbing his nose at Kadar."

Which reminds me. "Kadar?"

"First thing I did. I've contacted him and told him what happened." The twist to Hunter's face shows how that conversation went.

My mind already focused on getting the woman I've decided will be mine, back, I'm finding it difficult to concentrate on anything else. Only now do I notice the blood running down Hunter's arm. "You need medical attention."

"That can wait." My suggestion is dismissed.

As I look around I see two guards dead, and about ten wounded. As Hunter had said, any of the enemy left behind are dead, and I doubt will have anything on them that's useful or would give the identification of their employer away. No, the person who organised the abduction would be far too clever for that.

The flight attendant's tending to them with a first aid kit in hand. She'll be military trained just like the rest of the crew, even if she seems to think providing extra services to her passengers is in her resume. I've been on the receiving end of her offer many a time. Declining, of course. The old emir used to fly often.

Turning my mind back to the task in hand, knowing security at the airport will be doing everything they can, and that I'll only get in the way if I try to help or obliterate clues. I'm a fighter, not an investigator, and seeking answers from this mess will be up to them now.

I'm a man of action, and here I can take none. My hands curl into fists, wanting to take my fury out on the man standing in front of me. The man who, in my opinion, was responsible for allowing *my woman* to be taken. I want to take Hunter by the shoulders and shake him until he tells me exactly what happened here today. However, Kadar will be waiting, and Hunter, looking weak from the loss of blood and shock, will only want to go through this once.

We appropriate the car that's at last drawn up, and which was going to take Aiza to the palace. Now, instead, it's taking two men back to explain to the emir just how his sister was kidnapped the moment she touched down in the country where she had come to be safe.

CHAPTER 7
Aiza

Earlier

I found last night to be awkward. I had a bed, Hunter didn't, and I wasn't going to offer to let him share mine. That kiss in my flat, that state of arousal he'd had difficulty hiding when he'd seen me in my fet wear, his refusal to consider me playing with anyone else but him all gave away that he was attracted to me. Any little encouragement and he might want more from me than I would be prepared to give. Although he was a perfect gentleman and didn't push. That's not to say I wouldn't, in the right circumstances, be interested. He's a good-looking guy, has an obvious zest for life, and if he toned down the Dom in him I'd be tempted to take a chance. Like me, he can't seem to switch it off. I can't see myself acting the role of a sub, no matter how good the Dom is.

When I slip between the sheets there is another reason sleep evades me, what I try to put out of my mind without success. The events of the afternoon come back to me each time I close my eyes, with a force that jerks me fully awake. The thought that someone's been tracking me, listening to me. While I'd had company I could downplay the effect, but now I'm alone I can't stop thinking about it, nor wondering why, or to rid myself of the feeling of wanting yet another shower to wash the filth off, their actions making me feel dirty. What's their reason? Why am I being targeted? Is it for money? To get at my family? Which is more likely?

Of course, the final reason I can't rest is that tomorrow I'm going to be putting my head back into the lion's den and return to my family. It's not that I don't want to see my brothers—as a result of growing up as I had, they're little more than strangers. On my brief visits home I get on much better with their wives than I do them. Nijad's the closest to me in age, and even he's eight years older. As I toss and turn I go back to the perennial concern that both my father and brothers blamed me for the death of my mother at birth. Of course, no one comes right out and says it was my fault, but the stark truth is, if I hadn't been born she may still be alive. It's a burden I've carried with me all my life, and one which will stay with me until the end.

Oh, how I'd longed for a mother's presence growing up. My father never showed me any love or even affection, but then he never did to my brothers or anyone else. From the beginning I was viewed as a commodity, my marriage arranged before my first birthday. A marriage, which I hope, is no longer on the cards and won't be brought up while I'm in the palace.

A union between myself and Prince Rami of Alair would be beneficial to both countries, but I've lived too long in the West. I'm not prepared to give up my life for political gain. Having no idea what Kadar's view is now he's emir, I'm worried he might still think it a good match, and about the pressure he'll bring to bear on me to do my duty. *Of course, I can always enlist the help of Zoe, his wife.* Now I suspect she'd be on my side if I refused to marry Rami.

If Prince Rami was anyone else, and not the person I had been promised to, I might have wanted to explore a connection I'd felt between us at Nijad's wedding. With so many guests, I hadn't had time to find out anything about him other than he was good looking and seemed kind. It's not the man himself that puts me off, it's the thought that the match was arranged. If he tried to court me it would always be at the back of my mind that I wasn't really the woman he wanted, but one that was his duty to bed.

I like to hook up with men when there's no expectation of a relationship. That's why I enjoy playing in clubs. An enjoyable liaison with no strings attached. If I've ever thought about finding a serious partner, it won't be with a man who wants to control me or my life. Even within a marriage I'd want the freedom to do what I please, and don't consider that selfish. I'm committed to doing some good in this world, and wouldn't want anyone to expect me to stop. I hate that I've led a privileged life for no other reason than accident of birth when I see so much poverty and hardship around me. A man who wants a trophy wife would be disappointed.

I can't deny I've benefitted from the advantage that my family's wealth has brought me, except money isn't enough by itself. I'm sure many people less well off in financial terms hadn't been forced to live in an emotionless desert. I'm not even sure I know what love is. Or how to love. None has ever been given to me.

After tossing and turning all night, when morning arrives I'm irritable and tired. My sleeplessness, my fears about returning to Amahad putting me in a sour mood. Unable to help myself, I'm short and almost rude. Hunter reads me well, and after the first couple of attempts at conversation leaves me to stew by myself.

The journey to the airport is uneventful, our progress to the family jet relatively unhindered thanks to the diplomatic immunity I possess. Boarding the flight, I notice the flight attendant checking her uniform is fully buttoned up, as today a female passenger is on board. It's a moment of light relief as I recall she's been flying with us for years, and I'm certain the male members of my family have probably made use of her personal services in the bedroom at the rear of the plane. Hmm. Perhaps I should ask them. Or then again, maybe it's best not to know.

As we take our comfortable seats I stretch out in readiness for the six-hour flight, allowing myself to enjoy the luxury for once. Normally when I flit between countries it's on a commercial airline, in economy class, packed like sardines with little more than room to breathe. Sometimes I'm lucky to get that.

Take-off is smooth, and the flight attendant approaches once we're at altitude. "Princess, can I get you some refreshment? The chef's preparing breakfast."

Princess. I hate my title. It hangs around my neck like a millstone. Composing my features into a friendly smile, knowing she'd be horrified if I defied protocol and asked her to call me by name, I nod. "Coffee and an omelette would be lovely, thank you."

Hunter doesn't hold back, ordering a full breakfast which I think would feed a whole army.

"Really?" I raise an eyebrow in his direction.

"I'm a growing boy."

Boy isn't the word I'd use to describe him. His comment leads me to examine him, his long legs stretched out, t-shirt hardly containing his bulging muscles. No, he's not a boy at all. Hunter's all man. I look away fast before the blush appears and reveals my feelings. *If he wasn't a Dom I might be interested.*

After I've eaten I feel less out of sorts. I visit the bedroom where I find, as I'd remembered, some clothes that I'd left here. I finger the material of the delicate tunic and shalwar kameez, the loose cotton trousers that will be comfortable and cooling in the high temperatures I'm heading into, then move my hand along the rail, selecting instead a lightweight, long-sleeved tee and capri trousers. I avoid dressing in the Amahadian clothes, believing that would signal an acceptance I'm not yet ready for. A small sign of rebellion. There's little else I can do to show my reluctance I'm being forced home.

Returning to my seat, feeling relaxed, I rest back my head, and the sleep that eluded me last night at last catches up. I drift off, waking only when the plane is starting its descent.

"Feeling better?" Hunter grins as he asks, making me scowl.

While I'm still nervous, the nap has refreshed me, so relenting, I chuckle. "Much."

I detest coming back to Amahad because I'm pushed into a role I hate playing. But it is the place of my birth, and I do have an inborn fondness for it. It's that that drives me to look out of the window and admire the desolate while beautiful desert passing underneath, growing closer as the plane loses altitude.

"I love the desert." Hunter's surprised me. He nods to the ground flashing past below us. "I've spent many months in the south, overseeing security while the pipeline was being constructed. Got to know the tribespeople well. I have tremendous respect for both them and the land. It's a harsh existence."

I hadn't known that. I had assumed all Hunter did was provide close protection for myself and other members of the royal family. I didn't realise he got his hands dirty. Then I remember a tidbit I'd overheard once. "Don't you work for MI6 or something?"

The turn of his head and his evasion of an answer suggests that he does. Hmm. There's more to this man than I had thought.

He does give me something. "The oilfields and pipeline are important to more people than just the citizens of Amahad, Alair, and Ezirad. The West needs oil."

It's more than likely the British government would have a vested interest in making sure the project is a success.

I've flown back and forth so many times, the sudden change of direction as the plane veers away from its normal approach to the airport registers fast. "Hunter?"

"Report." He's pressed the button to communicate with the pilot.

"Sir, Princess. There's a fire in the terminal building. We've been directed to land on the second runway. Sorry for the abrupt turn. We're circling, then will be coming in to make our approach on the next pass. I'm sorry for the inconvenience. We were only redirected at the last minute."

"Anything that will affect us?"

"My instructions are to land. The fire is contained in the main terminal. Security has assured me there's no risk to this plane. They'll divert the escort to the correct runway."

His brow furrowed, Hunter's pinching the bridge of his nose. "I don't like it," he mutters half under his breath.

"The pilot and co-pilot are both ex-military," I try to reassure him. "They'll have liaised with security on the ground. If they say there's no problem, there probably isn't." Looking around I see the Amahadian guards who've been discreet and almost invisible up to now have moved to seats close by.

"Probably isn't good enough." Hunter doesn't seem at all reassured. "Not when it's your life at stake, Princess."

The plane has started its approach again. "It's too late to divert now," I observe.

"Do what I say, Aiza," Hunter warns me with a frown. "I know you object to anyone else telling you what to do, but please let me take the lead when we land. You stay behind me, okay?"

He reaches into his jacket and pulls out a gun. I'm surprised, and it confirms my earlier suspicions. He must have brought it on the plane, and due to the strict gun laws in the UK, a run of the mill bodyguard isn't allowed to carry one. Not unless he was employed by the military or in the armed police.

His preparedness starts me worrying. Sure, a fire requiring a last-minute change of plans is unusual, but surely there won't be danger awaiting us? Still... Pointing to his weapon, I ask hopefully, "You haven't got another one of those, have you?"

"Nope. And you wouldn't know what to do with it if I had."

While I can't help pouting, he's right. Unlike my brothers, I wasn't sent into the military or given any sort of physical defence training.

The plane touches down. A limousine can be seen with outriders waiting and a number of soldiers and security guards standing around. All seems normal. The steps are wheeled up to the plane, and I collect my handbag.

Hunter pushes me behind him as he stands at the top of the steps. Military men outside stand in two lines either side, waiting for my arrival. Hating all this pomp and circumstance, wishing I was descending instead in the midst of a horde of three hundred other passengers, I follow Hunter down the stairs. We've passed through the escort when the limousine pulls up to us.

A man gets out, Hunter steps back to let me in first, and before I realise what's happening the stranger has grabbed my arm and pushed me inside, following me in so fast he falls on top of me while slamming the door shut behind him. The driver pushes down hard on the accelerator and I'm driven away. As shots start sounding behind us my brain takes a split second to catch up and realise I've been separated from Hunter, and these are no friendly men taking me to my brothers.

"Let me out!" I screech, reaching for the opposite door handle, finding it locked. I struggle, but the man forcibly holds me down. It can't be more than a minute or two before the car comes to an abrupt halt, and I automatically clutch at the stranger to avoid being thrown off the seat.

The driver opens the rear door and pulls me out, the other man taking hold of my other arm. Protesting, trying to get loose, fighting to shake them off, I'm dragged to a waiting helicopter. I make it as hard for them as I can, though my feeble attempts count for nothing, and I'm again thrown inside, the two men accompanying me.

A harness is forced around me, one of my hands cuffed to the side of the seat, and then we're airborne. It can't be more than a couple of minutes ago that I was safe on the plane.

As the chopper rises quickly into the air I look down below, seeing the airport and the plume of smoke growing smaller.

Oh fuck.

"Who are you? What do you want with me?" I scream to make myself heard over the sound of the rotors. When the man at my side just looks at me blankly, I try again, this time using the language I'm rusty in. *"Min 'ant wa'ayn 'ant takhudhuni?"*

He understands me, I know it, as a slimy grin crosses his face. He doesn't deign to answer.

CHAPTER 8
Rami

I had two excuses to stay at the palace of Amahad rather than returning home to Alair. The first being the ongoing oil negotiations, and the second, and more personal reason, Aiza. The woman who's arriving later today. I can't wait to start courting her, optimistic of winning her over, of convincing her I'll be the best man for her, leaving her no choice other than to become my wife. That's what I've long dreamed for.

From my earliest memories my father had spoken to me about marrying Princess Aiza, and almost from the same time I had been determined I'd prefer to make my own choice. Why couldn't my older brother Ghalib do his duty and form an alliance through marriage? Or, for that matter, my younger brother, Nasir. As for my sister, Aazeen, she's been doted on since birth. Sometimes I think my father would run a blade through any suitor who tried to take her away, whether suitable or not. But it wasn't any of them. No, it was me who was promised and groomed to be a political pawn.

I wasn't vocal about my refusal, just non-committal, secure in the knowledge that my father would never force me to do something to which I was completely averse. Knowing when it came to it he might be disappointed, though would accept with good grace that I wanted some say in who would become my life partner.

Then, at Nijad's wedding I'd met Aiza, had seen she was no longer a young girl, instead a fully-grown woman. I'd been struck by her ethereal beauty, the depth in her eyes, and the overall air of mystery and promise on her face. Immediately attracted to her, I asked her to dance. She fitted into my arms as if she was made to be there. It had been hard to hide the evidence of my arousal from her, but I tried to treat her with all the respect with which a virgin princess should be awarded. I could listen to her musical voice for hours, and her magical laugh which sent tingles down my spine. I wondered if Allah had a role in pre-ordaining our coupling, wanting to return to Alair and ask my father to put marriage plans in place immediately, knowing I'd never find another woman her equal.

Even as that thought flitted through my head, I knew capturing someone like her wouldn't be easy. She'd need to be encouraged, wooed. And won. Even a prince like me didn't deserve her. I'd left the wedding with ideas in my head of how to get close to her. Thrawted as she'd disappeared back to Switzerland, and I didn't see her again. Or not until I was indulging myself visiting a BDSM club in Paris. I couldn't believe my eyes when I saw her in action, demonstrating how perfect she was for me. Not wanting to embarrass her, I'd slipped away before she could see me.

I'd first fallen in love with her, and now I was in lust with her. Watching from a distance, knowing that like me she wouldn't want the secret of her proclivities to be known. The fact I wouldn't be gaining a virgin bride in fact filled me with excitement. An experienced woman with the confidence to know what she wants, far more my ideal. She deserves that pedestal on which I placed her. No woman could be more perfect for me.

Today I'll see her again, and this time I won't wait any longer. I'll press my suit. When I lay on my charm there'll be no escape for her. Lowering my hand, smiling ruefully, I readjust myself in my trousers, wondering why I'd worn a suit today instead of my robes, which would have hidden my reaction to her. I'd dressed in western clothes with a purpose, wanting to emphasise my cosmopolitan leanings rather than coming over as an Arab, wedded to my land. My ploys carefully put in place to start getting her attention from the moment I greet her. The time for delay is over. She will be mine. And soon.

My suite of rooms overlooks the main palace driveway. I watched Kadar leave some time ago, presumably to collect his sister from the airport. Like a schoolboy, I find it impossible to keep my mind focused on the report I'm supposed to be absorbing, and return time and time again to the window, hoping the emir will soon be back, bringing Aiza with him. When he does, I'll find an excuse to intrude on their family time and be with her. It won't be difficult. Unless their wives are around, neither Nijad, Jasim, nor Kadar know how to speak to her. *But I do.*

Ah. It's Kadar. He's back. Surely it's too fast? I frown, expecting the formalities at the airport to have taken longer. As I watch, it's only Kadar who exits the limousine, gesticulating and shouting, surrounded by guards who rush him into the palace. A brief smile crosses my face. *Has Aiza upset him already? That didn't take long.* Then my mouth turns down, and I'm hit with a premonition. *Something's wrong.*

Quickly I put down the drink I've been holding, and as fast as I can make my way to the ground floor of the palace, hoping I can inveigle myself into any discussion that's going on. As I walk through the impressive and extensive hallways I don't have to think where I'm going, I'm just following the voices, several men, all shouting at once.

"Where the fuck is she, Kadar?"

"Kadar. Have you heard anything?"

"Ni, shut it. Let me think."

Then I hear Kadar talking in rapid Arabic, and as he's not being answered, I take a guess that he's on the phone.

The sinking feeling inside me grows as I grasp that the *she* they're discussing can only be Aiza. Hoping to Allah it's only that she's done something stupid and missed the plane, and it's nothing more than her normal shenanigans, I quicken my steps until I enter the atrium where guards and the Kassis brothers are congregating.

Jasim's the nearest. "What's happened?" I grab his attention. "Where's Aiza?"

He looks at me with no recognition, so lost in his thoughts, then shakes his head as he comes back to himself. "Aiza's been kidnapped. We don't know anything more at present."

Kidnapped? My heart skips a beat as I look around in horror. Kadar's not the only one on his phone, Nijad is too. As well as one of the uniformed guards whose uniform and medals show he's a senior officer.

I hear snippets of conversations. Conference room. All lines diverted there. Surveillance tapes. Air traffic control. Radar. Grade A… I surmise everything's being done to try and trace where she's gone.

Aiza's missing. My head reels with the information. *Someone's abducted her.* When she was coming to Amahad to be safe. *Was the plane hijacked?* What the fuck has happened? My heart almost stops beating in the concern for the woman I've loved from afar.

When Kadar uses his loud voice to instruct everyone to convene in the conference room, I follow them in, taking a seat around the table. Well, she's my future wife. It's my place to be here. If I hadn't dallied so long we could be married by now, and she'd have been safe in Alair. Safe, at home, and looking after my babies. My head sinks into my hands as it dawns on me there's a chance we might not get her back. I've heard Kadar's strict views on paying a ransom.

Suddenly two men burst into the room, one holding a hand to a bleeding arm, blood dripping from his sleeve. It's a man from Grade A Security who I recognise, having come across him when discussing how to protect the pipeline. His name's Hunter. His companion is Sheikh Rais.

Another man's hot on their heels. This one carries a bag looking suspiciously like one a doctor would use. As he makes a beeline for the man covered in blood I gather my summation was on target. Hunter and the doctor are shown to seats at the side of the table.

Stripping off his shirt, uncaring he's barechested and surrounded by sheikhs, high-ranking military men, and hangers-on like me, Hunter simply holds out his injured arm for the doctor to examine while crashing his other fist down on the table.

"It was a complete set up."

Kadar nods once. "The bomb that turned me and my entourage around. Then the incendiary devices that were set around the terminal. More to cause smoke, panic and disruption rather than serious damage. It did the trick."

One of the military men raises his hand. "I'm sorry, Your Excellency. The captain in charge of the guard diverted half of his men to go help evacuate the terminal."

"A decision any of us would have made, General Zaram." Nijad waves off his apology on his brother's behalf. "No one knew lives of civilians weren't going to be lost at that point."

Zaram lifts his chin, still looking upset. "With only half the guard remaining they were overpowered, put inside the hanger and tied up."

"Injuries?" Kadar snaps.

"They put up a good fight. Two dead. Two in a critical condition. Eight walking wounded. As far as the terminal is concerned, all members of the public were evacuated safely."

"And the fake guard that greeted you?" Kadar snaps the question.

"Any left behind were all killed, so we couldn't question them," Zaram confirms. "We have no idea who they were. Any alive got away in a second helicopter before we could free our men.

The room goes quiet as each of us wonder who we're up against, and in the brief silence a low voice can be heard. "You've got severe bruising over your ribs. I'd like to do an x-ray. And if you'll just lean forwards... Ah, yes. That's a nasty one over your kidneys. I think you should go to hospital."

"Just patch me up, Doc. I'm not going anywhere until I know Aiza's safe."

"Was the princess hurt?" I can't keep quiet any longer, and feel at least some relief when Hunter shakes his head.

"No. But they were rough with her when they dragged her to the limousine." He pauses and frowns. "I could see that she put up a struggle, though it was in vain. They overpowered her easily. Kadar," his eyes implore the emir to believe him, "I tried to get to her…"

"Damn it." Both Kadar's fists come down hard on the table, then he stands and proceeds to pace around the room, coming up against a technician who's hurriedly placing wires and plugging them in under the table. They dodge around each other, then Kadar starts pacing again. He swings around. "Rais?"

"Can't tell you much more than Hunter has said. Helicopters flew off, keeping under the radar. We only know the rough direction they were flying in. All airports have been warned to look out for them."

"What models?"

"I saw her dragged into a common enough R44," Hunter cuts in. "Four-hundred-mile range, however we've no idea where it came from."

"Identification?"

"No, Kadar." Hunter looks as distraught as I feel. So he should. *He* was responsible for the princess. I hope his arm's hurting.

"Fuck."

No one speaks, all thinking of something practical to suggest. The fact of it is, Aiza's even now being taken away by fuck knows who, and fuck knows where. Or why.

Kadar plants his fist on the wall, and I can see the tension in his body. He breathes in audibly, then lets the breath out on a sigh. I watch as his shoulders draw back, and then he comes back to the table, pulls in the chair he'd kicked away, and sits down. With elbows on the table he puts his head down into his hands.

Then he looks up. "I thought she'd be safe in Amahad," he notes sadly. "That's why I called her back."

"We all did, Brother," Jasim offers supportively.

"It was a snub. A thumbed nose in your direction, Kadar. And who would want to do that?" Rais's eyes are half hooded.

"Amir al-Fahri," Kadar says without pause. "There is no one else. No one else with this amount of organisation." He turns to Zaram. "Did your men notice anything about the men who overpowered them?"

Zaram frowns. "They were Arab, well organised. Well trained. Don't forget they had two helicopters to call on."

"To confuse us." Rais nods. "Anything to identify the dead?"

"We're working on it," Zaram replies. "We'll see if we can get any identification, though I'm sorry to say I doubt we'll find anything." He breaks off to speak directly to Kadar. "For my part, I agree with you. The only person who has the manpower to set up something like this is Amir al-Fahri."

"We've no fucking idea where he or his base is. We've been searching for him long enough." Nijad's face has darkened in anger.

"Ni, the whole fucking world wants to know where he is. He was behind that terrorist attack in London the other week. Or at least took credit for it." Watching him, I realise I've never seen the emir of Amahad looking at such a loss.

"The helicopter hasn't got a long range," Rais offers. "I'll get the desert tribes looking out for anything suspicious."

"I'll get the drones sent up. We can cover a lot of the southernmost desert." Nijad's brow is creased. "I'll make contact with Qudamah, enlist his help to look for her in Ezirad."

"All my men will be searching. I'll send choppers and planes up to look for any unusual activity," General Zaram announces.

"I'll contact my father. We'll do everything we can in Alair," I offer.

Kadar looks grateful, "Thank you, Prince Rami."

Hunter clears his throat. "I'll talk to Ben, and we'll get all ears to the ground seeing if we can pick up any rumours."

"I'll speak to Cara. See if she can pick up anything on the dark web."

"Good thinking, Nijad." Kadar nods at his brother, then scratches his beard and shakes his head. "That seems about all we can do until we get more information."

"What if we're wrong? We could spend all our time looking for the elusive al-Farhi, and someone else may have taken her?" Jasim's looking concerned. "They didn't kill her, they took her. They must have had a reason."

Nijad glances at his brother. "If it's a kidnap for ransom they'll make contact soon enough asking for money. What other motive could anyone have for taking her?"

"I'm happy to work on the assumption it's al-Farhi." Hunter's softly drumming his fingers on the table. "If it is, I think we'll know soon enough. He does like to boast."

The man from Grade A is right. He does. I frown. "Are you going public with this, Kadar?"

"You don't have to make that decision, Emir." Rais is glaring at his phone, the very modern device looking incongruous in the large hands of the fierce-looking desert sheikh. "Someone must have put two and two together at the airport and has already run to the press."

As one, we all get out our phones and see the headline alert. *Desert Princess Kidnapped.*

Kadar swears loudly. "Jasim, get a press conference set up. We don't have a choice, and more people on the lookout for any unusual activity can't hurt."

"I'm happy dealing with the press," Jasim agrees. "I'll set something up and you can direct any enquiries to me. Rather everyone got the same story than went off half-cocked and make something up. I agree, the more people looking for her, the better. Whoever's got her will have to take more care hiding her. He might get careless and make a mistake."

I watch Kadar's hands as they open and shut, under-standing his frustration. We can look all we like, pretend we're taking action. At the end of the day the ball is in the kidnapper's court. It's unlikely we'll find her unless we have one hell of a lot of luck.

"Whatever you can do, just go and do it," Kadar declares. "Sitting here isn't doing anything to help. We'll reconvene once someone's made any progress or there's been contact."

As the men around me stand I pause for a moment, worried sick about the woman I've decided I want in my life, mentally sending a promise. *Hang on, Aiza. I'm coming for you.*

CHAPTER 9
Aiza

The man sitting by my side smells rank. Unfortunately there's no way to escape getting a whiff of his body odour with every breath I take. I'm thankful it's not too long before the sound of the rotors changes as we begin a descent. My relief soon turns into consternation. We've not arrived at an airport, or any type of civilisation, but the middle of the desert instead. As the handcuffs are undone and I'm pulled out of the helicopter, I rub my sore wrist to get the blood flowing again and look around, seeing nothing other than sand dunes in every direction.

There might not be anything to see, but there is something to hear—a sound which gets gradually louder, a rhythmic thump thump noise announcing another chopper is approaching. As it comes into view I see it's much larger than the small four-seater that brought me here.

"*Almarhalat alttaliat min rihlatik,*" the unpleasant smelling man tells me uselessly. I'd already figured out that my journey hadn't yet ended.

I don't bother questioning him more or asking where they'll be taking me, as I quickly learned he wouldn't tell me, and I've too much pride to beg for information. I don't even bother to run or try to escape. I'm not crazy. Unequipped for survival, I wouldn't last long in the desert even if I could evade capture. As the only rational reason for my kidnap is presumably to hold me for ransom, I'll take my chances and do what these men want me to. That way I've a chance of staying alive rather than face certain death.

Shielding my eyes, I look away as the landing helicopter whisks up sand, only glancing back when the rotors stop turning. When I see two robed men descend and come over towards me, I wish I'd worn the traditional tunic and trousers today, feeling far too exposed in my tight capris and small tee when their eyes roam over me, pausing far too long on my breasts and ass.

The tall man in the lead wears a smirk. "Princess," he starts sneeringly. "Your carriage awaits."

Noting he's spoken to me in perfect English, I raise my head haughtily, wondering whether these men will be more forthcoming. "Who are you? What do you want with me?"

"All in good time. Now, please." He bends a little and sweeps his hand in the direction of the new transport, the smirk remaining on his face. He might be exhibiting the right behaviours, but I can tell it's all pretence.

I hesitate, eyeing the men who brought me here, while suspecting there's little I can do to persuade them to take me back again. They're hired thugs, bribery probably wouldn't work. At least the newcomer looks and smells clean. Keeping my shoulders and back straight, I walk towards the helicopter, accepting the hand of the man who helps me inside. This craft's far more luxurious than the previous ride, and there are three other men waiting inside, including the pilot. That makes five in total, far too many for me to take on even if I did know the first thing about self-defence. *A big gap in my education.* One I'll rectify if I get out of this alive.

I'm politely directed to a soft leather seat as if I was an honoured guest rather than a kidnap victim. Rejecting the offer of help, I do up my own harness. There'll be a time for protest and struggling, and this isn't it. Best to save my energy for when I need it. Looking out of the window, I see what looks like money exchanging hands. As I watch I run through in my mind the advice I had been given about what to do if I was ever kidnapped. The first, of course, was to avoid being taken in the first place, and that one I've already failed.

Keep calm and be co-operative. While that goes against the grain, complaining won't get me very far. Retaining a semblance of composure isn't easy, my heart's been pounding since the airport, and useless adrenaline is pumping through my veins telling me to run, to fight, to scream. I force myself to slow my breathing. *Think, Aiza.*

Everything depends on who they are and why they've taken me—whether it's for money or for political advantage. If it's the former, then I'm worth more alive. If the later, I might make more of a point dead. *Observe.* I eye up my captors, trying to memorise their features. Cataloguing that someone has money, this isn't a run of the mill craft. That doesn't comfort me. If I've been kidnapped by someone already rich, why would he, she, or they want more wealth?

If someone likes me, it's harder for them to kill me. Whether I find it easy or not, I'll be co-operative and cordial even if I can't bring myself to be friendly. Make sure they see me as a person and not a piece of meat to be sold or disposed of. Whatever happens, I'll keep my dignity. I won't grovel or beg. I'm a princess after all, even if most of the time I try to forget the position I was born into.

I'm going to be rescued. Kadar won't give up. I've got to remain positive. Whatever happens, I'll keep the thought of rescue firmly in my head.

All the men are now on the helicopter, and the rotors start turning slowly. I wait for take-off, but before we get underway one man comes and sits opposite, and another appears by my side.

"You'll be more comfortable this way, Princess."

Before I can ask what he means, my arm's grasped firmly, and a hypodermic needle appears in the second man's hands. *Oh shit.*

Seeing my body tensing, the first leans forwards and stops me moving. I feel a prick in my arm, cold creeping through my body…

I wake lying on thin mattress on a cold stone floor. The room's dark, and there's a sound from outside it takes me a moment to recognise. Wind howling and heavy rain blowing against the window.

I shiver and wrap my arms around myself. The temperature and weather tell me I'm not in Kansas anymore. Not in Amahad or the neighbouring countries. As to where I exactly am, well, I could be anywhere in the northern hemisphere.

Tears prick at the back of my eyes. Angrily, I wipe them away. *I won't give in. I won't give up.* Rescue will already be on its way. As I raise my wrist, in the darkness there's a brief glimmer of something glowing.

Thank fuck! They didn't take my watch. And it's an iWatch with 4G. I must be crazy, but can I? I haven't tested it before. It's worth giving it a try. I tell Siri to call a contact. To my surprise and delight, it works and connects.

"Kadar? It's me. No, let me talk, I have to be quick. I'm using my watch and I'm low on battery. Can you trace me?"

"*Aiza?* What the fuck? Where are you?" It sounds like I'm the last person he expected to hear from.

I keep my voice low. "I've no bloody idea, Kadar. That's why I'm calling you. Get a trace on my signal, fast."

"I'll get Cara on it. Are you alright?" I've never heard my brother sound so concerned before.

"I was drugged, but so far unharmed. Kadar... Hearing your voice... But I need to give you as much time as possible, my watch could go off at any minute. I'm in a cold, wet place, that's all I can tell you."

A sigh as if he doesn't want to break the connection, then, "I understand. Stay strong. We're coming for you."

My voice breaks as I speak words I've never uttered before. "Kadar... I love you. Nijad and Jasim, too."

In an equally unsteady tone he replies, "Love you too, little sister. We'll see you soon."

I end the call wishing I could have listened to his voice for longer. Wishing that I'd had more information to give him. Glancing at the face of my watch I see the battery indicator is already well into the red zone. Reluctantly I take it off, immediately feeling naked removing the one fashion item I'm seldom without. Looking around for a hiding place, I lodge it between the mattress and the wall. I don't want anyone to find it and destroy it before Kadar presumably gets Cara to work her magic. Sometimes it's a bonus to have a hacker in the family.

I'm scared, though try to force down negative feelings, just concentrating on the fact I must survive whatever the unknown is bringing to me. I stand and stretch, rolling my head, trying to get the stiffness out of my sore muscles while wondering again where I am and what my kidnappers want. My head is throbbing, presumably from the drug they gave me to make me sleep. And also from a healthy dose of stress.

I examine my prison. It's bare. The window is high on the wall, suggesting I'm in a basement of some sort.

There's a light bulb glowing dimly, illuminating my sorry surroundings. Apart from the mattress there's nothing else here. My bladder is full to bursting. Unless I want to relieve myself in a corner I'll have to suffer until, hopefully, someone comes and lets me out of here.

I yawn, but I've slept enough. Too much. Had I woken before I might have some indication of where I've been brought to.

I'm getting colder by the second, clothes worn for the harsh heat of Amahad no protection against the climate here. The fact no one's looked out for my comfort concerns me, suggesting my health and well-being isn't a priority. *Or is this an attempt to weaken me?* It won't work. I'm determined to stay strong.

Giving into fear isn't going to help. I pace the room, trying to find something, anything to give me a clue as to what this place is, or something I can use as a weapon. Disappointingly, though the bricks look ancient, none are loose enough for me to pull them out.

It's not too long before there's a noise at the door, the sound of a key turning. Facing towards it, I watch as it opens. There are two men outside. One nods as he inspects me. "You're awake. Good. Come with me."

Geez. No manners. Not even a please. Focusing on his abruptness instead of the butterflies swirling in my stomach enables me to walk out with my head held high.

I follow the man who'd spoken up a narrow stone staircase, emerging into a brightly lit area at the top. It's no help to realise I'd been right, and my prison had been a basement. Eyeing my surroundings, I want to learn as much as possible in case I'm given a chance of escape. It looks like a small stately home, or a mansion of some sort. I'm now in a large entrance hall and being led to a door off to the side. The man opens it and waves me through, then steps in himself and takes up position in front of the door, effectively trapping me inside.

There's a blazing fire in the fireplace, logs spitting and cracking, the sight dissipating the chill even before the warmth hits my skin. Two wingback chairs are placed either side, and one is occupied by a man I've never seen before in my life. Not that I'd expected my captor to be someone I'd previously met, however there was always the possibility. Someone familiar would have provided a clue or suggested a reason for my abduction.

As I examine him, he's looking at me, a satisfied smile playing at his lips. It's not a comforting sight. Trying to stay strong, I manage to suppress a shudder.

What am I supposed to do now? I haven't a clue how one should greet their abductor. My kidnapping training omitted that.

After what seems like a lengthy pause, he stands. "Princess Aiza Kassis." He comes closer, then walks around me, and my skin begins to crawl.

"You know who I am. How about you introduce yourself?" I'm proud my voice sounds steady.

"My name isn't important," he replies as he returns to my front. He stands too close, and his eyes once again sweep across my body, a critical expression as he reaches out his hand and waves to my clothes. "You don't look much like an Arab princess. It's easy to rectify that."

"What do you want from me?"

"All in good time. All in good time." He takes a step back. "First, you should shower and change into attire that hasn't been slept in."

He makes it sound like I had been taking a nap, not drugged for hours. A bathroom, though, sounds good. I still need to pee badly.

"Frank here will show you where to go." He nods at the man standing behind me. "When you've cleaned up, we'll talk."

Don't annoy your captor. Another kidnapping lesson comes back to me. So, I dip my head in agreement. I do feel dirty, and a shower will hopefully get rid of this lingering headache, as well as go some way to warming me up.

Taking my arm with one hand, Frank opens the door with the other. This time he leads me up a grand carpeted staircase and indicates a room at the top. Stepping inside, I find it's a well-appointed bathroom, but when shutting the door behind me, find it has no lock. That makes me uneasy. However, unless I want to wet myself I have to ignore that someone could walk in when they like. Feeling vulnerable and exposed, I sit on the toilet, where I sigh with relief as I can at last empty my bladder. Then after I've flushed, look at the window. *Escape?* They've anticipated that. The window's been nailed shut.

There's a radiator underneath it, and as is common in old houses, it's doing little to take the chill off the room. A draught is getting in from somewhere, and I'm still freezing cold. A hot shower would warm me... But there's a man waiting outside who could come in any minute. I debate for a moment. If I don't do as I've been instructed, will I be making things worse for myself?

"Best get in that shower, lady. Or my instructions are to put you in it myself."

The voice coming from the other side of the door and the threat has me moving. I shower quickly, even in the circumstances enjoying the welcome warmth I can feel seeping into my bones. When I get out and have a towel wrapped around me, the voice speaks again. "I hope you're decent. I'm coming in."

Wait? What? Before I can protest the door flies open. Frank scoops up my old clothes and puts a pile of new ones on the chair to the side. While he's in here I keep rock still, holding that towel as tight as I can. He doesn't even glance at me, just completes his task and goes.

"You've got five minutes." The warning comes from the other side of the wood again.

I rub myself dry, then look at the garments which had been left for me. The black should have given it away immediately, though it's not until I pick it up and shake it

Blood Brothers #6: Hard Choices

out that I see it's a fucking abaya that will completely cover me from head to toe. There's black underwear too, certainly not that which a modest woman would normally wear—a lacy black bra with cut-outs for nipples and pants barely worthy of the name with a convenient slit in the gusset. The juxtaposition between robe and undergarments so confusing, I can't understand it. But immediately am afraid. *What have they got planned?*

"Two minutes."

I hadn't realised how long I'd been staring. Having no option, I slide into the pants and put on the bra, feeling very exposed. For want of something to hide me, I put the hideous abaya over the top. Even in Amahad very few people, except maybe an old woman, cover up in such things. There's a hijab too, that wraps around my face.

With only my eyes now showing, I'm just in time as the door opens.

"These too."

These are hooker shoes. Black with diamante, and at least five-inch heels. *What the hell am I being dressed like this for?* My mind comes up with an answer. I push the thought back down, replacing it with a far more optimistic one as I remember the call I'd made. *Kadar's going to find me before anything happens.*

Tottering precariously, I hang onto the handrail as we descend the stairs and return to the room to find my abductor sitting once again in his wingback chair.

"Thank you, Frank. I take it she gave you no problem?"

113

"No, sir. She behaved."

"Good. That's very good. And wise of you, dear. I wouldn't have wanted to have to mark such perfection."

"Who are you?" I ask again, goosebumps of fear rising on my skin. "And why am I here?"

"My name isn't important." He waves his hand dismissively. "Although you deserve to know what I am." He pauses as though for effect before continuing. "You see, I'm a broker."

CHAPTER 10
Hunter

Eight hours since Aiza's been taken. Eight fucking hours and we've still no idea where she's gone or who has her. There's been no contact, no request for a ransom. We remain convinced it's the terrorist, though so far there's been nothing to confirm our suspicions.

"Ben, surely any kidnapper would have been in touch by now." While I wouldn't wish being held for money on any woman, it's the best fate I can imagine for Aiza now. She wouldn't be harmed and should be well looked after.

"Hunter, calm down. Fuck, man. I've never heard you this emotional about a case. I get it that you feel responsible, but you need to focus and think with your head. Think rationally."

As Ben's voice admonishes me down the phone line I realise he doesn't have the faintest clue just how much I'm invested in her safe return. Somehow that girl has captured my heart, and I need her back to show her what she's come to mean to me. Is it a case of absence makes the heart fonder? That she's now beyond my reach serving to amplify what previously were embryonic feelings? I'm more resolute than ever that she'll be mine, and that never will anything harm her again. *If we find her in time.* Realising I'm gripping the phone so hard I'm in danger of crushing it, I force myself to relax and do as Ben suggested and, with determination, bring my brain into play.

"Look, Hunter, sometimes kidnappers like to give the relatives time to worry so when they do make their demand they're more likely to agree to it. She could just be being kept on ice for now. We still can't rule out that option. Not just yet."

I draw in breath. "The longer there's no contact the more likely…" I can't even say it.

"What's up with you, Hunter?" My boss isn't stupid, as shown by the tone of his voice. "Are you…?"

"Yes," I interrupt him and admit. "I like her, okay?"

Ben snorts, then apologises. "Okay. That was unexpected." There's a pause while he absorbs the new information. "Look, you need to put any feelings you have for her aside. You've got to think logically and use your fucking head. Act like the professional I know you are. Jon, I, Ryan, and Seth are ready as soon as we come up with a location. We're staying in London for now, though we've already got a plane fuelled and on standby."

Ben and Jon are ex special services, both having had training in hostage extraction when they were in the SAS —in fact, they became instructors themselves. They're the experts who'll be advising how to get her back once we know where she is and who has her. I'm relieved to hear they're planning to come in person.

"I'll keep you updated, Ben."

"Do that, Hunter. While I know Cara will be monitoring everything, Nafisa's doing what she can too. We'll find her, Hunter. Fucking hell, man. I don't know how you'll take it from there. The first thing to do is to get her back. Just focus on that, okay?"

"Thanks, Ben." He's right. Any thoughts of making her my woman need to be put to the back of my mind. I can't do anything until we extract her from whatever situation she's in.

I end the call while walking out of the empty office I'd used for privacy and return to the conference room, finding it in uproar.

"What's going on?"

The nearest person to ask is Rami. He's actually got a smile on his face. "Aiza's made contact," he tells me excitedly.

What? My first thought is one of relief. *She's safe.* "How, where…"

"Hunter!" Kadar calls my name so loudly the buzz of other conversations ceases. "Come take a seat and we'll update you on the situation."

Almost knocking over the chair in my hurry, I sit down. In the interval between standing and having my ass on the seat, I realise had anyone truly known where she was we'd already be moving. My relief rapidly fades, transforming into anxiety again. My arm where it had been clipped by a bullet throbs, I make myself ignore it.

Kadar nods when he sees everyone's settled. "Right. It appears Aiza's got one of those iWatches that has its own sim card. As you know, her phone was discarded, presumably they didn't realise the significance of her watch. She's just called me." He breaks off. "Ah, Cara. Thank you for joining us."

"Kadar. Aiza's been in touch, I hear?" She sees me and gives me a quick smile, but just as fast turns her attention back to her brother-in-law.

"Yes." He waits another second so she can join us at the table. Almost in one motion she sits and opens her laptop, her hands hovering over the keys as her face flicks towards Kadar.

"What's the number she rang from?"

In answer, Kadar slides his phone down the table. Cara glances at the screen and starts typing.

"Time's of the essence. Her phone is low on battery so she couldn't talk long. All she could tell me was that she wasn't in Amahad anymore, and where she was, it was cold and raining." Kadar's brow is furrowed, and his hands play with his beard.

"Could be fucking anywhere," Jasim observes.

The emir clears his throat. It doesn't work, as when he speaks next he sounds husky. "She told me she loved me, and you Jasim, and Nijad."

"Fuck," both brothers exclaim, as they exchange worried glances.

It makes me sit up. I've seen Aiza around her family enough times to know such platitudes are never exchanged. The fact she's now told them suggests she thinks she might never see them again. My muscles tense, and if I didn't concentrate on taking air into my lungs, I'd stop breathing.

"Okay." Cara starts talking. "The good news is the iWatch version she's got has GPS, so I should be able to pinpoint her position." She's tapping again, then looks up. "I've found her, and I'll send you the coordinates." Tilting her head to one side, she looks confused. "She's in the UK. Scotland to be precise."

Well, that would account for it being cold and wet. I start to rise, then realise Kadar's still seated.

"Hunter. Sit down." He glares at me, then looks to his sister-in-law. "Cara. Send those coordinates to Ben Carter. He and his team are the closest. Jasim, Nijad. We'll all go..."

"Not a good idea," Rais butts in forcefully. "Your Excellency, it may have been luck they allowed her to keep her watch, or it may be a trap to lure the ruling sheikhs out of the country. The three of you can't all go."

"I want to go and rescue my sister." Nijad's face grows dark, and fury emanates off him at the thought anyone would suggest otherwise.

Kadar is staring at Rais, his eyes sharpened as though they could pierce the sheikh. Rais meets his gaze head on, a challenge in his eyes. After a pregnant pause, Kadar lets

out a loud sigh, makes a quick decision and backs down. "I
hate to admit it. I know you are correct, Rais. I'll stay.
Nijad and Jasim will go. She'll need family around her."

"And a woman. I'll come." Cara's eyes shine with
emotion, and it doesn't take a genius to guess what she's
probably thinking.

"I, myself, will obviously go." Rais doesn't expect any
argument, and he's not given any.

"I want to come too." Rami raises an eyebrow in challenge towards Kadar. "You know my views." After a
moment's consideration, the emir gives him a nod. I
frown, not at all certain I want the prince there. *I want to
be the one she runs to.*

"Hunter?"

"Yeah. I'll be there. I'm meeting up with Jon, Ben and
the Grade A team."

Kadar's looking pointedly at the bandage on my arm.
"Are you fit enough?"

"I'm fine." I dismiss his concern. "No real damage
done. Ah," I hold up my hand as a text message comes in,
"will you excuse me a moment, Ben wants me to call
him."

"Put it on speaker, Hunter. That way we can all hear."

I waste no more time answering. "Ben, I've got you on
speaker."

"That's good, Hunter. I need only go over this once.
Good morning, Emir."

"Good *afternoon*, Ben. What have you got for us?"

"The co-ordinates Cara sent us are for a fair-sized house in a remote area of the Scottish Highlands. The type that's used for a shooting retreat. We're trying to trace the owner. That's proving difficult. It appears to be owned by a shell company, and it would probably take less time to peel an onion layer by layer by the time we get to the bottom of it.

"What's the defence like?"

"That you, General Zaram?"

"It is."

"The house is in a decent sized clearing in the middle of a forest, long driveway heading up to it through open countryside. There's a small loch to one side. Difficult to approach with any degree of surprise."

"Any other way to get close?"

"Maybe via the forest to the rear? We'll be able to assess more when we're on site. Anything we're seeing could be old information. We're relying on Google Earth here."

"Satellite pass?"

"We're working on that now."

There's a strange sound on the line, and I can hear traffic. "Jon, myself, Ryan and Seth are driving to London City Airport now. We've chartered a plane and the pilot's already put in a flight plan to Aberdeen. I suggest you fly straight there yourselves. We don't want to waste time on this, so we'll hire a couple of SUVs and get there as soon as possible, which means we'll be ahead of you. Wouldn't want to take the risk they might move her."

We know where she is. Ben Carter and Jon Tharpe, two of the people I respect most in this world, are on their way to her. I allow myself to take in the first deep breath since I stepped into the room. With the time difference we should get there late afternoon local time. By this evening I will hopefully be seeing her face to face, checking with my own eyes she hasn't been harmed.

"We'll get moving, Ben. Keep us updated."

"All the way, Kadar. All the way."

Nijad looks up. "I've put a call into the airport. The jet should be ready when we get there."

"Thanks, Ni. Right." Kadar shakes his head, a pained expression on his face. "You can continue planning on the plane, there's no time to waste." He pauses before adding his last words, which seem to come straight from the heart. "Bring her home. Just…bring her home."

We stand, Cara comes over to me, Nijad takes her arm and puts her behind him. At any other time it would have amused me. For now I make no comment, and instead listen to what he has to say. "Hunter, we're going in armed. Don't care what the fucking British laws say. Come with Jasim and me and tool yourself up."

Music to my fucking ears. I have no problem with going in heavy. As for shooting anyone there, whoever they are, they deserve to die for laying their hands on my woman.

We travel light, no need for packing. We have no intention of hanging around in Scotland, our aim just to retrieve Aiza and then getting the hell out of Dodge.

Quickly summoned, a man who I'm told is Kadar's personal doctor is coming along with us, together with a medical team. Why is something I'm trying not to think about. General Zaram also has a team of men.

We are whisked through the airport and the plane starts off down the runway almost before we've done up the seat-belts. Once in the air we put our heads together and start to plan for every eventuality. Without knowing more until we get eyes on the ground, we're limited as to how much we can put in place. Various suggestions are thrown around of alternative scenarios, still unsure whether we're up against an international terrorist or a bog-standard kidnapper.

"You know, even if it's someone who's kidnapped Aiza for ransom, they've already got money to come up with the organisation they did. The soldiers at the airport, two heli-copters to take them away. Somebody seriously wants her," Nijad points out.

"We can presume they won't give her up lightly. They've got too much invested in this." Rais slowly nods.

"I and my men will be taking the lead," the general informs us. At his word I glance at the half dozen uniformed men sitting at the back of the plane. All looking like they mean business.

"No." Rais shakes his head. "I will lead."

"You're not in the desert now," Zaram retorts.

Nijad objects. "I'll take the lead. She's my sister."

"With me by your side," Jasim agrees.

"Sheikhs, you will both stay back. My job is to protect the royal family. I can't have you putting yourselves in danger."

Nijad and Jasim toss identical glares in Zaram's direction and give equally identical shrugs. "Kadar's got an heir now, and with Jasim's son, Eti, there's still a spare. We're not going to be left behind. The last thing I heard, the military works for the royal family."

Christ, this is heading for a clusterfuck. It's time I take charge. "You've got two experienced hostage negotiators heading up there now. Ben Carter and Jon Tharpe are ex SAS. They're experienced soldiers and will be in place to formulate an actual plan, unlike the theoretical ones we've been throwing around. They know what manpower's coming and will be able to assess what they need. Their expertise means we should help, not hinder them. And everyone rushing in blind would be an error of immense proportions."

"You're right, Hunter," Nijad agrees.

General Zaram's lips have thinned. He doesn't look impressed, though there's not a lot by way of valid objection he could offer. What I've said makes sense.

No further information has been forthcoming, the only update that Grade A have still been unable to trace who owns the property. Cara's at the front of the plane working diligently, trying to dig deeper, working her magic on the dark web. So far even she's had no success. We're still working on the basis we'll be going in blind.

The plane journey is tedious, the six hours seeming to be double that time. A man of action, I prefer to be out doing things. I take out the Glock that I'd selected from the palace armoury and check it for the umpteenth time, patting my pockets to make sure I've got spare ammunition handy.

Cara's walking towards me, presumably heading for the restroom at the end of the plane. On her way back she drops into the empty seat opposite me. "She'll be okay, Hunter."

"Of course she will," I reply as nonchalantly as I can, not wanting to give away, even to my oldest friend, how personally concerned I am about rescuing Aiza.

"No…" She leans forwards and takes one of my hands. "She *will* be okay."

I glance at her sharply. She's clearly known me too long and knows me too well.

"It's easy to see you care for her." As I start to deny it, she stops me. "We've been friends forever, Hunter. It's your body language. I've sat across from you in meetings before, and I've never seen you so wound up as you've been today. You care very much for her, don't you?"

I throw a quick look up the aisle, checking Nijad and Jasim are out of earshot. I lean forwards too, which means my forehead is touching hers. "I do, Cara. Somehow I fucking do. Never felt something like this about a woman before. She's got me tied into knots. I want her."

"She's not one of your playthings."

Our skin touching, I take comfort from my best friend's presence. We've known each other for fifteen years and have always been close. "I wouldn't toy with her, Cara. I can't think of anyone else. I think, I know... Fuck it. I want to marry her. Start a family with her. Kids, dog, white picket fence, the lot."

Her hands surround mine. "If you can convince her, then she could do a lot worse."

I give a wane smile at Cara's endorsement, then it fades. "If she's still alive." I voice the unthinkable.

"She's too valuable breathing." Cara tries to reassure me.

"For fucks sake!" Suddenly Cara's wrapped in Nijad's arms. "Can't you keep your fucking hands to yourself, Hunter?"

"Ni!" Cara bats him away. "We were just talking."

"You can fucking talk without holding hands."

"I'll hold your hand instead then, shall I?" Despite the seriousness of the situation, Cara's grinning up at her husband, and he's looking down at her with devotion in his eyes. Although Nijad's never accepted the unusual and completely non-sexual friendship between Cara and myself, I couldn't think of a better man for her. Even given the way that they'd met.

An announcement comes over the speakers.

"Sheikhs, gentlemen, Sheikha. Please retake your seats and fasten your seatbelts. We're just about to commence the final approach into Aberdeen airport."

CHAPTER 11
Aiza

A broker? Although the clothing that I've been forced to wear reminds me of the subjugation of women in some Arab states, I stand tall and proud. Letting him know if it was his intention, he hasn't been successful in making me feel degraded. "What's your name, and who do you work for?" My voice has a touch of arrogance. Unbeknown to him, rescue is on its way. When I get out of this I'll do what I can to bring this man down. To help, I'll get all the information I can. Of course, the longer I keep him talking the more time I'm giving to Kadar.

He sneers. "My name isn't important. I work for no one."

"Oh, come on." He's fuelling my temper. "Someone must have paid you to kidnap me."

A smirk appears on his face. "You're correct, of course. I get commission on whatever merchandise is purveyed."

"I'm not *merchandise*. I'm a person," I spit.

Now he gives an unpleasant laugh that sends chills down my spine, the tone disturbing as much as his next words. "Not anymore."

What has he got planned for me? I push down the thought. I've already got a very good idea, and if I allow myself to think about it, I'd collapse in a heap of tears. Still believing it's important to show no weakness, imperceptibly I take a deep breath then cross to the wingback chair on the opposite side of the fireplace to his, and audaciously sit down, identifying myself as an equal, a human being, not a thing.

He smirks again, leaning over to a small table, picking up a decanter and pouring amber liquid into a glass. He swirls it around, then takes a sip, smacking his lips, showing he relishes the flavour. He offers none to me. Replacing the tumbler on the table, he gives me a considered look. "It will be interesting, *Princess*, to see how long it will be before you lose that conceit. I would lay down good money that it wouldn't take long."

I breathe deeply, trying to slow the fast beating of my heart, hiding the palpitations caused by fear summoned by his words. Inwardly terrified, I raise my head in challenge and don't deign to give him a response. *Princesses don't beg for mercy.*

The silence extends. He breaks it. "You're no longer a princess, no longer anyone at all. From this moment on you're a slave. And that's what you'll be until you die. There'll be no chance of rescue. The sooner you accept it, the easier it will be."

I'll accept nothing of the sort. "In your dreams," I retort.

Another huffed laugh. "No, slave. My dreams will be your nightmare." He sits forwards. "You want to know your fate? You have been purchased. You already belong to someone else."

"I belong to no one."

"Slave, however much you try to deny it, you have been bought. Shortly Frank will deliver you to your buyer. I don't imagine you'll have any chance of escape. Your purchaser lives on a yacht—by the way, I trust you don't get seasick?" He seems to find the suggestion amusing.

It's a rhetorical question, I can see he doesn't expect an answer. I don't tell him I'm already feeling nauseous, and it isn't from any thought of the sea. Glad my olive skin will help hide that all the blood's drained from my face, I probe. "And who is this man?"

"Your new Master."

I examine the man who calls himself a broker. Middle-aged. Not unattractive. Gold rings on his fingers. If I met him anywhere else there'd be nothing to warn me how evil he is. "Why are you doing this?"

"Why? It's my business. Don't think you can appeal to my better nature. I don't have one. I don't even see you anymore, you're goods which I've sold." He frowns. "It's business, that's all. A lucrative one. Sometimes it's a valuable painting, sometimes an antiquity. And sometimes, a slave."

I'm learning nothing to help myself. A frown plays at my lips, not knowing how much time I've got, whether

Frank will take me away before Kadar has a chance to arrive. Wanting to drag this conversation out, I know I need to find the right question which will bring me some answers. A moment later, the obvious one comes to mind. The one I haven't yet thought to ask. "Why me?"

"Why you?" He tilts his head to the side as if wondering whether to answer. "Well, that's not difficult to answer. You're beautiful, and your master won't find it a hardship to break you. I'd enjoy it myself." He smirks at me as if I should be flattered by the compliment. "It's your relationship to Emir Kadar that's the point. Kadar will be destroyed knowing what's happening to his sister."

"You're going to tell him?"

He chuckles. "Oh, much better than that. He'll see with his own eyes." He picks up his drink and swallows again. "When your master takes your virginity—and you are a virgin, aren't you?" He raises an eyebrow. When I completely ignore his personal and inappropriate question, he continues. "He'll take you roughly and without care, and everything will be filmed. The video will be sent to your brother. When you're whipped, left bleeding, Kadar will see it all, every single stroke laying your back open. When your master wishes to share you with his friends, every scream, every indignity, every hole, Kadar will watch."

I look on, unable to conceal my horror as he adjusts himself in his trousers as if he is getting carried away relaying the horror that lies in my future and turning himself on.

Hurry up, Kadar. You must know where I am by now.

I hear a familiar sound, the rotors of a helicopter thump thumping, and my heart leaps in anticipation and hope. Which is almost immediately dashed.

"Ah. Our little chat is over. That is your transport arriving."

It can't be. Kadar needs more time. He's looking away as if he's already lost interest, dismissed me as though I mean nothing at all. According to him, I don't. Something tells me I can't draw this out. Whatever he's set in motion will play out without me being able to stop it.

I don't plead. Don't beg. Don't try to appeal to any conscience he clearly doesn't possess, as our conversation has shown.

There's a knock at the door, and Frank, together with the other, as yet unnamed man who'd accompanied me from Amahad enter. The broker, staying seated, simply nods as suddenly they surround me, pulling me none too gently from the chair.

Before I'm taken out of the room I pull back my shoulders and give my kidnapper the most arrogant look that I can. *The master he referred to may indeed break me. I'll not be leaving this man with the slightest satisfaction that he had any part in my destruction.*

I can't fight off two strong men. Determined not to break, somehow recognising they'd prefer to see me kicking and screaming, I force myself to walk calmly out of the room with them and to my fate.

My body might seem compliant, however my mind's whirling. If no one's coming for me, I, myself, will have to find some way of escape. I won't allow myself to be used. I'm a princess, not a slave. No, my rank isn't important, this fate shouldn't befall any woman. I desperately try to tamp down the thought that while Kadar knows I was brought *here*, the destination of the helicopter will remain unknown. *Kadar. Hurry up. Time's running out.*

If I'm gone, Kadar will question this man. From what I know, and usually try to avoid thinking about, Amahadian torture methods are both vicious and effective. In the circumstances, I've no doubt Kadar will employ them.

I just have to hang on until my brothers save me.

Wishing I was still wearing my iWatch, yet knowing by now it will probably have run out of charge, I allow myself to be seated in the helicopter. I'm already shivering in this inadequate clothing. Snowflakes are fluttering in the air, and in high-heeled shoes I wouldn't get far if I tried to run. I save my energy for when it's going to be worth it. *As soon as I get a chance, I'll take it.* As Frank climbs in the helicopter to sit beside me his jacket opens, enabling me to see a gun in the holster. *Now, if I could get hold of that...*

There's a headphone set by my side. As Frank puts his on, I do likewise. Immediately I can clearly hear what the pilot is saying. He's preparing to take off. As the helicopter rises into the air, I have an idea.

It must be worth a try. "I'm a princess," I start. "I have money. Take me to an airport and I'll give you any amount you like." If they ask for more than I have access to, Kadar would help. *What am I thinking?* My brother's more likely to trap them and kill them. That would be no more than they deserve.

I know they've heard me as Frank throws me a strange look, but no one answers. While they talk among themselves they ignore me, at times mentioning the package they have to deliver. It's apparent my kidnapper was right. They're already dehumanising me.

A sob rises. I stuff my fist in my mouth to stop it escaping, willing myself to stay strong. *Kadar won't give up.* While I'm not close to my brothers, by stealing me away they've insulted the monarchy and the country. That is what will be driving Kadar on. He wouldn't let such affront to Amahad go unpunished.

It doesn't seem long before the thumping of the rotors changes to a rhythmic thwack thwack thwack sound, which I know from my familiarity with such mode of travel means it's coming into land. *But where?* I peer out of the window in the gloom of the darkening skies—night falls early in this part of the world. I can see nothing beneath us, only the wane light of the moon reflecting off waves. *He told me I would be taken to a yacht.*

I hate the sea, a feeling that appears to be reciprocated, as each time I've been on a boat the movement of the waves makes me ill. Well, this man who's apparently bought me, and who I refuse to call Master, will get what he deserves if he tries to force himself upon me and I'm violently sick.

I swallow rapidly as we descend, giving myself a silent lecture, reminding myself to be brave. Despite all the years when I tried to forget my origins, I'm now repeating to myself, *you're a princess. Princess Aiza.* And no one, or anything that's done to me, will ever take my identity away.

The chopper lands with a slight lurch, making me clasp the harness, worried we'll be blown off the helipad into the sea. I can hear the wind outside, and already feel the motion of the yacht. My stomach, churning with fear, threatens to rebel.

Frank leans over and unfastens my harness and rips my headset off my head. "Out."

As the other man opens the door, I obey, knowing there's no point struggling to stay in my seat. Again I get a glimpse of Frank's gun. My problem is, unless I can immobilise him in some way, there's no way to get my hands on it. I'd only be using guesswork if I tried to fire it. As Hunter had pointed out, firearms training wasn't in my curriculum.

A man in white uniform approaches, gives a nod to the men who'd brought me here, then speaks to me curtly. "This way."

The wind's blowing, the snow's changed to sleet. Looking around I can't see far in the darkness, not knowing whether we're close to land or far out at sea, nor, if the former, which direction the coast is. If I tried to escape by swimming I'd probably die of hypothermia within minutes. I'm still not that close to giving up. With nothing else to do, I go through the door indicated, stumbling in my high heels.

The uniformed man leads, I follow, my eyes searching for some kind of weapon, but the hallway is bare with doors off the side. I start to get an idea this yacht is enormous, certainly much bigger than I expected. Soon we come to big double doors. He pushes them open, stands aside to let me enter, then disappears without a word.

I step inside, then pause with my back to the doorway. While the size of the boat had already led me to believe it's owner has to be loaded, his wealth is apparent by the size of the room and the furnishings within. The artwork on the walls appear to be originals, the gold fittings, I would guess, real and not gilt. I'm not unused to such opulence, having lived my formative years in the palace of Amahad, but to find it floating on the sea is surprising. The room is huge, larger than I expected, and when a man removes himself from the chair he'd been sitting in at the far end, I take a moment to examine him.

He's dressed in Arabian robes, his head covered. It's hard to tell his age, he's well past the flush of youth, lines betraying his years. Middle-aged is the closest I can place him. His mouth is thin, his nose aquiline, his eyes too close together.

He's tall and walks with a purposeful stride as he approaches me.

I pull myself up straight, refusing to cower.

He pauses a short distance away. "*Kunt tufadil alta-haduth biallughat al'iinjliziat 'aw alearabia?*"

Should I stay silent? Mute? Or face up to him? "English," I reply, as he asks me what language I'd prefer to converse in, deciding the only way to get information is to speak.

"English, *Master*," he corrects, adding, "Slave."

For a response I just draw back my shoulders.

He laughs. "Let me explain your situation. You are on my yacht, the *Master of the Sea*. An appropriate name, don't you think?" He pauses, I say nothing. "It has ten guest cabins as well as the master suite. Unoccupied now, of course, while we get to know each other. After I've trained you I'll start inviting guests. I have a crew of fifty who have their own accommodation. Fifty men and women who are fiercely loyal to me. It would be useless for you to try to bribe any of them. Any attempt will be reported to me and severely punished. Do you understand me?"

The last four words are snarled out, the suddenness hitting me like a physical blow. Still I offer no answer.

My lack of response doesn't appear to faze him. Instead he chuckles. "Oh, I'm going to enjoy breaking you." He stares at me for a moment. "You need to understand, I own you, completely. Your home is this yacht, and you will never leave. You will never put your feet on land again. You will be here for the remainder of your life, and how long that lasts will be completely up to me." His eyes, meeting mine so directly, seem to mesmerize me. "If you behave as I wish, I *may* reward you. Or I may punish you for my own enjoyment. If you don't obey me, you will receive retribution, the likes of which you cannot yet imagine. You are here solely for *my* pleasure. Nothing I do will ever be for yours. You are not a person, you're not a human being. You're not even an animal. You are my toy. Are you appreciating your situation yet?"

I'm shaking. However much I try to remain poised, the terrible words coming out of his mouth are affecting me.

"The only way you can make your life easier is to do what I say, when I say it. If I ask you to put your hand in fire you will do so for my entertainment. If I tell you to have sex with a dog, you'll do it." He walks behind me and then circles back to my front. "I don't expect you to pretend to enjoy anything I ask of you. I don't want your pleasure, real or faked. It's your tears, your screams that I desire. Are you understanding me yet?"

CHAPTER 12
Rais

I'm not one for sitting still for long periods. Even in meetings I prefer to walk around, quick to start fidgeting if I'm forced to remain in my chair. The long flight has tried my patience. Now, sitting in the SUV with Jasim beside me isn't helping to calm me. My leg bounces with frustration. My one desire is to get to our destination and rescue Aiza. The journey to get to her is taking forever.

"I suppose you look on her like a little sister, too?" Jasim asks, his eyes not missing my agitation.

Not fucking likely. Now's not the time to reveal my true interest. Kadar knows, of course, though he obviously hasn't enlightened his brothers. "I've known her most of her life." That's the truth, though the way I view her has decidedly changed over the years.

He seems to want to talk rather than brood in silence. "She used to annoy the hell out of me and Nijad. Always following us around."

A snort from the front seat. "We discouraged that pretty fast. When she born we were already at boarding school, only coming home for the summer holidays. We had better things to do with our time. Like learning to be men."

"And Kadar was being trained as a clone of the emir." I'd seen how the family had lived for myself while spending time at the palace and training in the desert alongside Jasim and Nijad.

"I suppose we were quite hard on her." Jasim closes his eyes for a moment, then shakes his head. "I can't think of one time we actually treated her as anything other than a nuisance." He glances at me with an apologetic shrug.

"She grew up before we noticed, Jasim. I couldn't say I know her at all," Nijad adds dejectedly.

Silence falls. I suspect they're wondering whether they'll get the chance to make it up to their sister. Not that the brothers know it, but while they'd been away getting on with their lives I had taken pity on the young girl, giving her her first riding lessons when she came to stay in the southern desert—another location where she was sent to be out of sight. Not then having an inkling the child I was leading around on a pony would grow into such a beautiful woman, independent enough to turn her back on her royal heritage and use her own money to fund charity work. The exact kind of woman I want by my side and in my life. The affection I'd felt for the girl having morphed into something far deeper and far more mature.

Hunter, driving due to his familiarity with driving on the left, has kept quiet during our discussion. He might have been concentrating on the road, or, not having known Aiza as a child, he wouldn't have had much to communicate. He does, however, speak now. "Aiza's an amazing woman."

"You seemed quite taken with her at my wedding," Nijad says, and I note that he seems much more relaxed with Hunter when Cara's not around. He's left his wife with the plane. She can continue to work there and, quite rightly, Nijad refused to have her exposed to any danger.

"I was," Hunter admits. "I spent time talking to her at Kadar's wedding too. I admit I've not had a lot to do with her in between, but we had interesting conversations the night I brought her here. I give you fair warning, I intend to get to know her much better."

I growl under my breath.

"Are you saying what I think you're saying, Hunter?" Jasim sounds amused.

"Why not?"

I could certainly tell him why not.

I see Nijad stiffen in the front seat. "I'm not sure you'd be right for her, Hunter." I'm surprised he's refraining from saying much else. It's well know he's always maintained his suspicions about Hunter's intentions towards his wife.

"Aiza's a grown woman," Hunter reminds him. "She should be allowed to make decisions for herself. If it's me she wants, you're not going to stand in my way, Nijad."

"I won't have her back only to lose her," Nijad starts, and quiets Hunter's interruption with a growl. "Neither will I prevent her doing what she wants to do. But I won't be pressing your case."

I want to throttle the man driving. At least now he's showed his hand I can be better prepared. Without giving my own interest away, I remind Hunter there's yet another rival. "I think you'll have a fight on your hands with Rami. He's made it quite clear that he's going to make a move." Rami, who I thought was my only competition, is in the vehicle following us. Behind are the other hired SUVs carrying the military men.

"Rami's far too weak for her. Oh, he's a decent enough chap, but Aiza needs a strong man. She needs a Dom, not a sub."

"Sub?" The man by my side laughs. "You think Rami's submissive, Hunter?"

"Actually, I think he is too, Jasim. He's like a puppy, eager to please." Nijad's summed up the prince well in my estimation.

"Perhaps Aiza would like to teach him new tricks." Jasim chuckles again.

Hunter's phone rings. He answers immediately, putting it through the car's speakers.

"Your position, Hunter?" Ben Carter asks, his voice immediately recognisable.

Hunter's head lifts as though he's consulting the Sat Nav. "About twenty minutes away."

"We've just got into position, had to hike through the woods at the back. While we were moving in there was a development I don't like. A helicopter arrived. Only stayed a few minutes, then left."

"It was picking someone up," Hunter replies quickly, his voice sounding strained.

"Or dropping someone off."

"Either way, I don't like it. What's the plan, Ben?"

"Ryan got close enough to get the identity of the helicopter. I'll try and find out if it's filed a flight plan. Jon's already trying to get it tracked by satellite."

He breaks off, and I hear murmured voices, then he's back. "We can't follow it on the ground. We'll stick to the original plan. If she's still there, we'll get to her, if she's not, hopefully there'll be someone in the hunting lodge who'll be able to tell us where they've taken her."

"Hold off until we get there," Nijad commands. "We go in together."

I crack my knuckles. If there's anyone there and Aiza's been taken away, I'll be asking questions to which they'll have to fucking respond, and in such a way that leaves them no other choice other than to tell us all they know. I might have watched my lieutenant, Mustapha, a time or two. He's an expert at torture.

Nearing the location, we pull off the road where Ben had indicated. The Grade A senior partners appear out of the trees as if by magic as we prepare for whatever might lie ahead. All of us having divested ourselves of our robes, and we're dressed alike in dark jeans, black jumpers and jackets. Leaving the warmth of the SUV, I pull my coat around me, noticing the cold which immediately starts seeping into my desert bones. Snowflakes flutter around me as I momentatily remove the jacket to slide on the armoured vest Ben's handed out.

Our group huddles around, and Jon updates us. "There's a rear entrance Ryan's already checked out. One man in the main room to the left of the hall. A butler and cook were seen in the kitchen. Two guards left with the helicopter, and there were three more that we saw."

We outnumber them, that's good. Ben gives us directions. General Zaram and his men will make the first advance along with Ben's team. Hunter will stay back with us. Once they immobilise the guards we'll go in and search for Aiza.

Armed with stun grenades, guns and knives, we're only paces behind them as attacks are made at various locations around the ground floor.

It's not a fair fight. Our attack took the people inside totally unawares, our trained soldiers easily overpowering untrained guards. Ryan and Seth run up the stairs to check out the rest of the house, with calls of 'clear' echoing as they look into each room.

Jasim, Nijad, Hunter, Rami and I go into the elegantly furnished room where our prey is sitting. Presumably the man who owns or leases this house.

As Jon appears shaking his head and says the words I dread to hear, "She's not here. Found the room where she was kept. In the fucking basement," I notice he's holding an iWatch in his hand, and then he slides it into his pocket.

Snarling, I throw myself at the Caucasian man who sits sneering, not even bothering to get up. My hand around his throat, I pull him up out of his chair, pushing him back until he slams up against a wall. "Where the fuck is she?" I spit at him, shaking him so hard his teeth rattle.

Unease appears in his eyes.

"Talk." Nijad approaches. "Don't mistake us for fools. Rais, loosen your hand. He can't say anything like that."

I hadn't realised the man's face is turning red as my hand constricts his airway. I loosen my fingers slightly, however don't let him go.

"Where's the princess?"

"I don't know what you're talking about," he gasps.

I've no patience. I hit him hard in the stomach. "Aiza Kassis. We know she was held prisoner in this house. Who are you, and why did you take her?"

My blow had knocked the wind out of him, but still he denies it. "You're mistaken, I don't even know who you're talking about. There's been no woman here."

Jasim comes up alongside his brother, taking the iWatch from his pocket and dangling it in front of the man. "This says you're lying." He glances at me and nods. "I've heard some of the methods my friend Rais here uses to get people to talk. They're quite inventive. I'm not quite sure I've got the stomach for it myself. Why don't we leave you alone with him for a while? Rais?"

An ugly grin comes to my face. "Sure, Jasim." There's nothing I'd like more.

Nijad puts his hand on my arm. "Just make sure he can talk. Doesn't matter if he can't walk, or ever fuck again."

"If you don't get results, I'll try myself." Now Rami joins in.

"He's wet himself," Jon throws in conversationally.

"I'll talk. I'll talk." The man is trembling, his face, at last, full of fear.

"Fucking talk then." Curling my hand around his neck, I throw him into the middle of the floor. "What's your name and what have you done with Aiza?"

Stunned by the force of hitting the floor, he pulls himself into a sitting position and brushes his hair back off his face. Wild eyes scan the angry men facing him. If he's seeking one to appeal too, he'll come up lacking.

"My name's Chris Germaine. I'm a broker." He shakes his head as though hating that he has to admit it. "I was paid to procure Princess Aiza."

Procure her? "Who paid you?" I advance menacingly.

"Sheikh Twafiq al Karim bin Ajam," he spits out as if he can't talk fast enough. "He bought her."

As Nijad and Jasim exchange glances, I stare at Germaine. There was something in the way he said it. "That's not all, is it? Who paid you to take her?"

"Twafiq..."

145

My boot kicks out and connects, oh dear, with his balls. He curls up. "I want the truth and nothing but the whole fucking truth," I roar.

"Twafiq," he cries out again, the word having two syllables punctuated by gasps.

I've had enough of this. I draw a long knife out of my boot and again advance. "Say goodbye to your cock…"

"Amir al-Fadi! It was Amir al-Fadi," he screams, and finally we've got the truth, and even if it's what we expected, it's not what we wanted to hear.

"Where's she now?" Jasim asks, the urgency in his voice making me look at him. "Where the fuck is she now?" His voice has risen in pitch.

I've never seen him loose control. It shocks me. "Twafiq?" I query, a cold feeling shooting through me.

"Bad fucking news, Sheikh." A look at Nijad shows he's just as concerned as his brother.

Roaring, I approach Germaine again. He shuffles back as fast as he can until his progress is stopped by a heavy armchair. Approaching ominously, with absolutely no mercy on my face, I ask again. "Where. Is. She?"

"The helicopter took her to his yacht. She'll be there by now. It was anchored in Lochaline, but his plan was to set sail. I don't know where she is now. That's the honest truth."

Out of the corner of my eye I see Ben heading out with his phone in his hand, Jon by his side. Although I suspect Nijad and Jasim already have a very good idea, I'm still in the dark and need Germaine to spell out exactly what's going on here. "What do you know, Germaine? Why did Amal al-Fahri want her kidnapped, and why did Twafiq buy her?" I ignore the fact he must have been payed twice. That thought alone makes me want to pull his fingernails out.

"I can't tell you. He'll kill me. You'll know soon enough. You won't be able to find her to stop it."

"To stop what?" Rami asks, his voice shrill. As he starts to rush at Germaine I hold him back. *He's mine.*

"Amir al-Fahri wants to destroy Kadar."

"And where does Twafiq come in?" My voice has dropped an octave. I'm barely able to speak through my rage.

When the answer doesn't immediately come I grab him by the neck, lift him up and dangle him, shaking him violently again.

He speaks fast, knowing it's the only way to get out of my hold. "He wanted a slave. He's going to fuck her and film it, and Kadar will get the tapes. He'll threaten to kill her if Kadar doesn't halt oil production…"

Again I throw him on the floor, ignoring the oomph of pain behind me. I turn and look at Jasim and then Nijad, my raised eyebrow asking a silent question.

"I know of him by reputation," Jasim starts. "He has slaves. They're never seen or heard of again."

"Why hasn't he been stopped?"

"No evidence. Or none that will stick," Nijad informs me.

Jasim nods at Nijad. "He wanted membership to Club Tiacapan when I still owned it. I denied it to him. Wherever he has played, he's been thrown out."

And my Aiza's with this monster now?

Ben and Jon return. "Coastguard's going to look for the yacht. The helicopter is one of Twafiq's, and luckily he's not a trusting sort. He's got tracking on it. Cara's managed to hack into the system and confirmed it's landed on the yacht."

"Can we keep tracking it?"

"Not much point. It landed then flew off again. All we know is where the yacht was when it did so."

Jon pushes past and stands hovering over Germaine, his face black as thunder. "What's the name of Twafiq's yacht?" he roars.

Germaine doesn't hesitate to spit out, "Master of the Sea."

Jon's got his phone out again. It only takes him a few seconds to google. When he turns back, he's shaking his head. "Shit." He pushes back his dark hair. "It's no small boat. It was only recently built for him. It can house 80 staff and 20 guests. Fuck knows how many people will be on board. It's close on one hundred metres long."

Fuck. It's hard to prevent returning to Germaine and kicking him, just to let my frustration out. Getting into this house was a doddle. Getting onto the yacht? That's going to be something else entirely.

CHAPTER 13
Aiza

As he stands there and lists the depravities he'll want to put me through, *for his entertainment,* something inside me shrivels. Hope. Hope that I'll get out of here and that rescue is coming. Or that it will arrive in time before he succeeds in what he wants to do. The things he said, they'd destroy me. When I cease providing him with amusement he'll kill me. And enjoy doing it.

He's *the devil.*

He's still studying me, still got me gripped in his thrall. He chuckles again. "You might think silence is your weapon, it doesn't bother me. I don't mind that you're not using words. Your screams, your cries, your pleading will be music to my ears. And you will scream, you will cry, and you will beg."

"Who are you?" I whisper, for some reason wanting to know the name of the man who intends to abuse me.

"Your Master." He steps closer and rips of my hijab, my long hair flowing loose. Then he moves back and snaps. "Take off the abaya."

I don't move a muscle.

He smiles and moves to the wall where he presses a button. In seconds the door opens, and two men enter. "Strip her."

They're rough, burly specimens, both looking like ex-heavyweight boxers, one's nose broken so many times it's gnarled with bumps. The other has a scar drawing down his mouth, giving him a permanent scowl. Automatically I flinch. I struggle as they grab hold of me, quickly finding I'm not strong enough to fight them. One holds me tight, the other doesn't bother gently undressing me, using his strong hands to rip the abaya right down the middle. The other slides it off.

I'm standing in front of three strangers in provocative underwear that hides nothing. Even though I keep repeating to myself I'm a princess, it's hard to remain composed.

The man who calls himself Master, who I've named the devil, imperiously waves his hand, and the two men step back. As if they've done this before, each take hold of one of my arms, stretching them out to the sides.

The devil comes closer, too close, invading my personal space. His breath, landing on my face, carries the mixture of mint and alcohol. His hands reach out, each touching a breast, circling over the flimsy material of the bra. He finds the convenient holes and widens them, encouraging my nipples to poke out. Then he pinches them, so hard tears come to my eyes, and it's all I can do to smother my cry.

Before I realise what he's doing, one hand shoots down and finds the open slit in the gusset of my inadequate underwear. His fingers slide inside, his touch on my dry folds making me cringe.

All the time he's been watching my eyes, seeing there the expressions I've no chance of hiding, however hard I struggle to compose my features.

"Oh, I'm going to enjoy deflowering you."

Then he moves quickly, ripping away my bra and pants in two quick movements. The men holding me seem completely impassive as he tells me, "You've no need for clothes. Now kneel."

I'll kneel at the feet of no man. But as I raise my chin defiantly, my captors push on my shoulders, applying such pressure that my knees fold. Knowing what's expected of him, Scarface puts his hand on the top of my head, forcing me to bow.

"Remember this pose. Whenever you see me, this is how you greet me. You stay like this until I give you a command."

Staring at the floor, I hear him addressing the men holding me. "You know what to do."

I'm pulled to my feet, and Broken Nose and Scarface pull me outside. Relief fills my body that I've been removed from the devil's presence, then I feel afraid again, as I've no idea where they're taking me. *To his bedroom?*

I'm led through the yacht, my position made clear to me as I pass uniformed sailors, staff who look like stewards, both male and female. They greet the men holding me in a friendly way. Once or twice my escorts even stop to make small talk. Not one person looks at me or acknowledges my nakedness, emphasising that I'm nothing here. It's as if I don't exist.

I try to seek a glimmer of sympathy, someone who might have enough compassion to help me escape. But there's nothing. Total loyalty, he'd told me. From what I've seen, he's apparently right.

We descend a staircase, heading into the bowels of the ship, the sound of engines louder here. A door is opened, I'm pushed inside, and I hear a key turning in a lock.

I look around where they've brought me. There's a window in the door, the only other light in this bare room coming in from the bulb screwed into a cage on the ceiling. It's dishearteningly like a prison cell. There's an uncomfortable looking cot, a toilet, and basin. Nothing else. No porthole so I could see outside.

My situation, my fear, and the movement of the ship combine, and I rush to the toilet and am violently sick. Wiping my face on the supplied paper, I sit back on my bare haunches, wondering what the hell I can do.

A sound from the hallway gets my attention. I turn quickly to see the devil standing there, staring in at me through the glass window. I wait for the door to open, relieved when it doesn't. Ignoring him, I search for a light switch to dim the room, soon discovering there's not one here, and that cage around the light is bolted to the ceiling. The smirk on my enemy's face shows me this is part of the degradation. Nothing I do will be private anymore. He, and anyone else, can stand and watch me whenever they want.

With no way of measuring time, I'm not sure how long he stands there without moving. Having given up looking for what isn't there, I face him and hold his stare, forcing myself to keep my hands to my side, standing brave and tall despite the circumstances. Not wanting to give him the satisfaction of being the one to look away first. In the end he turns and leaves. In no way do I feel I've won.

Going to the bunk I sit down and put my head into my hands. I could dissolve into sobs, they're not very far away. I could cry, could scream and beat my hands. It would be too easy to sink into despair, to imagine the devil actually doing the things he'd listed out. To envisage Kadar's face when he sees the videos, or Nijad or Jasim. Whether I've only got a distant relationship with them or not, they're my family. Knowing how I'd be distraught myself at the thought of any one of them being tortured, I can only imagine they'd be beside themselves, and moving heaven and earth to save me.

As they'll be doing everything they can now. It's only a matter of time until they find who's taken me, and where I'm being held. I just have to remember the resources at their disposal—Hunter and Grade A will be helping, *and* the authorities. No stone will be left unturned. The kidnapper I'd last seen at the house will be made to give up his secrets. Of that there's no doubt.

A strange clunking sound interrupts my thoughts. When it stops the engines become louder, and the movement of the yacht changes, becoming smoother. *The anchor's been pulled up and we're moving.* All the kidnapper will be able to say is where we were. *Is it possible to find a yacht in the wide ocean?*

Yes. It is. It has to be. Otherwise, just like the yacht, I'll be lost.

I wait. No one else comes to spy on me. I have no way of knowing the time. Eventually I lie on the bed, noticing there's been no blanket or sheet left for me, nothing to cover my nakedness, and the light remains on. Though it's warm enough, I feel so exposed. Everything I do, every time I do something that's normally mundane, like simply relieving myself, somebody could stroll along and watch me.

That knowledge means all my senses are on high alert. I can't sleep or even relax, just toss and turn, shutting my eyes momentarily then immediately opening them again to look at that window, unnerved by the feeling of people able to observe me when I'm at my most vulnerable.

I wait. And I wait. And I wait. Wanting an end to my isolation while equally hoping no one will come. I'm hungry and thirsty, forced to drink water from the tap over the basin, hoping it is suitable for drinking. In case it's not, taking only enough in my cupped hands to wet my parched throat.

Eventually the key turns in the lock and the door opens again. In steps Scarface and his mate, Scarface moving quickly to restrain me while Broken Nose fastens something around my neck. I hear a snick, then Broken Nose moves back. In his hand he's holding a leather leash.

Sliding my hands up to my throat, I find I'm wearing a collar. It's so tight it makes me gag, but there's no buckle that I can immediately find to loosen it. I don't get a chance to investigate further before there's a tug on the leash, the pressure he's applying making me fall forwards.

Scarface catches me, laughing at my discomfort. Another fierce tug, and I have to move or fall down. Knowing I can't do anything else or be strangled, I let them lead me along the corridor, up the stairs, and eventually into a dining room where the devil is sitting as though waiting to be served. Again no one's acknowledged me as I've passed them, and Broken Nose has been rough, jerking the lead hard even when it wasn't necessary. By the time I reach my destination, my neck is sore.

The devil waves and indicates a spot on the floor by his feet, and the lead gets me moving closer.

"Kneel."

I don't.

Broken Nose and Scarface make sure I do, pushing me down hard while yanking hard on the leash.

A waiter appears, and a plate of something with a
wonderful aroma of bacon is placed in front of the man
who thinks he owns me. Food is put on the floor in front of
me. It doesn't smell appetising and being served in a dog
bowl puts me right off, even had I wanted to eat at that
moment. Another bowl is lowered, this one of clean-
looking water.

"Get used to it," the devil tells me, and then proceeds to
dive into what I assume is his breakfast.

A few minutes pass, then he wipes his mouth on the
serviette. "Food is a luxury to be earned," he says casually.
"I've been generous offering you sustenance when you
haven't done anything to deserve it. And what do you do?
You ignore my generosity." He takes a cup and sniffs at it,
then takes a noisy sip. "Mmm."

The smell of coffee assaults my nostrils, making my
mouth water. *Don't beg.* I clamp my teeth together to stay
quiet.

Suddenly he stands, so fast his chair rattles as though it's
going to topple over. Taking hold of the leash, he pulls me
to my feet, and with his free hand swipes his used plate and
utensils off the table, sending them smashing onto the
hardwood floor.

Then he grabs me roughly and bends me over the table,
his upper body holding me down as he fastens the end of
my leash to an eyelit he's pulled seemingly out of nowhere,
and produces handcuffs, which, while I flail my arms, he

Blood Brothers #6: Hard Choices

easily forces around my wrists and attaches to other fastenings. Held down by my throat and my wrists, I can't move.

Allah! He's not going to…

I feel him leave me, hear a cupboard opening, and then there's warmth at my back again. Then I scream as something hits me hard over my backside. The next time I'm better prepared and press my lips together, trying not to let the cries out. But he continues, my buttocks, my thighs and my bum, continuing until I can't help whimpering, and then I'm begging him to stop. A few more strikes, and then, at last, my torture ceases.

He must have summoned them, because Scarface and Broken Nose reappear.

Out of the corner of my eye I see a crop land on the floor. Then hear the words, "Take my pet for a walk and get someone to clean this place up."

I wait to be untied, unable to move until I'm free. There's a delay before I feel a hand stroking across my bruised arse. I cringe at the unwanted rough touch.

"Her arse marks up well, doesn't it?"

"Yeah. I'm looking forward to fucking it. Reckon he'll let us break her in tonight?"

"He might. He's an impatient sod. Fucking love my job."

Broken Nose laughs. "Wouldn't have got it if we weren't such ugly buggers. The Sheikh loves the contrast, beauty and the beasts."

Scarface is chuckling too. "Specially when we both go at her at once. Will make for a great film. Might get some money from it too."

"D'reckon she'll bleed?"

"All the better if she does."

I feel a weight pressing into my back. "I'm a big chap," Broken Nose says straight into my ear. "When the sheikh's ready, I'm gonna rip this arse right up."

CHAPTER 14
Rami

For most of the proceedings I've stood with my mouth open, watching as the others expertly get information from Germaine, trying to take in all that he's telling us, trying to cope with my crushing disappointment. When we had landed in Scotland I'd honestly thought it wouldn't be long before we found Aiza. We'd have freed her, then I'd have comforted her. I had even been thinking of how to begin to prepare my suit—depending on what state we found her in, of course. Ready to lend a shoulder to cry on, arms to make sure she felt safe, soft words to soothe her. Yet we've been foiled. Again. She'd been swept away from under our noses. All my hopes shatter. Will I ever be able to tell her I love her?

Now she's apparently been sold as a slave and is on a billionaire's yacht somewhere out on the ocean, being subjected to Allah knows what treatment.

I observe the hive of activity in front of me, not knowing what can be done or what to suggest, appreciating my role is staying out of the way and letting others determine what to do next. I might be a prince of my country, however I've not had the same type of military training as was imposed on the ruling sheikhs of Amahad, a deficiency I've only just realised. *When I have a son, I'll need to do all I can to prepare him to cope with the kidnap of his future wife.*

Yeah, and the prospect of Aiza and I ever having a child is diminishing by every passing minute. I hate this feeling of uselessness. My hands shake with the frustration there's nothing I can do.

"You got everything you need?" Rais has walked behind Germaine. I watch Rais with a sense of admiration. He got results, the man he was questioning too terrified to do anything other than tell us everything he knows. I'd have approached it in a far more gentlemanly way and would probably have got nowhere. My skills lie in negotiation. The rough, rugged, *uncivilised* sheikh got the outcomes that I wouldn't have been able to. For that, he gets all my respect.

"Anything else you want to say?" Now Hunter's up in the kidnapper's face.

Germaine stutters, pain and fear creasing his face, and raises his hands. "I've told you everything I know."

"Amir al-Fahri. Where is he? How do you get in touch with him?" Hunter's stance is also admirable, like a wild animal holding on to his rage by a thin thread. If I was Germaine I'd be trembling too.

Germaine spits the words out, one after another, his voice as shrill as a woman's. "He contacts me, not the other way around. Money's transferred between Swiss bank accounts."

As my eyes to go Jasim's and then Nijad's, I see an almost imperceptible rise of their chins, then Hunter walks behind him, raises his gun and a shot is fired. Germaine falls to the floor, a large hole in the back of his head.

Ben Carter looks on impassively. "I'll get a team here for cleanup. Good job, Hunter, saved the country money taking this piece of shit through the courts."

Even though he's just killed a man, Hunter's face is calm. Me? I can't tear my gaze away from the man who a second ago was talking, and now his blood is seeping into the expensive carpet. He deserved what he got. He's stolen my woman away. In that moment I envy Hunter for being the one to pull the trigger.

"Got news from the coastguard." Ryan comes into the room, not even sparing a glance at the dead man on the floor. "They've found the yacht. It's heading out into the Atlantic. Coastguard are tracking it on radar."

"Have they got a reason to stop it?"

Ryan shakes his head. "It's already in international waters. But they're monitoring it."

Ben looks around the room. "We need somewhere to thrash this out."

"There's a dining room next door."

"That will do, thanks, Seth."

Noticing how the Grade A men work as a team, I find myself following them into a room where a dining table is laid for about twenty people. In a moment, all cutlery, plates, flower arrangements are brushed onto the floor as

Hunter, Ryan, Seth, Ben and Jon get laptops out and plug them into an extension lead that's appeared from somewhere.

Jasim and Nijad's faces are drawn, and it's not hard to miss the worried glances they keep exchanging. Rais sits opposite Ben, his features tight, his hands, resting on the table, are fisted. Suddenly feeling alone and out of the loop, I sit beside Zaram, and his men take up the rest of the places around the table.

"Can we call on the British Navy to help?" Nijad asks.

"Not without valid reason. Sheikh Twafiq is a distant member of the Saudi Royal Family. It could cause an international incident if we're wrong. If we're right, and he sees the Navy on his horizon, he could kill her and dump her body overboard. Christ, in this weather he doesn't even have to kill her first. She'd last no time before dying of hypothermia. No, the life of one slave wouldn't be worth his reputation or freedom." Jon pinches the bridge of his nose.

"We need to make a surprise attack. That's the only way we'll find her alive." My eyes flick to Ben Carter in horror. It hadn't occurred to me he could get rid of her, the evidence, like that. I go cold just thinking about it.

"Suggestions?" Rais wants to get down to practicalities.

"What do we know of the crew, Jon?"

Jon calls up something on his screen. "Cara's managed to get hold of the crew list, she's cross-matching it now. There's the captain and sailors, of course. They're paid well. Just how far their loyalty extends beyond working for a rich employer, there's no way we can tell, but I think we'll need to assume some, at least, are armed. Six trained bodyguards are definitely on board.

"Damn it." Jasim's hand thumps down. "We need more information."

"We need," Zaram sits forward, "to get on that yacht. Now let's work out how the fuck we're going to do it."

"I want Twafiq dead," is my contribution. He's laid hands on the woman I already consider mine.

"Goes without saying that's what we all want." Nijad surveys the faces of every man at the table. "We've got to be smart about this. In my view, every man or woman who gives their loyalty to such a man doesn't deserve to live." He pauses, then emphasises his point. "Amahad can't afford a war, nor can we at this point in the oil negotiations. We can't do anything which would harm diplomatic relations between us and the Saudis. Twafiq is a dead man. However, who kills him must be kept quiet. We can't publicly take responsibility."

"We need to scupper the yacht. Sink it with all hands on board once we've rescued the princess." No one disagrees with Zaram, but first we've got to get on that boat.

Jon's nodding at Ben and raises his chin at Ryan sitting opposite. "We go in at night. A stealth operation by parachute."

"Where are we going to get the paratroopers?"

Mumbling something under his voice that sounds suspiciously like, "Mia's going to kill me for this," Jon raises his voice to an audible level. "You've got them right here. Me, Ben, Seth and Ryan."

Zaram raises his hand. "Two of my men are trained." I presume he brought his most experienced soldiers with him, ready for any eventuality. The two he points to nod and seem quite happy at the thought of being dropped onto a ship in the middle of the ocean in the dead of night. In fact, one is actually grinning.

"Won't they hear a helicopter or plane?" I've no experience with such matters.

"They would. Though not if we free fall from altitude, deploying the parachutes only when we need to." My stomach rolls at just the thought.

"Hunter, get Nafisa to contact Major Salter." Hunter purloins Ryan's laptop and starts tapping, presumably sending an email. Ben explains, "We might not get official help, but Salter's a good man. He'll get us a plane and have his most experienced navigators and analysts on it."

"You can do this?"

Ben shrugs. "A night time drop? Sure, piece of cake in a ground location. On a moving ship? Fuck knows. But we'll give it a damn good try."

"What if you miss?" To me it sounds like they'll be trying to land in the eye of a needle. And one that's hidden in a haystack.

"We'll be kitted up for survival. We'll have a chopper come by to pick us up."

"What are you thinking of using?" Nijad queries.

Jon answers. "BT80 multi-mission parachutes."

Nijad and Jasim again look at each other. "We're going with you. You can buddy up with those."

"Sure can." Jon grins. "The tandem master can have a passenger strapped in front of him."

"I protest. No." Zaram looks apoplectic. "I can't allow you..."

"With respect. You've got fuck all say in this. We're not in Amahad now."

"I want in." Rais, though not looking particularly happy with the prospect, offers to go.

Not wanting to look like a wimp, I raise my hand. "You're not leaving me out of this." My offer isn't made easily. The thought of free falling out of the sky is not even on the list of things that appeal to me. But I'm not going to be left behind. If there's a chance to save Aiza I'll willingly put my life in someone else's hands.

"It's best if my men go," Zaram says with determination.

Sensing the debate is going to override our objective, Ben bangs his hand on the table. "Who's going depends on the next stage of the plan and what expertise we're going to need once we're on board."

Seth's nibbling at the end of his pen. "You don't want any survivors?"

Ryan's nodding at his colleague as if he understands. "From what you're saying, we get on the yacht, rescue Aiza, then get her clear. Whatever happens to the boat after that no one really cares. As Zaram says, we'll scupper it."

"Except, Twafiq must be dead." I make that clear. Rais growls and jerks his chin in agreement. Like me, he wants no chance of that animal making it out alive.

"What you thinking, Seth?"

"Underwater explosives. We punch a large hole in the hull. When the boat starts to sink, all focus will be on saving it."

"And raising a distress signal and getting into lifeboats..." It's clear from the flicker of excitement in Jon's eyes that he's playing devil's advocate.

"We use a jammer." Hunter shrugs. "Block radio communications. Sabotage the lifeboats too."

"Except for what we need to get us off."

Ben grins. "Sounds like a plan. Get the captain to think a fucking engine's exploded. They'll start running around like headless chickens trying to fix it before realising they've got visitors."

"Anyone going into the water, I can deal with." Seth, who I'd thought was a mild mannered and quiet man, seems to have turned on a different personality—one which leaves me to be grateful it won't be me facing him underwater. *No, I'll be dropping through the sky.*

"I think Nijad's buddy system is the right one. There's six of us who can parachute in, which means there'll be a dozen of us if most double up." Jon's brow is creased. "Nijad and Jasim, I don't want you along. Zaram's got a good point." As Nijad stands, his chair falling back, Jon holds up his hand. "You disappear at the same time Twafiq does? That's too much of a coincidence. What you both need to do is to return to Amahad, tonight. Take Cara, go cuddle your babies, act as if nothing's wrong. Leave it to us to get Aiza while you protect your country."

Nijad doesn't like it. Jasim, however, more of a diplomat, puts out his hand and encourages Nijad to sit again. Once he does, he turns to him. "Jon's right, Ni. We've trusted our lives to these men before, now we must trust them to rescue Aiza."

Jon lifts his chin, and I hear the sigh of relief from Zaram. "I will be one of those going."

Nijad rounds on him. "Same applies to you, General. We cannot risk losing someone with such international visibility. If we're going home, you do too."

"I can go." I've already made my decision.

"Rami..."

"No, Nijad, listen. You're not going to stop me on this. You know my intention toward your sister. My feelings towards her are too strong to just stay on the sidelines. I need to be part of her rescue." My eyes, full of determination, meet his.

"Your father?"

"Would understand. There's nothing to link me to Aiza." *Not yet*, I add under my breath. "My disappearance wouldn't be linked to Amahad. No one apart from the people in this room know I'm connected to the rescue mission. I can disappear, and no one would connect me to Twafiq's death." What better way to give up my life if it means saving Aiza?

"And I." Rais sounds determined. "I don't have a reputation outside of Amahad either to protect or to lose. I'm a desert sheikh. Unknown internationally."

Ben looks around the table and sums up. "So, we've got me, Jon, Ryan, Seth and...?"

"Alaa and Yarub." Zaram indicates the two paratroopers on his team.

Ben continues. "Hunter, Rami and Rais will buddy up."

"Faiza, Hafeez and Latif will go too." Three more of his men seem pleased they're not going to be left behind.

Am I the only person nervous of jumping from thousands of feet in the air in the dark?

"Seth and Ryan will drop first with Hunter and Latif." He gets a chin lift from the man so named and continues, "Seth will set the explosives, Hunter will be prepared with the jammer, and our radios will operate outside the jamming range. *After* Seth's ready, we'll descend before pandemonium breaks out. Jon, I and Ryan will disarm the crew. Alaa and Yarub will scubber the lifeboats. Rais and Rami, your job is to locate Aiza and get her to the deck safely. Faiza, Hafeez and Latif will go with you."

Ben's phone rings. He answers right there at the table, and from his side of the conversation it's clear to see he's talking to his friend in the SAS, Major Salter, who's received permission for a nighttime training session, hastily arranged to keep his troops in a state of readiness. The logistics are discussed—where to meet, and the equipment to be provided.

It appears our rescue mission is a go.

CHAPTER 15
Aiza

After a humiliating tour around the yacht, luckily inside only as I'd freeze on the exposed decks, I'm led back down to my prison in the depths of the boat. Already I wish death on everyone I've met. It wasn't, as Twafiq had made it sound, to allow me to stretch my legs. Instead it was an exercise in degradation. And to impress on me again that no one would lift a finger to help me.

I was unable to appropriate any weapon or anything that might help me escape. Of course I couldn't. I was led around naked. I'd tried to walk around with my head held high, to project an image of a strong woman not fazed in the least she wasn't wearing any clothes. It hadn't been easy forcing my hands to stay by their sides, feeling the lecherous glances from the male crew members burn into my skin and the assessing looks from the opposite sex. I refused to think that my hips are too large, my breasts, unsupported by a bra not as firm as perhaps they might be. That's not even counting the embarrassing stripes on my backside and thighs. Every critical look was a blow to my pride.

I was glad to have that leash, if not the collar, removed and at last be left to some semblance of privacy in my room.

Now sitting on the mattress, eyeing that window in the door, I know it's just an illusion. Anyone could walk past and look at me all they want, just like an animal in a zoo. I finger the too tight leather around my neck, which seems to have no way of unfastening it. It's designed to make me feel owned. *I belong to no man. And never will.*

Time passes slowly. I don't have to try hard to convince myself that being ignored and abandoned is better than being taken in Twafiq's presence again. After what seems like a lifetime I hear something outside, and Scarface opens the door, allowing a woman whose head is concealed by a hijab to come in. She hands a tray to Scarface, then places two plastic dog bowls on the floor. One has water, the other same sort of unappetising-smelling food.

As she turns to go I take my chance, gambling that the uneducated looking Scarface speaks no language other than his own, and ask in quickfire Arabic, "*Sawf tusaeiduni alhuruba?*"

As she shakes her head I realise she's not going to help me escape. Shaking off my disappointment, I stand and snap in my best Domme voice. "*Limadha tusaeid hula' alrajal?*" Her eyes fall to the floor, giving no answer why she's helping these men. I draw back my shoulders and continue to ask questions. When I imperiously demand that she replies, she tells me at last that Twafiq is a good man. That he treats them well. If I behave, he'll treat me right too.

"You're his submissive." I switch to English at last.

She smiles, and a glow comes to her face. "We all are," she replies.

"Enough!"

I'm surprised Scarface hasn't interrupted our conversation before. He must be confident she's not going to help me at all. Twafiq's obviously got her so brainwashed she sees nothing wrong in his treatment of me.

The girl's ushered out, the door closing behind her. I eye the offerings she'd left. Sinking to my haunches, I pick up the water and hastily drink, then put my hand into the bowl of food, picking up something that doesn't look as bad as the rest. Then throwing it back down as my stomach revolts.

I'd rather starve. At least that would be a way to get out of his clutches. Starvation is one choice I can make.

I sit back and wait for a summons, relieved as it doesn't come, and in such a state of anxiety I wonder whether lack of food or a heart attack will kill me first. My heart's constantly thumping in my chest, my senses hyperaware. I don't want to be taken in front of the cruel sheikh again. Nor to start the depravities he must have planned for me.

Soon all I can hear are the rhythmic sounds of the engines as other noises from the yacht quieten. Footsteps cease walking so often overhead. While the light coming into my room is the same, I've a feeling that night has arrived and everyone else is winding down to sleep.

I lay on the mattress, not allowing my mind to switch off, just resting, trying to regather my physical energy. *Next time I see him, somehow I'll kill him.* There must be a way, I just need to find it. *If I can get my leash wrapped around his neck, maybe I can strangle him.*

Despite my best intentions, the past hours of wakefulness and tension, together with the motion of the ship, make me drift off to sleep. I'm woken by a loud bang, and quickly become conscious that the thumping sound is missing, the engines have stopped. Adrift in the ocean, the yacht starts to rock, and I dry heave at the protests from my empty stomach, expelling the water I'd drunk into the toilet. I get to my feet and find it hard to balance, certain the floor has started to tilt.

Oh shit! Are we sinking?

I peer through the window, straining to see or hear what's going on. Shouts are sounding from the upper decks, and it can't be more than a handful of minutes before men dressed in overalls—engineers?—are rushing past. The yacht's got a decided list now, and they're running up hill. I'm shocked to discover my feet are in icy cold water.

I bang on the door, no one stops to open it. Clearly too worried about their own safety, dismissing me as not a person to be rescued, considering me only an animal they can leave to die in a trap. My ear to the wood, I hear someone shouting and I'm able to make out they're yelling something about lifeboats.

They're abandoning the yacht? Are they leaving me here to drown?

The water's now up to my ankles, and rapidly moving towards my knees. Whatever has happened, the yacht appears to be going down fast.

I start praying—not that I'm a practicing Muslim—but now I'm begging for rescue, and then, as the water reaches my thighs, for all my past sins to be forgiven.

I can't feel my legs, the cold water has made them numb. Will the sea or hypothermia take me?

Something knocks into my pelvis. I jump, looking down to see the plastic dog bowls floating.

I try hammering on the door, my teeth chattering with the cold. Then the lights in the hallway, together with the one in my room, flicker and go out, leaving me in complete darkness. My lungs heave as panic overwhelms me. I open my mouth and let out a piercing scream. Then another. Then another and then again, doing what I promised Twafiq I wouldn't, begging for someone to save me until my voice is hoarse.

The water's lapping at the bottom of my breasts, and I feel the cold seeping into my bones, numbing me entirely. I wonder whether I'll pass out before I drown, hoping that might make death easier.

I can't stop fighting, can't allow myself to give up. Feeling water slosh around me, I bang on the door again, my hands feebly beating against the wood that's preventing my escape.

Taking in as deep a breath as I can, I let it out in the loudest screech possible, suspecting they might be hearing me on the upper decks and are ignoring me.

Suddenly I become aware that the distant sounds I thought were sounds of the yacht protesting its imminent death are something different. Popping sounds that sound like gunfire.

Is it a rescue?

The water's up to my neck. This is a big yacht. If someone's come for me, they've got to search it and find me. By the time they do, it might be too late. All they'll be rescuing is my dead body.

Another rush of water seeps in as the boat lurches again, and I lose my footing. Trying to make my paralysed limbs move, I'm forced to leave my place by the door and swim across to the wall where there's the most air. Discovering fast how hard it is to tread water when I've lost all feeling in my limbs. Keeping my mouth above water is almost impossible.

Don't give up.

Seawater fills my mouth. I splutter and cough and spit it out, struggling to lift my head out of the liquid that's intent on killing me.

My mouth's covered, I can only breathe in through my nose. *Just give up. Let yourself go under.* As I long as I hear the sound of a battle going on, I refuse to stop fighting.

175

Until I don't have the option any longer. There's no air pocket left. Water seeps into my nostrils, my chest burns as I automatically inhale. Unable to fight anymore, my body goes limp.

CHAPTER 16
Hunter

I t's probably not a good time to tell anyone I've no head for heights. From the windows of the plane, the clear, starry sky enables me to make out the lights of the yacht very far below, looking more like a toy than something we could actually land on. Eying my fellow jumpers, I see the experienced skydivers appearing excited and exhilarated, ready to do their job. The other 'passengers', seeming much like myself, tense but focused. We're all dressed in black clothing, and that, together with the dark parachutes, should hide our descent. The plane's flying high, so the yacht will ignore us.

As I'm buckled into a harness I hear others speaking in their headset. Luckily Zaram's men speak perfect English, so only one language is used for those last-minute instructions. Although I speak fluent Arabic, it would be hard to string words together in that language at the moment. My hands feel sweaty, my heart's hammering in my chest. *If men were meant to fall from the sky we'd have been given wings.*

"Just let me drive. All you've got to do is hang on." How the fuck Ryan can sound so calm is beyond me. "Relax, man. Just enjoy it." I can't even be embarrassed that my teammate has sensed my distress. I make my mind focus on Aiza. I'd do, and am doing, all that I can to get to her. To save her. Then to plan how to keep her at my side.

"Ready to go in five." Sean will be making the first drop into the water. Latif, another with underwater experience, is going along with him. As well as the jammer, Ryan's equipment includes a rope ladder to enable them to get back up the side of the yacht.

I'm a part-time bodyguard and intelligence officer, not a skydiver. While I've never had the slightest inclination to throw myself out of a plane before, there's probably not much I wouldn't do when it comes to Aiza. The thought of what Twafiq might be putting her through is probably far worse than jumping into the night sky. That's what gives me the incentive. If, as my mind seems to expect, that parachute I'm so suspicious about fails to open and we crash and die on impact, at least I'll have died trying. Ryan, it seems, is full of confidence and has no such doubts.

As we hear the countdown begin through our headsets, the door opens. I take one last look around the interior of the plane, noticing the two sheikhs are looking decidedly pale. Rami looks quite nauseous. Having company in my misery helps me feel a bit better, so I give them a cheeky thumps up as Ryan steps into the void, and then we're falling, following Sean and Latif, who I can't make out far beneath us.

After a slight tumble Ryan gets us right way up. As the air rushes past far too fast, it's hardly possible to catch my breath. I'm wondering when the fuck he's going to open the parachute, having to clench my fists in an effort to ignore my every reaction to pull every rope in sight. As the ship hurtles up towards us, I know he's leaving it too late. Something must have gone wrong...

Then a jolt, and our downward progress is drastically slowed. We start to float through the air, and I make myself a promise—I'm never doing this again in my life. *Fuck, Aiza. You're going to be my woman, and I'll ensure you're kept safe and out of harms way.* Since she'd been taken at the airport it's all been action or planning, the few minutes of floating through the air giving me time to analyse my part in her abduction. Now I wonder whether I could have done anymore to prevent it. *Fuck, I failed you, Aiza. I'll not let you down again.*

We're going too far to the right, Ryan makes an adjustment. Then to the left, then out over the stern. Luckily my teammate knows what he's doing. Soon the helipad on the top deck of the yacht is rushing up to meet us. Remembering my instructions, I prepare to bend my legs, and we land, curling and rolling.

With expert ease, Ryan has the parachute rolled in seconds and back in his pack. He takes out the jammer, turns it on and finds a secure place to hide it.

Communicating with hand signals, we follow the route learned from the blueprint Cara was able to obtain, and quietly start descending the stairs. Guns equipped with silencers and lethal knives in our hands, we make our way to the bridge. Ryan signals, *two men*.

Like thieves in the night, we enter. With no remorse or second thoughts we slit their throats, their blood running and staining the otherwise immaculate wood. Ryan indicates something. The wheel's making small adjustments by itself as it continues to take the yacht on its preprogrammed course.

Suddenly there's a loud boom breaking the quiet of the night air. *Sean's done his job.* The yacht lurches. We leave the bridge, going to the lower deck where Ryan throws the ladder over the side.

"Jon and Rais have gone into the water."

Hearing they've missed the ship, anxiously I look out into the darkness, unable to make out anything in the black sea. Then the ladder bucks, and within moments Sean's on top, followed by Latif. He turns, and like us, looks out over the water.

"Gust took them off course," Latif notes. "Saw them veer off to starboard."

With relief I see the ladder's moving again.

"How long since you last did that, Jon?" Rais queries the man appearing behind him.

"Too fucking long." Jon shakes the water out of his hair as well as the implied insult, then replaces his helmet. "Come on."

Without wasting any time, we go first to the crew quarters. Ben's already got a number of sailors and engineers corralled in the mess room. I go to help, checking for weapons and disarming them. Ryan and Seth disappear, coming back with officers and the rest of the crew, methodically searching this part of the boat. Faiza, Hafeez, and Latif head to the staff quarters. Up to now most have been sleeping and we've taken them by surprise.

The captain makes the most fuss, but he quiets down with my fist to his jaw.

"Hunter, go after Rami and Rais. They've headed to the master suite," Ben instructs.

He doesn't need to tell me twice. I turn and run through the central hallway leading to the state rooms in the bow, clearing each room as I pass. Alerted by the listing of the ship, two men looking like bodyguards suddenly appear ahead of me. Using their surprise to aid me, I take them down with two bullets.

Stepping over their bodies I carry on, finding Rais and Rami stumped by two massive, locked doors. Not unexpected. I take out the small explosive device from my pack and we retreat to a safe distance. The C4 does its job, the doors hang from their hinges.

Inside, a man in Arab clothing is hidden behind two men who look like they've previously had arguments with Mike Tyson. I don't hesitate, shooting as soon as we enter, and both men fall. Rais rushes forwards and checks, finishing one off with his knife. My silencer's crap now, the sound hardly deadened.

The man left standing must be Sheikh Twafiq. To give him his due, he's standing up straight, his face betraying no emotion at the death of his men. As Rais advances, although he must know his yacht's compromised and seriously damaged, there's no fear in Twafiq's eyes. Instead, his cheeks flame red and his body is quivering with unsuppressed rage.

"How dare you?" he spits out. "Who do you think you are? Are you pirates? You have no business boarding my yacht."

Rais roars, and one punch with all his strength behind it has Twafiq flat on the floor. "We're asking the questions, you piece of shit. Where's Princess Aiza?" He's not asking nicely. To encourage an answer, he raises his knife and pins one of Twafiq's hands to the floor. Then takes out another blade and does the same to the other.

Trapped and at Rais's mercy, Twafiq lets out a snarl of rage. He stares unflinching into the desert sheikh's eyes. Though he must be in considerable pain, he doesn't show it. "She's not here."

"She's on this yacht. You bought her, you fucking sorry excuse for a man."

Trapped and threatened, Twafiq only laughs. "You won't find her."

Has he already killed her?

I watch as he lifts his head and gives a gloating look down the room, the direction towards the stern which is sloping downwards. The lower decks must be filling with water.

My eyes go to Rami's. In a split second we both understand.

"Finish him, Rais." My gut tells me we haven't got much time.

"Leave him with me." Yarub, quiet up to now, nods at Rais. "I'll make him hurt, I promise. Go find the woman."

Though it's clear Rais wants to deliver retribution himself, he nods his thanks to Yarub and then comes to Rami and myself. "She's down at the stern."

"Yeah, I picked that up." I'm already moving.

We run through the staterooms, calling out. A couple of members of panicked staff are returning to this deck, obviously having found the lifeboats are sabotaged. Angry and confused, they have weapons at hand. We're better prepared and trained, and soon take them out. Swinging around a corner there's another huddle of frightened men. A short gunfight, and we've got them beaten.

Taking the first set of stairs, we start to search, throwing open doors left and right. When we can't find her, we go down to the next level and do the same there.

The expressions on the faces of Rami and I are mirrored.

"Where the fuck is she?" Rami shouts in despair, banging his fist against the wall.

"I don't know. She has to be here somewhere," Rais yells as he runs for the next set of stairs.

These lead down to the engine deck. Beneath us seawater is slopping around. The yacht suddenly lists further to the side, and the bottom of the stairwell now has water waist deep. We don't hesitate, just go straight down. Rami starts wading off towards the bow, yelling her name in a voice thick with despair, while Rais and I eye up the deepening water in the other direction. The boat's well down towards the stern now, the engine room must be totally submerged.

Creaking sounds come from all around us mingled with mini waves from the water sloshing. Then there's roaring noise, which I suspect heralds the yacht's final death throws, but I'm not giving up. The sheikh and I exchange grim glances, and I know he's on the same page. We'll find her, or die trying.

Suddenly I signal him to still. "Hear that?" I thought I heard a weak cry.

Rais heard it too. "It came from down there."

Quickly I speak through the radio. "Sean. Get down to the engine deck with your diving equipment. Quickly, man." Knowing there's no time to waste, I don't bother waiting for his acknowledgement, just step forwards into the freezing cold water.

A slushing by my side shows Rais is coming with me. We wade, then the water's up to our chests, then our necks. As we push on, the rapidly rising water is to my chin now, and still coming up as the ship lists even further towards the stern. *The ship's sinking.* Still neither Rais or I have any other thought than getting to Aiza, even if I'm starting to think there's no way we'll get to her in time. I'm not leaving without her.

The water comes up over our heads. I start to swim, noting with dismay how little space there is between the water and the ceiling. Submerged, our comms have been knocked out, the only light coming from the waterproof torches we hold. We communicate with hand signals as we try to fight against the flow, hanging onto the handrail to stop from being swept away. Creeping forwards *too slowly*, we come to a locked door. A quick glance at each other, then try to break it down. Under the water our kicking has little effect. I dive to check the lock. My lungs soon start burning. I need air, but I'm not leaving Aiza. Although my brain is shrieking self-preservation, somehow I remember a skeleton key is part of my pack. Hoping to fuck I don't drop it, I take it out and have the door opened.

I'm feeling dizzy from lack of air. Rais doesn't look much better as we swim into the dark, neither of us going to give up.

I swim like a dog quartering the land to flush game, and then, fuck, the beam of light from my torch shows me a lifeless body floating at the back of the small space. Kicking my legs, I swim forwards, taking her in my arms, then making one last effort, start to swim back the way we've come. Rais swims on his back, one arm clutching my shirt, helping both me and my burden along.

The burden that's naked, unmoving. *Aiza! You can't be dead.*

The water's now up to the top of the stairwell, it's only when my head rises above it I can gasp in much needed air. My lungs heave as I take the next set of stairs. As soon as we're in a steeply sloping but dry corridor, I set her down and immediately start performing mouth to mouth.

"Come on, Aiza. Fucking come on!" I scream, wanting to shake her, but instead lower my lips to hers again.

Rais is doing compressions on her chest while I breathe my life-giving air into her mouth.

Sean's finally arrived. Thank God I didn't wait for him, we'd have been too late. His footsteps falter as he sees what's on the ground.

"Is she?"

As I raise my head I spit out. "No." My denial forcing me to keep trying again. Her body's so cold to touch, in the light of the torches it's blue.

Compressions, air, compressions, air. Neither Rais or I will be giving up. Rami's appeared and drops by my side. "Let me take over." He tries to push me out of the way.

I snarl back. No one is doing this for Aiza other than me.

Then, *thank every god there is*, she coughs, and sounds like she's choking, I turn her to her side and she's violently sick as all the water she's swallowed and breathed in is expelled.

Sean appears with a dry blanket in his hands, purloined from a state room the water's not yet reached.

"Hunt...?"

"Hush, don't speak. Save your energy. We've got to get off of this boat."

"I think it's sinking," she informs us weakly.

I chuckle, though the situation is far from amusing. "We've already figured that out."

I stand, holding my so precious *and alive* bundle in my arms, and start to carry her up the stairs, Rami and Rais reaching out to touch her as if to reassure themselves she's really there.

Then we come to a halt. *Christ, I thought we were home free.* Standing dripping with blood from where the knives had pinned him to the floor, and with the extra wounds Yarub had inflicted, is Twafiq. He's accompanied by half a dozen of his men carrying automatic rifles, all pointed at us. Without being told, I know Zaram's man has to be dead.

My radio's out, luckily Sean's isn't. I close the gap between us, speaking loudly so his mic picks up my voice. "You've lost, Twafiq. All we want is the woman we came for. Let us go, and you concentrate on saving your yacht."

A muttered sound escapes Sean. Yeah, well there's no point telling Twafiq that Sean's so efficient at this job there'll be no saving his yacht now.

"No. I keep the woman *and* my yacht. If my yacht can't be saved, *my slave will* be going down with me."

I snarl that he still thinks she's his. "No one's coming to rescue you, Twafiq."

"Then we'll die together." He looks at the bundle in my arms. "It would have been a waste if she'd just drowned, so thank you for saving her. If I only have a short time to live, I can still make good use of her. Give my slave to me."

Aiza gasps in horror. I squeeze her, letting her know there's no way I'm giving her up.

It looks like there's no way out of this without bullets flying. In the narrow stairway, ricochets might hit us even if the bullets miss. I can't put Aiza down to get my gun. It's a standoff.

Then rapid gunfire comes along the corridor behind Twafiq. As his men turn around to face the new threat, Sean raises his rifle and rains fire from this side. Twafiq jerks, his eyes blazing in anger as his body jumps like he is being pulled with strings like a marionette, and then he falls to his knees, his mouth working, trying to curse us until the end.

"Get out of here now!" It's Ben and Jon appearing from different directions at the top of the stairwell. "We've got most of the crew contained. There may still be more, but this ship is going down fast. This way. Quickly." Jon and Ryan take the lead, pausing at every corner and the top of each stairwell until we reach the lower deck level at the stern, now well down in the water. The Amahadian soldiers have secured it, have already launched the motor-boat which is floating well above the yacht's usual docking area.

Rami quickly jumps in first, holding his hands for Aiza. I don't want to let her go. The boat's rising and falling with the swell of the waves, and I can't risk trying to board holding her. Taking a deep breath, I drop her into Rami's waiting hands. Then I'm onboard, the rest of our team following. I indicate to Rami that I want him to pass her back to me, however this time it's him who's not going to relinquish his prize.

As Rais shouts to me to hurry the fuck up, I give up trying to take her and move up the boat. Ben does a head-count. With the exception of Yarub, who, as I feared, is dead, we're all present and correct. Sean cuts the line tying us to the yacht, then someone starts the engine and we're off, moving fast out over the sea. When we're a clear distance away, Sean presses a button on a handheld device, and another loud explosion finishes off the Master of the Sea, taking its owner and crew to the bottom of the ocean, its secrets and horrors hopefully intact. With any luck it's sunk over one of the deep areas which can be up to two thousand metres deep.

Ben's standing, his sea legs keeping him steady even though the boat's cutting through the high waves, his hand shading his eyes and looking back at the slowly disap-pearing yacht, flames hissing as they're extinquished by the sea.

Jon, his long-time partner, tugs at his arms to make him sit down, then, when seated, turns and shows he understood his friend. "Ben, leaving them alive could have started a war. Put oil production back decades. We couldn't leave any witnesses."

"There were no good people on that yacht." A small voice speaks up from under the blanket in Rami's arms.

"Can we go faster?" Rami asks. "Aiza's shivering."

I suspect Aiza's trembling with shock as well as shaking with cold. I have to resist snatching her back and giving her the comfort she needs. Someone passes a foil blanket, which is placed over her.

I'm betting this boat's going as fast as it can, and swallow down my own plea to increase the speed. Aiza needs medical attention.

CHAPTER 17
Aiza

Even though the blanket and Rami's strong arms are around me, my teeth are chattering so hard I start worrying that I'll break my jaw. I'm gazing across at Hunter, who's training his eyes on mine as though willing me to take some of his strength. I keep mine open, half of me fearing I'm still asleep, trapped in the midst of the worst nightmare of my life, and that it's just transformed into one of the best possible dreams I could have. I'm frightened if I close my eyes I'll wake up to find myself back drowning in that room.

The boat launches into another wave, then slams back down. I welcome every bit of discomfort, as it helps me believe I'm alive and my rescue is real. Although there are things that don't make any sense.

Why am I in Rami's arms? A man I've only met a few times before. Hunter and the others from Grade A, that's understandable, but what the hell is Rais doing here? And the soldiers, talking as quietly as they can over the wind and the waves, have Amahadian accents. Are they the desert sheikh's men? Why would they be part of my rescue at sea off the coast of Scotland?

I feel weak, tired, emotionally drained, and my chest hurts, both inside and out. I want nothing more than to relax and accept the comfort of the strong arms surrounding me, but comfort like this is unfamiliar. I had no mother to love me, a father and brothers who were distant. I'm a Domme. I give aftercare to my subs, no one's ever given any to me. I didn't want or need it.

I'm fighting sleep, and refuse to give in. The blankets do nothing to ease my bone-deep cold. I'm so chilled, so close to unconsciousness I fear if I give in I might never wake up.

The boat goes on through the night, battling against the monotonous sea that seems to threaten to capsize us. Although I've already almost drowned once tonight, I'd prefer death by the sea to torture at Twafiq's hands. Twafiq. The man who was killed in front of my eyes. The man who'll never buy another human being to keep as a slave and treat like an animal ever again. He's dead. I moan as I remember his threats and promises, and Rami tightens his arms, but even while my body is held securely, my mind can't help fearing he escaped and will be coming for me again. I shiver uncontrollably.

At last we arrive at a small port, then there's a hasty transfer onto a helicopter. The flight doesn't seem long, and soon I'm boarding the Kassis family jet at Glasgow Airport. As I take in the familiar surroundings, tears fall from my eyes. *I never thought I'd see anything from home again.*

"Rami. You can put her down now." I feel a growl through my chest, then the voice speaks again more sharply. "Rami. Put her down. The medical team need to inspect her."

I'm placed on a wonderfully soft, comfortable bed. The one in the bedroom at the end of the plane I realise. Then I hear the voice of the flight attendant. "Gentleman, out, please. Sheikhs, you too. Let the doctor tend to the princess, please."

My eyes fall on Rais. I've seen the rugged sheikh many times in my life. Have watched him prove his riding and fighting skills in tournaments between tribes. Have seen him as a leader of men. Never have I seen the possessive expression that I do at that moment in his eyes. His piercing stare seems to probe into my mind, asking without words if I'm okay. I answer with a small nod, and then he turns and is gone.

Rami tries to linger, Hunter jostling him for a position in the doorway. The flight attendant's all business and shoos them away.

Then the door closes. The doctor waves to the nurse and discreetly turns his back as she steps closer. Whisking off the blankets covering me, she replaces it with something like another shiny foil blanket, this one thicker than that had been wrapped around me in the boat.

"Heat blanket," she tells me, then sticks a thermometer into my ear. "Hmm. As we expected, your core temperature's quite low. This will bring it up quickly."

She then puts a cuff around my arm and proceeds to take my blood pressure and pulse. She calls out the readings to the doctor, who now comes back to my side. "Any injuries that we don't know off?" he asks.

I place my hand on that damn collar which is still around my neck. "Can you get this off?" I turn my head so he can see what he's dealing with.

"Hmm. There's a catch."

"I know. I tried to undo it."

"Nurse. Can you see if anyone has anything to pick a lock with?"

Only a minute later and I hear a commotion which quickly dies down. Ryan comes in with a smirk. "They're fighting to see you out there," he explains, taking an instrument out of a rolled-up toolbag. "Let's see what we're dealing with here. Hmm." His face creases in concentration, then there's a snick, and at last the blasted thing comes free.

Immediately the doctor steps forwards. "It's caused some nasty bruising, but hasn't broken the skin.

Ryan's holding it as if it were a poisonous snake. "Son of a bitch." His eyes widen as he looks at me, then views the lock. "I take it you don't want to keep it as a souvenir?"

No, I do not. "Take it away, please."

Ryan holds it between thumb and forefinger and removes it, and himself, from my sight.

The nurse is busy checking my temperature again and making a happy click with her tongue, which suggests I'm doing okay.

"Any other pain?"

Now that darn thing's gone I can concentrate again. "My ribs."

"Do you mind?"

I give him permission, and he pulls down the blanket. I don't give a damn. After the number of people who've seen me naked after the past couple of days... The thought brings tears to my eyes and I stifle a sob.

"I'm sorry." He misunderstands. "I just want to check what we're dealing with here. You may have a cracked rib from when they were trying to revive you. We'll check at the hospital when we land."

I realise there's something I haven't asked. "Where are we going?"

"Home," he says. And when I raise a quizzical brow, elaborates, "Amahad."

After all the time I've spent trying to avoid the country of my birth, knowing I'm going to Amahad sounds the most comforting thing in the world. As long as I get there this time.

Without communicating with words, the nurse appears at his side, a hypodermic in her hand. I narrow my eyes.

"It's a painkiller and sedative."

As I shake my head, not wanting to lose control again, the flight attendant who I thought had gone, speaks. "Your body needs rest, Princess. Don't fight it, you're safe. You're on the Kassis jet, your family is waiting for you. The plane is full of people who'd already proven they'd give their lives for you."

As I bite my lip, still undecided, the nurse makes the decision for me, tapping a vein and then inserting the needle before I can make further protest. I try to fight it, but sleep pulls me under.

I wake as the plane is preparing to make the descent into the airport I first arrived in only a little more than forty-eight hours ago. The flight attendant has laid out clothes on the bed, and the nurse hovers in case I need help getting dressed. As I sit up I feel woozy, knowing the memory of Twafiq's touch makes me feel dirty.

"Have I time for a shower?"

"No, Your Highness. There'll be plenty of time later to wash the saltwater off. Rest was what you most needed. That's right, sit up gently. Your ribs are probably going to be sore for a while."

I shudder. Suddenly scared that history is going to repeat itself. "The airport...?"

She laughs. "I think the whole Army is there. There's a couple of tribes who've sent their warriors too. No one will take you again. Emir Kadar has the hospital surrounded."

"No hospital," I interrupt. I just want to get to the palace where I know I'll be safe. *The palace.*

She purses her lips, clearly not happy. "I'll ask the doctor."

"No hospital," I repeat adamantly. Calling on my inner strength, I sit up and slide the tunic over my head, then put my feet through the legs of the shalwar kameez. I bend my head, resting it in my arms before taking a deep breath and shakily getting to my feet and pulling them all the way up. I take the couple of paces required to bring me to the door, then turn the handle and step into the main part of the plane just as the pilot announces we should take our seats for landing.

The flight attendant's quick to settle me into the nearest seat, and sits down beside me, helping me do the seat belt up. I see Hunter's face pop up from the row in front, and he gives me a wink.

Then, looking out of the window, I see the desert coming closer, see the runway appear, the airport buildings, the clonk as the wheels come down, and then the plane lands.

My heart starts to pound in my chest and my hands clench, remembering last time I was here and the start of my nightmare.

The plane taxies up to the main terminal. No diversion today. The steps are wheeled up, then the door opens. I'm holding my breath then let it out in a rush when my oldest brother appears at the entrance hatch wearing such a look I've never seen before on his face, and would never have expected. His eyes search up and down the plane, and eventually land on me at the back. He hesitates, his gaze fixed on mine, and slowly comes over, his pace quickening for the final few steps. I stand, a little unbalanced. His arms come out, and then I'm being dragged into his body and up off my feet.

Pulling back my head, I'm amazed to see tears flowing from his eyes. "Sister. Dearest sister." His words come out as a sob.

Part of me was expecting he'd admonish me for getting kidnapped in the first place, for putting myself at risk and not being where I should have been. Now I see none of that matters. He's just pleased to see me safe. *He's not my father.*

Reluctantly he lets me slide down his body until my feet are on the ground. Still his arm steadies me. "Can you walk?" he asks quickly.

"Yes. I can." Or at least I think I can.

"You're going to…"

I put my hand up and cover his mouth. "I'm coming to the palace, Kadar. I need to be home."

I see him having a silent conversation over my head with who I suspect is the doctor. Then he puts me at arms' length and studies me. Slowly a weak smile spreads over his face. "Home," he confirms.

I feel jittery and my chest aches as I descend the steps with my brother's support. My eyes scan in every direction, wary of danger. As the nurse had said, it looks like the whole Army's here or, at least, a very large part of it. Armed soldiers in every direction.

At the bottom of the steps, Nijad, Cara, Jasim and Janna are waiting, emotion clear on their faces, but Kadar waves them away. I'm grateful he doesn't want to overwhelm me at present. My whole family is here. Now I'll have the chance to get to know them all over again. Or, perhaps, for the first time.

In the limousine Zoe's waiting, a toddler on her lap who I realise must be my nephew, Ra-id. He looks at me curiously, his thumb going into his mouth, and then turns to his mother for reassurance.

"This is your Auntie, Ra-id. Aunt Aiza." Her kind, warm eyes find mine, gentling as I look at my nephew before returning to those of her son. "Something tells me you're going to be very good friends."

Nobody minds when I rest my eyes on the drive back to the palace, my body still exhausted from the stress as well as the sedative given to me. I'd never expected to find a comfortable silence with my oldest brother, and know he must be biting his tongue wanting to learn all the details from me. At one point I open my eyes to see him starting to speak. He's giving something to distract him as my sister-in-law plonks his son on his lap while giving me a wink.

After watching him play with Ra-id for a moment, the difference between him and our father stressed once again, I allow myself to give in to the drugs still circulating around my body and doze.

I awake when the limousine pulls up. The palace is just how I remember it. Ornate. Opulent. Oppressive. I pause at the steps leading to the grand entrance. This time it's Jasim who comes to greet me and takes my arm, understanding immediately why I faltered. "Give it a chance, Aiza. It's not like how you remember."

I try to refute that's why I stopped. Being afraid of a *place* seems unreasonable. "I have been back since Father died."

"Only for a brief visit for various celebrations. And then, like me, you probably didn't open your eyes and see what was around you. A building can't hurt you. It's only the people inside that can do that."

At that moment there's a high-pitched squeal, and a little girl runs across the marble flagstones where, as a child, I was only ever allowed to walk, and would have been spanked had I made such a sound. She's holding the hand of an equally excited young boy.

"Aunt Aiza. Aunt Aiza. Mummy said you'd be coming." I sink to my knees as an ebullient child throws herself trustingly into my arms. "Hello, Zorah. And this little rascal must be Eti."

Quickly bored with his new aunt, as though he doesn't see what all the fuss is about, Eti staggers across and is swept up into his father's arms. "See?" Jasim holds his son to him and raises his eyebrow towards me.

I do see. My fears of regressing back to my childhood are swept aside by seeing the very different people living here now. And, that the servants are dipping their heads in greeting, no longer bending double or prostrating themselves on the ground.

"Emir! I need your signature…"

I catch Kadar's rueful eye and realise there are some things that never change.

CHAPTER 18
Rais

R ais, come. Sit." Noticing Kadar looks weary, I enter the room and take the seat across from his desk. He tries to stifle a yawn, and then looks up apologetically. "Raid had a disturbed night."

His admission tempts me to smile. The previous emir wouldn't have had a disturbed night for such a reason. Children slept out of sight in the nursery, and never stayed in their parent's suite. "Is he alright?"

"I think he was overexcited. Woke at two determined to go and play with his new aunt."

His aunt. Aiza. "How is she?" I don't say her name, it's obvious who I'm talking about.

Kadar drums his fingers on the desk, giving himself time to formulate the answer. "I'd say remarkably well and back to normal. Fuck it, Rais. How the hell do I know what her normal is?" He stands and goes to the floor to ceiling windows in his office and seems to look out at the flowers blooming in the garden. "Physically she's recovering well from her ordeal. Her ribs weren't broken, just bruised."

"Has she told you much about what happened to her?"

I see some of the emir's tension seep away as his shoulders relax. "Twafiq toyed with her. Played with her mind. Made her promises, threats more to the point of what would happen, and I've no doubt he would have carried them out. Praise be to Allah he didn't have a chance to rape her." He suddenly turns, his eyes blazing. "He took a crop to her. Made her walk around that damn yacht naked with his henchmen leading her around in nothing but a collar and leash. She's still got fucking bruising around her neck."

My hands tighten. If I didn't have short nails they'd be cutting into my flesh. It's a physical pain to hear exactly what was done to her. She neither asked for or deserved anything like that. If she has recovered, it shows just how strong she is, proving once again how ideal she'll be for me. I need that strength in a wife.

Kadar shrugs as he continues. "She spends all her time playing with the children. Yesterday they were clambering all over her as though she was a damn climbing frame. That's what got Ra-id so worked up. I went to see her, she was laughing, smiling..."

When his voice trails off, I prompt, "But?"

He shakes his head. "There's an expression in her eyes that shows her mind wasn't fully engaged. That she's using the children as a distraction. She..." Instead of completing his thoughts, he changes the subject. "Rami's officially asked me for her hand in marriage. I've given my permission for him to propose to her." His eyes flick to mine to see how I'm taking it.

My fists tighten even more, though I keep my voice calm. "Rami isn't right for her." He's a good enough bloke. He'd impressed me when he'd stepped up to parachute onto the yacht, like me, putting his fear behind him to rescue her. It doesn't change my mind, I know she wouldn't be happy with him.

Again Kadar's shoulders rise and fall. "It's her decision whether she wants the prince or not. I'll support any agreement she comes to with him." Sweeping his robes around him, he retakes his seat behind the enormous desk, an ancient relic left over from his great grandfather's day. The monitor sitting on top shows how Kadar's made it his own and brought it into the twenty-first century. His eyes meet mine. "It was a match my father proposed. Rami's known about it almost since his birth. Was brought up to expect it. As were we all."

The fuck he has. "Another one of your father's dictates you can reverse," I remind him. "It's no longer Rushdi sitting behind that desk."

He looks at me sharply. "I would never force Aiza to do anything she didn't want. But..." His face twists as though he finds something distasteful.

"But?" I prompt impatiently.

"From what Aiza said, I wouldn't need to push her in his direction. It seems like she's made up her mind. When he makes a proposal, she's indicated she's inclined to accept."

It takes a moment for me to digest that she's even thinking about agreeing to his offer. I stand so quickly it makes the chair rock. Leaning over the desk, my palms flat on the ancient wood, my voice rises as I tell him again, "Rami is not the man for her."

"Sheikh! Remember yourself."

Kadar's growl has me sitting back down. Once I'm seated, though in no way any calmer, he holds up his hand. "I *know* that."

He does?

"I'll put it into my language. Rami's a good man. I've never heard anything to his detriment. Brave. Hell, he jumped out of a plane to go rescue her." Kadar seems impressed.

Has he forgotten I did that myself?

The emir hasn't finished. "He's submissive. Anyone could see it."

"Aiza's not," I state firmly.

He looks at me with tired eyes, and now I understand part of his exhaustion is down to his worries about his sister. "You might know better. I don't understand her, Rais. Never took the time to know what makes her tick while my father was alive. I grew up accepting her marriage would be for the sake of Amahad. It should be easy for me to give my blessing on the match and pleased it's all come about as planned."

"Instead, you're not." That gives me hope.

A knock at the door interrupts us, and Ma'mun enters, a tray of refreshment in his hands. He puts it down on the conference table and pours two coffees, bringing them over. I take mine and place it on the desk. Kadar holds his cup between his hands. He thanks his personal assistant, then, when we're left alone once more, starts speaking again.

"What do I know of her, Rais? We left her in Switzerland, basically forgot about her, thinking of her as nothing more than a pawn in the service of Amahad. She had us fooled, had her own dreams that she followed. Lived a life I had no idea she even had in her mind. She worked her arse off to get a degree, and from what I hear has been doing good work for a charity." He smooths his hand down his beard. "Instead of living in luxury, she's been using her allowance for the good of others. She's an incredible person, and we should never have dismissed her as we did, or believed she was of no consequence. Sure, she made some mistakes, only because she thought she wouldn't be allowed to continue what she was doing unless she was free."

I nod. She fooled everyone into thinking she had no value, was spending her money on clothes and a good life, when that couldn't be further from the truth. Every word he's saying emphasises what an excellent wife she'd make for me. I test the water. "You think Rami would be wrong for her? You'd prefer her to continue to have that freedom?"

"Marrying Rami would give her a sheltered life. One similar to that she would live here. She'd be the mother of his children. A diplomat's wife."

That life would slowly kill her. I can imagine the light fading out of her eyes when she was living such a secluded existence. "She needs a challenge."

He shakes his head then drains his cup. "It appears that she did. I'm not sure she does any longer."

"She's been through something terrifying." I think out loud. "Rami's a safe haven. She'd be protected in Alair."

Kadar raises his chin. "And out of the sights of Amir al-Fahri. So far, al-Fahri's not got on the bad side of Alair, and there's a good chance he'll keep it that way. I think it's a safe bet that being married to Rami might give her the protection she thinks she needs."

I cock my eyebrow. "You think al-Fahri will come after her again?"

"No one can rule it out. He wanted to get at me through her."

I take a breath. "I'd lay down my life for Aiza, Kadar." I thought I had when I jumped out of the plane, using the freefall time to make my peace with Allah. To keep her alive, I wouldn't hesitate to do it again.

"I know you would, Sheikh," Kadar says absently. "As you proved time and time again. You're loyal to all the royal family."

"Emir, you misunderstand me. My views haven't changed." I slash my hand through the air. "I don't believe she's thinking straight if she's considering accepting Rami. She needs a strong man. Someone to stand up to her. Someone she respects, and who respects her back. Despite Rami's formal approach to you, I would like your permission to show her what I have to offer."

He gives me a look which is completely unreadable, and for a moment I worry about the gun I know he has concealed under his desk. Then he does the last thing I ever expected. He starts to laugh.

Feeling disgruntled, I protest his reaction. "I don't see what's so amusing."

He gets himself under control. "Rais, I don't give a fuck who she marries, or whether she marries at all." Wiping his hand over his face, he becomes serious again. "If a desert sheikh wins her I would have no problem. I'm just amused that so many people are sniffing after her. Hunter's declared his intention as well."

That news doesn't surprise me. Hunter's been quite upfront. I've got a few cards up my sleeve myself.

"She'll be in the nursery. Seems that's where she's happiest at the moment." Kadar reaches for a file, opens it, then takes out a scrap of paper and peers at me over the top. "Well, why are you still here?"

Now it's my turn to grin. I stand, dip my head politely, then leave to find the woman who seems to have bewitched all the men who cross her path. *I'm the one who's going to win her.*

My first thought when I see her sitting cross-legged on the floor is how beautiful she is, and the second, how I'd like that to be our child she's holding. I'm thirty-four years old, and since my first attempt at marriage had never had the slightest inclination to settle down. That was because no one has ever held a candle to Aiza. Her beauty has ensnared me from the time I first recognised her as a woman, and in the intervening years it had been her I'd seen in my dreams.

Just the sight of her brings an unusual softening to my face. However, when she looks up and sees me, she stops smiling like a switch has been thrown. A brief explanation to the young girl, then she stands elegantly and comes over.

"Sheikh Rais." She greets me politely. I can't help but notice a shadow has come over her face.

I bow low. "Princess."

She indicates the balcony, then leads, and I follow her out. This part of the palace faces the sea, an unfortunate view as water is probably the last thing she wants to see after almost drowning. I'm not surprised that she puts her back towards it.

"I haven't been able to properly thank you for coming to rescue me." She can pretend with the children, their innocence keeping dark thoughts at bay. Seeing me, however, must bring it all back, as the light slowly fades from her eyes.

I make her a promise, one from the heart. "Always, Princess."

She laughs self-consciously. I worry there's no mirth in it. "I hope I'll never need rescuing again."

I think she does. She needs saving from making a terrible mistake, and the sooner the better. "You can't marry Rami." I dive straight in without preamble.

I've shocked her. Her eyes open wide, and her mouth opens and works, and it's a few seconds before she speaks. "You've been talking to Kadar," she accuses.

Unable to deny it, I shrug.

She glances back into the room, seeing the nanny has taken over playing with the children, and then looks at me, then down at her feet. "Why not? It's what was planned for me all along."

"He's not the right man for you, Aiza." I'm firm.

She shakes her head slowly as she peers up to look into my eyes. "I'm struggling to understand why you think it's any of your business, Sheikh Rais. This is between me and Prince Rami." There's a bit of her old spirit reappearing.

I decide to show her why it's my business. I take a step closer to her, inhaling the perfume that surrounds her, nothing fancy, just that of her shampoo and soap she must use. It's intoxicating. I've entered her personal space. She steps back to evade me, being halted when she comes up against the edge of the balcony.

She's stepped out of view of the windows. Behind us, the sound of children playing fades into the distance. All I can hear is my desert warrior blood rushing through my veins, her closeness causing my cock to swell, luckily hidden beneath my robes. Like a predator I stalk her, the gap between us closing until we're just a few millimetres apart. Reaching out my arms, my fingers curl around her upper arms.

Her mouth opens, but I don't give her a chance to speak. Instead, taking advantage, I quickly move my hand, cupping the back of her head and tilting it upwards, and at the same time bringing mine down.

My mouth finds her lips. She tries to close them, I'm too fast, my tongue pushing inside, meeting hers.

Her taste is everything I'd dreamed of as I ravish her, holding her tight to me. Not letting go of her head, my other arm snakes around her back and pulls her in close, my hardness resting against her soft stomach, leaving her in no doubt of my desire.

She's pliant, and also responsive. Hesitantly her tongue starts toying with mine. *I'm winning.*

The sound of the door to the suite opening interrupts us and brings her back to herself. She pushes at me hard with both hands, and immediately I step back, giving her space. Her eyes wild, now at least have life in them. Without turning to see who's entered I tap my finger against her nose.

"*That* makes it my business. I promise you, Princess, this isn't finished." I cock my eyebrow to question if she understands.

She swallows and looks bemused. Before she can answer a man coughs. I move back to the doorway to see who's entered, stifling a groan, then, remembering my manners, greet him as pleasantly as I can under the circumstances. "Hunter."

"Sheikh Rais. I was looking for Aiza." I indicate her standing at the edge of the balcony, out of sight of the doorway. "She's here. We were just...talking." I brush past him and go into the nursery, pausing to pat Eti on the head and admire a toy he seems proud of.

"Hi, Hunter." Aiza sounds shy, and as she comes in behind me to greet the man from Grade A, I glance back, unable to suppress a smile as I notice her lips are swollen. "Rais was just leaving."

Nice try. "We haven't finished our *conversation*, Princess."

Hunter's looking from me to her, and then back again, his jaw tight as he senses the tension in the room. He comes closer, effectively putting himself between us, his back turned towards me. "I was hoping to talk to you myself."

"It seems I'm popular today." Her words are light-hearted, though not in her usual tone, giving away that she's nervous.

Hunter's raising his hand, daring to touch what is mine as he gently traces her face, his fingers trailing down to that fucking circle of bruises yellowing on her neck. The only thing that stops me slapping his face away is when she backs out of his reach. Hunter lets her maintain her distance. "How are you feeling, Aiza?"

"I'm fine." She lies. I know she's not telling the truth. The right words are coming out, while her eyes say something different. She's far too meek, not the spirited woman who immersed herself in a worthwhile career.

"I don't think you are, Aiza," Hunter contradicts, able to read her as well as myself.

"Look, I'd love to stay and chat, but you'll both have to excuse me. I promised I'd go see Zoe this morning, and I'm already running late." Her words sound hurried, and she seems on edge.

It's an excuse, reassuringly one which applies equally to both of us. I'm happy to leave as long as Hunter's also being dismissed. I don't want to heap more pressure on her. Making sure I catch her eyes, I bow my head respectfully, then fix my gaze on hers. "Of course, Princess. We'll pick up where we left off later."

She moves so fast she's almost running as she leaves Hunter and I alone—well, alone except for the nanny and the children playing at our feet. When Hunter nods and turns to go, I follow him out.

He waits for me in the corridor. "She's far from alright."

My thoughts exactly. He might be my rival, but we both have her best interests at heart. "You know about Rami, I take it?"

His eyes meet mine. "That he's going to ask her to marry him? Yes." Hunter puts a finger and thumb to the brow of his nose, and I gather he also came running as soon as he heard. "He'd be no good for her," he says, proving he's on the same wavelength. "Though I can see why she thinks it's an attractive option at the moment."

So can I. Marry a prince of Alair and her risk of abduction will fade. "At the moment, yes," I agree. "He's safe."

Hunter sighs loudly. "She'd get bored in no time."

"Rami wouldn't challenge her. He'll wrap her in cotton wool and adore her." I'm thinking aloud.

He nods, showing he's on exactly the same page, then looks at me sharply. "What the fuck are you doing, Rais? Don't think I can't recognise the signs of a woman who's just been kissed."

I raise my chin and look straight into his face. "Throwing my hat in the ring."

Again, a little more slowly, he dips and raises his head. "Can't say I didn't see it coming. It's not what I expected, Sheikh. I can't see what you've got to offer her. She wouldn't be happy living in Amahad as much as we know she'd suffocate in Alair, whatever she might be trying to persuade herself of at the moment.

I gaze up the corridor in the direction she'd turned, then glance back. "I want her to be happy, and I think I can give her that." I know exactly how I'm going to tempt her to stay. I don't tell Hunter. One doesn't show one's opponent his cards.

He looks at me curiously as though wondering what game I'm playing, but sees I'm not going to disclose my hand. "We'll agree to disagree on that one. There's one thing where both our thoughts coincide. We've got to stop her from running to Rami. That would be the worst mistake of her life."

"Does she really want the prince?" I wonder aloud. "Or is she just seeing him as someone who can keep her away from danger? Or, even worse, after all the trouble she's caused, mistakenly thinks, is this a way to repay her family?"

CHAPTER 19
Aiza

I refuse to think about my body's traitorous reaction to that astonishing kiss Rais had given me, or my automatic reaction to return it rather than push him away. *How dare he just take what he wanted?*

I didn't object, that's for certain. Had he asked, requested, I'd have refused. I couldn't have predicted he'd just take what he wanted, nor in doing so, blow me away. I never had an inkling he thought of me in that way. Coming right out of the blue, I reacted purely on instinct, any ramifications far from my mind. A kiss I can't deny I've always longed for, though not once had expected. *I never dreamed he might want me in return.* His timing couldn't have been worse, not now when I've all but agreed to become engaged to another man.

I had to get out of the nursery, a flimsy excuse anyone would see through. Rais on his own is overwhelming. Add Hunter into the mix and the amount of testosterone in the room became unbearable. All I could do was run away.

When I've put sufficient distance between me and them, I lean against the wall to get my breath and catch sight of myself in a mirror opposite. Reaching up my hand to finger the signs of the bruises still visible at my neck, flashbacks make me put out my other arm to the plaster-work for much needed support. Memories of being dragged around naked with a leash and dog collar, being dehumanised with the promise I'd never be able to make a decision for myself ever again. The ability to say 'no' taken away from me.

What Rais did should have frightened me. Instead it aroused me.

Unable to understand my reaction to the sheikh, I decide to forget about it instead. Pretend it never happened and hope he never speaks of it again. Certainly I never will. Pushing away from the wall, I continue to my destination. Despite saying I had to meet Zoe, I had no such meeting, but decided anyway to try and find her, thinking a woman's company far less dangerous. The emira isn't in her suite of rooms as I discover when I knock and receive no answer. Belatedly, I remember she'd had plans to go out and visit some schools today. Zoe's not the type of wife I'd ever have envisaged for my older brother, though anyone could see she's absolutely perfect for him, determined to do her part and not live the life of a sheltered queen. It's clear while Kadar worries about her, he makes no move to restrict her activities, which some-times leave her exposed. He's softened from the brother I remember. His actions, his obvious love for his wife and his son, convincing me more than words could ever do, how he's a different man from our father.

As I retrace my steps to return to my own quarters I continue to think about the family I hadn't given much thought to over the years. They were like names on paper, a genealogical history. It's as if I've only got to learn about them over the past few days. Nijad's kidnapped wife, Cara, turned out to be the best thing that could have happened to him, and she's now virtually the country's finance minister in everything but title, as well as a world-renowned computer hacker, of all things. Jasim's wife was the one who gave up her chance of fame and fortune to marry my middle brother. Now pregnant again, Janna seems more than happy being a wife and mother, though I know she's been talking to Zoe about developing a music scholarship programme in schools. Although I'd never known my own mother, it was no secret my father had kept her closeted in the palace, and she never had the chance to live her own life…

"Aiza." A shout from behind interrupts my thoughts and gets me swinging around.

"Prince Rami." I feel the first genuine smile of the day come to my face. Whether I'm having doubts or not about my hasty decision to consider accepting his proposal of marriage, his enthusiasm for life is infectious.

It had been embarrassing meeting Rami for the first time after we'd returned to Amahad, remembering how he cradled my naked body so gently on the boat that carried me away from yacht. He'd come to seek me out the next morning, his affable and bubbly personality quickly erasing any awkwardness between us. Ebullient in his compliments, he'd taken my hand and told me he intended to ask Kadar formally for my hand in marriage, a proposition I hadn't immediately dismissed and, instead, found myself indicating that while I wasn't going to rush to commit, I might very well accept.

I could do a lot worse than marry a prince of a neighbouring country, the union consolidating the already warm relationship between Amahad and Alair. I'd always known it was my dead father's wish, and in the past had rebelled against it. There's no doubt it would make my family happy.

In other ways too, Rami's perfect for me. I'm a Domme, he's submissive. He'd spend his life trying to make me happy. *What kind I life would I have?* Fulfilling his expectations and needs? A sub serves their Dom, while the Dom or Domme has a responsibility to care for their submissive. In a marriage, a twenty-four-seven relationship, he'd be more of a slave. An exhausting union. I'm not sure I could cope.

"I wondered if you'd care to walk in the gardens?" It's forty degrees celsius out there. Living in England for so long, I'm having to get used to the high temperatures again. But some of the garden is shaded, and it would be pleasant to just sit and listen to the fountains play. Soothing after my emotions have been tugged so many different ways today.

Feeling bold, I reach out my hand and take his. A natural enough thing to do in the UK, but here... Seeing that Rami looks like he's won the lottery as he wraps his fingers around mine and squeezes, I wonder if I've been a bit too forward and am sending a signal I'm not quite ready to send.

The heat doesn't bother him as much as myself. He stands in the sunlight, a bold silhouette as I hog the shade offered by a palm tree. He advances, puts one foot on the bench and leans forwards with his hands clasped on his knee. His attention caught by a colourful bird flying over-head, one of the parrots that used to live in the harem garden, he half smiles, then brings his attention back to me.

"I don't believe you've been to the royal palace in Alair, have you? I doubt you'd find it wanting."

I study my hands resting in my lap. Most of my life I've tried to leave my royal life behind, and that includes living in palaces. Since I was taken and sold, the continued security sounds more than attractive.

"Have you any residences abroad?" I don't know very much about him. Perhaps it's time I learned about my potential husband-to-be.

He puts his leg down, turns around and sits beside me. He smells fresh, as though he's just showered, his white robes gleaming in the bright light. His thigh, so close yet not quite touching, seems to give off warmth. He's an attractive man, only three years older than me. "There's a family mansion in Paris, and of course, one in London, in Mayfair."

Of course it would be. One of the most expensive places to live. I shudder, not yet able to remember my last night in that city, finding out someone had been keeping tabs on me.

He's regarding me carefully. "If you didn't want to make your home in Alair, we could live overseas."

"Would you still work?"

He shrugs. "Wherever I go, I'll always be an ambassador for my country, that goes without saying. The oil negotiations will wrap up soon and can be left to the executives of the joint oil company we're setting up."

I keep up to date with news from my homeland. AmaOil is the joint merger between Amahad, Alair and Ezirad.

"I'd be okay living here for a while." I leave the 'here' vague. I could mean Amahad or Alair. Rami doesn't seem to have much purpose in life, and that disturbs me. Suddenly I need to ask, "What do *you* want to do, Rami?"

He leans forwards, audaciously placing a kiss to my forehead. "Whatever makes you happy."

What would make me happy? I think of everything I had desired to do. Working with the charity to get sick children the help they needed, dealing with visas and permits to get them out on their own and into the right country for treatment. Knowing what officials I have to bribe. Suddenly it all seems overwhelming. The woman who did that is in the past. Even though I started it, now I don't want to extend this topic of conversation.

"Kiss me." The words escape before I can hold them back. I know it's not a fair thing to ask, aware I'm conducting an experiment. When Rais had his mouth on mine I forgot my name. I want to see whether Rami can stir anything like those feelings.

"With pleasure." A gentle hand tilts my face as he brings his head down slowly, brushing his lips against mine. I open, giving him permission, and our tongues touch and meet. He inches closer, his arms come around me, my hands clutching at his robes, pulling him nearer. I place my hand on the back of his head, my fingers taking hold of his headdress and ensuring I position his head where I want it. He makes no complaint as I take the lead.

My tongue sweeps into his mouth, tasting the coffee he must have recently drank. I increase the pressure, then slowly come back to myself, first letting go of his headdress, then dropping my hand still holding his robe. Tactfully as I withdraw my permission he immediately retreats, pulls away, then gazes at me with a look of adoration on his face.

I found his touch arousing, different. He let me be me, he didn't try and impose himself. *Unlike Rais.* Or, I suddenly remember, like Hunter's kiss, which happened, it seems, so long ago in London.

"I'm sorry," I start, genuinely perplexed at my behaviour. At leading him on.

His smile widens. "It confirmed I was right to ask you to marry me." I notice him widening his legs and know the kiss hadn't left him unaffected. Instead of making sure I was aware of his arousal like the desert sheikh, he's being gentlemanly and hiding it from me.

In my head I curse Rais, wishing he'd never touched me. This morning I was content to let the plans my father had made sweep me away, marry the man who'd keep me safe and never challenge me. Now I don't know what to think.

I stand, fanning my face. It's no excuse when I tell him, "I'm getting hot, Rami. I need to go in."

He stands and leans down, speaking into my ear. "I'm feeling a little heated too, if you want the truth."

My cheeks start to burn, and it's not because of the sun.

He walks beside me as we enter one of the state rooms, closing the door behind us. There's air conditioning here, and I relish the cooler temperature. A servant appears, looking slightly out of breath.

"Prince Rami." He bows. "Emir Kadar has requested your presence in his office."

Politely apologising for having to leave, Rami sweeps out of the door. As he does, a man steps from the shadows. I jump, my heart leaping in my chest. My hand rises to cover it as with relief I recognise who's stepped out.

"You make a habit of kissing men?" Hunter asks, seeming more amused than annoyed. Embarrassed he must have noticed my swollen lips earlier, and now caught me with Rami, I don't deign to answer, and instead point my feet towards the door. He stalks across the room, blocking my progress. "If you're trying out all your suitors today, there's one you've missed." With his foot he pushes the door closed, then leans back against it, his arms folded across his chest.

"Who?" I ask shakily.

"That would be me."

I shake my head. *No more kissing today, it's getting me in trouble.* Would I leap at another chance to taste this dominant man? Dressed in jeans that show the delicious outline of his arse, and the undeniable bulge exposing he's already turned on. A tight-fitting t-shirt does nothing other than showcase his impressive muscles.

He leans forwards and down so his mouth's at my ear. "Kiss me, Aiza," he demands.

No. The kiss in London had been an act, a ruse to confuse the people listening to me. It's not something I thought we'd repeat. *What would it be like to mate our mouths for real? Would he let me have control?*

"Kiss. Me," he repeats, making no move to initiate contact himself.

All I need to do is turn my head and…

I turn my head, and as if by accident my mouth meets his. I tell myself I was only going to utter another refusal. Instead, he takes advantage, pushing his lips against mine.

We touch with nothing but our mouths.

"Open," he instructs, and it must be the reverberation of his words against my face that makes me comply.

Tongues meet and explore, sliding as though in a dance. I fist my hands at my sides, determined not to encourage him not to take this any further. *I wish that he would.* The feelings he's bringing to the fore make me want him to bend me over the couch and take me, thrust his cock into me, make me scream….

Tell him what you want.

I can't.

His lips are soft, his tongue invasive, movements mimicking what he could do with another part of his body. I lean into him, trying to let him know without using words how much he's turning me one.

He doesn't press his advantage, pulling away and ending the kiss when he's explored my mouth to his satisfaction. He rubs his nose against mine. "Kadar wants me in the meeting too, Princess." He's smirking, the bastard. *He knows full well what he's done to me.* "We'll have to finish this later."

Stunned, I say nothing as he departs. When he's gone, a growl of frustration comes to my throat. Seeing a hapless cushion, I go to pound my fist on it. *What the fuck am I doing?* Kissing three different men in one morning *and* getting aroused by them all? Including, as I've told Kadar, if not in those precise words to the man himself, that one I have every intention of marrying.

Perhaps it's the heat I'm not accustomed to that's making me act out of character. Boy, in their different ways, each of those men can kiss.

CHAPTER 20
Rami

Kadar's seated at the head of the conference table in his large office, his brow furrowed. Rais is already there, and so is Nijad. The latter looks up and acknowledges me as I walk in.

"Prince Rami. Thank you for coming promptly. We're waiting on Jasim and Hunter. Hunter should be on his way, Jasim's just finishing up on a phone call."

Drumming his fingers on the table, Kadar looks impatient to begin. I wonder why I've been called here. Could be anything—trouble with the pipeline or the drilling site. I purse my lips, hoping I'm not going to hear bad news which could upset me on this near perfect day. That kiss I shared with Aiza leads me to believe she's closer to agreeing to my marriage proposal than I could have dreamed.

I'd give her the world, whatever she asked for. My only desire to serve her and make her happy for the rest of my life. I have no real ambitions of my own, content to make hers mine. She'll never want for anything with me.

The door opens and closes. One more seat is filled, and then the sound of another chair being kicked out. Lost in my reverie, I don't take much notice until I hear Kadar start to speak.

"Hunter. Take a seat, I want to get started."

His gruff voice alerts me, and I scan those invited. Rais, Nijad, Jasim, Hunter and myself. The others look as mystified as myself. No meetings were scheduled today.

"What's this about, Kadar?" It's his youngest brother who sounds anxious.

Now I'm looking more closely I see how tight Kadar's features are, and how his body is giving off small tremors as he glances around the table and then begins. "I got a phone call earlier. I think you should all hear it." He presses a button on his phone. Like my father, the king of Alair, all the emir's official calls must automatically be recorded.

"Emir Kadar."

"Amir al-Fahri."

There's silence while Kadar obviously takes in the name. Then, "I'm listening," he says in a brusque tone.

"I want your sister."

A moment of silence, then, "You're not having her. You've already hurt her enough." You can hear the conclusiveness in Kadar's voice.

"Pah. She was rescued before my plan was put in place."

"Leave her alone, Amir. She's under my protection," Kadar growls.

"I'm going to offer you a choice, Emir, which I think is fair. Your sister, or I'll come after your children. Your child, Nijad's, and Jasim's. Even the unborn child in your wife's womb."

"You dare threaten me?" Kadar's enraged voice thunders through the small speakers.

"It's not a threat. It's a promise. An expression of intent, if you like."

We all exchange glances, and Nijad and Jasim start speaking, causing Kadar to pause the call.

"It's too personal." Hunter's looking surprised. "Amir al-Fahri is a known terrorist. He kills indiscriminately just to score points. The USA, the UK, Europe. Hell, even Africa hasn't escaped. Or he'll swoop in and direct a hit on a person of importance. He doesn't warn in advance, or if he does it's in vague terms to cause the most worry. He's not known for making personal threats or bargains."

Kadar's nodding. "Listen. It will become clear." He starts the recording playing again.

"What do you want with the Kassis family, Amir?"

"Revenge."

"I don't understand why."

There's a pause before the terrorist answers. "Because of my son. He died on Amahadian soil, and I suspect you were behind it."

"I don't recall…"

"Then let me refresh your memory." Amir's voice is raised now. "His helicopter crashed, the bodies were buried by your tribespeople and were never found. I think you'll remember the *accident,* as you call it, in the southern desert."

"I recall an accident which claimed four lives. The helicopter was assumed to be flying too low. Or maybe flew into a sandstorm. Burying bodies fast is the way of our tribes. They would have thought they were paying respects, rather than leaving bodies to rot under the sun or be eaten by vultures. As far as I know, the identities of the men in the helicopter were never discovered. All we know is that four people were buried."

"That day my son didn't return. Neither did the woman he was running around with."

"Conjecture at best."

"Oh, no, Kadar. It's enough evidence for me. I've stated my terms. An eye for an eye, a tooth for a tooth. The debt must be repaid. I want Aiza in revenge for my son."

"That is not going to happen."

"Then you lock your palace up tight. In the end it won't matter what you do, I'll find a way in. I'll hit you when you least expect it. A day from now, a week, a month. Next year. I won't stop until I've taken all the next generation. Is a sister you barely know worth losing all that?"

Kadar presses the button a final time. "I'm afraid I lost it at that point. Nothing further productive came out of the conversation."

"What do we know about al-Fahri's missile capability?" Nijad looks across at Hunter.

Hunter notes something down. "I'll have to check. But yes, that is a possibility he'd be able to get his hands on something. So far it's been suicide bombers or other types of attacks. He's not used missiles to date. To our knowledge, that is."

"Security at the palace is tight." Jasim nods at Nijad. "If he thinks he can get in to take out the children, he'd be wrong. I think you might right. He must know how well protected we are here, it might be something big."

This is out of my league. Because oil was found as a result of the Amahadian survey, coincidentally in a field running under Alair, the terrorist has always focused on Kadar's country, the aim to unbalance the world economy, not wanting more oil to come onto the market. As Amahad has led the exploration, and the pipeline runs across their land, Alair has been kept out of his sights. However, my future wife appears to be right in them.

"I'll marry Aiza immediately. Take her to Alair. Hell, take her anywhere to keep her safe and out of his clutches."

"No." Two voices growl in unison, making me look up sharply. Rais and Hunter.

"The threat will still be there." Hunter's face looks tight as he explains. "Amir al-Fahri doesn't give warnings lightly. It's a promise of action, not intimidation. We all need to be prepared." All eyes are on him, we all know he's more than a Grade A operative and assume he works in intelligence. "He doesn't always succeed, and we've been able to foil some plots. If he says he's going to attack, you better start getting ready."

"We, as being MI6?" I ask, wondering if he's going to be straight for once.

Hunter shrugs. He's not going to admit it.

"We fight." My eyes go to Rais. The fierce looking desert sheikh looks murderous. No stranger to battle, I'm not surprised that suggestion came from him.

Kadar's staring at him. "I'm all for direct action. But against what? Amir al-Fahri's a phantom. No one knows where he is, otherwise the battle would've been taken to him long before now."

Rais doesn't look like the emir's comments have bothered him. He shrugs. "We draw him out."

Looking interested, Nijad leans forwards. "And how do you suggest we do that?"

Rais gives a twisted grin. "We lure him into a trap." As all eyes go to him, he puts a hand to his forehead and talks as he formulates a plan. "I take Aiza to the Desert Palace in Zalmā. That takes away any reason for him making an attack here."

"Not happening," I tell him forcefully. "The Desert Palace, as I understand it, is smaller and more open to attack."

Rais spares me a dismissive glance. "I don't think it's up to you."

"I've asked her to marry me!" I protest. "And…"

"She's not your wife yet." Kadar stops me, giving me one of his haughtiest looks. "Carry on, Rais, I'm listening."

Rais nods. "It's obvious al-Fahri's got the hots for her. He'll pull out all the stops to take her. We'll be prepared and take him instead."

Hunter looks interested. He lifts his hand. "Number of reasons why I don't think Rais's idea should be dismissed out of hand." He pulls at his first finger. "One, al-Fahri will know she won't be there for good. She'll not want to be confined to the desert at all knowing her, so this has to be a temporary measure. If he's going to try to take her there, he won't wait long before making his move. He'll think it an easier target to attack." He pulls at the second finger. "Secondly, we can put all our resources in one place…"

"The Haimi will be out in force." Rais refers to his tribe, their reputation as warriors being known as a legend even in Alair.

"Agreed, Rais. Thank you."

"Thirdly, we can have intelligence officers descend on the place." He pauses and puts his hand down. "I'll have to check in, though I reckon this is the best chance we've ever had of getting this bastard once and for all."

"Cut the head off the snake and another will grow."

"Rais, my old friend, you're right. Hopefully it will take them time to regroup after al-Fahri is gone."

The way they're talking, he'll be dead, not languishing in a prison cell. And fuck it if I don't think that's the best thing to happen to him. He's after my woman, after all.

Jasim's face looks pinched. "She's not going to like risking herself as a target again."

"If she stays here," Nijad says, looking equally upset, "the lives of our children will be at risk. Aiza loves all the kids, she's not going to want to put them in danger."

"I will speak with her," Kadar states. A shadow comes over his face, and I don't understand why. Is he thinking she will refuse?

I try to put myself in her shoes. She's been through too much in the last few days. The woman who sat next to me on the bench was not the feisty woman I remember meeting before or seeing while I was abroad. In many ways, this softer version is more appealing, more *fitting* to be by my side. And definitely easier to handle. I don't like confrontation, either between myself and my future wife, or if I'd need to sooth over any feathers she ruffles.

"She's not herself," Hunter observes, voicing my own thoughts aloud. "She's not the same woman I spent the night with or brought here on the plane.

Nijad growls, "I hope you didn't mean that the way it sounded."

I want to smile. Nijad's always had a thing about Hunter and his wife. Now it appears to extend to his sister as well. But I'm also interested in the answer. *Hunter wouldn't have, would he?*

Hunter raises a brow as he turns to the youngest Kassis brother. "Are you suggesting I'd act anything other than professionally?" he challenges.

Nijad gives him a steely gaze, though he doesn't reply. Instead, he looks at Kadar. "I shall, of course, go to Zalmā."

As Jasim goes to speak Kadar stops him. "No. The three of us will stay here. We can't divert all our forces to the desert city, in case al-Farhi decides it will hurt us more to harm our children."

Nijad and Jasim exchange glances, seeming to have a silent conversation, obviously realising the need to protect their offspring. Then together they give identical nods. I've noticed it before, but you could be fooled into believing they are twins. "We'll stay." They even speak at once.

Kadar continues, "Rais. You'll be in charge of security in the Palace of Zalmā. I expect you to move into the palace."

"Of course, Excellency."

"I'll go too." I want to stay close to Aiza and play my part in keeping her safe.

"Prince, that's a generous offer. But as we don't know when he will strike, you may be there for a while."

Raising and lowering my shoulders, I inform him, "I can stay as long as it takes." As the second son I don't have an official role in my country and my presence wouldn't be missed. Espcially if my father knew I was courting Aiza.

"Then we must thank you." Kadar raises his chin.

"Hunter?"

"I'll have to clear it with Ben, though there's no doubt he'll send a team from Grade A, and it's almost certain I'll be heading it up. I've spent the most time of anyone in the southern desert."

"I'll be in charge." Rais seems to want to make that clear. He glances at Hunter and then to myself.

Well, somebody has to be. Too many people shouting orders could lead to confusion. I nod. Hunter's a little slower, then he agrees too.

"I can't stress on you how important it is to keep Aiza safe." Kadar still looks worried.

"Why does she have to be there?" Hunter asks. "We can dress someone up to look like her, take the decoy down there under massive security, while sneaking Aiza out of the country."

Kadar slowly nods, and then smiles. "I like that plan."

"I don't," Rais snarls. "Here we can put all our resources into protecting her. The Haimi and myself will die before they see any harm befall her. If she goes somewhere else, we won't have any guarantees al-Fahri might not find her. He's got his fingers into far too many pies. She'd need to stay completely out of sight."

Hunter's nodding. "In her current state of mind, I believe she needs friends around her."

Nijad doesn't look convinced. "Grade A could provide protection."

Their representative at the table shakes his head. "Again, our men could be recognised. We'd have to use operatives that can't be connected to her. If she's going to be exposed, I'd want our best men on it. The vast majority of those have provided services for Amahad in the past."

Kadar wipes his hand over his beard. "A way-out-there thought... What about that motorcycle club in America? The one that gave Zoe's friend, Sophie, protection. No one would think of looking for a princess in the Satan's Devils compound."

Even the name makes me shudder. No, I don't want my woman associated with men such as them, however much Kadar might like the idea.

Again Rais growls. "Fucking bikers. That race was rigged. Had to be."

"The Native American won fair and square, Rais. No doubt about it." Nijad grins as he toys with his friend.

And then the penny drops. They must have been the strange group of leather-clad men who attended the emir's wedding. I still remember how astonished Rais was when one of them proved he could ride a flesh and blood horse well enough to beat his best warriors. I smile, then immediately stop. The desert sheikh is not looking amused.

"It is an option. In my view, Aiza's been through enough and needs to be in familiar surroundings. Why don't we keep that suggestion on the back burner in case we need a plan B? Devil works with the Satan's Devils' computer guy a lot, so can always ask them for assistance."

Nijad's nodding. "Cara talks to them too. Strange bunch of men, but their hearts are in the right place."

Kadar nods and grows serious again. "I'll speak to Aiza, and unless she raises a valid objection she'll be going to the southern desert. As for myself, I'd prefer her to stay on Amahadian soil."

I nod, conceding his point and agreeing with him. *Until she's my wife and comes to Alair.*

CHAPTER 21
Aiza

I'm trying to focus on a book—I'm rereading one of Dexie Sanders—when there's a loud knock at my door, and Kadar enters the sitting room of my suite. As I go to rise he waves me back down, then comes over and seats himself on a chair opposite. Removing his headdress, he places it beside him and immediately looks less formidable.

"How are you, Aiza?" He stares at me, concerned.

"I'm good," I say lightly, trying to put him at ease.

"Really?" One brow rises.

Shrugging, I don't know what to say. If truth be told, I'm not sure who I am anymore. Physically I've recovered, even those darn bruises around my neck have faded completely. Inside me, though, something has changed. I've not got the confidence that I previously had. I'm constantly jumping at my own shadow, thinking it's someone coming to kidnap me, and each night I have nightmares that I'm still on that yacht, even though logically I know Twafiq is dead and won't be coming back.

"I'm sorry, Aiza."

I tilt my head to one side. "For what?" He had no part to play in my abduction.

Suddenly he stands, his robes swirling around him. He walks to the side of the room and then back again. "Because I don't know if you're back to normal or not. How can I tell? I don't even know you."

"Kadar…"

He spins. "No, Aiza. Let me get this out." His hands brush over his shortly shorn hair. "When we were children it was understandable. The age difference between us meant that three older boys had nothing in common with a little girl playing with dolls. Our training and education took us away from you." Again I go to speak, his palm held towards me forestays me. "There was no such excuse when we became older. When our father died I should have done more to get to know you."

For a second time I shrug. "I was settled in Switzerland."

A snide glance. "But you weren't, were you?"

Pursing my lips. I grimace. "Not all the time, no."

"You weren't out partying with your girlfriends as everyone thought. You were studying. Something I hadn't given you credit for or even believed you would do. Fuck knows why."

Again, my tilted head prompts further explanation.

"You're a Kassis. Intelligence doesn't keep to the male line."

I laugh. "Our father thought that it did."

"I'm not our father." He's certainly not. Our father would never have credited me with having a brain. To him

I was just a commodity to further his political aims. Not only was I female and otherwise worthless, in his view I'd murdered my mother by being born. Rushdi had wanted nothing to do with me.

"I'm sorry, Aiza. I'd like to make up for not making the effort to get to know you in the past."

"There's nothing to apologise for, big brother." I smile.

"Yes there is. I called you home because you had been threatened. If it had all gone to plan I would have lectured you, admonished you for how you live your life. I would have treated you the same as our father would have done." The admission surprises me. "When you were kidnapped, that's when it hit me. You're my sibling as much as Jasim and Nijad. While I don't always agree with their choices in life, I understand them, as I know them. I've never taken the time to get to understand you." Again his hands tunnel through his hair. "I didn't know how you'd react, what you were feeling. Whether you could be strong, or whether they would break you."

Now I rise, going over and taking both his hands in mine and doing something I never thought I'd be doing. Going on tiptoe, I plant a kiss on the cheek of the emir. "They didn't break me. Damaged me a bit, but I'm still here. I will get over it. Especially with the help of my brothers."

His hands encircle mine. "I'll never dismiss you again, Aiza. I want to have the chance to find out more about the person you really are."

Tugging gently on one hand, I lead him over to the couch. I sit down, and when he copies my action I squeeze his fingers. "I'd like to have a chance to learn about you, Kadar. It's not all your fault. I've been avoiding coming home, as I couldn't get the thought out of my head that you might want to control me in the same way as our father. I'm a person in my own right, not a pawn to be used for Amahad."

Reaching out the hand I'm not holding, he tenderly brushes a tendril of hair out of my face, tucking it behind my ear. An affectionate gesture, and I find myself leaning into his touch. "Rushdi expected you to marry Rami. I know Rami has asked for your hand. I want you to know that I'll support you, whatever your answer is."

"Thank you, Kadar." I look down, and then back at his face. "I think I'm going to accept."

He doesn't have the reaction I thought he would. Instead he frowns. "Oh, Aiza. I only ask you do nothing in a hurry. Make a decision you might come to regret because you've just come through a horrific ordeal. Think it through carefully, take your time. If you do agree to marry Rami, make sure that you're doing it for all the right reasons."

I thought he would have been delighted. That he's cautious gives me cause for pause. Maybe he's right and I shouldn't decide so hastily. Having gone quiet, Kadar mistakes my reason.

"I want you to know, you needn't have unnecessary worries. Rami knows."

Now he's confused me. "Knows what?" I turn to look at him again.

Kadar won't meet my eye. "That if you did take him as your husband he wouldn't be getting a virgin bride."

"What the hell?" As thought it had burst into flames and burned me, I drop the hand I'm still holding.

Now he turns back and raises an eyebrow, and there's a smirk on his face. "Seems you're more like your brothers than we gave you credit for. You've been seen playing in clubs." He grins, then grows serious again. "There, I do know something about you. I just wanted to reassure you if you were worried about having to come clean."

What conversations have my brothers been having about me?

Feeling myself flush, I realise the fact that Rami might be expecting a virgin bride had been the last thing on my mind. While we might share the same taste in entertainment, I don't want to discuss BDSM clubs with my brother. "I appreciate you coming to see me, Kadar. Though I have doubts it was just for a catch-up chat?" Something tells me there's more to his visit, and I'd rather talk about something different.

"No. There's something I need to discuss with you." Watching him closely I see a cloud pass across his face, then feel myself pale as he explains about the new threat against me.

Now it's my turn to stand and start to pace. "Of course I need to leave the palace." There's no doubt about it. I can't bear the thought of the children being at risk. "I'd prefer not to go to the desert."

"I'm not asking you to sleep in a tent, Aiza. You will, of course, be staying in the palace."

"Who says I wouldn't like staying in a tent?" I wink at him cheekily. "In fact, that sounds much more exciting."

He snorts. "I told you I didn't know you."

"Well, I don't live as a pampered princess." I'm serious again as I walk to the other side of the room and then back. "Have you any idea how long I'll be there for?"

"To be honest, I've no idea, Aiza. You'll not be in the back of beyond, you know. There's WiFi in the palace. And telephones. The office areas have been completely modernised."

I nod, then place my fingers to my lips as I start thinking, caught unawares by a bubble of excitement thinking of visiting the desert. I haven't been to Zalmā since I was a child. I used to love playing in the palace where everything was far less formal than here. Though the circumstances are not particularly thrilling, there are worse places I could be.

"Rais will be in charge of your security. He's calling on the tribes, particularly his own, the Haimi, to provide warriors." The Haimi have a fierce and well-deserved reputation. If anyone can keep me safe, they can. "Oh, and Rami has invited himself along. I think he wants to press his suit."

Rais will be there. And Rami. My hand goes to my lips as I remember the kisses earlier today. Huh. All I need now is for Hunter to complete the trio.

"Of course there'll be a team from Grade A which will be led by Hunter."

I turn away and put my hand fully over my mouth to suppress the burst of laughter that tries to come out. Fuck knows what I'll be getting myself into. Then I grow cold and wrap my arms around myself. I'm still not over my previous kidnap, and now I'm setting myself up to be taken again.

Eyeing my big brother, I admit, "I'm scared, Kadar."

Kadar gets to his feet and comes over, taking both my hands in his. "Amir al-Fahri wants you. Wherever you go, Aiza, you'll be looking over your shoulder. If I could do anything to spare you that, I would. We've talked it through, and I believe this is the best way to protect you. Al-Fahri is wanted the world over. MI6 and the CIA will be getting involved, and Britain's sending some SAS, America some SEALS, maybe even a Delta Force team. The Australian SAS want in on it too. The upshot is we'll have the best intelligence we can get, and the most highly trained men all with one aim in mind, the capture of al-Fahri and his top men. And by taking him, they'll save you."

My eyes narrow. "Would he really expose himself like this?"

"I've questioned that myself. I think in this case, yes. He's got a real hatred for Amahad. Even before the death of his son, we kept foiling his plans."

"Did you kill his son?"

A strange smile comes to Kadar's face. "No, he was actually shot by an Englishwoman. She works for Grade A. But," he taps my nose, "that stays between us. As far as al-Farhi and the rest of the world know, his son disappeared, or was most likely killed in a helicopter crash."

Pleased Kadar trusts me enough to tell me the truth, I think over what he's told me. Although I know the best laid plans can go wrong—I've recent example to show me that —everything being put in place seems enough to protect me. While my heart sank when he first told me I remained a target, I feel better knowing there's so many people who are trying to keep me safe and, most importantly, remove the threat for good.

The thought I'll be with Hunter, Rais and Rami both amuses and scares me. One thing I do know about all of them, I couldn't ask for anyone who had a greater desire to keep me out of harm's way.

"I'll do it. When do I leave?"

Kadar lets out a deep breath. "As soon as possible. I'll go and see what the arrangements are and make sure you get to know them."

He collects his headdress, puts it on, then walks to the door. With his hand on the door handle, he turns and smirks. "Oh, and if you weren't already aware, you might like to know part of the harem has been converted into a dungeon.

My mouth drops open as he disappears into the corridor. *What the hell?*

Because of the threat to the children, plans are put in place fast. It's the next morning when I'm yet again getting into a helicopter, this one a twelve-seater. Serious looking military men armed to the teeth are flying with myself, Rais, Rami and Hunter. It's a two-hour flight to Zalmā, and we'll be landing at the helipad at the desert palace.

For most of the way I stare out of the window. While I've lived so long away from my country, love for the desert is in my blood. I get sheer enjoyment from simply watching the sand pass by underneath. The dunes, the shadows cast by the sun, the outcrops of rocks and the occasional herds of desert gazelles. It gives me a sense of peace, only broken when over the headphones I hear the pilot talking to the airports, who are monitoring air traffic and radar, making sure nothing's coming to intercept us.

It's a reminder that this is no pleasure trip. I'm being dangled as the proverbial carrot to catch an international terrorist. It's a sobering thought.

When I get my first glimpse of the palace my heart leaps, and I feel as I did as a child seeing it for the first time. It's a beautiful building, some parts over a thousand years old, and surrounded by an oasis of colour. The gardens are maintained for the people of Zalmā to enjoy. As my hand settles on a key in my pocket, I feel a buzz of excitement. Nijad had passed it to me with a wink as I was leaving, and with one word, "Enjoy." I'd been too flabbergasted to respond with anything other than a stunned nod.

And then had turned away, wishing I'd been able to stay and get to know all my brothers better. Hopefully it won't be too long until I can come back. It seems we have at least one thing in common.

The key brings a smile to my face. If Jasim had a hand in designing it, it would probably be quite a place. *I can't wait to explore.*

The helicopter lands, ending my thoughts about dungeons, and soon I'm entering into the atrium at the rear of the palace, admiring the incredible brightly lit space, a glass ceiling letting sunlight stream in. It strikes me as smaller than I remember it, though that's understandable as then I viewed it through the eyes of a child. The palace staff are all waiting, their heads dipping quickly up and down as I pass.

"Welcome, Your Highness." A woman steps up to me. "I am Lamis. Sheikha Cara's personal maid. She's asked that I be of service while you're in residence."

"Thank you, Lamis." I follow her as she leads me up the magnificent staircase and along the hallways. The palace, just as I had remembered, seems more intimate and friendly than that in Al Qur'ah. She opens the door to the royal suite, the one my brother occupies when he's here. It has two bedrooms, a comfortable looking sitting room and a dining area.

Rais steps in behind me, his low voice growling in my ear surprising me. "I will be staying in here with you. You need someone with you at all times."

I swing around. *Here? With me?*

As I open my mouth to clarify, Hunter interrupts. "Not so fast, buddy." He frowns at the desert sheikh. "I'm her close-protection officer."

Rami scowls. "I've asked her to be my wife. I should be the one to stay."

Lamis is standing with her arms folded and an amused look on her face.

"Are there other suites close by?" I ask her.

"Two," she confirms. "Each with two beds."

"Can you show them to my friends?" As they all open their mouths to protest, "Look, you'll be close by in case of trouble. I'll be fine by myself."

"No," Rais says firmly. "Close by isn't near enough. I'll sleep on the sofa. That way no one can get in without me knowing. My goal is to keep you safe, Princess."

"In that case, I'll take the second bedroom. I'll only be a shout away," Hunter says tersely.

Rami looks like he's going to stamp his foot. "I've said I should be the one to stay with her. I'll take the bedroom... Or share yours, Princess?"

Confounded by his presumptuousness, I'm momentarily stunned.

The others aren't struck so dumb. "No!" Rais and Hunter roar in unison.

I look from one to the other, and then at Rami standing behind. There's an argument brewing if I'm not careful. "Look..." I try to come up with a compromise. "Why don't you toss a coin for it. Or it's probably a large enough bed, why don't two of you share the second bedroom?" I want nobody sharing mine.

Hunter looks at Rami and tilts his head to the side. Rami thinks for a moment, then nods. I take it no one wants to risk losing a coin toss.

That the three of them will be close by does give me some level of comfort and shows how seriously they're taking my protection. Still, I can't help saying, "I hope none of you snore," as I turn away, giving Lamis a wink, which makes her giggle. My only problem is, with the three men here I can't have a good look around and try to find that secret door. All I know is it must be somewhere in the royal suite.

Lamis makes a move to leave us, pausing only to ask, "You want to eat dinner here, or downstairs?"

"Downstairs will be fine." I cock my eyebrow in the direction of the men, daring them to criticise.

Rais nods. "That's a good idea. When we go down, I'll introduce you to some of the tribal leaders. Everyone's concerned about your safety, so they've come along themselves rather than just sending their men."

"Who?" I'm intrigued.

"Sheikh's Ghalib and Jibran. Sofian and Khalaf."

Ghalib I remember from my youth. He must be getting on in age now—he seemed old then. Yet perhaps not, anyone over the age of thirty appears ancient to a child. I make a snap decision. "Invite them to join us for dinner."

Rais gives his version of a smile, an expression I've noticed is rare for him. It seems to be one of approval.

Indicating the main bedroom, I let them know I intend to take a few minutes to myself. "I'm just going to go freshen up."

The sitting room was becoming claustrophobic with all the posturing and testosterone flying around in it. I'm relieved to close the door on the three intense men and have some feminine time to myself. I open the door to the bathroom—it's large with a shower that could probably hold three. A huge tub with jets, a sink, commode and bidet.

The bedroom itself is dominated by an enormous bed. I throw myself on it, bouncing as I land. Hmm. More than comfortable. If this is my temporary home, I've so far got no complaints. I roll over onto my stomach. Hang on, what's that? Scrambling to my knees, I crawl up the bed and inspect something I saw on the headboard. *Eyeholes which can only be for handcuffs.* Nijad, you bugger. I laugh out loud, then get off and start having a good look around. There are fixings all over the bed. *Now I know what my brother and Cara must get up to here when they're in their official residence.* I never suspected. Perhaps I should have known. Jasim did used to own a BDSM club, and Nijad is very alike. And of course, he put in a dungeon.

Is Kadar...? Yeah. Well, he told me as much. He's a Dom as well. So that makes four of us. There certainly are traits that run in the family.

There's a curtain over something to the side of the bed. Curious, I pull it aside. *A door.* Excitement bubbles inside me as I open it to find a worn stone staircase leading downward. *It must lead to the harem.* A quick thought for the men in the next room. *They won't miss me if I don't take long.* Then I'm carefully making my way down, eager to explore. Halfway down on the left is a short corridor, and I suspect I know where that leads to. That will probably be the lookout where the sultan would select his women for the night. Ignoring that for now, I continue on, coming to another door. This one is locked.

Taking the key from my pocket, I place it in the lock. *It fits.* I'm holding my breath as, with hands shaking with excitement, I push the door open. It's dark, I can see nothing. I fumble for a light switch and, *oh shit.* It's one of the best equipped dungeons I've ever seen. Certainly the best of the private ones, and while small, easily rivaling many clubs. A St Andrews cross, a couple of spanking benches, a bondage table. There's even rigging set up along one side. Some equipment I don't immediately recognise. Whips, crops and floggers adorn one wall, and just looking at them arouses me, imagining the sound of them meeting flesh. Walking over I take a paddle and weigh it in my hands, thoughts taking shape in my head, wishing I had someone to play with.

CHAPTER 22
Hunter

Fuck! That didn't turn out how I wanted. Trust Rais to jump in before I got a chance to explain she needed her close protection officer nearby. During the journey I'd formulated a strategy to win her, and that didn't fucking start with two others sharing her suite. Well, Rais can take the couch, and I hope it's uncomfortable. Though I won't be in much of a better position, sharing a bed with the prince.

It's a setback. Now I'll have to come up with another plan. Adapt and improvise—I'm used to doing that. As I deal with the disappointment that I'll not be the only one staying in the royal suite, I eye up my rivals, thinking I've surely got the drop on them. That kiss shared with Aiza yesterday? It had left me walking around with a semi-hard cock for the rest of the day. There's something about her that my body responds to, and I'm pretty sure hers reciprocated. If we'd been left alone together I was going to press my advantage, seeing just how many of my instructions she would obey. *Kiss me*, I'd told her, and *fuck me*, she did.

The memory gets my cock swelling again, and I turn and walk away, pretending to check out the second bedroom. The bed is large, and while I'm not relishing sleeping with another man, it's big enough so we can both keep to our sides. Perhaps I'll put pillows down the middle. Don't want him to roll over in the night and get handsy in his sleep. Uh uh. That we've decided to share the room will make it harder to relieve my cock. I suppose there's always the privacy of the shower.

The positive is I'll hear Rami if he decides to try his chances and enter her room. Yeah, and I'm going to keep that door open. Got to keep my eye on Rais as well.

Rami's also interested in checking out the accommodation and comes into the bedroom, his eyes landing on the bed. His sneer reveals he's about as keen to share as I am, as he grates out, "Don't know why we're all staying in here. She only needs one of us."

A slow shake of my head as I realise he's being obtuse. "Don't be a fool," I reply. "It's obvious. You think you've got a claim on her. It's clear Rais does too."

"Rais?" His forehead scrunches up, one eyebrow rising. "He's a desert sheikh. She wouldn't look twice at him."

Fucking privileged asshole. He's probably dismissed me as just the bodyguard

"And why the fuck not?" The comment's snarled out from behind us.

Rami has paled, as would I if I were in his shoes.

Swinging around, he tries to explain. "Rais, just look what I can offer her. We can live anywhere she wants. America, Britain. You're tied to the southern desert. You think she'd be satisfied with that?"

Rais steps closer, one hand on the hilt of the wicked looking scimitar in his belt. "I think that's up to her, not you." Rapidly, Rami nods as Rais turns his attention to me. "And Hunter here, he wants her too."

I shrug. I'll be saying nothing to contradict him. The prince looks at me, his mouth gaping. His wide-open eyes move to the sheikh, then back to me again. "All of us?" His voice sounds shrill.

A barked laugh escapes me. "The prince, the sheikh and the bodyguard. It sounds like the start of a joke."

"I'm not finding it amusing," Rais grumbles.

"I kissed her," Rami suddenly spits out, as if that gives him any advantage.

Rais growls and steps towards him. Feeling I ought to prevent bloodshed, I toss out, "I did too." I pull back my shoulders, ready to take the sheikh on, when instead he starts to chuckle.

"And me."

It's a ludicrous situation. Three grown men almost coming to a fight about one woman. Rais is poised, Rami's on his toes, and I'm squaring up. Then suddenly the tension breaks and we're all sniggering. Rais slaps Rami on the back, Rami shakes my hand, and for some ridiculous reason, it feels like a bond has started growing between us.

"So, which one of us does she like?" Rami ponders. "She did give me the signs she was seriously considering my proposal." His face falls. "I can't marry her if it's another she wants."

I shrug. "She's kissed all of us. Yesterday morning for me."

"And for me."

"And me."

A sudden fit of laughter has me doubled up while part of me wonders why I'm finding it amusing and not being consumed with jealousy. I put it down to the control I have as a Dom, possessing the confidence that it will be me she'll choose in the end.

Having laughed too, Rais is quicker getting himself under control, and looks over his shoulder. "Talking about Aiza, where the fuck is she? How long does it take a woman to freshen up?"

I could reply it might be hours, however under the circumstances we find ourselves in, I exercise caution. "I think we should knock and gee her up. She could have fallen asleep." As we exchange worried glances it appears we're on the same page. None of us had checked out the bedroom, assuming no one could have got inside. *Shit.*

Rais is first at her door. He knocks. Then knocks again harder. The door stays shut and there's no answer. He glances at me, and I nod. The knob twists, so at least she hasn't locked herself in.

The door opens to reveal an empty bedroom. Pushing past, Rami goes to the ensuite bathroom, where the door's ajar. Applying a little pressure it opens fully, revealing she's not in there.

Pulling my gun out of its holster, I start to inspect the empty room. Rais's scimitar has come out of its scabbard, and in the other hand he has a semi-automatic.

"Where the hell has she gone?" Rami asks anxiously, his eyes examining the empty room.

A cold feeling grips at my gut. We've not been here two hours and she's already been stolen. Fucking useless bodyguard I'm proving to be. Again.

Rais and I spring into action. Pulling open cupboards, looking under the bed—there's some bondage hooks there. However, we can't find *her*. *Where the fuck has she gone?* She couldn't have disappeared into thin air.

"Over here!" Rais has pulled back a curtain revealing a door and a secret passage.

Fuck! Why didn't I check this room out before I allowed her to come in here?

Rais is already moving, and I'm hot on his heels as he goes through the hidden doorway, pausing to hold my arm out to Rami. "You're unarmed," I explain quickly. "You stay here. Someone has to stay to raise the alarm if we don't come back."

He nods quickly, without question responding to my instruction.

Paying him no further attention, I follow Rais, going as fast as we can on the narrow and uneven stone staircase while trying to keep quiet. My heart's beating fast, terrified what we might find at the bottom.

There's a corridor off to one side, a quick inspection showing a boarded-up room. We make a quick decision to continue on downward, where the next twist in the stairs reveals light leaking out from a partially open door.

After an unnecessary gesture for me to be quiet, Rais carefully pushes it open. And…

For the second time this afternoon I'm laughing so hard my stomach hurts. Rais is stunned, his eyes wide as he notes his surroundings.

There, in the middle, is the woman we thought we'd lost. Standing, holding a paddle in her hands, testing its weight. *Fucking Princess Aiza.*

"What's up, I heard laughter…" Rami slams into my back as he tumbles down the last few steps. I hold him up, then turn my attention back to the object of my desires, my cock finding the whole situation very interesting.

Aiza looks like a rabbit caught in the headlights. "Oh shit."

Rais stalks towards her. "Oh shit?" It sounds like his voice has dropped a few octaves. "Did you come here to play, Princess, or are you just curious?"

"Oh, she likes to play alright. Don't you, Aiza?" I contribute. "Though you seem to be lacking someone to play with."

"Play?" Asks an all too eager voice behind me.

Rais completes a full circle as he turns to survey the room. "Hmm. The equipment here has possibilities."

"And she knows them all, Rais." To my knowledge, Rais has never been in a dungeon before. Will it turn him off to know this is the lifestyle Aiza enjoys? The one which I'm very familiar with.

"I expect she does." Damn. It doesn't seem to have fazed him.

"*She* is standing right here." Aiza all but stamps her foot as she starts to recover her composure.

Which I immediately shatter again as I close the gap between us. In this environment I naturally take charge. All other roles and responsibilities have gone out of the window. Here I'm a Dom, as Aiza is going to discover. Ignoring the other men, I rasp in a deep voice, "All this arouses you, doesn't it, pet? Don't deny it. I can smell you from here."

Violently she shakes her head.

"One," I tell her with an amused twist to my mouth.

"No," she refutes loudly, showing she knows what I'm implying.

"That's two. Just keep it up, Aiza."

She pushes against me, turns her face up and sneers. "I'm not your sub. I don't have a submissive bone in my body if you haven't noticed. You won't be laying a hand on me."

"But I might." Rais employs a lazy drawl. "She scared the fuck out of us, Hunter, by disappearing like that. How many for giving us such a fright?"

"At least five."

"Ten," Rami says. When we both turn to look at him, he shrugs. "I enjoy being spanked. That paddle she's holding, fuck, she's getting me hard."

Aiza starts. She seemed to have forgotten she was holding it, and now embarrassed, puts it down. Conveniently, in my view, on a spanking bench as her action draws my attention to it. She glares at me, then at Rais and Rami and says forcefully, "Look, no one's getting spanked, paddled, or doing any spanking or paddling. Time must be getting on now. I don't want to be rude being late if the desert sheikhs have been invited…"

"There's plenty of time." Rais advances, placing himself at her back. As though we'd planned it, together we take a step nearer. She tries to slip out of our human sandwich. I put my hand on her shoulder to stop her. Rais copies me, gripping the opposite one. She's squashed between us, and I'll be fucked if she's not flushing, and this time it's not with embarrassment, but barely concealed excitement.

If Rais is in the same state that I am, she'll have two hard cocks pressing against her. Over her head, I stare at the sheikh. He stares back, and a corner of his mouth turns up. *He's enjoying this.* Rais might not have experience of playing like I have, probably doesn't even know he's a natural Dom. A strange thought comes into my mind.

Perhaps we could share her? My cock grows harder at the thought. *Perhaps that's what she wants?* This is no virgin princess squashed between us.

"Fuck, that looks hot."

The voice pulls me out of my reverie. I'd forgotten Rami was here. His presence gives me more food for thought. Turning slightly so I can see him out of the corner of my eye, I beckon with my spare hand. "Come here." Then I follow my instincts, take a chance and test him. "Kneel."

Immediately the prince falls to his knees, and his face fills with pleasure.

Aiza starts to protest. She looks uncomfortable, and when she tries to look up into my face, she can't meet my eyes. Hmm.

"Look, Hunter. Whatever you're thinking, I want no part of it."

"You're turned on, Aiza," I drawl.

"I'm not." While the dilation of her pupils betrays the truth.

"Rami, why don't you check to see whether she's lying."

He doesn't immediately understand what I'm asking.

Rais does. "Is she wet, boy?" he thunders.

Aiza's eyes open wide, and her jaw drops. Her signs of protest are overtaken by the way her breathing speeds up and she flushes. I'm watching her carefully, every minutiae of her expression I'm analysing. Any sign that she really doesn't want this, I'll make everything stop.

Although her mouth might be gaping, no words to stop us come out, nor does she physically make any move to halt the prince who's almost panting with eagerness as he pushes her tunic up and pulls at her loose trousers so he can slide his hand inside. He must brush her clit, as she gasps and her pupils enlarge.

Nothing in her reaction makes me think there's a need to tell Rami to back off.

She's enjoying this.

Rami sounds happy as he announces, "She's very wet. She's dripping."

As he pulls his hand away I grab hold of his wrist roughly, pulling his fingers to my mouth, sucking off her delicious essence. Then Rais's hand snakes out and captures Rami's from me, his tongue cleaning off the remaining moisture I'd missed.

We are all stunned. No one planned this. No one orchestrated it. It just happened. And fuck it, it seems right. Aiza's the first to recover, looking at me, then down at Rami, and then tries to glance over her shoulder at Rais.

"We can't," she whispers. She sounds disappointed.

"Why the fuck not?" I question, while acknowledging it's a ludicrous situation and has taken us all by surprise. *We came together so naturally.* It's something I, for one, would like to explore. Being sensible, taking it further now might be a mistake, especially as Aiza looks panicked. Raising my hand to her face, I stroke her cheek while raising my chin to Rais. "I think we should talk about it before we do anything more. Give ourselves time to cool off." Speaking for myself, that might take quite a while. My cock's so hard it's nigh on painful.

"I, I..."

"I've not known you lost for words before, Aiza." Rais nuzzles her neck as he speaks. "Don't panic, don't overthink it. Don't run when we leave here. Don't deny that something's happening here. Something which to me feels fucking right."

"I don't know what you mean, what you're suggesting." She stiffens in our touch, and as one, both I and Rais drop our hands and she's free. She glances at Rami, then as fast looks away. "Look, let's go upstairs. Lock this place up. Throw away the fucking key. It's dangerous for us to be here."

I can't lose her. Can't have her scared and running. Softly I tell her, "Dangerous? I thought it felt quite safe to me."

"We're hidden away. Easy to defend even if anyone were to find us," Rais adds in support.

"That's not what I mean, and you know it." She steps to the side and away from us. Her hands flutter. "I think we need to forget this ever happened?"

"I don't want to forget," Rami says eagerly. "I want to explore it further."

"What's the matter?" I ask. "You've played in clubs before." A situation like this can't be alien to her. Then, in the past she's always been the Domme, never acknowledging her submissive side before. I'd take a bet that's what's spooked her.

Her back's to us now. "Only with strangers. Not with…"

As her voice trails off I realise what else she's worried about. "Not with men you're attracted to. You just enjoyed the control, with no emotional attachment."

Now she's moving, storming off. Turning back looking at the tableau in front of her—two dominant men standing, one sub still kneeling on the ground. She waves her hands dismissively. "I can't, alright? I just can't."

Idly I say as she flees the room, "Stand, sub," only vaguely aware that Rami's almost jumped to attention. I had no doubts he'd obey. "What do you think that's all about, Rais?"

"We overwhelmed her." He looks at me with a slight grin on his face. "I don't think any of us saw that coming. I think you're right." He nods at Rami. "Any of us could have regrets later. Let's have some space. Either we never talk about it again…"

"Or we take exploring further."

Rami's face, which had fallen as Rais finished speaking, now lights up again at my words. He puts out his hands and gently touches our arms. "I, for one, will have no regrets unless it causes awkwardness with Aiza. Neither will I refer to it in the future if she doesn't want me too."

"I can't forget," I tell them both. "She still deserves a spanking."

Rais grins. For him, widely.

CHAPTER 23
Aiza

By the time I reach the bedroom I'm shaking like a leaf. *What the hell just happened?* I'm no stranger to seeing a woman with multiple men, however, I never thought that would be me. The woman in the middle was always submissive, and I'm not. I can't lie though, when I felt Hunter and Rais's hard cocks pressing into my back and my front, their hands holding me firmly, I did nothing, just forced vague and vain protests come out of my mouth, then even abandoning that and simply allowed myself to feel.

What about Rami? Fuck. He was so compliant with the instructions Hunter had given to him. Then both other men cleaning my essence off his fingers... That was soooo hot. My cheeks flame as I rerun the scene in my head.

Hearing multiple heavy footsteps climbing the stone stairs, my hands clench at my sides. *They're too much.* My head's spinning, my body throbbing with need. Adrenaline coursing through my veins in confusion, not knowing whether I was to flee or fight. Or simply take what they're offering.

I can't. They'd overwhelm me. Shit. They already have.

I can't turn to face them, just listen as they talk.

"Yeah, Hunter. After the trouble with Abdul-Muhsi a year or so back, I'd trust any of the other sheikhs with my life and hers. You've got no worries on that score."

"Do we need more men? My father would probably send some."

"Can we park that idea for now, Rami? There's a balance between having enough to protect the princess and having so many we might scare al-Fahri off. Then this will never be over."

They're not discussing what just happened.

"Are you ready, Princess? The sheikhs will have arrived by now."

I start at the direct question. As my hands touch my cheeks I can feel them still glowing. "Give me five minutes?" I haven't yet had enough time to process what went occurred in the dungeon. I'm kidding if five minutes is going to be enough. Five years probably would be nearer the mark. The three men I fancy, all for different reasons, are offering me something I never could have dreamt about.

"You've got it." Rais says, almost indulgently, and then the three of them go past and out into the sitting room.

They've got themselves together. I must as well. I walk into the bathroom, still unable to deal with the events of the last half hour. Scared, intrigued and, damn it, excited when I consider what might happen later tonight when we all return to the suite. Splashing cold water on my face, I look into the mirror and give myself a pained smile. Three men have all made it clear that they each want me. I could handle that. What's out of my league is that they might want me together.

I don't understand why any of these fiercely independent men would even consider it. How could they work together? That's what they had done, worked as a team as though they'd been doing it all their lives. Hunter and Rami frequent clubs, so maybe it's not so unusual for them. But Rais? That was completely unexpected.

Brushing my hair, then scrunching it into a bun, I give myself a final inspection, deciding I'll pass, no longer looking like someone who's just been ravished. *By three men.* Slipping into my princess persona, pulling back my shoulders, I steel myself, then enter the living room.

It's as if nothing unusual had just taken place. Two minutes later I'm walking through the palace, Hunter and Rami at my side, and Rais bringing up the rear protecting my back. Glancing in turn at the men walking by my side, they're completely unaffected. It's as if nothing's happened at all. Can I do that? No, revealing a submissive side that I didn't even know I had has shocked me to my core. I can't forget, though I'll do my damn best to pretend that I have.

We enter the smaller intimate dining room where a table which can seat twenty is covered with gleaming plates, cutlery and glassware. Jugs of fruit juice have been placed in convenient spots. Remembering that this palace is dry, I wonder if Nijad has a secret alcohol stock which I can attack later. I need a drink, and I'm not ashamed to admit it. Yeah, a whisky or vodka or two might help settle the butterflies in my stomach.

As a wizened man comes over and bows, I try to force all thoughts of Hunter, Rais and Rami out of my head.

"Princess Aiza. It's been a long time since I've seen you. I don't know if you remember me? You must have been this high then." He holds his hand about a metre off the ground.

Inclining my head, I respond with a smile. "Sheikh Ghalib. Of course I remember you. It's good to see you again." He half turns and beckons three other men over. "I don't think you've met Sheikhs Jibran, Sofian and Khalaf."

I bow to each. "Welcome, sheikhs. And how are the Niyaha, the Alah and the Makka? And of course the Hagra, Sheikh Ghalib?" Politely I enquire about their tribes, glad I could recall the names.

As they offer polite answers, Rais touches me on the shoulder and guides me to a seat at the head of the table, then sits himself to my right, Hunter's on my left, and Rami next to him. It's only then I realise everyone's been waiting for me to take my place. It's slightly unnerving being seated in top spot, then I remind myself I've chaired enough meetings of the charity before. I can do this.

Food starts to arrive, it's appetising aroma overcoming my nerves and making my empty stomach growl. Luckily quietly enough no one else hears it. Remembering I'm a representative of the royal family, I don't want to do anything to disgrace myself.

I glance around the table. "Thank you all for coming and giving me your support."

Khalaf, a tall, intense looking man, seems to answer for all of them. "We've got a lot of money invested in the oil field, Your Highness. We want to get al-Fahri off our backs as much as you want him off yours. A chance to have a permanent solution will benefit us all."

"Your safety comes first, Your Highness. But it also suits our purposes." Jibran backs him up. "While al-Fahri's breathing we're all hyper-vigilant about protecting the pipeline. When he stops, we'll be able to be proactive, and not reactive all the time."

The others nod in agreement.

Sofian goes one step further. "The oil money will raise the standard of living for all our tribespeople. There was no shortage of volunteers determined to take al-Fahri out."

As I study them I realise that a man fighting to protect what is his is likely to give more than soldiers working for pay. For these sheikhs and their men, it's more than a job, it's a bone-deep need to ensure they can provide for their families. For the first time I feel confident we can beat al-Fahri. Whatever he throws at us.

"Princess. You've spent most of your life outside of Amahad. Even so, you're as much part of this country as any of us, and part of the royal family. We'll serve you as we would the emir or your brothers." Ghalib is intent with the vow that warms me inside.

I reach for some bread, break it, then look up. "Kadar has instigated some changes."

Jibran sits back, patting his mouth with a napkin, smirking as he looks at the other tribal leaders. "He has. Some more questionable than others. Women drive cars now."

Ghalib swears under his breath, and Sofian snorts and puts up his hand quickly to stop the mouthful of juice he's just taken spitting out over the table. He points to Khalaf. "Think you might have something to say about that."

"Fucking woman," Khalaf swears. "Clipped the wing of my Jeep crossing a junction."

"She was a learner." Rais tries to pacify him.

"Which proves my point, doesn't it? Men have a natural ability when it comes to machinery."

Casually I place my roll on the plate. "You're lucky yours was just clipped. My car was written off." I let a pregnant pause stretch out, then elaborate, "By a man."

Hunter guffaws, Rais changes the subject. "Kadar's penalty reforms have of course been put in place."

Shaking his head, Ghalib informs us, "Prisons are filling up. It was easier just to kill a man who had offended."

Despite the sheikhs sounding critical of the changes Kadar has brought, I do sense an underlying pride in his efforts to move Amahad into the twenty-first century. Well, perhaps bring it up to the twentieth century at least.

As if to prove it, a ping announces someone's received a text. Jibran grimaces apologetically and pulls out his iPhone and glances at the message. A beam crosses his face. "I apologise, Princess. My sister is in hospital having her first baby."

"Has she had it?" Sofian asks eagerly.

"Yes, a healthy girl."

As congratulations go around the table, it's another thing I hadn't expected. In my father's time women had babies and men weren't involved. The fact Jibran was worried about his sister, and that they're all celebrating the birth of a female child, is heartening. I start to relax.

The rest of the meal proceeds smoothly, then coffee is served and plates cleared. I notice Jibran, who's phone is now back into his pocket, looking at me thoughtfully. "And you, Princess. I hear you've been no slouch."

Not understanding, I put my head to one side.

"Your charity. I understand you helped a boy from Ezirad to get the help he needed. You managed to get him into the States and to the best doctors. Fuck knows how you did that. He's alive, and without your help he wouldn't have been."

It's surprises me he knows about that. My work isn't advertised. "That was a hard one," I agree. "Getting a Muslim into the US nowadays is nigh on impossible. I nearly gave up. Somehow we managed it. Now I understand he's back home and thriving."

Rais's hand lands on mine, and he squeezes it. Quickly I glance at the other sheikhs. They don't act as though they've witnessed anything inappropriate.

Realising we've avoided talking about plans, I ask, "So how's this going to play out?"

Nobody asks me to explain what I'm talking about. "Princess, you don't need to worry tonight. We've got the palace surrounded and extra guards inside. No intelligence reports that al-Fahri's on the move yet. We'll plan in more detail tomorrow."

I shoot Rais a look. "I'd appreciate being part of it."

It's Hunter who responds. "Aiza, I won't let you be left in the dark. If you don't know what's happening, where and who to run to if it comes to it, you'll be an easier target to snatch."

Rami's nodding. "I agree. Unless the intelligence people demand secrecy, you'll be included in all the discussions. He glances at the other sheikhs as he talks, and they don't seem to have a problem.

It's not just women getting behind the wheel of a car that's changed since I was last here then. I've had nothing but respect from these men tonight. *If I discount what happened in the harem earlier.*

Sensing the atmosphere changing in the room, I realise the meal, and the discussion afterwards, is wrapping up. If I tried to start up further conversation people would wonder what I was doing. *None of them will stand up and leave until I do.* I've enjoyed this evening more than I thought I would. No one has treated me anything other than an equal. Things like Jibran's delighted reaction to the birth of his sister's baby giving me much to think about.

Now I can tarry no longer. My mind starts to wonder what's going to happen when we get back to the suite. Glancing at the three handsome, very different men waiting for me to rise, my thighs clench as a familiar need starts to grow. My head tells me to run into my bedroom and lock the door. My body's got entirely different ideas.

I stand, and already my heart rate's sped up. *If I want any of them, I could have my choice. Maybe all three of these men would be mine.*

Taking my leave of the sheikhs, my escorts get into up position once again, and we retrace our steps back along the corridors and up the staircase to the royal suite. I bite my lip. There's something they don't know—and quite obviously don't expect—and maybe it's time I come clean and tell them.

With three large men surrounding me, their masculine odour overwhelms me. I feel myself becoming more and more aroused at the thought of what could possibly happen if I give them the word. I'm scared, and worried that my revelation is going to change the delicate dynamics. If I give in to them, what if I do something that breaks their newfound friendship up? What if that leads to their focus not being on catching the terrorist, and instead intent on fighting amongst themselves? Can I take that risk?

Why on earth am I contemplating giving in to them? If I hadn't played in clubs I'd be outraged at the memory of them all having their hands on me at once. It's not the way a normal woman would behave, or even think of or want. I can't do this, can't let their joint masculinity engulf me.

No, There's too much risk. I'm not here to enjoy myself, I'm here to try and divert a terrorist's attention away from the Palace of Amahad so the next generation of the Kassis family can stay safe. Whatever my need, my wants or wishes, I've got to keep thinking with my head. Which means I need to politely say goodnight, go to my bedroom and turn the key in the lock that I noticed earlier.

We reach the suite, Hunter opens the door. As I lift my foot to step inside, strong arms come around me and hold me back, and glancing behind I see it's Rais. Hunter steps in and looks around, then opens the doors and disappears into each bedroom. He's far longer in the master bedroom, and I realise he must be checking out the dungeon.

"All clear." He tells us when he comes back into sight. Rais puts his hand to the small of my back, his palm seems to burn me. Hunter's standing only a metre or so inside the door, blocking my way. As I near him he gives a smirk and holds out his hand as if to give me something. Automatically I reach out mine to take it. "I think you ought to keep this somewhere safe." I look down to see the key to the harem that no one remembered to lock earlier.

My face glows, comprehending the significance. *He's given the choice to me.* I straighten my back, the movement moving me away from Rais's touch. "I don't think I'll be using this again," I warn them, while my body's screaming, *Yes you will.* My head tells it to shut up and be sensible.

CHAPTER 24
Rami

I watch Aiza almost run as she disappears into her bedroom, and the turn of the key in the lock sounds loud in the quiet of the room.

Rais is looking at Hunter with a puzzled expression on his face. "You think she means it?"

Hunter smirks. "No. She likes to play too much."

I tap my fingers against my knees. "She's a Domme, Hunter. Not sure she's used to being told what to do."

"She's a challenge," he replies thoughtfully.

It's time I stood up for myself. So I do, literally as well as metaphorically, getting to my feet. "*And*," I begin forcefully, "she's mine." We were all swept away in the dungeon. Things happened that perhaps we shouldn't have done with me and my future wife. *Nevertheless, I was the only one touching her intimately.*

Rais lifts an eyebrow. "How do you work that one out?"

"I'm the one who asked Kadar for her hand in marriage. It's been the understanding between our two countries since she was born."

The desert sheikh's brow creases as he puts his arm over the back of the couch and crosses one leg over his knee.

"Actually, you're not. I've spoken to Kadar too." As shock spreads over my face he continues, "I've been wondering, Rami. Why you? Why not your oldest brother and heir to the throne? If there's to be a match between Amahad and Alair, surely that would be the best pairing?"

I draw myself up to my full height. "Do you not think I'm good enough for her, Sheikh Rais?"

Hunter scoffs a laugh. "It's not that, *Prince* Rami." He stands and comes over. As tall as me, we're looking eye to eye. "Do you really think it would be a match made in heaven? You said it yourself, she's a Domme. And you're quite clearly submissive."

Rais, still lazily relaxed, lets his dark eyes meet mine. "You're a prince, Rami. How's that going to work in the real world? Your princess ordering you around..."

I shrug. I can't see anything wrong in that at all.

Suddenly Rais is on his feet. He's taller than Hunter, and this time I do have to raise my head to meet his fierce gaze. "When you've got an army bearing down on you. When a terrorist attacks. What are you going to do then?"

I swallow. Alair's not suffered in the same way as Amahad. The king is not like Kadar's predecessor, ruling with a government, and not in autocratic ways, so there's been no unrest with the desert tribes. We've not been the target of a terrorist organisation, because we didn't have oil reserves before. Now that we do, it's a possibility that we, or I, might be tested in ways I've never previously been. Of course, I've had military training, but I've not been at the front line.

There's only one answer I can give him. "I'd protect her with my life."

Hunter's watching our interaction carefully. He goes to a drink cupboard and pours himself a glass of amber liquid. While alcohol isn't officially served in the palace, it doesn't surprise me that Nijad keeps the royal suite stocked. He waves the bottle at Rais, who dismisses it. I, in turn, nod.

After bringing my drink over, Hunter leans back against the ornate cabinet. "Aiza's not a creature of the desert, Rais. So what would *you* have to offer her, Sheikh?"

Now Rais seems even taller. "What do you know about her, Hunter? What would you know about her needs and desires? I've known her all her life."

Hunter shakes his head. "With all due respect, I think you know fuck all about her. Neither of you knew what she did for a living. All you knew was she was living a privileged life in Switzerland, when actually she was in England. Or travelling the world playing in different BDSM clubs."

Rais makes a gesture of dismissal. "She's sewn her wild oats. It's time for her to settle down. Grade A didn't know much better..."

"We weren't supposed to be looking after her then. She had no need of additional security in what was supposed to be a secure compound."

"I've not failed her. Nor will I. And any settling down there will be with me." I decide it's time to put my foot down and make my position clear.

Hunter looks thoughtful. "She responded to all three of us in the dungeon." He's right, she did. Playing for fun is one thing, and while I enjoyed submitting to Hunter and wouldn't turn down the opportunity to do it again, committing to Aiza for life is something entirely different.

"As she would to anyone if she was playing in a club," I reply indignantly. "That has no bearing on who takes her hand in marriage."

Rais swings around. "I don't know what the fuck happened in the dungeon." He rubs at his forehead. "I can't deny it seemed to all fall into place."

"What if she does want to play again?" Hunter seems set on the idea. "Think what the three of us could offer her." My mouth drops open at the suggestion, and the man from Grade A laughs and points his glass towards me. "I know she plays as a Domme, however, she responded to me as a Dom. And you play the part of the sub, so that part of her would be satisfied too."

Rais snorts. "Where am I in this scenario?" Both eyebrows now rise as he queries Hunter. I'm surprised he hasn't dismissed the idea out of hand.

"You're dominant too. You must know that."

One corner of Rais's mouth turns up. "Too dominant to share. On a permanent basis at least."

This is getting ridiculous. "She's mine. I've proposed to her." I realise I sound like a petulant child, and know I've got to tone it down. I'm a prince for fuck's sake. If I'm not careful I'm going to lose the woman I've been half, if not fully in love with, since I danced with her at Nijad's wedding.

Hunter's phone chimes just as mine pings with a text. Rais takes his out too. The American sets down his glass, Rais sweeps his robes behind him and moves to the door, and I follow behind. After addressing the guard outside, making sure one takes up station inside the suite, Rais leads the way down through winding corridors of the ancient palace, down the ornate stairs, and from there to a modern looking conference room.

General Zaram's already seated at the head of the table and looks up as we enter. He stands and looks like he's going to move until Rais lifts his hand, indicating he should stay where he is. We find empty seats at the table and sit down. Hunter nods at his colleague, Ryan, and I notice there's other military men seated around. Rais leans forwards and raises his chin towards the elderly sheikh, Ghalib.

Once we're settled, Zaram begins. "I apologise for disturbing your evening, but this information can't wait. Amir al-Fahri knows where Princess Aiza is. In one way we've been successful. It's at least turned his attention away from the Palace of Amahad."

"He knows she's in the Desert Palace?" Hunter asks for confirmation.

"Kadar received another communication. This one said there was nowhere Aiza could hide where she'll be safe. Al-Fahri indicated he's happy playing this game, and emphasised he's playing to win. That Kadar would be brought low, knowing there was nothing he could do to protect his sister, and despite his efforts, she would be taken." The general breaks off, wiping a hand over his face.

"He wants to kill her?" Hunter asks in his drawl. I notice the American side of him comes out more under stress.

The general shakes his head. "No. He made that quite clear. He intends to take her so Kadar knows she's alive and suffering. Until all progress on the pipeline is stopped and, presumably, until he's exacted all the revenge he needs for his son."

Ghalib sits forwards. "Don't like to see women brought into our wars, but we depend too much on the oil. Can't give in to al-Fahri's threats."

Isn't she worth more than a few barrels of oil?

"We've got to stop him. Once and for all," Rais interjects. He glances around the table, sparing a moment for each of the key players. "I'll remind you, this is what we planned. Al-Fahri has got her so far in his sights, he might get careless. We watch, listen, and plan. It's our best opportunity to take him out. Get rid of this threat once and for all."

A man I don't know in a suit raises his head from the tablet he's been watching. "There's troops gathering just beyond the border into Ezirad. It could be his men."

"He's going to take the palace by force?" I ask while cursing the sultan of Ezirad for being so weak and having no control over the borderland on his side.

"We can't rule it out," General Zaram replies.

"I'll get my men, and those of Jibran, Sofian and Khalaf to meet them on this side if they're going to cross." The elderly sheikh bangs his fists on the table to punctuate his point.

"Hold on a moment, Ghalib. We're only going to get one chance at this. They've got to be stopped. Any weakness on our part and our forces could be decimated. If that happens, not only will that leave Princess Aiza unprotected, but the infidel will be able to invade our southern desert. Worse, make their base in Zạlmā." Rais stares him down, then turns to the man in the suit. "Your intelligence is from satellite, I presume?"

He gets a stare back, though the man, presumably from MI6, isn't going to reveal his sources.

Rais raises his chin towards Zaram. "First, we need to know the size of the force, their armament, and where they're heading."

"I agree." General Zaram turns his attention to Ghalib. "Let's get down to figures. How many men…"

"Stop." I stand up, then lean over with my palms flat on the table. When everyone's eyes come to me I continue. "You're reacting exactly the way they expect us to react." I wave my arm around the table. "You're all military men. You see the enemy and want to face it head on."

Zaram's not happy that I, not even a citizen of Amahad, have interrupted him. "Prince Rami, you forget," he starts, "Amahad has been fighting border wars for decades, if not centuries. We are well versed in stopping our foes crossing into the southern desert."

"And that's the point." I stare him down. "Your focus is preventing people coming in." I wouldn't deny it's not without good reason. Jihadists have been trying to infiltrate Amahad for years, unhappy that the northern half is multi-cultural. Alair, on the other hand, is far more traditional, and not such a target for those wanting to start a religious war. "You might be right, Zaram. On the other hand, you could be wrong."

"It is never wrong to stop an army invading." Ghalib's stern gaze makes me feel like a small boy. Nonetheless, I hold my ground.

"What's the result if you move the troops and make a show of force at the border?"

Rais sucks in air. "We leave the palace security weakened."

Hunter's looking at me with something akin to respect. "You're suggesting it could be a decoy."

I nod and take my phone out of my pocket. "There's one way to find out without moving our troops." Though it's late at night, I place a call, and being who I am, am quickly connected.

"Sultan Qudamah. Greetings." I put it on speaker phone.

"Prince Rami. To what do I owe this pleasure." Qudamah speaks a slightly different dialect, so we both talk slowly to make sure we understand each other. Perhaps placing the call at this table was indiscreet. All eyes stare at the phone as though looking at the man himself.

"I've received some worrying information, and I seek to have your opinion on the matter."

Qudamah can be heard clearing his throat. "Go ahead."

"I've heard there's an army gathering on your northern border. As you are aware, Alair and Amahad have a peace treaty with Ezirad."

The sultan's quick to read between the lines. "If there is such a force, it is nothing to do with us. We stand only to gain from continued peace between us."

"Your confirmation is welcome, Your Excellency. Nevertheless, it appears there is an army getting prepared. Our Amahadian allies can see no alternative other than to ready themselves for invasion. If Eziradians are involved, retaliation."

"I reiterate, Prince, war with Amahad is the last thing on our minds." The tone suggests I've caught Qudamah wrong-footed, and now have him worried.

"That's good to know. As a war with Amahad would also be a war with Alair." My stress on the word *war* is entirely intentional.

Qudamah sighs audibly. "What do you want, Prince?"

Now I know I've got him where I want him. I never believed it was Eziradian troops, just wanted to put the fear of Allah into him. "I want to confirm the size of the force that has gathered. And the nature of their equipment."

"It may be our own soldiers performing manoeuvres in the desert. We do undertake such exercises."

"You can easily find that out."

"I can."

Rais looks like he's going to speak. I wave him down, wanting Qudamah to believe he's only dealing with Alair. "Have there been any heavy troop movements through your country? Tanks? Artillery?"

"That I can also discover. If the infidels are gathering, you can assure your father that my military will make a joint attack with the Amahadian Army. The protection of the oil fields and pipeline is of paramount importance to all our countries."

I thank him, ask him to get back to me without delay, and then end the call.

There's silence around the table. Zaram's regarding me with wide open eyes.

"That's helpful, Rami." Rais sounds impressed. "You seem on good terms with Qudamah."

I shrug. "We need to know what we're dealing with. Qudamah's not got a good hold on his country, we all know that. His own position is fragile. If the oil fields bring the dividends we expect, he's strengthened and less likely to face a coup. It helps to remind him that he needs to keep both of our countries onside."

As I retake my seat, Zaram's looking at me respectfully. "You don't believe there's a force gathering for invasion?"

"I think we need to be sure," I reply. "I'd prefer all the resources we have concentrate their attention on protecting the palace. Leave us weak and exposed, we could lay ourselves open to another form of attack."

Hunter indicates he's got something to say. "Amir al-Fahri hasn't been caught because he's clever. He's performed acts of atrocity because he plans well. *If* Rami is right, and the information is meant to divert our Army, or at least part of it, away from the palace, then where we are right now is where we should stay."

Ghalib is looking thoughtful. "I agree with Hunter. There's a chance we might already be under attack. From within."

Zaram leans forwards. "What do you mean?"

Sparing him a quick glance, he looks at Rais. "Remember what happened to the Emira? How she was taken when the palace guards were replaced by Abdul Muhsi's men?"

"I could never forget." As Rais's face darkens, I recall the story. Of course, Zoe wasn't Kadar's wife at that point, and her kidnap was arranged by her ex-partner. How it was orchestrated is something we would do well to bear in mind. "The palace security has been tightened up. Each guard carries a photo pass now," Rais continues. "Even so,

I suggest we do a one-off sweep to check them carefully, then check them in and out when they come on or go off shift."

"The household staff too, as well as the guards." Hunter's nodding in agreement. "We should trust no one at this point."

CHAPTER 25
Aiza

I didn't sleep well, hovering between remembering the arousing sensation of having three men around me alternating with something akin to disgust that I allowed myself to enjoy it. The idea in itself doesn't concern me — that I was the one in the middle does. If I had submissive tendencies I would have been out of this world with delight having all their attention on me. Unfortunately, I haven't. That I got any enjoyment from a situation where I had absolutely no control is what unnerves me. I acted out of character, allowing two men to dominate me. It can't happen again.

Embarrassed to face them, I delay as long as I can before getting out of bed. After showering and dressing, mentally gearing myself up, I gingerly step into the living room only to find after all that fretting I'm alone in the suite except for a guard standing by the door. My first reaction is one of relief, followed quickly by curiosity as to where Hunter, Rais and Rami could be.

"Good morning, Princess." The guard smiles reassuringly. As recognition dawns I give him a broad smile.

"Good morning, Zaki. It's good to see you're still here." I'm surprised to see him, having thought he'd been promoted years ago and would no longer be a lowly palace guard.

"Princess," he acknowledges. "Sheikh Rais asked for volunteers of faces you'd recognise so you could be assured at all times of your safety. I head up the palace guard now at the Palace of Amahad. Nonetheless, I answered his call along with Safwan and Dharr. You'll always have someone you recognise and remember on each shift. Each of us will have three additional guards assigned to protect you, The rest of my team are standing outside the suite now. You have no need to worry, all of us have sworn to protect you."

Belatedly I notice the extra flashes of rank on his shoulder. Seeing him, though now greyer and older, takes me back to when I was a child. Zaki, Safwan and Dharr had been merely corporals in the palace guard then. Whenever I left the palace with my nanny they'd tag along. Young soldiers at that time, and while they weren't the only guards I went out with, those three were the ones who made it most fun, taking some time to play with a little girl. He's changed, he's filled out, his muscular build stretching at his tunic, and from the medals he wears, he's not been idle over the intervening years. I get a warm feeling inside. None of the royal family can forget what happened to Zoe and how she was taken from the desert palace because all the guards and household staff had been replaced by

Abdul-Muhsi's men. That Rais had thought to make sure I recognised the guards is reassuring.

When Zaki opens the door to introduce me to his team, a guard I don't know turns away and speaks quietly into his radio. When he turns back he lifts his chin towards me. "I've ordered you a late breakfast, Your Highness."

Thanking him, I'm introduced to the others, then I return to the suite, feeling more relaxed than I have done for a long time. I'm a strong woman, yet having been so recently kidnapped, the worry of being abducted again constantly plays on my mind, however much I try to put it behind me. It's encouraging to see my protection is being taken so seriously.

I'm just finishing off a plate of delicious pastries, and on my second cup of coffee when Rami enters. My eyes flit behind him, but he seems to be alone. After giving him a nod of greeting, I raise my coffee cup to my lips, wondering if he intends to refer to yesterday evening. If he does, out of the three, I'm glad it's him I need to tackle first. Swallowing a mouthful of the thick, bitter-sweet liquid, I try to summon my inner Domme.

"Princess…"

I turn to face him and raise an eyebrow, seeing nothing other than a guileless smile on his face. "Prince?" When he doesn't elaborate, I take the initiative. "Where are Hunter and Rais?"

"Hunter's speaking to the intelligence people. Rais is talking with General Zaram. I think they'll be tied up most of the day."

Placing my cup back on the saucer, my eyes narrow. "Has anything happened, Rami? Anything I should know about?"

He comes closer, sweeping his robes around his as he sits on the couch opposite. "We're just taking precautions. Tightening up security around the palace."

"It seems an awful lot of people are tied up with trying to keep me safe."

He gives a quick shake of his head. "It's not just about you, Aiza. Though you know your safety is paramount. It's to prevent the insult to Kadar and your country. And to try and capture Amir al-Fahri once and for all." He breaks off and nicks one of the pastries I hadn't eaten. "There are some CIA officers flying in today. Everyone wants a chance to take him down. We just have to formulate a plan that will work."

"Nothing's worked yet. Amir al-Fahri has always slipped through everyone's hands." I stand and take my coffee cup and plate over to the sideboard where breakfast had been set out. "I don't understand what's so important about me that gets an international terrorist so hot under the collar. I understand he wants to get revenge on Kadar. Surely there are other ways?"

"I wish I could say that it's you, however it's not. You're incidental, a tool al-Fahri can use. Yes, it helps that he can combine payback for his son's death while taking us on." He pauses and brushes some stray crumbs off his beard. "In the end it all comes down to one thing. Oil. If al-Fahri could, he'd destroy all oil exports to the West. He thinks that would bring them to their knees. In that respect, you're simply a tool, a way to get Kadar to cease production." Rami gets to his feet. "Come. Enough of this. Take a walk with me in the palace gardens. You should get some fresh air rather than staying cooped up."

Here I'm safer... That's stupid. Who would be able to get me here in the palace? Amahad couldn't have more people with one single focus, keeping me out of harm's way. Suddenly the idea of seeing something other than these four walls sounds attractive. When I nod and move to the door, Rami puts his hand in the small of my back.

Outside in the corridor, Zaki and the other guards leave their post and fall in behind us. One, who seems to be the communicator, lets someone know what we're doing. Although it's all designed to save me from danger, inside part of me rebels, longing for the independence and freedom I had in London. *Will I ever be able to go back? Or is this my new normal now?*

We walk through the palace, along beautiful hallways and down the magnificent staircase, then through the back to the atrium. Looking through the glass doors I see guards lining the walls, each vigilant and alert. Then we're out into the heat of the day, and I feel the burn of the sun almost immediately, and am, for once, grateful for the headscarf I'm wearing.

Rami seems totally unaffected by the rays blazing down, however notices my discomfort immediately. Leading me around the palace, we enter into what I remember used to be the harem gardens. I can't help glancing at the newly filled gap in the wall where the rogue sheikh Abdul-Muhsi had blown a hole in the wall, enabling Zoe to be kidnapped. Though the stonemasons have tried hard, they haven't been entirely successful in making the new bricks match the old, leaving it standing like a memorial to what happened that day. Though hot, I shiver at the reminder of the lengths some people will go to. Today I see fully-armed guards lining the walls, preventing anyone's approach.

"Here. It will be cooler in there." Rami points me to the interior of the old harem.

The harem at the Palace of Amahad had been renovated at the suggestion of Cara, it holding a special place in her and Nijad's hearts. In fact, that was why Zoe had come to Amahad in the first place, as she'd been an architect and landscape gardener. It's now used, and successfully, as a venue for hen parties. I'd cracked up when I first found that out, wondering how they'd ever persuaded my austere brother to embark on such a venture.

The harem at the Desert Palace isn't in such need of repair, and instead remains, though unfurnished, just as it's been throughout the centuries. Apart from one major exception. It's now been cut in half. One half, only able to be entered from the royal suite, has been converted into a dungeon at Nijad's request.

The part Rami's leading me into is the part left unaltered. Glad to be out of the direct sunlight, I walk to the edge of what used to be a bathing pool and sit on the stonework surrounding it. A beautiful mosaic is still there at the bottom, though it no longer holds water. I stare down at the scene, amused to see Cupid armed with his arrows.

Rami's eyes follow my gaze, and he grins. "I wonder how many arrows hit their targets."

"I suppose it depends who was the ruling sultan at the time." Until my great-grandfather's day, Amahad was two countries, the southern desert having its own ruler, until economics forced it to unite with the more prosperous north. "If he was kind and handsome, quite a few." My eyes look around the harem. "I doubt many were like that." Sensing Rami is looking at me, I turn. "What?"

"You're a romantic at heart, aren't you?"

"No." I shudder. "I can't think of anything worse than being forced to submit to a man you haven't chosen."

He huffs a laugh. "You wouldn't submit to any man at all. Any sultan would have hell on his hands with you."

I mock punch his arm. "Thanks a lot."

"You're welcome." The mirth slips from his face, and now his dark eyes become intense and lustful. He places a hand under my chin and gently raises my face. His intention is clear as he leans in towards me.

"Rami." I place my fingers over his mouth.

His free hand pulls mine away. "Hush. Just give me this. You're a beautiful woman, in beautiful surroundings."

I shouldn't encourage him, but he's so darn handsome himself it's hard not to want to see if he can deliver. Shooting a glance outside to check the guards focus is on what's going on outside, not inside the harem, I don't move towards him. He doesn't need me to, completing the journey himself. Soon our lips are touching.

Of their own volition, my hands go to rest on his shoulders. He doesn't force the kiss, lets me set the pace, and it's me who's anxious to taste him. I press my tongue against the seam of his lips and slip inside as he opens. He's fresh, clean. His taste is from breakfast, a slight lingering bittersweet flavour. He's sampling me too, my open eyes see his nostrils flaring.

Our mouths move against each other, our lips pressing together. Tongues sliding as though in a slow dance. It's nice, but... My eyes flick to the wall separating what remains of the original harem and the dungeon, and my thoughts go to what I could do with him were we the other side of the brickwork.

He'd let me do whatever I wished. He'd place himself under my control, trusting me to make him feel good, which means I'd get satisfaction too. He's a prince, with a heavy load to carry representing his country, and just for a while I could make him forget his responsibilities. The thought of having him at my mercy has my arousal growing.

As I'm lost in my thoughts, he starts to pull away, breaking the contact, replacing it with another as he rests his forehead against mine. "Marry me."

I breathe in deeply. Before I can reply, it's now Rami's turn to place his fingertips to my lips.

"Hunter and Rais both want you."

My forehead creases. Hunter, yes. I'd have to be blind not to have noticed he'd been attracted to me that night in London, and if I'd have succumbed, would have wanted to play with me at Club Tiacapan. If I'm honest about last night, it showed he's the wrong man for me. He's a Dom. We'd clash, that's the problem, pure and simple. There's no denying his good looking boyish charm would be attractive to any woman unless she was no longer breathing. His physique leaves nothing to complain about either. It's his personality that puts me off. He wouldn't be dominant only in the dungeon.

Now Rais? Though I can't deny, in last night's moment of weakness when I let them surround me he'd had a very obvious physical reaction to me. Nevertheless, the thought that the rough-looking, desert-living sheikh would dream of me as a pairing is laughable, even though there's a part of me that wishes it could be different.

"I admit, I want you to commit to me, before they start making moves on you."

Again, I sigh. "Rami, I'm sorry if I've misled you. With everything going on, I'm not sure I want to get married at all. Or not just yet. There's too much I want to do with my life."

His hand holds mine. "I don't mind a long engagement. I'll follow you anywhere, Aiza. I'd never stop you doing what you want to do." He stops, and then surprises me. "Even if you wanted to experiment with Hunter and Rais. As long as it's me you're promised to." He looks at me earnestly and repeats, "Whatever you want, Aiza. You can have it."

That's the problem. Perversely, while I don't want a man who'll always tell me what to do, I don't want anyone simply hanging onto my coattails. I don't want a doormat. I cast a sideways glance and realise I'm doing Rami a disservice. I'm thinking of him as weak when he's anything but. As a diplomat and representative of his country, he's a natural born leader. However, from what I saw last night in the dungeon, in the bedroom he needs someone to take charge.

So why am I even hesitating? Isn't he my perfect match?

The problem being, the kiss we shared was pleasant enough, satisfying, and undeniably arousing, but it did nothing to make my blood really race.

"Our marriage was destined from the time of our births, Aiza. So why fight it?" He raises his hand to my face and gives a wry smile. "Or is that the problem? If we'd met as two strangers, would things be different? Do you feel pressured?"

I don't answer, knowing that could be part of the problem and what's holding me back. The thought of my father controlling my actions even while he's cold in his grave.

Rami sighs, and his hand drops away. "Maybe we shouldn't rush this. Once al-Fahri is caught we could start over. Date, get to know each other better. It's hardly the best of circumstances right now."

The situation is what it is. Which makes it difficult to think of doing normal things like dating again.

Will I ever be free of this cloud hanging over me?

CHAPTER 26
Hunter

W here the fuck is she?" Pushing back the lock of hair that's fallen over my forehead, I look around the empty suite in disgust. It would be easier to protect Aiza if she stayed where she was meant to be.

Rais enters the living room. "She's walking in the gardens with Rami. Safwan, the head guard just told me."

"She should be here. Not wandering around. Especially not until we've done a complete check of all the personnel in the palace."

"Add in a security sweep for bugs." Rais sends me a sharp look.

"We checked before we brought the princess here."

"Well fucking check it again." Storming over to me, Rais adds, "If someone has infiltrated the household, it would be easy enough to plant more."

Chagrined, I have to agree. My face is tight as I tell him, "We'll do daily sweeps."

Rais disappears into the second bedroom. When he comes back out he's disrobed and is now in jeans and a tee. He'd look like a man you'd be happy to go to the pub with—if you didn't mind all the other customers leaving.

He tops me by about five centimetres, and I'm not short by any degree. His hair hangs to his shoulders, and I won't be requesting the name of his hairdresser anytime soon. He has a short beard which he attempts to keep trimmed, a straight nose in an aquiline face, a scar through one eyebrow, and piercing dark eyes which seem to see right down into your soul. His air is that of one much older than his thirty-four years, making the four years between us seem like a much larger gap.

Technically he's got little power. The military are in charge of this operation, acting under Kadar, and Grade A have also been employed directly via the emir. Rais has grown into his unofficial title of the Desert Sheikh, ruling over the other tribal leaders. He's a natural born leader, and a force to be reckoned with.

The other night, in the harem, for the first time since I did my Master training, I'd felt myself being topped.

Which is crazy. Rais isn't a Dom in the way that I am.

"I'm still not happy Aiza's not in the suite." I go back to the original subject, a little peevishly.

Rais throws himself down on a couch. "I understand, Hunter. Though we can't keep her cooped up all the time." He frowns. "Could Rami be trying to get the jump on us?"

"I fucking hope not. The prince couldn't handle her." Aiza wouldn't accept if he proposed again, would she? *She might, if she's still spooked after last night.*

299

"He handled the meeting well enough. Got us to put the brakes on what could have been a knee-jerk reaction. The more I think of it, the more I believe he was right." Rais taps his chin thoughtfully. "I was impressed with him."

"He's a good diplomat, certainly." I'm man enough to concede Rami's worth.

"I don't like an enemy I can't see. Same as any fighting man." Rais shrugs. "Tell me there's a buildup of troops and I want to be there, forcing them back. I wasn't thinking. Rami stood up and told me I was wrong to my face. Don't underestimate him, Hunter."

I go and sit on the couch opposite. "I like the man, Rais. That doesn't mean he's right for Aiza."

I'm fixed with a steely stare from those black eyes that don't allow me to know what he's thinking.

His silence encourages me to keep talking. "I mean, it should totally be up to Aiza, shouldn't it? I worry she's getting pressure from Kadar to do the right thing." Pinching the bridge of my nose, I feel I'm on the right track. What other reason could there be for Aiza even considering him?

"The right thing being?" Rais tilts his head.

"To marry Rami to form a liaison between Amahad and Alair. If he's playing on that, putting pressure on her…"

Rais stands and walks to the drink cabinet. As he pulls out a bottle and two glasses, I nod my head. "Kadar has assured me she can make her own choice. Rami thinks he's in love with her. He's always been attracted to her."

"He doesn't know her."

As Rais returns with a glass for me, he sits back on the couch. "That's the one thing you've said that's correct." At least we agree on something. As I start to relax, Rais continues, "You don't understand her either."

I splutter and choke as the malt goes down the wrong way, then when my fit of coughing has finished, sit forwards and put my drink back down on the coffee table. "I think I understand her more than you do, Rais. That night in the dungeon, I knew exactly what she needed…"

"I allowed you to take charge."

Allowed me?

"Now stop right there, Rais. The dungeon was probably a new experience for you. For Aiza it was like coming home. I'm a Dom…"

He slashes his hand through the air angrily. "You think I don't know how you label yourself? Fuck, man, I've been friends with Nijad for years. I watched Nijad develop into the man that he is. We were close as children, even closer as men. We talk about everything. I know what he does, I know what the dungeon's for. Just because I don't give myself a fancy title or use specialist equipment, don't dismiss me as not knowing what I'm talking about."

As he speaks he seems to grow in front of my eyes, authority radiating off him. He's not threatening me, just letting me know I was wrong to challenge him. I find myself unable to continue looking at him, and standing, move to the windows.

Looking down I see Rami and Aiza. It looks like they're on their way back. They're not holding hands, or even walking particularly close. From here their body language suggests that if Rami had been taking his chance to press his suit, he's probably been unsuccessful. A weight lifts off my mind.

As they disappear around a corner I continue looking out, not seeing the beautiful blooms that are kept flowering for the people of Zalmā as well as residents of the palace to enjoy. Instead, I'm thinking, realising I've been putting people into boxes. Being arrogant to think that I know more about them than they do themselves. I *know* I'm a Dominant. I can't be any other way. It's reflected in my choice of career—a protector—and the way I like to control my women in bed. Why hadn't I seen Rais is similar? He protects a whole desert and its people. In the dungeon… While I might have got Rami and Aiza to give me their submission, I certainly had none of his.

"Tell me why you want her, Hunter." Rais' deep voice leaves me no choice.

"She's beautiful inside and out. She's got a fire inside her."

As I pause, trying to string my thoughts together, Rais interrupts. "And you want to put that fire out? Control her? Make her submit to you? Would that make you feel like a man?"

"That's not what I want to do…"

I feel a presence behind me and know Rais has left the couch and moved close. "Are you going to give her a nice house? A family? *Love* her, worship her? Make her feel like the most cherished woman in the world? Help her succeed in whatever she wants to do?"

"I'd give my life for her."

"Of course you would. I have no doubt about that." As I glance over my shoulder, he's smiling wryly. "It's the unwritten part of your job description." Now he's by my side. "Would you nurture her, allow her to grow, give her what she desires?"

"Yes. Obviously. As a Dom that's part of my job."

"Would you give up your career for her, or leave her alone for long periods of time?"

I decide to challenge him. I've had enough of him putting me on the spot. "You want her too," I accuse.

I'm answered first by a gruff laugh, then, "Why do you think I've never married again, Hunter?"

I have no idea... *Oh fuck.* The answer slams into me like a freight train. I pause, knowing once I've acknowledged it I'm going to have to deal with it and find some way to move on. "Because you were waiting for her to grow up."

He doesn't confirm or deny it. Just stands beside me, looking out into the gardens below.

I try to lighten the situation. "We could duel for her. Swords at daybreak. Winner fights Rami..."

"You wouldn't have a chance, Hunter." He's not bragging, just matter of fact.

While I keep myself fit, I have to be on top of my game to provide bodyguard services, there's no doubt that he's speaking the truth. His prowess at unarmed combat is renowned.

Rami's challenge doesn't bother me. However, Rais is a force to be reckoned with. I'm not offering, just finding out where I stand when I ask, "You want me to step aside?"

Rais turns to face me, a wealth of seriousness in his eyes. "I want you to think about why you want her. And what for. Whether you can give her the kind of life she deserves. Or whether you just want to break her, bring to the fore her submissive side and know that you've won. That's how I read you, Hunter. I can't see how you could make her happy that way."

"At least I don't live in Amahad. She won't need to pretend to be a princess anymore."

He sighs. "She *is* a princess. Whether she's here acting like royalty or living in a slum going to work on the tube every day, she deserves to be treated like one." Again he looks me in the eye and says something perceptive. "She needs to be the important one in the relationship. She needs support to do what she wants to do. She's special, she deserves the world being given to her. She's been trying to take that in her play in the clubs, not understanding it would be given to her freely."

He's right. I suddenly realise it. Aiza's been trying to wrest that control from the men that she plays with, without comprehending she doesn't need to lift a finger to receive it. His grasp of the situation makes me acknowledge there's a possibility all I feel for her is only a fleeting passion, and question whether I can be the man that she needs.

While I may be able to draw out Aiza's submissive tendencies, never letting her have the control that she craves in the same way she needs air to breathe would break her. Would I be able to conquer my inner Dom and be the man that she requires? I frown, wishing we hadn't started this conversation, it's provoked too much self-examination. Deep down, I know that he's right.

Tamping down my competitive spirit, I look him in the eye. "If you believe you can be all that for her, I won't stand in your way."

Then he says something completely out of left field. "Perhaps I wouldn't be able to be everything for her, Hunter."

I stare for a moment, uncomprehending, finding myself hoping, not wanting to jump to the wrong interpretation. I test out the waters. "You'd consider sharing?"

I watch his Adam's apple bob as he swallows, and a pained expression comes over his eyes. "It's not what I want, Hunter. What makes *her* happy is what we should be considering here."

If she became mine, would I allow another to touch her? I turn away and walk back across the room. Sharing a woman isn't something I haven't done many times before. Fuck, I've played with Ryan and Seth often enough when it's been for pure fun, no emotion involved. *Has Aiza even been between two men before?* The thought that she might have has my cock thickening.

"Rami might satisfy her other desires." Rais has turned to face me, the smirk on his face showing he's noticed the erection I'm unsuccessfully hiding.

"Her other desires?"

"When she feels the need to be in control."

He's suggesting a foursome? Could that work? Rais has put forward some strong arguments. Perhaps together we can be the relationship that's right for her. It's something to think about seriously, and decide how much I want her, and whether I still want to be part of this fight. This proposal means I'd still be close to her. It has merit, I finally decide. Before I can formulate an answer the door opens, and the man we've been discussing walks in.

"Where's Aiza?" I snarl, even before the door has closed.

Rami stops abruptly, his welcoming smile slipping from his lips. Under my scrutiny he looks uneasy. His eyes go to the floor as he explains, his words tumbling out one after the other. "Lamis waylaid her. She's gone to discuss the clothes that she needs, she didn't bring many here. Zaki, the head guard, is with them along with his men."

"Lamis has been part of the royal household for many years." Rais notices my concern and tries to put me at ease. "Her absence gives us space to talk to Rami."

It does indeed. As Rami raises his eyebrows, I wonder if this is happening too fast. It's one thing to play in the dungeon, and my thoughts after last night were that would be fun. As for the future, I was determined to make my play for Aiza, believing I could be the one to satisfy her. Now I've ended up seriously thinking about sharing her, and not just a temporary arrangement, but something permanent. Letting not just her, but the enigmatic sheikh into my life. And to add in a submissive? My brain might have trouble getting on board with the idea, but my lengthening cock seems to approve.

Rais's head's cocked towards me. I take a split second to decide. Fighting for her is out of the question, and we all seem to have parts of us that together make a good sum total. Taking a deep breath, I leap into the unknown.

Once we've brought Rami up to speed, it's surprisingly easy to get him on board. There's a visible stress being lifted off him. Rais is right. In his element he's got the strength to match any of us. With a woman, he's out of his depth. There's joy in his face at the thought of being the bottom in any sexual relationship, and while his robes hide his reaction, I'd be surprised if he hadn't got hard during our discussion.

"So, let's get this straight. What we're talking about is a polyandric relationship." Rami's voice can't disguise his excitement.

Rais nods. "She'll only be able to marry one man. We will, of course, have to exercise discretion." For a woman to take multiple husbands would not be looked upon kindly in either of the countries. Even Westerners would have some difficulty accepting it.

"Keeping it quiet won't be hard." I add my thoughts. "We've all got a reason to stay close to her. Even when this is over, Kadar will insist she has better protection."

"Kadar won't be a problem," Rais contributes. "He's open minded"

"Jasim used to own a kink club." I smirk. No, I don't think there'd be a problem with her family.

"Of course, I'll be the one to marry her," Rami states confidently, his face full of charm.

Rais again seems to grow another few centimetres as he contradicts. "No. I will."

Rami opens his mouth to argue, then snaps it shut. His eyes fall to the floor, unable to challenge the dominant sheikh. I watch their interaction with interest.

"We've got time to decide, and she might have a preference. It would be hard enough putting any of us forward, let alone three." I frown, wondering how this is going to go.

"I will marry her," Rais insists again.

"Why?" Rami gets up the nerve to ask.

Rais gives him the full force of his intense stare. "Because you would take her to Alair. Hunter would take her to London. With me, she'll stay in Amahad."

I scoff. "Good luck with that, Sheikh. I don't think there's anything less likely to tempt her." I remember my vow that I'd get her away if there was any pressure put on her to stay. No, I've still got a chance to have her all to myself. What Rais is offering would never hold any appeal for Aiza.

CHAPTER 27
Aiza

Given the tension of the past few days, spending the afternoon with Lamis and the other maidservants was exactly what I needed. After a brief period of awkwardness, and until I finally got them to start calling me Aiza instead of Your Highness, we found we had a lot in common. Shared history for one thing. Although I'd been out of the country, I'd still kept a close eye on what had been going on, and they'd filled in some of the details I'd missed. Some of the more salacious ones at that.

Lamis's eyes had glazed over when she told me details I hadn't known of how the romance developed between my brother, Nijad, and Cara, obviously enthralled by the love that they share, and that she'd been there from the beginning watching it grow. From an older woman I heard stories of my brothers when they were younger, and some of their retold antics had me wiping mirthful tears from my eyes.

I lingered longer than I had expected, enjoying their company. Part of my extended visit down to my reluctance to return to the suite. In any lull in conversation, my mind had gone back to this morning, and Rami's renewed marriage proposal.

The more I think on it, the less right it seems to be. Then, should my personal preferences have any place in this scenario? My attempt at living like a normal person hadn't worked out too well. I'm not sure I could ever go back to how I was, knowing I'm scared to be independent again. If I resumed using public transport and walking the streets, I'll always be looking behind me. However much I try to forget it, I'll always be a target simply because of the accident of my birth. It might not be al-Fahri. Even if we defeat him once and for all I'll always be at risk of being taken by someone else wanting to use me against my family. Even if not for political purposes. It could simply be money. The richer the oil makes Amahad, the more I'll be under threat. At the very least I'll have armoured transport and bodyguards wherever I go, cramping my style.

I could change my identity. Oh, I'd love to do that. Though the only way that would work is to give up my family. It's only been recently I've had a chance to get to know them. Give up seeing my nieces and nephews grow? I couldn't do that. I can't disappear.

Which makes marrying Rami an ideal solution. If I need to have bodyguards and live in a palace, I could do worse than moving to Alair. Perhaps I could continue to do my work, with the additional prestige of coming out as a member of the royal family rather than just using my money and brain.

I'd only be a figurehead. Other people would be doing the work I love, and it's them who'd be celebrating their successes. I wouldn't have the same sense of pride knowing I'd arranged everything. No longer able to bribe people, as I'd have to maintain an air of respectability.

There's one big obstacle against me throwing everything in with Rami. While he's pleasant enough, he wasn't the one to get arousal flooding through me last night, or send me running with my tail between my legs into my room—or not directly. *It had been the combination of Rami with Rais and Hunter.*

Rami, alone, wouldn't be enough. And, outside of the bedroom, however much he thinks he'd be able to give me a life I'd enjoy... I've been to Alair. I even like Rami's father, King Asad. While the country is not as suffocating as Amahad was under my father's rule, it is still very traditional. There's nothing inside me that would be content with being a trophy wife.

I stay to eat with the women, knowing I'm delaying returning and facing the men. While my lengthy presence here could be questioned, Lamis seems to understand I need this time to regroup. Eventually, I can't put it off any longer, and begrudgingly, wishing I was staying alone, return to face the music.

Zaki nods at the guards, then opens the door of my suite and steps inside. Even though I can hear male voices, he doesn't forget his guard duties, checking the suite out before I enter, presumably in case anyone's being coerced. Then, at last, he waves me in.

Immediately I put my foot over the threshold I feel something has changed. The atmosphere is different, a camaraderie between the three men that wasn't there before. Rais looks fresh from the shower, his long hair hanging to his shoulders, forming curls as it dries. Rami, also in Western clothing, is staring at Hunter as though waiting for him to take the lead. Hunter's eyes fix on mine, one eyebrow raised.

"You've decided to join us at last," Rais observes.

"Have you eaten?" Hunter asks.

I walk in, undoing my headscarf and putting it down over a chair. "I don't have to answer to you. My guards knew where I was, and yes, I've had dinner."

"Be careful, Your Highness," Hunter growls.

"Careful? *Careful?*" The way he's just spoken to me gets my blood raging. "Where I go, what I do, is none of your concern." I draw myself up to my full height, which isn't very impressive when faced with these three tall men, and gird my mental loins with my most regal poise. "I'm grateful for your protection. However, this palace is sewn up tight. I know my guards will have informed you where I was, who I was with, and what I was doing." In fact, I'm surprised they didn't report back about the food I'd consumed. "I don't need permission from you to spend some time away from the suite."

Hunter draws closer, and disappointingly, I have to crane my neck to look at him. "Kadar left your safety in our hands, *Princess*. That means one of us should be with you at all times."

"For goodness sake! I suppose I should be lucky you don't mean one of you should sleep in my bed."

I realise immediately that was probably the last thing I should have said, so quickly change tack. "I have my guards, and I'm not stupid. I won't be leaving the palace alone." I'd even been reluctant to walk in the gardens this morning, as Rami should know. Though when I glance at him, the expression on his face also looks censoring. "I'm totally protected here."

Rais comes over, Hunter steps aside. "You were with Lamis?"

"Yes," I confirm, cautiously, wondering where he's going with this.

"And who else?" While his tone is quiet, measured, there's an underlying menace underneath.

I filter my words very carefully. "Some other maids."

"You knew all of them?"

"Well, of course I didn't. Some…"

I've fallen straight into his trap.

Now it's Rami who gets off the couch and starts crowding me too. "A sweep of everyone who works in the palace is currently underway. Identity cards are being checked and matched against the database that issued them. Soldiers are being vouched for by their captains and

majors, household staff by their supervisors. Your sister-
-in-law, Cara, is doing a check of all employees' backgrounds and their current financial positions. We cannot
afford to take anything for granted where your safety is
concerned."

I bite my lip. I can't argue with what they've said. That
it's over the top, in my opinion, just shows how seriously
they are taking this threat.

It's time for me to back down. "I'm sorry." I look from
Rais, to Hunter, and then at Rami. "I didn't think."

Hunter closes the gap between me and him. "Princess,
you didn't know our concerns. There was no reason for
you to mistrust people in the palace. Hopefully, the
security check will show nothing untowards. We've had
the suite checked for bugs, and it will be checked twice a
day from now on. We don't want to make you a prisoner,
but we want you to be safe. One of us will be with you
unless you can personally vouch for everyone you're
meeting with."

My eyes can no longer meet his, and drop to the floor,
reminding myself this is how they're showing they care for
me. Still feeling like I've been reprimanded, I wave at the
door of my room. "I'm going to have a nice long bath and
an early night."

"No."

My feet have already turned in that direction. Hunter's
moved fast, putting himself in front of me. Suddenly
nervous, I look around at the three men who are

surrounding me. If I'm not wrong, there's hunger in their eyes, and it's not food they're wanting.

"Your safe word is red," Hunter says lazily.

My eyes flit to his. *What?* It doesn't take a genius to understand him.

"If you want to go to bed. Alone. Use your safe word."

My mouth opens to spit it at him. Something makes me swallow it back down. I look at Rais, so magnificent and masculine, then at Hunter, so commanding. Then at Rami, who can't keep the look of anticipation off his face, and a part of me starts to throb.

"I can't do this." *I'd love to.*

"You're not using your safe word, Princess."

That's all it would take. They wouldn't follow me or try to persuade me. A shiver runs down my spine as Hunter steps closer, into the escape route I'm still considering taking. Rais moves behind and is crowding my back. I try to force my features into a haughty expression. I'm obviously not successful.

With a sudden, unexpected move, Hunter steps back, and putting his hands on Rami's shoulders, moves him in front of me. "Kiss her," he instructs in his most dominant voice.

Rami doesn't hesitate, doesn't give me time to protest. His hands come out to cup my face, and his mouth is on mine before I can utter a word.

"Open for him," Rais growls from behind me, and oh shit, I'm doing just what he says.

Rami is gentle, his touch so sweet and loving as his tongue touches mine, at first hesitantly, then sweeps into my mouth. One hand moves to the back of my head, controlling me, not allowing me to evade him. It seems following instruction gives him the impetus to take charge, precisely what was lacking this morning.

My stomach clenches, a delicious shiver runs down my spine. Still keeping it gentle, Rami ravishes my mouth, as if wanting to imprint my taste on his mind. I breathe in his perfume, an aftershave mingled with that of a man.

Just when I realise, hands circle around me, palming my breasts over my clothes. My nipples peak as I moan into the mouth of the man so expertly kissing me.

Then I catch up. Wrenching my head out of Rami's grasp, I get out the word I should have uttered before. "Red."

Shrugging off Rais's hold, I step away, my lungs heaving as though they've sucked all the oxygen out of the room, and I'm having difficulty breathing.

Hunter looks surprised, Rami disappointed, Rais impossible to read.

I look from one to the other, then longingly at the door to my bedroom.

"Aiza?" Hunter asks cautiously.

There's something that needs to be said, I just don't know how to say the words. I feel panicked, like a deer caught in a trap. *I want this.* I don't. *I do.* Do not. In the confusion the words bubble up which explain my hesitation and come out before I can stop them. "I'm a virgin."

They all look like I've slapped them. Hunter turns and walks away, then spins around, one hand smoothing over his face. "You can't be."

Now it's out, I can't take it back. "I am."

Rami's looking confused. "I've seen you playing in clubs." His head's going backwards and forwards in dismissal.

"Not the rumour I heard," Rais grumbles behind me.

"I think I would know," I snap.

Hunter moves quickly, his hand snaking around my head and twisting into my hair. "Explain. You've played as a Domme."

I lower my eyes, not wanting to have this conversation. I could tell him to get lost, that it's none of his business. Put a stop to everything now... But Rami's kiss, directed by Hunter, felt so good, even now my body's buzzing, crying out for relief.

"I let my subs bring me to orgasm with their mouths or fingers. I've never let anyone go all the way."

"You've never had a man's cock inside you." Without me noticing, Rais has moved closer again, the hard organ he's just mentioned pressed into my back.

Another rush of arousal, and I'm so tempted.

"Have you been saving yourself?"

"Yes. No." Hunter releases his hold so I can turn to face Rais.

He's wearing a wry smile. "Which is it, Princess?"

"I don't really know. I just wanted it to mean something." I like to play, anything else I've been holding back.

I've seen women with two or more men in clubs many times, and always wondered how it would feel to have so much attention, so many cocks all at once. I've never seriously considered being in that position myself. If I had ever imagined it, it would have been me directing what they were doing, not being at the mercy of one, let alone two Doms.

The idea excites me. The idea turns me off. My body is throbbing, my clit pulsating, while my brain's firmly putting on the brakes.

Hunter is watching me carefully as though reading the myriad of emotions crossing my face. Eventually he raises his head and speaks over mine. "Under the circumstances, I believe Aiza has a lot to think about. I suggest we let her go to bed and think about whether she wants what we're offering."

That's the best suggestion I've ever heard… No, it's the worst.

The three of them exchange glances and seem to have a silent conversation. Then Rais takes charge and gives a little prod to my back. "Go to bed, Aiza. We'll talk in the morning."

Escape. Free at last, I hold my head high and start moving towards the master bedroom.

"Oh, and Aiza?" I pause at Hunter's voice. "No making yourself come."

I refuse to give him the satisfaction of any reaction. *Not play with myself? When they've got me so riled up?* How can I think of what they're offering without needing relief?

If I do what he says it's going to be a long, torturous night. Out of their hearing, I huff.

CHAPTER 28
Rais

D o you think she'll follow your instructions?" Rami's still staring at the door Aiza's just disappeared through, once again the key turning loudly in the lock.

Hunter barks a short laugh. "If she doesn't then she's going to get her ass reddened."

I look at him sharply, trying to quell the sudden awareness inside that if anyone's going to be reddening anything of hers, it's going to be me and my hand.

"A virgin, eh?" Rami's shaking his head, and at last turns around to face us. "Never saw that coming. It's true, I didn't see her going into private rooms in the clubs. Obviously I didn't have eyes on her at all times, and just assumed."

"Doesn't change anything, does it?" Hunter doesn't seem fussed. "Just means we have to take things a bit slower."

Rami puffs himself up. "You realise this puts things in a different light…"

"No, it doesn't." Hunter and I exchange looks, having said exactly the same thing at the same time. At least there's something we both agree on. Any dream Rami's got of riding off with her into the sunset alone has got to be quashed.

After he huffs, Rami comes with us to sit at the table, and we start throwing around some ideas. As we talk about practicalities and what a woman like Aiza would want and need, he starts to get on board. By the time we go to our beds, or me to the couch—hopefully for the last time—we've all agreed to a plan. And it's me who's going to kick it off in the morning.

Being called to an early meeting, Hunter, Rami and I leave Aiza sleeping after I'd double checked and reassured myself she was sufficiently protected by trustworthy guards.

The reason for our summons being a report from Sultan Qudamah. Rami had done well contacting him before we'd taken action. The sultan had found no reports of heavy artillery moving in Ezirad, and further inspection of the satellite footage by the experts in Grade A and military intelligence suggested what we'd taken for tanks were actually mock-ups, and there were fewer bodies than the number of tents would suggest. Everything pointed to it being a decoy. Rami got a metaphorical slap on the back for being on point.

Rami and Hunter remained behind—Rami to update his father, and Hunter was engaged with whom I'm certain are his colleagues from the intelligence community, even if he refuses to make his relationship official. My part played for now, I return to the suite mid-morning, nodding at the guards standing outside the door. Entering, I'm unable to miss the flare of anxiety in her eyes, or the way she looks behind me, and the relief when she sees I'm alone.

She's in the sitting room, and crumbs on the plate suggest she's just finished a late breakfast, and I take a moment to study her before putting my plan into action.

"Are you ready to go out, Princess?" I ask, immediately sensing she's nervous. The sooner I get her out of this suite, the quicker that tension will slip away. My aim is to make her totally relaxed today.

Her brow creases. "Out? Where? Yesterday you wanted me to stay in the suite."

"I'll be with you, so no worries there. I want to show you something." At this point I'm keeping it vague. I'm also keeping my distance, though what I'd rather do is sweep her up into my arms, take her into the bedroom and change the status that she astounded us by announcing the evening before. We'd taken that into consideration in our discussion.

She frowns. "What? Shouldn't you be working? Planning to take down al-Fahri or something?"

"We've had our morning meeting while you were catching up on your beauty sleep. Don't worry, everything's in place. Hunter and Rami have everything under control."

I read her pout as disappointment she's missed it, and if she'd been awake and ready there wouldn't have been any harm in her coming along. As it is, she can't complain. She was the one who locked her door and slept in.

"If you're not going to tell me where I'm going, you'll have to tell me if I'm alright dressed like this." As she stands and twirls, I look to check, and immediately wish I hadn't. She's wearing capri trousers that hug her legs and outline that firm arse beautifully, and another one of her tight t-shirts that emphasises her pert breasts. The ones I had my hands on last night for far too short a time.

"Maybe a loose blouse?" I suggest, my voice sounding like someone's choking me. Then feel sweat on my brow as I watch her arse swaying as she walks into the bedroom. She comes out moments later with her arms decently covered. Not that I give a damn, but not being a tourist destination, the people of Zalmā are more conservative than those of the more cosmopolitan north.

She's ready in no time, and I walk by her side as we go through the palace, finally leading her out through the main entrance. She pauses and looks back at the magnificent building behind us, glowing white in the sunlight against the background of a clear blue sky.

"I'd forgotten how beautiful it is." She breathes out, the air whistling through her teeth.

Not as beautiful as you are.

I allow her a few more seconds to take it in, and then prompt her. "Come."

Looking around, she sees a lack of transport. "We're walking? Is it safe?"

I don't miss that shiver of fear. "They'll be with us." I incline my head towards a dozen men who are waiting in addition to her usual four guards, this morning headed by by Dharr, a seasoned fighter and a man of whom I approve. They immediately surround us when we reach the end of the driveway. "It's not a long walk in any event. I just thought you might appreciate some fresh air and want get outside the palace walls." From the way her nostrils twitch at the perfumed flowers around us, and her features seem to relax, I reckon I'm right. A woman like Aiza doesn't like to be cooped up.

Some people are lining the sidewalks, others coming out from shops. I greet them with a wave. They know who I am, and for some unknown reason they seem to like me. A man raises his phone and snaps a photo, making the security perk up.

"Yjb 'an yakun manaeahum 'akhadha fawtughra?"

I shake my head at Dharr. "No, let them take all the pictures they want." As I speak I pull Aiza in closer, feeling pride that the photos will show both of us together.

She stiffens and says quietly, "Is that wise? Some of those may appear on Facebook, and if they do, we've told al-Fahri exactly where I am."

We haven't told her he already does know, or of his second phone call to Kadar. We hadn't wanted to worry her more than she already is. Leaning down, I murmur into her ear. "That's what we want. Keeps him away from Al Qur'ah and prevents him carrying out his threat to the children." I glance up at a building and see the light glint of an automatic rifle. I've got snipers on every high point keeping a look out. Every action possible taken to ensure her safety today.

I see a slight straightening of her back, even though she can't completely suppress the shudder at my reminder of the risk to the children.

It's not a long walk, and after only a few minutes I pull her to a stop, pointing with my index finger to a massive building in front of us. In fact, it's more than one, linked by chrome and glass walkways. Although built a few years ago, it's been expanded and brought up to date. "I wanted you to get the full impact." If we'd come by car we would have been driven up to the front, and she'd have been unable to get an idea of the scale of it.

"What is it?" Her eyes are wide as she takes it all in.

"Our hospital," I explain.

"Wow." Turning to me, her mouth drops open. Then she swivels back around to face front again. "I didn't expect anything like this. It's bigger than the one in Al Qur'ah."

I'm quite happy to explain, "It serves the whole of a southern desert. Some people from Ezirad come for treatment. From further abroad as well. We have the ultimate in trauma treatment centres, as the military are stationed here."

"The border wars."

"Yes," I agree. "Though due to the oil field we're now at peace with Ezirad, still the jihadists try to get across. Our border controls are attacked regularly, and unfortunately our troops get injured. Come. I've arranged for you to have a tour."

Shaking her head in disbelief and wonder, she enters the building, clearly appreciating the cleanliness and the facilities. We go to various units, and doctors, as arranged, take time to talk to her. She's particularly interested in the cardio-thoracic unit and the oncology department. I stand back as she questions the doctors, watching her delight when they agree if they're unable to do something they'd happily welcome a specialist from another country. Just as I'd hoped, I can see her mind whirring.

It's late afternoon before we return to the palace. Aiza's quiet and deep in thought all the way. It's only when we're nearing the suite she stops and addresses me. "My status means I can get anyone into Amahad, can't I?"

"You can. Zₐlmā's got an airport that can take the biggest jets." It's run by the military.

I keep quiet, not wanting to be the one who plants the idea that she could do excellent work for her charity if she were to be based here. I'd prefer her to come to that reasoning herself. She, herself, doesn't instigate any further conversation as we make our way back to the palace.

I breathe a sigh of relief once we're back inside the walls. It had been a slight risk taking her into Zₐlmā today, however I'd known seeing is believing, and going to the hospital would be better than me simply describing it. She'd been well protected, the visit secretly arranged, nevertheless the tension seeps out of me when I know that once again she's completely safe.

Hunter's in the suite when we return. We exchange nods, me letting him know the day had gone as planned, and while he greets her, he doesn't stand or crowd her or say anything to make her uneasy. His relaxed posture encourages her. Once she realises Hunter, too, isn't going to refer to the previous night, she begins to speak. Animatedly, she relates to Hunter all that she's seen, and starts coming up with ideas. Ideas that suggest she's considering staying local. Taking a seat, I relax back with my hands clasped behind my head. Stage one complete. Successfully.

Rami appears, and like Hunter, simply acknowledges everyone when he comes into the room, nothing in his language or behaviour referencing back to the evening before. We order dinner to be brought in and eat it. It's only when we've had a catch-up conversation, allowing her time for her food to go down, that we put stage two into action.

I excuse myself and enter the bedroom. When I re-emerge, I've lost my robe and headdress, and am dressed only in dark denim jeans, and I haven't done the top button up. My shoulder length hair hangs loose.

My movement catches her attention. Looking up, she swallows fast. If I wasn't already hard in expectation, the sight of her throat working would have achieved that result. *If it was my cock in there...*

Hunter stretches lazily, then sits back, his arms straight out to either side, resting on the back of the couch. Rami walks out of the bathroom. He's also disposed of his robes and is wearing jeans and a sleeveless top that showcases his muscles.

As the levels of testosterone rise in the room, Aiza stands, looking like a she wants nothing more than to turn and run.

"Stay where you are," Hunter barks.

Immediately she stills, her hands fluttering as if she doesn't know what to do with them. "What's going on?" She glances at me, licking her lips without knowing what she's doing, and definitely not noticing the effect it has upon me, and then looks away, choosing to address herself to Hunter.

"Rais is going to help you with that, er, issue you mentioned last night."

Her eyes widen, and she seems to have difficulty finding words. In the end plumping for a question. "Rais? Issue?" I swear her voice is an octave higher.

"Yes." That's all I say.

Her eyes snap quickly to me, then back onto Hunter. She doesn't pretend not to understand. "Why Rais?" She attempts to inject some humour, though her voice squeaks as she asks, "How come he drew the short straw?"

Ignoring her lame and totally untrue joke, Hunter shrugs. "As he's going to be the one to marry you, it seems fitting."

"Marry me?" This time she's squeaking as she swings around to Rami. "You were the one who proposed."

Rami throws himself down on the sofa next to Hunter. "I'd still marry you in a flash, sweetheart. I've been persuaded this way is better."

She's looking totally lost. Her eyes flicking wildly between us. "What if I don't want to marry any of you? Or have help *solving my issue*." She uses her hands to put the last three words in quotes. "This is crazy. None of us know each other."

"I've known you forever, Aiza," I correct. "I've watched you grow from a child into a beautiful woman."

"I too." Rami adds. "I was brought up with the know-ledge I was going to be tied to you. Every time we met, every time I saw you, I knew that wasn't going to be a chore."

She looks at Hunter and sneers. "We've only just met."

He refutes it. "I've been around even when you didn't notice me. Providing security. Staying out of sight meant I was doing my job. When I first saw you, there was an immediate attraction, which I don't think you can deny was mutual."

"What if I want someone else?" She sucks her lower lip into her mouth. "Sure, I can't deny there's something between us, I'll admit that. I've been attracted to many men…"

"Though you might well have been, you've never acted on it, have you, Aiza? Last night, habiti, it wouldn't have taken much of a push for you to give yourself to three men."

Her olive skin, much paler than mine, does little to hide the pinkening of her cheeks. Her dark eyes flash, and it's me that she challenges as her voice returns almost to normal as she sneers, "Marriage, Rais, really?"

I step closer, crowding her space. "Marriage. A lifetime commitment. A lifetime of loyalty. You already know I'd give my life for you."

"You've not mentioned love," she blurts out.

"I'll love you." Rami stands, his face far gentler than mine. He smiles at her nervously.

She stares at him, her brow creasing, her voice cracking again. "But you're not the one proposing to marry me!"

"Rami will visit. Make his second home here with us."

"What?" Her voice goes to the top of the range once again.

"I'll be here as often as I can. With the three of us, Aiza, you'll never be alone."

She shakes her head. "With the three of you I'll probably wish I was."

"Aiza," Hunter snaps. "Here is the ideal base for your charity. You must have seen that. We can work with you smoothly the way to get sick kids here and any specialists needed. You'll have your mahr, the bride price from Rais, that you can use as you want to. Rais will be the stability this relationship needs, that's why he's going to be the one who puts the ring on your finger."

I've moved behind her. My hands rest on her shoulders, and leaning down I murmur to her, "I'm a man of the desert, Aiza. Not one for words. Agree, and I'll show you with my body just how much you mean to me."

She shivers, and I see her nipples peaking, betraying how far she is from immune to my touch.

"You three hardly know each other."

"What's the worst that can happen?" Hunter challenges again. "You'll be married to Rais. If something happens to me or Rami, you'll have your life with him."

She suddenly twists in my hold, turning to look at me. "Rais, this is crazy."

I press my advantage. "The only crazy thing would be if you pushed me away." For tactile confirmation I move my fingers gently up and down her biceps, feeling goosebumps rise on her skin.

She draws in a breath and lets it out on a sigh, then pulls away from me. *Fuck it. Have I lost her?*

For a moment I think she's going to retreat to her room. If she did, we'd let her. It's not our intention to force her, or even use pressure on here. I sigh. *We did our best.*

She turns around before she gets to the door and comes back, coming to a halt equidistant between us. She folds her arms around herself, then spares a quick glance to each of us in turn.

"Twafiq bought me as a slave. I wasn't his first." She pauses and lets that sink in before spelling out, "He'd have used me and killed me. Accidentally or on purpose."

Another break. "Or I'd have died trying to escape. I knew I hadn't got long."

"Habiti..." Fuck, I don't want her going through it again, even if only in her head.

"No, Rais. You've had your chance. Please let me speak." She waits, and when I reluctantly nod, carries on. "I didn't expect to be kidnapped. But life happens, doesn't it? Things you can't prevent. Yes, I'm a virgin. I was saving that. To give to someone. Certainly not for a man like Twafiq to steal."

"Habiti..." I try to stop her again.

She's almost talking to herself. "Now al-Fahri wants to take me again. For another buyer? Who knows. If there's the slightest chance of him taking me... Well, I'd rather experience my first time with someone I, myself, want."

I don't like her reasoning, however it's led her to the conclusion I'd hoped for. "With me?" I ask, hopefully, advancing on her again.

Her eyes go to Hunter, and then to Rami, and then landing back on me.

Hunter moves nearer. He lifts his hand and puts it under her chin. "You have all of us. You'll *have* all of us. Just not for your first time."

She shivers and unfolds her arms.

CHAPTER 29
Aiza

I must be certifiably insane to even be considering this. There's no real reason why I've held on to my virginal status, no conscious decision, there's just never been a man I wanted to give it to before. I play in clubs, and though while I let men service me, they've all been submissive by my choice.

Perhaps I was waiting for someone more dominant than me? Now I've ended up with not one, but two. Then there's Rami, he hasn't got a dominant bone in his body. Each of them with something different to offer.

It's preposterous to give a single thought to this ridiculous idea. A bizarre arrangement that I should dismiss out of hand. Rais is standing far too close for me to think rationally. I sneak a peek at him from under my eyelashes. He's standing there, tall, ruggedly good looking, a scar I hadn't noticed before running over his bare, hairless chest down his abdomen and disappearing into those unbuttoned jeans. I have the sudden impulse to follow it down with my tongue to see how far it goes.

I realise with a start that I've been staring, transfixed on the body that proposes to become one with mine. While

I've been feasting my eyes, Rami and Hunter have advanced towards me.

I look in a daze at the hand Hunter's extended to me and take it automatically, at the same time as Rais murmurs into my ear, "Come."

Rami's got the door open, and I let Hunter lead me through. *Not to the dungeon. Not for my first time...* I needn't have worried, as Hunter stops me facing the foot of the bed.

"Rami?"

As if Hunter's already given him instructions, I feel the prince's hands reaching around me, sliding my blouse off my shoulders, his mouth nuzzling at my neck, then drawing back to pull the tunic up over my head. Wrapping my arms around my chest I try to hide, but eager hands gently push them back down, encouraging me to submit. My bra drops to the ground. I've been undressed before, bared my breasts. That was only when I've been the one in charge. For some reason I can't analyse, having the decision taken out of my hands sends a shiver of excitement down my spine.

Picking me up, Rami gently puts me onto the bed, then his mouth descends and takes mine in a kiss which rapidly becomes urgent. His tongue sweeps into my mouth, his lips moving enthusiastically over mine. As I give in and simply allow myself to enjoy the experience, I feel hands at my breasts, then two mouths working in tandem. Arching my back, I give in to the sensations that start overwhelming me, shooting my level of arousal up into the hemisphere.

Fingers tracing, lips soothing, tongues circling, and teeth nipping. My clit's throbbing almost painfully, and I writhe on the bed as I try to seek some relief. Masculine aromas surround me, I can't distinguish one from the other. I moan into Rami's mouth.

Now my left breast feels neglected as a head pulls away, but Rami takes his place, and someone is taking my trousers off. Wantonly, I raise my hips to help, desperate for someone to touch me, to give me some relief.

"You're fucking beautiful," Rais's deep voice informs me as he bends my legs at the knees and pushes my thighs apart. Opening my eyes, I find him kneeling at the end of the bed, and our gazes lock. His expression is tight, as though he's having difficulty controlling himself. He resembles a warrior preparing for war. And tonight, I'll be the victim of his onslaught.

I groan once again as he lowers his mouth and starts kissing his way up my inner thigh of my right leg, then his mouth fixes on me, and I feel a nip, the small bite of pain adding to everything else that's overloading my senses.

As he pays the same attention to my other thigh, his hand gently strokes the one he's now neglecting, and I start to wriggle, wanting to force him to make his way up. Remembering who and what I am, I give him an instruction.

"Lick my pussy. Make me come."

He slaps my thigh and barks, "You're not in charge. I am."

His voice, that tone which oozes authority, seems to vibrate through my body. For a second I panic, never having relinquished total control before.

Hunter raises his head a few millimetres only to say, "Your safeword's red. Don't forget you can use it." His breath washing over my wet nipple makes it peak even more.

I've always been the one giving subs a safeword. Until we came to the Desert Palace and these three men ganged up on me, I've never had the need to use one myself. Never given anyone control over me. I feel adrift, out of depth, not sure what I want. The jerking of my body which I can't stop tells me I need some relief. Even my skin seems alive, and as a hand strokes my stomach I twitch.

Then Rais plants a kiss to my clit, and I jump. The attention they're paying to my nipples, the little bites and stings of pain zoom through me. I try pleading. "Please, Rais."

"I'll give you what you need, habiti. Be patient."

Then ignoring that bundle of nerves that want his attention, he places a finger inside me.

As my body automatically tenses at the intrusion, Rais growls, "Fuck, she's tight."

His words make Hunter and Rami groan, and I almost scream with frustration as my nipples tingle and another zing shoots through me. My clit must be swollen and pulsing.

Rais adds another finger and starts scissoring them inside me. My hips rise to try and get him deeper, all I provoke is a short laugh. Then I feel him breathing over that throbbing bundle of nerves which seem to be on fire. My stomach muscles clench and unclench, my desire overwhelming, almost painful. I momentarily consider saying my safe word, then remember that they'll stop.

I could finish myself off.

If they're making me feel this good already… I choke the word back down, wanting, *needing* to see what else they can do.

At last Rais puts his mouth where I want it, circling his tongue around that tight bud, then sucking and licking. I try to raise my hips to push myself against him, his strong arms hold me down.

"Don't come," he instructs. *The bastard. What?*

"Rais…"

He ignores me. "Hunter?"

I feel Rais removing his hand, his mouth leaving my needy clit. Moaning with frustration, I open my eyes to see what's happening. Rais is directing Hunter to take his place on the bed, and now another hand's touching me, and another mouth is on me. *He'll let me come.*

"Don't you dare," Hunter says with a laugh.

Oh, the times I've taunted a sub. Used cock rings until they had sweat running down their faces. Now I'm being paid back. I thrust down with my hips to get more pressure, but Hunter moves his head away.

Then my attention is caught by Rais, who's removing his jeans. He's commando underneath, and fuck, his cock's enormous. Knowing how he intends to use it, the sight of it makes me catch my breath.

I know we'll fit, most people do. But that monster is so large it doesn't look normal. Its purplish head looks angry, and I see the veins protruding....

Rais catches my eye and reads my unease. "Leave us," he instructs. I breathe a sigh of relief that even while it's only Hunter and Rami, we won't have an audience. Now the moment is near, I'm anxious enough. Especially having seen his size, he's thick as well as long.

The door closes, and we're alone. Rais comes to the head of the bed, curling his hand around my head, taking hold of my hair and turning me to face him. He stares into my eyes for a moment. "We don't have to do this if you've changed your mind."

"I'm nervous." With my admission, my arousal begins to fade. While a moment ago I'd have done anything he wanted, the enormity of taking this step hits me.

"You're going to be my wife."

"Do I have any say in this?" I try to lighten my voice and make it into a joke.

His expression grows serious. "I've spoken to Kadar and got his blessing."

"To marry me or defile me?" I snap.

He looks amused. "The latter comes with the territory." His hand trails down my stomach, my skin quivering at his touch. He moves to resume his position at the foot of the bed, and once more puts his mouth on my traitorous clit. As his talented tongue and lips work, my arousal rushes back. Soon I'm shaking, trembling, my muscles tightening, my head leaning back.

His deep velvet voice rumbles, "You're going to come with me inside you."

Before I can get enough breath to speak, I feel pressure, something too big is trying to get inside me. All the while his fingers are strumming my clit, and I don't know what to concentrate on. The burn of his invasion or the desperate need for release.

I squeeze my eyes shut, feeling a sudden thrust which hurts. Then he stops moving and leans over me, both his hands now touching my face, stroking my cheeks in a soothing gesture.

"Look at me, habiti."

I shake my head.

"Open your eyes."

As the pain starts to recede, I peer through my eyelashes and see a gentle expression on his face that I've never seen before.

"Your pussy feels amazing, habiti. Ah…" As I experimentally squeeze my muscle, it's his turn to squeeze his eyes shut, and a look of pure satisfaction comes over him. I do it again, he pulls back a little, then pushes in.

That feels good.

"Aiza," he begins as he gently slides in and out. "Fuck, I wish I wasn't wearing a condom for this. I can't wait to take you bare." His hands tighten around my face. "No one else ever will. Any child will be mine, understand? I want your ring on my finger and my baby inside you."

My stomach convulses. My eyes open wide. "I…"

"I'm not going to rush you, though you can take this as fair warning. One day I want you pregnant."

I didn't even know he wanted to marry me until a short time ago, so what I'm thinking is ridiculous. It must be my fear that despite all the precautions al-Fahri will get to me, or just send an assassin to kill me, there's part of me wishing I could experience everything now. *Why wait?* When I'd been playing with the babies back in Al Qur-ah, I'd longed for one of my own. To have Rais's baby.

The sensible part of me makes me keep quiet.

He's giving me time to get used to the size of him, his gentle thrusts keeping us both aroused and making thinking difficult.

The pain has gone, I feel stretched, almost split in two. My body jerks with need, and I want him to move to assuage this yearning for release. "Just fuck me, Rais."

He grins. That's when I realise I have no idea what I've just asked for. I feel so full, then empty as he pulls almost all the way out, then thrusts back in, then repeats. He's hitting something I wasn't sure existed inside me.

Placing both hands either side of me on the bed, he takes his weight on his arms and lets himself go.

I cry out as sensations wash over me. He growls and lowers his head, his teeth nipping at a tender spot on my neck. I can't hold back any longer, and come with a scream, my body shuddering and shaking beyond my control.

"Aiza," he shouts. "I'm going to come."

I can feel him swelling, his balls banging against me with every thrust. His words, *his intention*, make me go tense again, and as he roars his completion I come again with him.

He stills inside me, his body shuddering as he pumps his cum into me. I'm twitching uncontrollably with every thrust. His mouth meets mine and completely ravishes me, his tongue mimicking what his cock has just done to my body.

My lips feel swollen when he finally pulls away. His cock slips out of my body. I'm completely drained, unable to move as I feel the bed dipping and hear water running in the bathroom. Then he's back and cleaning me up.

I open my eyes to see a satisfied grin on his face, and that the cloth he's holding is tinged with red. I shake my head despairingly, realising he's enjoying seeing the proof.

"What? I'm a sheikh."

"Would it have mattered if I wasn't?" He seems to be taking too much pleasure in the evidence of my now lost virginity.

He fixes those dark eyes on me. "Not in the least. It's you I want. It's just a bonus knowing I'm the first man to have you."

"You could have been a bit bloody smaller," I grumble.

"Sore?"

I wriggle my hips. "Just a bit."

"A bit?"

"Okay, then, a lot. Satisfied?"

He throws the flannel in the direction of the bathroom, then lays down behind me and pulls me into his arms. "I'm more than satisfied, habiti."

The touch of his mouth nibbling and kissing my neck is so gentle for such a rugged man.

As my sexual euphoria fades, the strangeness of it all catches up with me. *I hadn't expected Rais to make me feel so good. Is this what I want? Or have these men, Rais swept me away?* Suddenly the speed with which everything's happened slams into me, and I stiffen in his arms.

He notices immediately, sitting up and turning me over. I turn my head away, he moves it back. I close my eyes, squeezing them tight, but can't prevent the tear from trickling out.

"Speak to me," he commands.

I give a quick shake of my head, wanting to be left alone to come to terms with what's happened here tonight.

"Habiti?" When I don't respond, he wipes the tear from the corner of my eye with a calloused finger. "I've just had the best sex of my life, and with the woman I'm going to marry. Now she's crying. Why, habiti? Tell me why."

I don't cry. This isn't me. Despising my weakness, I sit up fast, making him hiss. I grab my shirt from where it was discarded by the side of the bed and tug it back on over my head. Then, disregarding my underwear, slip on my trousers. It's only then that I speak.

"Why? Why am I upset?" I waggle my finger at him. "Well, let's just see. Maybe it's because I've been railroaded into something I'm not sure I want. Playing with you, Hunter, and Rami in the dungeon is one thing. But this," I point to him, then back to myself, "this between us, what you want, isn't what I do."

He gets to his feet, his full nakedness on view in all its glory. "I'm not what you want?" His face grows tight, it's hard to discern whether it's with anger or disappointment.

Whichever it is, it does nothing to dampen my anger, which seems to have appeared out of nowhere. "What do you think you are, Rais, Allah's fucking gift? Why should I want you? Why should I want to tie myself to a desert sheikh and be trapped in Amahad? I've fought all my life for the chance to be free, and you want to constrain me."

"I gave you a fucking choice! You could have said your safeword, or fuck it, just told me no, asked me to stop. You didn't."

Ignoring the fact that he's spoken the truth, my anger continues to rise. "You took advantage of me when I was feeling weak. When I hadn't recovered from being kidnapped. My mind's not in the right place, you should have known that. I'm not a fucking doormat for you to walk over. I'm not a submissive who's going to kneel at your feet or jump to your command. And you wonder why I'm upset?"

He prowls closer. "I took advantage?"

I wave my hand dismissively. "You all did. It's a fucking game to you."

"A game?" he growls.

"A game," I confirm. "Oh, and I've no doubt Kadar gave his blessing. He's managed to trap all the Kassis siblings now." I pause. "Well, he's failed. He's not trapping this one. As soon as I can I'm out of this godforsaken country. I won't be returning again either. Fuck Rami, fuck Hunter…"

A snide grin spreads over his face. "I'm sure they'd love to fuck you."

"I never want to see them again. I'll ask Ben to assign someone different…"

My voice has risen to such a volume it must have carried to the men in the next room. My bedroom door bursts open, making me swing around. Hunter's there, his face thunderous. Rami's trying to peer past him, his expression concerned.

Hunter looks from Rais to myself, and then back to the desert sheikh again. "How the hell did you fuck this up, Rais?"

345

CHAPTER 30
Rais

How did I fuck this up? I haven't a fucking clue. I thought she'd been right there with me, and she had been. She enjoyed it as much as I had. So why this sudden anger? What's caused it? In my mind I replay what she's said, one thing sticks out. Narrowing my eyes, I focus on her. "Hunter, Rami. Out."

Hunter stands his ground. "I don't think so, Sheikh. Did you force her?" As the idea dawns on him he steps closer.

I swing around, my eyes locking on those of the man from Grade A. "Well, did I, Aiza?"

There's a little gasp behind me, then she denies it. "No, Hunter, he didn't."

"You hurt her then."

Seeing the way his hands are fisting, I'm pleased when again she replies.

"No."

It's not quite the truth, though any pain wasn't intentional, I'd done my best to prepare her. I'd beat Hunter into a pulp if he wants to take me on, but I doubt it will make Aiza feel any happier to see the walls of the royal suite dripping with blood.

"Look, please. Will you all go? I want some time to myself." Her voice trembles, the sound making my heart clench. Time to brood is exactly what I'm not going to give her. Under the circumstances I can't. It's not what she needs.

I push past Hunter and open the door. "Give us some space."

"You gonna sort this, man?" Hunter's still glaring at me, clearly reluctant to leave.

"I'm going to have a damn good try. Rami, I want you to leave too."

Rami doesn't know what to do or say, he's not a man who likes to take charge. Give him a direct order, though, and he seems more comfortable. Once they've left, I lock the door and pocket the key.

Aiza's eyes are wide and staring. "Rais, please. I want to be alone."

Ignoring her, I start opening the drawers at the side of the bed. Ah, second one down has got what I'm looking for, and that goes into my pocket too. Then I walk over to her.

"Do you trust me, Aiza?"

"Yes. No." She seems flustered.

I stare deep into her eyes. "Tell me honestly. In all the time that I've known you, have I ever given you reason not to trust me?"

At last her gaze meets mine, and then just as fast she looks away. She shrugs. I haven't. That's all the answer she can give me.

"You're hurting," I tell her, knowing it's the truth.

She huffs a laugh. "I'm not that sore."

My lips curl slightly. "I didn't mean that." I tap my fingers gently against her forehead.

"I meant you're hurting in here. Trust me to help you."

Another quick glance at me. "What are you going to do?"

"Come." I hold out my hand, she places hers in it, and I lead her over to the door hidden behind the curtain.

As she pulls back my fingers tighten so as not to lose the contact. I turn to see her shaking her head. "No, Rais."

"Yes." I'm as firm as I can be, and then repeat again, "Trust me." I change tack and taunt her. "You afraid?"

"Of course not," she scorns.

You should be. Opening the door, I wrap my hand more firmly around her wrist and pull her with me. If she really protested or fought me I'd let her loose, but she doesn't, and allows me to lead her down the stone stairs. I let her go briefly while I select the right key from my pocket then open the door to the converted harem.

I hadn't taken much time to explore yesterday, so after flicking on the light I take a moment to look around. She jerks her hand away from my hold, wrapping both arms around herself as though she's cold.

I spy what I hoped to find. A nice comfortable chair. Well, comfortable for me that is. Putting my hand on the small of her back, I encourage her across the room, taking in the other equipment as we pass, thinking of how I could make use of it on another day. *I've got ideas. I've been friends with Nijad a very long time.* I stop in front of the chair.

"No."

Somehow she's guessed my intent. Raising one eyebrow, I remind her, "You earned a punishment as I remember."

"From Hunter."

"Well, you'll be taking it from me." I sit down. "Over my lap, Aiza."

"Red."

"Uh uh. I admit that while I might not be into the life-style, Aiza, don't think I'm ignorant. A safeword doesn't get you out of a punishment."

Her eyes blaze. "It does if I never want to see you again. If I'm going to take the first flight out of here and disappear."

"And that's earned you another one." My voice is quite calm, belying the anger her words cause. "For not taking your safety seriously."

"I don't feel particularly safe now." Her voice shakes a little.

I hold out my hand to her. "Come on, Aiza. The sooner we start, the sooner it will be over."

"Then you'll get out of my sight?" She glances at me hopefully.

"If that's what you still desire," I agree, knowing it's the last thing that I want. I've got one chance to bring her back to me, and I can't afford to cock this up.

"Of course it will be what I bloody want," she mumbles softly, at last putting her hand in mine.

I jerk her, unbalancing her, and she tumbles into me. My strong arms have turned her so she's over my knees, her arse in the air. She squeals as I pull down her silk trousers. Without delaying and giving her no time to protest, I spank her. She yelps.

"Relax. It won't hurt so much."

"You bloody relax. Then you won't hit so hard," is her spirited reply.

I spank her again. Then again. Then give her the next five. Her body is still rigid, at least she's stopped trying to get away.

"Isn't that enough?" she huffs out, trying to sound braver than she is.

Not by a long way. In Nijad's words, she's trying to top me from the bottom, but I've got this. Keeping my voice firmly controlled, I ask, "Tell me, Aiza, why didn't you say how badly your kidnapping was still affecting you?" *Spank.* "Why did you let us believe you'd gotten over it?"

"Because I had, have."

A harder spank. "Stop lying to me."

"Stop hitting me." Now there's a sob.

"Speak to me, Aiza. Tell me what's upsetting you." My voice is low and calm.

"I can't." There's an inflection that tells me she's not speaking the truth.

Spank. "You can."

Another sob, followed by another. *I'm starting to get through to her.* I change what I'm doing, massaging my hand over both reddening cheeks, then spanking again, followed by more soothing.

"They treated me like an animal," she sobs out. *There it is.*

"How, habiti? How did they do that?" I've heard the plain facts of it before, although she hasn't let anyone know how she felt about her treatment.

It's like the floodgates have opened. "The room where they left me had a window. There was no privacy. It was more like a kennel... I, I never thought I would get away. I gave up hoping for rescue. I have nightmares I'm still back there. I dream about it, even during the day."

There's more. I spank more lightly, then massage again, not to hurt her, just to give her focus.

"He was going to let his two disgusting men take me at once. He was going to film it for Kadar. He was going to break Kadar by showing him how they broke me. Rais, I said I would fight, death before dishonour, but, but I wouldn't have had a chance. There was nothing I could do. Everything, all my control was stripped from me. I felt like the trapped animal they said I'd become."

I put her up into my arms as the tears come in earnest. "They would have hurt me, degraded me. They wanted to use me for their entertainment. Nothing would be out of bounds. I was powerless, Rais. Helpless. If you hadn't come..." She sobs into my chest.

"Shush, shush, darling. I did come. *I'll* always come."

"And now he's going to get me again, and I'm just as helpless." She's so scared.

I rush to reassure her. "No, habiti. Not this time. You've got me, Hunter, and Rami. Let alone a whole army protecting you and keeping you safe. Shush, babe, I've got you. I'll always hold you and keep you safe."

Her arms around my neck are almost strangling me, I don't protest. I'm not into this dominance and submission —well maybe the fun part—I've not thought myself capable of carrying out a punishment before, however, I needed to get her out of her head. Needed to get her to open up to me. Needed to make her let go and let me in.

I'm rocking us both, her sobs still coming fast.

"Is there more, darling? Is there anything else I need to know?"

Her hands tighten even more, telling me my suspicions were right. There's more to it. Something else Twafiq had done? "Twafiq and his men are all dead, habiti. They won't be coming for you again."

"I know that."

At last her sobbing turns into hiccups, she lifts her head from my shoulder, and at last loosens that grip around my neck. She reaches out her hands and cups my face, staring into my eyes so sadly. I catch my breath.

"I thought this was right, Aiza." I couldn't bear it now if she pushes me away, knowing I've selfishly pushed myself on her in all types of ways today. *Did we take her choices away? Am I just as bad as Twafiq.*

She rolls her head back and stares at the ceiling, then she looks down and gazes at me, almost as if she's memorising every detail of my face.

"I can't do this, Rais."

A flicker of fear burns within me. *I can't lose her now. I've taken what I wanted too fast.*

"Do what, Aiza?" My voice catches.

"I can't marry you." The words I dread and have no wish to hear.

"Why the fuck not?" She struggles as if she wants to get down from my lap. If this is the last chance I'll have to hold her, I'm going to hang on as long as I can. "Is it the arrangement? The suggestion of Hunter and Rami?"

"The arrangement," she parrots. "That's part of it."

"Go on." Whatever protests she's got, I'll find a way around it.

Suddenly she straightens and sits astride my lap, her pussy hovering over my cock. The words she's uttering prevent it swelling. "You've asked for this, alright? It might not be what you what to hear and might not make sense to you. Rais, you remember taking me to Switzerland? When I was eighteen?"

I nod. I do. I haven't forgotten a single moment when I've been in her company. Could probably recite the number of times I got a glimpse of her across the room. I recall that journey well, when she first left for finishing school, and it was me that had taken her. None of her family wanted the chore. "I remember," I tell her.

She shakes her head sadly. "That was when I knew I was attracted to you."

What the fuck? My hands, which had been stroking, soothing her, still. I think I even stop breathing.

She nods as if I've spoken aloud. "Pretty stupid, huh? I fell in love with a desert sheikh."

She fell in love with me? "You didn't say anything. Aiza, if that was the case, why did you stay away? Why didn't you let me know? Give me some sign?"

"To avoid making a fool of myself. Like I'm doing today. You were out of my reach. I knew you'd never look at me." The words tumble out as if a floodgate has been opened. Her defences so far down she can't hold back the truth.

Words which shake me to my core. Words which crack the stone shield around my heart. It hits me then. If I hadn't already stopped taking air into my lungs I would now, as it's my turn to cup her face with my palms, and I hold my breath for the answer, hoping against hope my intuition is right. "Were you saving yourself for me, Aiza?"

She shrugs. I grin.

Her eyes fill with tears again. "Stupid, huh? I'm in love with you, Sheikh Rais. I think I always have been." The words I've longed for, yet never expected or dared aspire to hear.

"So why the fuck," I ask, wonderingly, "are you pushing me away?"

"I've just made it easy for you, haven't I?"

I don't understand and raise my eyebrow.

"You get your trophy wife who follows you around doe-eyed, waiting to be shown some affection..."

"Stop. Right. There." My sharp voice and command silences her. When her eyes meet mine again I've a full smile on my face. "We're on the same page, habiti. I've longed for you as long as you have for me. Six fucking years I've been waiting for my chance."

She rears back, her mouth dropping open. "Rais, what, what are you trying to say?"

I put it plainly, as my heart swells to bursting. "I don't want a trophy wife. Fuck, I could have had any I wanted over the many years since my wife died. I want the one woman I love. And that's you, Aiza. I was going to take you any way I could. If that meant having to have Hunter and Rami in our relationship, I would have agreed to it, just so you could be happy."

As her mouth gapes again, I take full advantage. My lips meet hers, at first just in a gentle caress as I try to assimilate that this beautiful woman wants me as much as I do her, that her longing for me matches mine. Placing her hand around the back of my head, she pulls me to her, her action deepening our kiss, making it more urgent. Now my cock comes back to life and starts to lengthen, and it's nigh on impossible to remember that tonight she'll be too sore. She arouses me like no one else.

Our mouths mate, there's no other word for it. Without breaking our connection, she moves closer, still straddling my lap, and now our bodies are touching. She lifts up and gives a little wince as she rests on her bare arse. The arse that's bearing my handprints.

I'd thought Hunter and Rami had more to offer than myself. I'd pushed myself in, inserted myself until we became a trio. I'd have a small part of her even if I couldn't have the whole package. Her declaration of love has changed everything, and all the possessiveness I'd tried to push down rises to the surface.

Suddenly my fingers entwine into her hair, and I pull her away, staring deep into those dark eyes that mirror my own. "You're mine. *Mine.*"

There's still a tear at the corner of her eye. I watch as it traverses the soft, smooth skin of her face.

"What's the matter, habiti?" She tries to pull out of my hold. I don't let her. "Speak to me, darling."

She swallows, and then starts to speak. "Rais, I can't believe this is happening." Me neither. A declaration of love, a confirmation that she reciprocates my own feelings was not what I'd expected tonight.

"I'll give you time if you need it."

Her fingers grasp my arms and tighten. "I don't need time to know it's you that I want."

"But?" I'm sure there's one coming. Despite how I want her to be only mine, I know her experiences, how she likes playing. It's her needs that are important. *I'll take her anyway I can.*

"Rais, I don't want anyone else." *Fuck.* Have my ears heard right? Are they hearing just what I want her to say? I need confirmation.

"You don't want Hunter and Rami to touch you?" My voice sounds hoarse. Again, I still as I wait for an answer, and loosen my grip on her hair, which allows her to shake her head.

Her eyes cast down, and although she mumbles, the words are clear. "If that had been the only way to have you…"

I snort a laugh. Her thoughts are so fucking close to mine. "Habiti, I'm yours, only yours, if that's what you want. And if you only want to be mine, so be it."

She leans close, her cheek resting against my bare chest. "What will Hunter and Rami say? They've got expectations…"

"Don't worry about that. You've given me the words now I'll make it happen. You're mine. Only mine. They'll have to accept it." If it means I pick up more scars to get my point over, so be it.

As she snuggles in closer I stroke her soft hair, grinning into the empty dungeon. *They've lost. I've won her.* She's an incredible prize.

CHAPTER 31
Aiza

I barely remember Rais carrying me out of the dungeon last night, mentally and physically exhausted. When I wake in the morning, finding myself held in his strong arms, everything that happened last night returns to my mind.

My face is flushed, embarrassed as I twist to face him, memories of the words we had spoken slamming back into me with full force. He doesn't give me a chance to speak, instead his mouth comes down onto mine, ignoring my morning breath. I give in to the sensation of being loved by the man I never thought would look twice at me. When he at last pulls away, I raise my hand and touch his face, tracing the scar over his eye.

"How did you get this, Rais?"

He yawns, then grins. "That was courtesy of Nijad. I think when he was about ten. He got the better of me."

"And this one?" I trace the slightly raised red line running over his torso. He flinches as my light touch tickles him. "Nijad and I had gone riding, came across jihadists trying to cross the border. There were six of them, two of us."

He's still here, so they must have come out the victors. "One got in a lucky strike. Nijad took him out."

For a moment I envy how close he is to my brother. Before I realise, if I marry him I'll be as close, if not closer. For the rest of my life. It seems too much like a dream come true. I need to confirm things said in the dead of the night. "Rais. Are you sure you want to marry me?"

He rolls onto his back, taking me with him. I try to ignore the very hard evidence of his arousal beneath me. "After my first wife died, I refused to bow to any pressure to marry anyone else. I enjoyed my freedom too much." He places a soft kiss to the top of my head. "There was this annoying little girl who tried to get Nijad to play with her. I thought she was cute."

"Cute?"

"Yeah. Cute. Then you started to grow up, I started to like the young girl you became. Then when you were eighteen and had developed into a woman, I started to notice other things about you, and that you weren't a pain anymore."

Giggling softly, I tell him, "I'm glad about that."

"You're right about when it started. It was that first trip to Switzerland. The first time we'd been alone together. My tribe started to hint again I should marry before I got too old. I always refused. I'd found the only woman I wanted to commit too, and if I couldn't have her, I'd stay a widower."

"Don't you need an heir?" Most tribes pass the leadership through the male line.

"Need, no. Want? With you? Yes." Placing a hand either side of my head, he gives me an explanation. "I've been grooming my nephew, Fuad, to take my place. He'll make an excellent leader."

Now I'm confused. "So if..." I break off, the thought is incredible. "*If* we had a son, wouldn't that put Fuad's nose out of joint?"

He laughs. "The Haimi have different rules of succession than the other tribes. We elect a leader on merit, not just on birth lines. If the successor isn't up to it, the tribe will vote in someone else."

"Wouldn't you want your son to follow in your footsteps?"

Now Rais surprises me. "It depends on what a child of mine wants. Being a warrior will be in his blood, but he might not want to take on the leadership. He might want to be doctor or a scientist instead."

If it was possible to love Rais anymore, that would seal it for me. He wouldn't pressure any child into a life they hadn't set their heart on.

Suddenly he turns me over and looms over me, making me remember I'm totally naked. His quick grin where I'm more used to seeing a scowl makes me relax. When he moves down, his mouth sucking one of my nipples, my back bows with the pleasure.

Both nipples are peaked and overly sensitive, and electricity is sparking, alighting my throbbing clit by the time he finishes his administrations. He moves down, kissing my stomach on the way, his short beard tickling my skin. When he reaches that so sensitive area between my legs I'm already on fire, ready to go over at the slightest touch. As he breathes over that hub of nerves my muscles go tight.

"Come for me."

His mouth suddenly sucking is all that it takes. I tense, my body going rigid as I attempt to process the wonderous feeling washing over me. I've never come so hard before as he continues to stimulate my clit. I forget to breathe, only taking in air when my lungs start to protest.

Before my muscles cease convulsing I feel his hard cock prodding my entrance, and then working in through my swollen tissue, momentarily wishing he hadn't somehow found the time to cover himself with latex, wanting to feel him skin on skin. Although I'm still sore, I welcome the burn as I yield to him, and the man I've loved for so long from afar invades me. My physical senses combing with my mental joy, and my legs come up to surround him, hooking my feet over his back, allowing him in even deeper.

He responds, starting to move faster, quickening his pace until he's hammering in, taking me up to the point of no return once again. I gasp as I tighten around him. He responds with a groan.

"Habiti," he shouts in warning.

Then I'm there, my back arching as incredible waves wash over me, my muscles clenching and almost trapping him inside.

With a roar he comes and empties himself inside me.

With his weight on his hands he lifts his body, staring down into my face, then planting a soft kiss against my lips. "You were worth all the time that I waited. I knew it would be good, but never imagined anything like this. And knowing I was your first? Habiti, that was a bonus I never expected."

I could have given my virginity a hundred times before. It's not as though I hadn't had offers, yet I'd never wanted to take that final step, though I've lost count of the hands and mouths I've had on me. Now I know why I'd always hesitated and what I told him in the dungeon last night was the truth. *I was waiting for him.*

When his now flaccid cock falls out of me, he signals I'm to stay put as he goes to dispose of the condom, then administers to me once again, getting a washcloth and cleaning me. His hand rests on my stomach.

"Would you mind carrying my child, habiti?"

Covering my hand with his own, I smile. "I'm marrying a caveman. Don't think you'll give me much choice."

He gives a half laugh, then looks serious. "You'll always have a choice, habiti."

I sit up and wrap my arms around him, not wanting to look into his face. "Why do you think I work with children, Rais?"

"Because you always wanted one of your own?" he suggests tentatively.

"With the right man." Now I realise I wouldn't have wanted a baby with anyone else.

"Fucking hope I'm the right man then, as the way you drain me dry, reckon we'll have results the first time I plant my seed in you."

There's a quivering feeling in my stomach as I realise I hope that he's right. I start to hope we can get married fast.

As I hear voices from the next room, and then someone trying the door handle, Rais closes his eyes, breathes deep, then opens them again. "Time to face the music I think, habiti."

Frowning, I start to pull away. "I need a quick shower first…"

He holds me back and speaks into my ear. "You go shower, I'll go front it out."

"We should do this together, Rais." I've never run from confrontation.

He shakes his head. "No, it's on me. I changed the rules…"

"We both did," I correct him.

"Nonetheless, you leave this to me." As I go to object once again, he continues, "You're my woman now, and it's my job to protect you. From anything. That includes saving you from two disappointed and potentially angry men." He stands, pulls me up, holds me for a second, then points me in the direction of the bathroom. "Go take your shower."

His voice, so full of authority, gets me moving, and I'm standing in the shower before I know it. As the water blasts down on me I can't stop worrying about Hunter and Rami's reaction, only hoping they accept with good grace that the best man won, and that there won't be bloodshed.

After I've dried and dressed, I brush out my long hair and return to the bedroom, unable to hear any sound coming from the living room. Taking a few deep breaths, I've got my hand on the door knob, summoning up the courage to open it, when a loud explosion rocks the palace.

Hesitating no longer, I pull open the door, bursting out in the living area, my heart beating so fast I feel faint. "What was that?"

Rais is on the phone, Hunter on the radio, Rami's nowhere in sight. The guards are running in as additional multiple explosions can be heard along with gunfire.

Coming to my side, Rais puts him arm around me, drawing me close, his presence immediately calming the worst of my anxiety. I try to listen. There's so many voices it's hard to get any information from the sharply barked questions.

"We need to get the princess to safety." Dharr makes himself heard. "The outer walls have been breached."

"The troops are holding the attack off for now."

There's a shattering sound of glass being broken. It's the windows to the suite. Something's thrown in and there's another smaller explosion which has my ears ringing. I can just make out Rais's shout.

"Out now!" Rais's arm is around me and half lifting me off my feet as he runs me through into the bedroom. We're quickly followed by Hunter, Dharr and the other three guards.

I'm starting to cough as Rais pushes me through the hidden door. Almost tumbling down the old worn stairway, I would have fallen were it not for the sheikh's strong arms holding me up, my heart pounding and my lungs heaving as whatever was thrown into the suite starts to choke me.

He leads us through the door leading down to the dungeon, stopping to lock it to buy us more time. I'm starting to panic. *Why's he leading us here? We'll be trapped. There's no way out...*

Suddenly I'm swept up into strong arms as Rais tears around the play equipment, coming to a stop at the opposite wall and puts me down. Pulling back a dresser which must be lighter than it looks, then pressing a code into a modern keypad that's appeared. As soon as the hidden door in front of us opens, an alarm beeps. Rais is quick to enter another code. He stands back until everyone else has passed, slides the dresser back into place, then the door, which I now notice is steel and heavy, closes behind us, and a final sequence of numbers is entered.

It's only then I realise we're descending again as we go after the others, and now we're moving fast down a long twisting corridor, our progress punctuated by bouts of coughing as we each try to rid ourselves of whatever it was we breathed into our lungs.

We've gone a long way when Hunter, in the lead, calls a halt. Listening, I can hear no footsteps behind us.

"They can't follow us," Rais tells them. "I changed the number sequence on the door when we came through. It's reinforced steel and will take them time to blast their way through." His hand comes under my chin and he examines my face, then continues grimly, "I spoke to Ghalib. Everything's prepared in case we had to resort to this option."

I'd worried about Hunter's reaction when Rais had told him about our change of plans. Any anger he had is put behind him, he's all business again now. "Thank fuck you did. Is he in position?"

"I checked before we left the suite. He'll be there ready and waiting, yes."

Waiting? Where and for what?

Rais then bends over and coughs. My own throat is tickling, and my head's still woozy.

"What was that?" I ask. "What was thrown through the windows?"

"Stun grenade. And a canister of gas."

"Poisonous?" My lungs are burning.

Hunter moves back to reassure me. "No, just meant to incapacitate. They want you alive, Princess."

Thank goodness I was with men who knew what to do. Talking of men, I suddenly remember what I'd forgotten in the confusion—Rami's missing.

"Where's Rami?" I ask urgently, worried we'd left him behind.

Hunter glances at Rais accusingly, then at me. "Rami didn't take Rais's announcement very well. He stormed off. I don't know where he went."

My hand covers my mouth. "He could be hurt…"

"It's you they're after," Rais reminds me.

I think of the prince, so gentle and kind. I might not want him as a husband, or, after being with Rais even in as part of a polyamorous relationship, I hate to think that he might be injured, worse, if he's dead. If he's killed on Amahadian soil, that would be disastrous for our diplomatic relationship with Alair. There's only one thing to do.

"We must go back." I'm determined.

"Princess…" Hunter looks worn. "On my part, I didn't take kindly to Rais's declaration, or the decision the two of you made. For now, we must put all that behind us. Rais will take you somewhere safe, and once you're away I'll go back and look for the prince." He glares at Rais. "That's my job. Yours is too look after Aiza."

Rais gives him a sharp nod. "We better keep moving. Ghalib will have had enough time."

Hunter agrees. "More than enough. Thanks to you, Rais, we were prepared for this eventuality."

They start moving forwards. Grabbing his hand, I pull Rais back. Though I'm anxious to get moving, this tunnel feels claustrophobic, and I need to know how much longer we'll be hiding down here. "Where are we going? What is the plan?"

"Only very few people know about the tunnels under the palace. There's three different exits. Ghalib's waiting at one. Even if they followed us down, it would be guesswork as to which escape route we're taking."

Dharr speaks for the first time. "Not even the guards were informed, Your Highness. So you can be assured they won't even think of following us."

With a direct attack on the palace, I don't think I can be assured of anything at all. There's clearly nothing else to do but get moving. I accept Rais's hand, refusing to be carried again. The effects of whatever we breathed in at last seem to be fading.

The tunnel seems to go on forever. We come to a fork, Rais unerringly takes the lefthand path. Now there's choice of three, and he heads straight on. I begin to feel we're never going to get out of here, when we come to a set of steps going up. Dharr takes the lead now, Rais holding me at the bottom as I watch the guard cautiously ascend.

"All clear," he calls out.

Not knowing where the stairs will lead me, I follow Rais up the worn steps, realising these passageways must have been hidden under the palace since ancient times. The harsh daylight of the morning sun hurts my eyes when we emerge, and I have to shade them and blink until I can focus properly.

I'm not given long to adjust. Ghalib appears, all business today, the friendly grandfather-like figure totally missing. "Sheikh."

Rais bows and returns the greeting.

"This way, Sheikh, Your Highness."

Now the light no longer hurts my eyes, I see Ghalib's tribesmen surrounding a monstrous looking helicopter. This is no friendly craft designed for transporting people from A to B, this is a serious looking military machine.

"Aiza, come." It's only when Rais tugs at my hand I realise I've stopped moving. "We've no time to dawdle."

"Hunter?"

"I'm going back to find Rami." Hunter takes my hand, squeezes it, then lets it drop. "We'll talk later."

Before I can worry that *later* might not come, I'm being helped into the helicopter, buckled into the front seat and putting on headphones which have been handed to me. Without delay, Rais sits behind me in a seat higher than mine. Feeling it's a strange arrangement, I crane my neck to look behind me, and watch him do some pre-flight checks, and then we're rising into the air.

As we go higher I look back below, seeing the destruction to the beautiful historic palace, which brings a sob to my throat, and, as the figure of Hunter disappears from sight, the sudden realisation that I may never see Rami or him again hits me, and tears start to fall from my eyes.

Rais stretches forwards and gives my shoulder a squeeze. "Stay strong, Aiza."

CHAPTER 32
Hunter

This isn't over yet, I think to myself as I allow myself to linger for a few seconds while watching the helicopter rise up into the air. *Not by a long shot.* Even had I been able to pilot the military craft myself, Rais is probably the best man to watch over her as they fly across the desert. Whether he's the best man to marry her, I'll pass on that for now. Whatever Rais thinks, I haven't given up. He thinks he's possessive... He hasn't seen possessiveness yet. I *will* take her away from him.

A throat clearing gets my attention. I pause a moment longer to watch the helicopter become just a small speck in the sky, then I turn to Ghalib. "Prince Rami is in the palace. We need to get him out."

"My job here is done, the princess is safely away. Now my men are at your disposal."

"What's been going on, Ghalib?" I'm out of touch. In the tunnels there'd been no radio or phone reception.

He wastes no time updating me. "It was a targeted attack. Explosions to get our attention and keep everyone busy while they tried to invade the royal suite from the air."

"How did they know that's where she'd be?" I wonder aloud. It's a fair assumption, but logically she could have been anywhere in the palace. "Did they make multiple entries?"

"No, just the one. Apart from a small task force who tried to distract us, they concentrated on entering the royal suite."

They knew she was there. At that particular time. As I follow Ghalib and his men back to the main palace entrance, thoughts are going fast through my mind. *Someone inside the palace must have been in contact with the terrorists.* And Rami had disappeared right before the attack. A coincidence? Did Rais just give him the excuse he'd been looking for? Had the perfect reason to be gone and out of danger just fallen into his lap?

No, It's impossible. Rami wouldn't turn on us like that. He'd been part of her rescue from the yacht. *He's been around far too much.* My sixth sense doesn't like it.

As we turn the corner, my eyes look into the now empty sky. *Rais had played a part in liberating her from Twafiq too.* Now he's flying Aiza away. What if he's a traitor, bought by Amir al-Fahri? If I suggested such a thing to Kadar he'd deny it in a flash. But unlike those closer to him, I can distance myself and look at things logicially. I've not been brought up alongside Rais, the most powerful of the desert sheikhs. What a coup if the terrorists have managed to get him onside. *What would that mean for*

Aiza? On that helicopter he's in charge of communications. If he's turned bad, there's no way to warn her.

A big part of me no longer trusts him. He changed his tune quickly enough when we gave into his demands to marry Aiza. Having had her, he no longer wants to share her. Though he gave no actual promise, he led us to presume he was on board with a four-way relationship. Then he went back on his word. *Has he now stolen her?*

My phone rings. I answer.

"Sheikh Nijad."

"As far as I know Rais has her safe." While I give him the reassurance about his sister, my eyes look at the empty sky again, a niggling doubt in my head.

"Where is he taking her?" As I repeat Nijad's question, I realise I don't know. In the rush to get her away I'd not asked. "Al Qur'ah, I assume."

"No, I don't know… Yeah, he might do that." Yes, Rais might take her into the desert to one of the tribal camps. I seethe with frustration. Turning, I hit my hand against the roughly hewn palace wall, hard enough to graze my knuckles. *Why hadn't I found out?*

"No, Sheikh. Prince Rami got separated from us…"

"Yes, I'm sure King Asad is concerned. I'm going to try and find him."

"Look, Nijad, I've been taken up with keeping Aiza safe. Let me get a status update and I'll get back to you. We've all got to be sensible about this. Best you stay in Al Qur'ah until we know more about the situation."

I end the call, cutting Nijad off in mid flow, and hope-fully having stopped his first impulse to come to Zalmā to see the damage done to his palace and take over operations himself. He'd only be one more royal we'd have to protect. Christ, this thing's all gone to hell in a handbasket. What a fuck up.

The palace grounds, normally so peaceful, full of aromatic flowering shrubs and well-maintained lawns, look very different now. Bodies lie strewn across the ground, odd body parts too. I see two arms and a leg which are clearly not from the same torso. Women are huddled, wailing and weeping, obviously evacuated from the interior. Our side has vanquished the intruders, and soldiers are guarding captives.

General Zaram is close by the doors. As I approach he gets my attention, asking urgently, "Well? Princess Aiza?"

"Sheikh Rais has taken her." I leave my statement ambiguous. Until someone proves I can trust the man, I'll be as suspicious of him as anyone else. "We got separated from Prince Rami."

The general nods grimly. "The prince is safe. He was with us when the explosions started." He nods towards the uninjured men being held captive. "We're going to start interrogating them now." To punctuate his words, he waves his hand in instruction for his men to start leading the prisoners away. "Do you want to come with us?"

Recognising Mustapha, Rais's lieutenant, the man whose methods of torture are renowned and certainly not condoned by the international community, I decline. I'll focus on working with the intelligence people instead. "I doubt if you'll get much from them. Foot soldiers I imagine."

"You might be right." He rubs at the tip of his nose. "Apart from the ones who attacked the royal suite directly, they weren't as well trained as our men. We'll give it a try. We've not much else to go on."

Leaving him to it, I walk inside the destroyed atrium, carefully picking my way through the glass that's fallen from the ceiling, my face twisting in disgust as I see one of Zaram's men lying dead, a shard obviously having pierced him. Others, injured, are still being led out of the ruined palace, and military engineers have already started cataloguing the damage and roping off areas which are unsafe to enter.

Luckily, the boardroom where we hold our meetings has survived unscathed. I enter to find a discussion in full swing.

"Hunter. The princess got away safe?"

Wishing I had a sign I could hold up rather than constantly answering the same question, I nod to Bertram, who I know is with the CIA.

"Bloody business this is." Kentwell, my boss at MI6 has come over.

"We got any more info?" I hate feeling out of the loop.

Kentwell sighs. "Going through all the palace staff and guards now. They were cleared on the official check. What we do know is the place was sealed up tighter than a gnat's arse, and everyone in the palace at the time of the attack had the right to be there."

"Hey, Hunter." Ryan gives me a slap to my back. "Good to see you're okay."

"You too, man. Casualties?"

He nods gravely. "Three household staff and five guards were killed in the explosions. Jibran lost a man in the fighting, and Zaram another couple more. Oh, and Seth took shrapnel to his arm. He's with the medics now. He'll be back as soon as his dressing's been done. Fifty or more walking wounded, none of them serious."

It could have been worse. Raising my hands in the air, I clap loudly to get everyone's attention. "Let's get seated and organised and thrash this thing out." Someone has to take charge, and Zaram hasn't reappeared yet.

When chairs have been pulled out and asses planted, I begin. "Sheikhs Nijad and Jasim are chomping at the bit to get down here. For now I've dissuaded them. I don't want any more lives put at risk until we get to the bottom of the attack today." I break off, and my eyes roam around the table. "Someone knew exactly where the princess was going to be at that precise moment in time."

"You're right, Hunter. That's our summation too. The bombs were meant to distract us, together with a half-hearted attempt to storm the palace. The real attack was from the helicopter."

"The men who entered Aiza's suite from the air were no unseasoned fighters. The attack was similar to one our SAS would carry out."

Bertram nods at his English counterpart. "Sure was. That's who Zaram needs to focus on interrogating. They'll be al-Fahri's trusted troops, not cannon fodder."

"And the ones best prepared not to talk," Kentwell replies.

So that's why Zaram's using Mustapha.

"The bombs were interesting," Ryan starts, and I raise my chin to give him permission to continue. "The main damage was caused by the three dropped from the air. There were four others, more localised explosions from devices planted in the palace."

"We got people looking for clues?"

"Yeah. Already found a timer. It's a sophisticated device."

I brush back my hair with both hands. "Did we not fucking check for bombs?"

"We did," Ryan confirms. "Last search was early yesterday morning. They must have been placed between then and the attack."

I catch his eye and hold it. "So that clearly shows it has to have been an inside job."

He doesn't flinch. "It does."

"Motherfucker," Bertram spits out.

Now it's the CIA man I focus my eyes on. It means we've failed—we being the intelligence community. Our ears to the ground and eyes open means we should have been forewarned. *Perhaps if I hadn't been so blasé in thinking we were safe and trying to get in Aiza's panties this wouldn't have gone down like it had.* Nevertheless, it did. The time for remonstration will have to come later. Now we've just got to get on and work with the hand we've been dealt.

"I've got two suspects in mind," I begin, causing all eyes to snap to me. "I've no evidence at all, but I don't think we can sweep this under the rug."

"Spit it out, man." Kentwell leans forwards to encourage me.

"Prince Rami." I pause for that to sink in. "It seems convenient how he was missing from the suite when the attack occurred."

Kentwell and Bertram exchange glances. It's the former who speaks. "Anything suspicious about him leaving?"

I can't tell him the truth. That he'd just heard from the man himself that Rais had just stolen Aiza away from him. That he'd become too emotional and overcome by loss and disappointment. Instead I shrug. "We had a slight disagreement."

"Was he behind that?"

Again, the truth. "No, it was instigated by Sheikh Rais."

Before we can say anything more there's a knock at the door, and one of General Zaram's senior officers enters. "Sorry to interrupt you. I thought you ought to know. The helicopter taking Sheikh Rais and Aiza has disappeared off the radar. We can't raise it by radio."

Fuck.

I dismiss him, he's clearly just the messenger. When the door closes behind him, I say what I would have thought was the unthinkable. "My second suspect is Sheikh Rais." My suggestion elicits an audible gasp, yet following on from the soldier's information, there's not as much shock as there'd otherwise have been.

"He got Rami out of the room. Reduced the men guarding her by one," Kentwell observes.

Ryan stands so quickly his chair topples and almost falls. He leans over, putting both palms flat on the table. "Not Sheikh Rais. Not in a million years. Rais would never betray his country like this. I *know* him. I've worked beside him…"

"People can turn. Or be turned," Bertram butts in drily. "Never say never."

Ryan gives him an incredulous look. "If he was working for al-Fahri I would know it. No man's worked harder than Sheikh Rais to get the oil field up and running. He's provided his tribespeople to ensure the pipeline is protected. It's not Rais. I'd stake my life on it."

Bertram gives him a pointed look. "Doesn't mean he can't be bought. Perhaps he's not getting what he wanted."

Last night he was.

Ryan looks angrier than I've ever seen him. "I trust Rais. Kadar trusts him. He'll have used his desert knowledge to get Aiza completely off the grid. If we can't find her, neither can al-Fahri. That makes more sense than what you're suggesting." He shakes his head, then scoffs. "Waste energy trying to find dirt on the sheikh? You'll be looking in the wrong direction, delaying looking for the real culprit and playing into the terrorist's hands."

Kentwell raises an eyebrow at me. "He's got a point."

While it's hard to accept my suspicions of Rais may be biased and come more from his seduction of the woman we're trying to find, Ryan, who's said a lot for a man who doesn't normally speak, has made sense. There's a sinking feeling inside of me. *I was meant to protect her. Now I've no fucking idea where she is.*

CHAPTER 33
Aiza

The inside of the military helicopter certainly isn't the luxury travel I'm used to. However, Rais expertly handles the controls of what he's told me is an Apache, one of the fastest helicopters in the world. To ease the tension, he told me I'm sitting in the gunner's seat, and have weapons at my disposal should I want to use them. I'm tempted to try out the machine gun.

Sitting up front, I have a perfect view of the scenery. As we fly over empty desert, leaving the palace far behind, my heart beat at last begins to slow. I'd been terrified by the explosions, the gun shots, reminding me all too much of my recent rescue from Twafiq's yacht and sending me back into a state of panic. My one comfort, if I could have chosen the man to be here with me, I couldn't have picked anyone better than the man now in the pilot's seat behind me. The man I've loved from afar for so long, and who I've agreed to marry. Casting a quick look over my shoulder, his eyes catch mine and he gives one of his rare, fleeting smiles. Making me recall, with something akin to amazement, that he said he'd wanted me as long as I've wanted him. For a second time he reaches and squeezes my shoulder before he returns his attention back to the controls.

Why, at eighteen I was attracted to him, I don't know. He's not handsome in a pretty-boy way, and there's something dark about his countenance, as though it's hiding something underneath. All my life it's been impossible to read him. Dark impassive eyes always scanning his surroundings, his body always tense, as though readying itself for a fight. At times he's reminded me of an unexploded bomb, just waiting for a trigger to set him off.

Last night he afforded me a glimpse of the man underneath the façade. Even now I can't be certain which is the real desert sheikh. The one who was so gentle and caring as he took my virginity? Or the stern and brutal man I've known all my life. Is it that he's an obvious bad boy that I'm completely enthralled?

Desert life isn't easy. While Kadar rules the country with diplomacy, taking, and keeping leadership over the fiercely independent desert sheikhs needs a strong man, someone who isn't afraid to demonstrate his strength. The rumours he's killed his opponents with his bare hands are whispered in the corridors of the palace of Amahad, and on just one meeting with Sheikh Rais, no one has difficulty believing them.

His prowess in battle during the border wars was unequalled. He'd left his military rank behind him when he returned to his desert home.

A sudden cold shiver runs through me. In the palace, surrounded by my guards and my friends, he hadn't seemed so overwhelming. Now I'm alone with him, it's a different matter. *I owe him my life.* But at what price? My lady parts throb in memory of last night, my heart swelling as I recall his declaration of love, while my head counsels caution. There's something thrilling, exhilarating, as well as frightening being alone with such a man as we fly over this desolate place.

Staring ahead I realise the helicopter's flying very close to the ground, Rais expertly navigating over the sand dune, the craft dipping and rising as we follow the profile of the land. "Why so low, Rais?"

"I'm keeping under the radar so no one can follow our route."

Biting my lip, I don't question him, though there's something unnerving about his answer. Okay, I wouldn't want al-Fahri to be able to track us, but our own military? They'll want to know where we've gone. "Rais, did you pre-arrange our route with General Zaram?"

"No," he says tersely, and I risk turning again and glance at his face. He breathes in deeply and lets out a sigh. "You should have been protected in the palace, Aiza. The damage from the explosions could have been contained, a direct attack thwarted. *Yet they came into your suite.*"

"That's where they'd expect me to be, surely?" It makes sense. It's where I spend a lot of my time.

"In your suite? The whole time? *At that precise moment?* You could have been anywhere in the palace, but you weren't."

My mouth purses, my mind focusing on the words he stressed.

"Princess, if I have to spell it out for you... There's a traitor in our midst. Someone who is in contact with al-Fahri and told him exactly where you were at that precise time."

My hand covers my mouth and I feel sick to my stomach. "Who, Rais? Who would want to see me captured?" *For torture or rape.*

"I don't know," he admits shortly. "Hence my reason for getting you away. Back at the palace they'll have come to the same assumption and will be trying to discover who betrayed you. For now, it's safest if *no one* knows where you are."

No one other than him. He handles the chopper with ease, flying as though he's one with the machine. His concentration purely on the task in hand. Which may explain why, since we've taken off, he's dropped the term of endearment he'd started using for me. I feel uneasy. For the first time since I met him, I wonder whether I'm right to trust him. *Can any man be bought...at the right price?*

A curt exclamation, and I see his hands tense on the controls. Seeing him staring straight ahead, I can't miss what he's noticed. *A sandstorm.*

"We can't fly into that." I might have lived mostly out of the country, but at heart I'm a girl of the desert.

"I'm aware of that. We've still got some miles to go. I'll fly as far as I can."

"Can we go around it? Or turn back?" It's a bad one from the look of it.

"We can't outfly it, and it appears to be quite extensive. No, we'll go on, then land if we're no longer able to fly."

In advance of the storm I can already feel the winds buffeting our small craft. "Go up, Rais," I warn him when the first particles of sand start to hit us and visibility is getting poor. "We're too low, we could fly into a dune…"

"I'm not risking us appearing on radar."

The thwack thwack of the helicopter blades starts sounding different. I look back at Rais in dismay as he starts to battle with the controls. He seems confident, so say nothing, just trust he knows what he's doing.

"We're going down now, Princess. Brace yourself, we might roll."

I check my harness is holding me tightly, and then reach up to the handhold.

"Hold on," he warns me again as I feel the dip as the helicopter descends to the ground. Visibility is almost nil now.

It's not a perfect landing, and as we hit the sand hard the harsh winds blow, and for a moment I think the craft will turn over. Rais cuts the engine. Before the rotors stop turning he's undone his harness, then reaches over to help me with mine. He gets out fast, and quickly comes around my side, holding out his arms to help me down. Reaching for my head scarf, he pulls it up over my face.

Immediately the sand is choking. Bowing my head, I turn my back, buffeted immediately by the strong winds. Then steadying arms come around me, leading me away from the helicopter. Once out of the helicopter's path, in case it should turn over, Rais crouches to the ground and pulls me to him, putting his larger body in the path of the wind, bracing himself to give me shelter.

It seems to last for hours. In reality it's only minutes before the sandstorm passes. Quickly the winds become lighter, the sun again beaming down from a clear blue sky. Analysing it's position, I know it's midday and have a new concern. *I'm going to fry out here.*

As the sound of the storm dies, Rais unwraps himself from me and goes to look at the helicopter. Soon he's shaking his head.

"Will it fly?"

"Not until the air intake is cleaned."

As I expected, but not as I'd hoped, it's on foot from here. "Where are we going, Rais?"

With his hand still hovering over the hot metal, he turns and speaks over his shoulder. *"Alwadi Aljameel."*

The Beautiful Valley, I quickly translate. I've heard about it from Cara, yet have never seen it myself. A picturesque place in the mountains where a river reappears for a short distance, leading to green grass and trees in an otherwise sparse desert. Nijad had taken her there shortly after their wedding. A romantic retreat. Water and shelter from the sun, nothing could sound more wonderful in this heat.

A look at my companion's face suggests he hasn't got romance on his mind. Ignoring me, he pulls a satellite phone out of his pocket and places a quick call. He's giving what sounds like coordinates.

"Who are you talking to, Rais?" I'm hoping he's making contact with Zaram.

"My men," he answers economically.

"Can we get word to the palace?"

"No. I told you before, I don't know who we can trust. Come. We need to get moving." He looks up into the sky. "The helicopter will be easy to find, we need to put distance between it and us."

"Rais…" I'm already sweating, and I haven't even taken a step.

"Princess. You must do this."

He sounds so distant. My lover who held me so tenderly through the night seems to have completely disappeared. *He's focus is on getting me to safety. But…* "Is this what it's going to be like?" I snap.

"What?"

"Our married life? You barking orders and expecting me to obey them?" That's not the kind of man I want.

Suddenly he's in front of me. "Princess, how much do I need to explain? There was an attempt on your life today. You can bet even now al-Fahri has men searching for us.

He'll use all the technology he has at his disposal. My duty, as your future husband and as your subject, is to protect you and keep you safe. Right now I can't afford the time to baby you."

"Baby me?" My voice rises in disgust at his term. "I'm asking for you to treat me like an equal."

He raises his eyes to the heavens as though seeking strength from Allah, and then lowers them to me once again. "Princess, my only concern is for your safety. Everything else must take second place. And that means we have to start walking now."

Huffing, knowing I've no other option, I start making my feet move, one in front of the other, grateful my trainers that I'd worn today are at least protecting me from the hot sand. Pulling my headscarf up over my head, I do what I can to protect myself from the harsh rays of the sun, starting to wonder whether I really know this stranger walking beside me.

His hand reaches out and takes mine, pulls me to a stop and turns me around to face him. Placing his fingers against my forehead, he tries to smooth my worry lines there. "Habiti, I'm not being fair to you, am I?" He shakes his head in despair. "I've never had a relationship with a woman I love. You're going to have to put up with my overbearing ways while I'm learning how to do this."

As I go to speak, his fingers move down and cover my mouth.

"That doesn't mean you can't call me out on it. At the moment, getting you somewhere safe is my number one priority. Here," he waves his free hand around at the nothing that surrounds us, "I'm in my element, and you not in yours. You have to trust me to do what's best for you."

I remember his only attempt at a relationship was an arranged marriage that only lasted less than a year. I've less experience than him. Not wanting to get involved is part of the reason I've got my needs fulfilled at clubs. We're both new to this and feeling our way. As the circumstances are not the best to start out, I decide to cut him some slack.

"Which way?"

That rare smile passes over his face again as he points. "We'll go straight in that direction, skirting the dunes where we can."

Then I ask the question I don't really want the answer to. "How far?"

Leaning forwards, he places a soft kiss on my lips. "Just keep putting one foot in front of the other, Princess."

Wondering how he knows where he's going when the only thing to guide us is the sun, I do what he says.

Quickly overheating, I try to put all other thoughts out of my mind than getting to our destination, that beautiful valley, where, if I remember correctly, Cara said there was a pool where I'll be able to swim and cool off.

We don't waste energy talking, just plod onwards and onwards again. After a while Rais stops and takes a water bottle out of the pack he'd liberated from the helicopter, and I gratefully gulp down mouthfuls of the warm but welcome refreshment, and then it's on we go again.

The sun beats down relentlessly, the dunes not high enough to give any shade. At first I think I must be seeing a mirage when in the distance I see horses appearing. I don't draw attention to what I believe my delirious mind is conjuring up. As they come closer, I realise it's not my imagination, and I pull Rais's sleeve, worrying whether their friend or foe.

Seeing the concerned look on my face, Rais reassures me. "My men."

They're approaching so fast, there's no need for us to continuing walking. Soon desert warriors are surrounding us, foaming horses kicking up sand. A rider comes up with the reins of a free horse in his hands. Taking the reins from him, Rais jumps astride and holds out his hand.

"You could have brought one for me," I tell him, laughing, suddenly lighthearted that we've been rescued. Then I take his hand and jump up behind him, my hands going around his back.

CHAPTER 34
Rami

I have no idea what you are talking about." Imperiously I stare at Hunter, not understanding the accusation he'd just thrown my way. "I had absolutely nothing to do with the raid on the palace, and I can't understand why you think that I would."

Hunter's gaze is unflinching. "You conveniently left the suite just before the attack."

My eyes go to Hunter's colleagues, Ryan and Seth, who are standing by the door impassively with their arms folded. Seth has a bandage on his left bicep. I then look back at Hunter and frown. Surely he doesn't want to go into this in front of his colleagues? From the expression on his face, it appears he thinks there's nothing to hide. I decide to be as discreet as I can.

"As you know, Hunter, I had just been turned down by Aiza. I came here expecting her to become my wife, when instead it seems she has chosen to throw her lot in with the desert sheikh." Still enraged at the events of the morning, I can't bring myself to say his name. "In the circumstances, you of all people should understand my disappointment, and that I needed to get away and put distance between her and myself until I'd come to terms with the new situation." Personally, I doubt I ever will. I'd had my dreams so tantalisingly close to being achieved, only to have them swept away.

"You left Aiza when you should have been protecting her?" Ryan sounds critical, and put that way, perhaps he's right to be.

"I didn't leave her at risk. Hunter and Rais were there, as well as the guards outside."

"I still think it was suspicious." Hunter's not giving me a chance to explain. "A prince doesn't run in such circumstances."

I stand, drawing myself up to my full height. "Believe what you want. This prince just wanted to get away. I couldn't trust myself to speak to her at that moment, and if I stayed longer in Rais's presence, I would have tried to kill him. So I went to see General Zaram and catch up with the latest information."

"And to the part of the palace that survived unscathed."

Frustrated, I turn on him. "What do you want me to say, Hunter? That Alair's secretly working with al-Fahri to sabotage the oil fields that will bring riches to our country?"

He shakes his head. "I don't believe Alair had anything to do with it. However, I do understand the dissatisfaction that comes with being a spare. Fuck, I saw it in Jasim often enough. Your brother is heir to the throne. When he marries and produces a son, you'll be completely surplus to requirements. You might be setting yourself up to get your satisfaction in other ways."

"By working with al-Fahri?" I'm shouting now, frustrated I'm unable to get through to him. Marching across the room, I lean over him, my knuckles to the table. "I *love* Aiza. What I feel for her doesn't go away just like that." Clicking my fingers I emphasise my point. "Even if she has thrown herself at that...that savage." I spin on my heels, quickly turning away. Then just as quickly going back again. "Just where has Rais taken her? What's the latest on her location?"

Now I've gone on the offensive, Hunter's eyes open wide as I continue. "What has got a fucking stink to it is that Rais declares undying love for her out of the blue and decides to make her his wife. *Then* the palace is attacked, and he's the one who knows the secret tunnels and spirits her away in a helicopter that we lose track of shortly after takeoff." I thump my fist down onto the table, making the jug and glasses on it jump. "Have you considered for one second that Rais might be acting for al-Fahri? That he might even now be delivering her into his clutches?" One glance at his face shows that he has. I nod. "So why are you wasting time questioning me? *I'm* still here, and Aiza is not. Maybe we should be trying to find her instead of wasting time."

"I'd stake my reputation on Rais being innocent," Ryan tells me with a sneer. "He'd not do anything to hurt the royal family. He'd give his life for any of them, and that includes Aiza."

I swing around. "You're hung up on me being a second son, surplus to requirements. That I've got a chip on my shoulder. That equally applies to Rais. Rais is an ambitious man, a blind man could see it. He holds the title of leader of the desert sheikhs, yet he's not *the* desert sheikh, is he? That's Nijad's role, even though Rais uses it for his own. What if *he's* fed up with his lack of opportunities?" I'm infuriated I can't seem to get through to these men.

Hunter's fingers are pinching the bridge of his nose. When I go to press my case further, he waves me down. "Give me a moment to think."

Mumbling, "You're wasting time," I resume my pacing. *Aiza, where are you? Are you safe?* When we find her, I'm going to redouble my efforts. Until Rais's ring's on her finger, I'm not going to give up. She was mine, everyone knew it. If Rais has harmed one hair on her head he'll die, and as painfully as I can make it.

At last Hunter rises and fixes me with a glare. "I don't trust you, Rami. And I don't trust Rais. Fuck, right now I trust no one except for my colleagues who've nothing to gain." He glances at Ryan. "Rais's knowledge of the palace is longstanding, yet the fact he knew which tunnel to take, and knowing the keycode does make him a suspect. I hear what you say, but someone had to plan this. Someone who could communicate with al-Fahri and get the message to him. We can't rule anybody out."

"What about the guards?" Seth speaks for the first time.

"The head guards were all old-timers, brought back for one purpose, to keep the princess safe. Their men were all handpicked," Ryan informs his colleague. "To be certain, Cara's rechecking their backgrounds."

"The guards were handpicked by Rais." Seth sends a look of apology towards his colleague. "But then, lots of people knew where she was. It could be one of the palace servants who brought breakfast. Hell, the chef who prepared it…"

"It could be anyone," Hunter says patiently. "Which is why we're looking into them all. Again." He brushes back that lock of hair which seems to fall constantly over his forehead. "Look, let's go and see what the latest is, what General Zaram has found. And I want a word with Ghalib, see if he knows where Rais was headed." He gives me a stern glance. "You, Rami, you're coming with us. I want my eye on you at all times."

As there's nothing I'd rather be doing, I've no problem with that. Checking, I ask him, "As friend or foe?"

Hunter snorts. "That remains to be seen."

Hunter leads the way, I follow. Ryan and Seth at my heels show me I'm far from out of the woods yet. As the Grade A man pushes the door to the board room open, General Zaram nods at us. It's easy to see how troubled he looks.

"What's the latest?" Hunter wastes no time asking.

Zaram shrugs. "The helicopter hasn't made it to Al Qur'ah. Nor anywhere else, it would seem."

Bertram raises his hand to get our attention. "It's a heavily armoured helicopter. Difficult to shoot down, and the sheikh would be able to protect himself from attack. It was one of our most sophisticated helicopters."

"With what range?" Hunter asks as he pulls out a seat.

"Two five seven nautical miles. That's just under three hundred miles on the ground."

Hunter's not looking pleased. "They could be over the border in Ezirad or Alair."

"Exactly," Zaram agrees. "Qudamah has all his airports on alert..."

"A helicopter doesn't need a fucking airport," Hunter snarls. "Nor even a helipad. We're looking for a needle in a fucking haystack." He looks over at Ghalib, who doesn't look as concerned as the rest of us. "Did Sheikh Rais mention where he was taking her?"

"No, he did not. And I didn't ask him."

"Why the fuck not?" Hunter looks like he's going to explode.

Ghalib suddenly leans forwards, his hands clenched in front of him. "Because I know the sheikh will only have Princess Aiza's best interests at heart. There's already been one leak of information, who knows who could have over-heard if he'd told me? I didn't want to know, so I didn't ask him. One thing I'm certain of is that she'll be safe."

"Are you sure of that, Sheikh?" Hunter's drawl comes to the fore. Then he snaps. "You're staking Aiza's life on it. Rais could be compromised in some way."

All at once the doors to the conference room burst open. Nijad and Jasim have arrived, both men looking near identical with matching expressions on their faces. Hunter's shaking his head. Something tells me he isn't happy at their appearance.

"Update," Nijad barks almost before he's cleared the doorway. He might be the younger sheikh by eighteen months, but his three-year banishment to the desert has sharpened him more than his brother, who'd spent that time in a more civilised London.

Neither brother look happy when they hear there's nothing to tell them, that no progress has been made.

"Are the drones up?" Nijad gives a satisfied nod when he's told that they are.

"Weather reports?" Jasim proves he's not entirely clueless in this environment.

"Sandstorm about a hundred miles east."

Both brothers exchange looks. "Get surveillance up in its path. Have we got satellite footage?"

"Ben's examining that back in London."

A servant arrives carrying a fresh refill of coffee, and pastries are put on the table. I take one aimlessly, more to give my hands something to do rather than satisfying any real desire to eat.

"Have men checked his settlement?" No one's mentioned that yet. From the derisive looks thrown at me, I have to concede that would have been the first place they looked.

Having taken a seat, Nijad pulls a coffee cup towards him and fills it. "The objective of Aiza coming to the palace was twofold. One to keep her safe," his scowl shows what he thinks of how that turned out, "and secondly, to catch Amir al-Fahri."

"We've spectacularly failed in the first, Brother," Jasim butts in, then his eyebrow rises. "What's your thinking, Ni?"

"I'm thinking Rais doesn't give up. He's always got a plan B."

I notice Hunter's sideways look at me and know what he's thinking. Is Rais's plan to protect Aiza, or to betray her?

Zaram's watching the two sheikhs carefully. "What, from your knowledge of Rais, would be his main objective?"

"Rais wouldn't see Aiza harmed, however," Nijad's face twists, "the prosperity of Amahad relies on the success of the oil endeavour. And the biggest threat to that is al-Fahri."

Now Hunter's eyes are wide open as he looks at me. "You say there's less chance of Rais having sold out to the terrorists, but a greater chance he'll use Aiza as bait?"

Nijad and Jasim look at each other, then give identical shrugs. Jasim leaves the floor to Nijad. "The desert is a harsh place, Zaram. You know that. Rais takes his responsibilities very seriously."

"Aiza could become collateral damage?"

Another shrug from the princes. "I know Rais, he'd do anything to protect her. But in ensuring her future safety, he might take risks."

"Then it's imperative we find them." From what I've heard, there's no chance I'm going to let Rais marry Aiza. He might have a plan B, I've reverted to my plan A. She's going to marry me, even if I have to drag her kicking and screaming off into the sunset.

CHAPTER 35
Aiza

R ais's tribesmen waste no time getting underway. As soon as I've secured my hands around his waist, Rais presses his heels into the side of the horse and it leaps forwards. Making his way to the front, Rais squeezes his legs once again and the horse breaks into a trot, and then a canter. When its flanks start heaving, Rais pulls on the reins and his horse and the horde behind us drop to a walk in deference to the heat of the sun.

The horses plod on, their footfalls monotonous. I try and digest everything that's happened over the last twenty-four hours. My mind drifts. I feel safe here, up behind Rais, protected by his warriors. As my tension seeps away, I grow sleepy. A sudden tug on my arms has me waking.

"Sit up in front of me. You can sleep then, Princess, I'll hold you."

"I'm alright," I reply, shaking my head to clear it. "How far do we have to go, Rais." Looking ahead I see a mountain range coming closer. The sight brings hope that we're nearing our journey's end.

"Not too far. It won't be long until we start to climb."

It isn't. The horses prick up their ears and put more spring in their steps, presumably as they smell water and grazing ahead. We seem to be approaching solid rock, then as we start to climb towards it, a cleft appears, and behind that, a path winding up a steep-sided ledge. I eye the drop-off warily, one false step and you wouldn't have much of a chance. Rais is relaxed and confident, so I rest my head on his shoulder, trusting that he'll keep me safe.

It's a fair distance. When we reach the plateau of the valley, the trek's been worth it. Tapping his shoulder, Rais stops the horse and lets me slide to the ground. I stand, on grass, looking around me in wonder. The sounds of trickling water reach me, and I can't stop myself going to explore this unexpected slice of paradise in the middle of the desert where an underground river emerges for a short while to keep the valley flourishing.

"It's beautiful, isn't it?" Rais had also dismounted, passing the reins of his horse to the rider behind. He stands, his front to my back, and puts his arms around me.

"Gorgeous," I agree. "Is that the pool Cara told me about?" I pull away and move forwards, looking with delight at the calm rock pool, large enough for swimming.

Rais moves his men on to give us some privacy. "You want to take a dip?"

That sounds glorious after our long walk and ride. "Your men?"

"Are discreet. Go ahead. They'll stay well out of the way."

Needing no more encouragement, I unwrap my headscarf then slip my tunic off over my head. Bending, I untie my shoes and kick them off. Finally, I step out of the light linen trousers I've been wearing, then lacking the patience to delay any longer, dip my toe into the water that's cooler than I expected it. Then I remember that the river comes up from beneath the mountains.

I step in deeper, until I'm up to my waist, my hands in the water moving it gently back and forth. A sudden splash throws water all over me. Rais, stripped naked, has simply dove in. He comes up with a quick shake of his head, which sends more water over me.

"Two can play at that game." I laugh, filling my cupped hands and retaliating.

I shouldn't have teased a desert sheikh. He stalks towards me, water parted by his strong thighs, reaches for my hand and tugs me in. Off balance, I slip right under. I suppose it would look odd, a tribal warrior and princess having a water fight in an oasis in the middle of the desert, though being playful with him feels so right. For the first time in hours my worries slip away. I feel carefree and happy.

As Rais swims, I tread water, watching the man who's fired my fantasies for such a long time, hardly able to believe that he's mine. His body is muscular without an ounce of fat, his waist narrow, tapering down to slim, powerful hips, making me dampen with arousal as I remember those loins powering into me last night. As I look down into the crystal-clear water, I see his cock, magnificent and aroused, and I shiver, then lick my lips.

He stands, the water up to his shoulders, and this time, as he stalks me, there's different intent in his eyes.

"Keep doing that, and I'll forget I've got no condom with me."

"Doing what?" I reply innocently, my tongue coming out to moisten my lips once again. *I shouldn't encourage him.* But he did propose to me, and in the heat of the night I accepted. Would the risk be so dreadful if I got pregnant with this man's child?

He's moving slowly, giving me every chance to back away. The more I imagine his seed shooting up inside me, the more my nipples peak and my clit throbs. *I must be mad.* Must have lost my mind somewhere along the way. I'm not going to say no.

"One last chance. One last warning, Princess."

I stand my ground, conveying my decision by the fact I haven't moved.

He closes the gap between us, his mouth crashing down on mine, his hand going behind my head, anchoring me to him, his rock-hard cock digging into the soft flesh of my stomach. "I can't wait," he tells me. Then without warning, places my hands on his shoulders, moving swiftly to places his under my arse and lifts me. I yelp and grab onto him for balance.

Shoving my underwear aside, his cock prods my opening, a growl comes from his throat as he realises I'm more than ready for him, and with one hard thrust he pushes inside.

"Fuck me," I cry. Whether in shock or as an instruction, I'm not sure myself.

He takes it as the latter, growling and surging up inside me, starting a rhythm my body immediately responds to.

My fingernails are digging into his skin, but he makes no complaint. Just starts thrusting in harder, water in the pool sloshing around us, the waves we're making matching those in my clenching stomach.

"Rais, *Rais.*" I'm shouting his name without knowing why, not thinking anything other than how close I am. My muscles start squeezing him, my body shaking. I'm so close... He moves, changing the angle, taking me right to the edge.

Supporting me with one strong hand, the other moves around to my clit. He rubs it, teases it, then there's that pinch and his mouth takes mine and catches my scream.

Then he draws back. "Aiza," he snarls as he releases his cum inside me, pumping and pumping as though he doesn't want to waste a single drop.

He continues to hold me. Thinking it must be straining him, I try to put my legs down. He forces me to keep them wrapped around him. "You're mine," he tells me, repeating the words of last night.

"I'm yours," I tell him, my voice sounding shy. Letting a man come inside me seems even more intimate than letting him inside my body when he's protected.

We kiss again, with less urgency this time. Still without letting me go, again he frees one hand and releases my breasts from the confines of the bra, then lowers his head and lavishes attention on first one, then the other. As he uses his teeth to nip, a new zing of arousal shoots to my clit, which starts throbbing again. As my internal muscles twitch, I can feel him swelling inside me.

Again? So fast?

"Can't get enough of you. The feeling of being inside you, skin to skin. It's the best fucking feeling in the world. See what you do to me, Aiza?" He throws back his head as he starts moving again, slow slides in and out as he hardens, his features set as if in concentration, his eyes squeezed shut. Then he quickens his pace until he starts hammering.

I don't need extra stimulation. Automatically I clench down on his cock as I come once again, an orgasm which seems neverending, extended by the relentless pounding inside. As my body twitches uncontrollably, I feel another building again, and then I'm coming for a third time as he wrings every possible response from me. I don't think I've anything more to give, then a fourth, albeitly weaker orgasm has me taking him with me.

My head falls against his shoulder. I'm exhausted and drained. As he slips out of me, he carries me back to the bank, gets out while still holding me, and puts me down on the grass. Then he collapses beside me, his arm flung up over his eyes, his chest heaving as much as my own.

When I can breathe something akin to normal, I lean over, placing a kiss to his chest, then curl up onto him, his free arm pulling me into his side.

"I love you," I tell him sleepily.

"I know you do," he replies. It wasn't the answer I was looking for, but then, he just demonstrated what he felt for me in the pool.

It's not long until the sun dries us. He sits up, pushing me towards my clothes. "Get dressed, Aiza."

His tone sounds odd, his voice different. But then, perhaps it's back to business again. He'll have to find out what's happening back at the palace. They must have communications here somewhere. Of course, he used his satellite phone to summon his men. A call to the general in Zalmā and we'll find out what we need to do next.

As I look around I realise I wouldn't mind staying in this magical place a little longer.

A jangling of bridles makes me look around, and I see a man appear with two horses. A blush comes to my face as I realise we hadn't been totally alone.

Rais walks over and thanks the man, then leads the horses over. "Do you need help mounting, Aiza?"

It had been Rais who taught me to ride, a skill I've never lost. I shake my head, and bouncing a couple of times on my left leg, throw my right over the saddle, gathering up the ornate reins in one hand.

Rais keeps a hold of them. He looks up and into my eyes and says intently, "Everything I do, I do for Amahad."

Then with that enigmatic statement that I don't know how to respond to, he releases my reins and mounts his own horse, squeezing his heels and leading the way through the valley. As the path is only single track, I can't move alongside him, so any questions I want to ask will have to wait.

A couple of disgruntled neighs get my attention as we pass a coral where horses are grazing, two having a slight difference of opinion. Otherwise the peace of this valley is undisturbed except for the odd voice I hear. Soon we're approaching a huge black tent which has seen better days. As the path's widened a little, I pull up next to Rais.

"Is that Nijad's tent?" I ask in wonder. It looks like it could have been here a couple of years.

"Yes. No one bothered to remove it. Little bit battered and faded now, though still serviceable enough inside." Again I remember Cara telling me of how romantic Nijad had been here in the beautiful valley. At the time I couldn't credit my brother being as she'd described him, so tender and starry-eyed, yet apparently he was. There's no doubt over the past three years he's definitely changed. No one could be sceptical of the love they share with each other. Looking at Rais, I hope we get to the same stage. Two halves of a whole.

We dismount. Two of his men come to take the horses, and I pause for some reason, reluctant to go into the tent even if it means I'll be in the shade. I'm entranced by this valley, content after our lovemaking, relishing the relaxed feeling after everything that happened earlier today. The peace I feel here making the fear I'd felt earlier seem a long way behind me.

"You coming inside?" Rais asks, clearing his throat as his voice comes out hoarse.

"Just enjoying the scenery." Turning, I place my hands on his robes and raise my face, wanting to feel his lips on mine, my beautiful man in this beautiful place.

He indulges me, but only briefly, then turns me, and with his hand firmly in the middle of my back, pushes me through the tent flap.

"I expected you before now." It's a stranger's voice. Harsh and stern.

"We made a slight detour. The princess wanted to refresh herself."

Who is it?

"I began to think you were having second thoughts, Sheikh." Slowly a man appears out of the shadows, his cruel countenance has me stepping back, bringing me up against Rais. Rais's hands grip my upper arms, forcefully, stopping my retreat.

"I have no second thoughts. This is the right thing to do for Amahad."

As he approaches, I notice he's not as tall as Rais, although far more heavyset. He wears a headdress, which doesn't hide his small eyes, nor the bushy beard masking his chin. He's Arab, but I can't tell anything more, except that he speaks English with a perfect accent.

He nods quickly at the sheikh behind me, then speaks to him while keeping his eyes on me. "It will take years for you to see any profits from the oil revenue. My money will allow you to kickstart the projects you want to see completed for the tribes. New schools and medical facilities. A lot of good for your people will come from what you are doing here today."

What is Rais doing? I grow cold as things start to fall into place. Those things that had previously made me feel uneasy all start to add up.

"Ah, Princess. I see you are putting two and two together. Let me introduce myself. My name is Amir al-Fahri. I am very pleased to make your acquaintance in person today."

I can't stop myself. This man is responsible for so many deaths worldwide, my hand seems to move of its own volition as I wrench my arm out of Rais's firm grasp and slap the terrorist across his face.

It's no match for the one he gives back. I would have fallen to the floor if Rais hadn't been holding me. I wait for Rais to protest, to protect me. Apart from a slight tightening of his grip, as he pulls me back and his hands take a more secure hold, he says nothing in my defence. Instead he says harshly, "Can we get on with this?"

"All in good time." Amir continues walking around me, as if eyeing up a prized camel. "I wasn't sure if you'd go through with this, Sheikh. You've gone up in my estimation."

"I got you into the palace, didn't I? And got her out without raising suspicion."

I turn, look at the person I'd trusted, respected all my life and had let down my barriers and admitted I loved him. I put as much hatred into my expression as I can. Then I spit in his face.

CHAPTER 36
Hunter

I'm frustrated as hell and going out of my mind with worry. We've still no reports of where the helicopter landed, whether it crashed in the sandstorm, or of where Rais and Aiza might be.

Mustapha has found himself on the other end of interrogation techniques when we try to discover whether Rais had divulged his plans. If he knows, so far he hasn't told. Nazam sent people to Rais's settlement, however there's been no positive news from there. The desert sheikh seems to have disappeared into thin air. All we know is that his elite team of men has also disappeared, together with his current heir and successor, his nephew, Fuad.

I pause in my pacing and rasp, "What we've got to consider, Nijad, is whether Rais is attempting a coup."

Nijad's hand slashes through the air before I've even completed my sentence. "Rais wouldn't do that. I'd trust him with my life, Cara's life, and that of my daughter, Zorah."

"Ni's right." Jasim backs up his brother. "Nothing Rais has ever said or done leads me to believe he'd act against the good of Amahad, and that includes Aiza."

Ghalib is deep in conversation with Jibran, Sofian and Khalef. After a moment he speaks louder, sending an accusing look my way. "Sheikh Rais has never given any indication he'd turn traitor."

Why can't they see that any man could sell his soul for the right price? My hands clench and unclench, rage bubbling up through me as I try to find something, *anything*, that will persuade them I'm right. Rais has turned on his own people. I'm certain of it. I prepare to give them the one piece of news they haven't yet heard, standing to deliver it. "The night before last, Aiza told us that she was a virgin."

"No way… Innocent? Aiza?"

I know what he's thinking. Hell, I had thought the same way myself. "Sure, Jasim, she's into BDSM, and she certainly played. Though she's never allowed her subs to go all the way. She was saving herself." As Nijad and Jasim exchange raised eyebrows, I continue. "Last night Rais made sure to change her status. And asked her to marry him. She agreed."

"I still don't believe it." Jibran's shaking his head. "The princess is a beautiful woman. I don't blame Rais for making a move."

Jasim's staring at me and raises his hand to Jibran. "He could have made his move anytime over the past six years, since she turned eighteen."

By my side Rami growls. "Everyone knows she was promised to me. He shouldn't have touched her."

"By our dead father," Nijad snarls. "Not the present emir. If Aiza wants to marry Rais, there's nothing stopping her, and I for one would be pleased."

"Kadar would be too. It would strengthen the union with the southern desert. Aiza could do much good work here." Jasim, now having absorbed the news, seems quite happy.

They're getting off track. "Why now? Why this timing?" It doesn't make sense to me. "As you said, Jasim, he needn't have waited. He could have asked her to marry him at any time."

Jasim shrugs. "Perhaps she was more interested in marriage now. She'll have gained a protector in Rais. Maybe it was the right time for him to ask her."

Nijad's eyeing me cautiously. "Did he force her?"

Guiltily I think that we all did in some way. Almost pushed them together. "She seemed happy enough with the arrangement." I frown as I remember her and Rais fighting, and would give my eyeteeth to know what that was about. Things had happened so fast this morning, I hadn't had a chance to ask.

Sofian shakes his head. "That goes against him being a traitor. If he was going to kidnap her for al-Fahri, he'd have devalued her in his eyes."

There's general agreement, and I slam my fist on the table. "Perhaps he took his chance, as he knew she'd disappear and he'd never get it again. Perhaps that was part of the bargain." Straightening up, I run my hands through my hair. "How the fuck do I know what he was thinking? Look at the facts. He's taken her with him, and now they've both disappeared."

Khalef's looking bemused. "It makes more sense to me that he loves her and wants to protect her. Otherwise, why did he take her?"

"He took her to get her out of the palace," Ghalib explains patiently. "He had it set up in case there was a direct attack on her. It's lucky he did. She might have been trapped and hurt. Or kidnapped."

"No, she wouldn't." Zaram comes into the conversation and contradicts. "If she'd have run out of the suite her guards would have protected her. It didn't take long to get the palace back under our control. The attacking force was too small to overpower us."

"They might not have been expecting us to be so well prepared. After all, that was the idea of bringing her here. To take Amir al-Fahri if he turned up."

Bertram and Kentwell have walked in while Zaram was speaking.

"But he didn't turn up," Bertram says. "The soldiers he sent were far from the cream of the crop. Unseasoned fighters who know nothing of battle at all. If that was his advance party, then he fucked up. And that's not something he's known for."

"His soldiers are quite disgruntled now," Kentwell observes. "They've given up all the information they have, which doesn't amount to anything. They are paid mercenaries, and not good ones at that. They didn't even know who the paymaster was."

"Except for those that entered the royal suite." I'd seen for myself, they were well trained.

"Unfortunately they can't give up any secrets. They're all dead. Zaki and his guards made certain of that."

I return to the table and retake my seat. "Sheikhs, General. I know considering Rais has turned is thinking the unthinkable, but nothing else adds up. He devised an escape route with a two-seater helicopter ensuring nobody else would be able to travel with them. That route was called into use when there was an attack on the palace which didn't have the slightest chance of success, but at the time when someone close to her knew where she was. Now we don't know where he is, or, more to the point, where Aiza is. Or what's fucking happening to her." Again, I bring a hand down heavily on the table. "In my opinion we must agree we've got to treat him as the enemy, at least for now. I'd put top dollar that he'll lead us straight to Amir al-Fahri."

Zaram's staring at me. It's hard to tell whether he's with me or not until he shakes his head and glances across at Nijad and Jasim. "I'm sorry, sheikhs, I wouldn't be taking that bet. Hunter is right. It's the only thing that makes sense. There had to be some benefit to making a futile attack on the palace, and I can't imagine what else they had to gain. The result being that the princess is missing and Rais is the only one who knows where she is."

Nijad puts his head in his hands, then clasps his fingers together and peers over his clenched hands. "Cara's not found anything in the backgrounds of any of the staff, soldiers, or guards who have access to the palace. No strange payments going into bank accounts." He turns to Jasim. "I'm sorry, Jas, as it stands, try as I might, I can't think of any other explanation myself."

Jasim's face tightens. "So all the time we were thinking Aiza could be safe because she's with Rais, we might have been wrong."

Zaram's phone rings, he answers immediately without apology. Unashamedly all discussion stops as we listen in, unable to interpret the reason for the call from his one-word responses at his end of the conversation. The call's short.

Replacing his phone on the table, Zaram looks around. "They've spotted the helicopter. It's obviously been downed in the desert." He tosses Nijad a look of respect. "You were right. Rais must have been forced to land during the sandstorm."

"Aiza?"

The general shakes his head. "They can't tell. It does look like the helicopter made a controlled landing."

Christ! That's one thing. If they'd crashed, we might only be finding dead bodies inside.

"I want the satellite images analysed." Nijad speaks again.

"I'll arrange that," I offer. It's what I want to do anyway.

"I'll get my boys on it too." Bertram offers the services of the CIA.

"I want to get out there. If they're trying to walk out…"

Jasim's level of concern matches mine. I want to be there too. Doing something, anything, rather than sitting, talking, has to be better.

I point to Jasim and Nijad, both pilots. "We'll take a couple of helicopters to the location. Check things out. Make sure the helicopter was forced down because of the weather and not by enemy fire."

"Have you seen the Apache?" Bertram asks incredulously. "It's fully armoured. Would take a lot to down that. One reason, I thought, why Rais chose it."

"Hunter is right," Nijad starts. "We'll go to where we know she last was. If they're on foot or hurt, then we'll be able to help."

"Take Zaki," Zaram suggests. "He's a good tracker. If there's any footsteps to follow, he'll find them."

My gut clenches when I hope he won't be leading us to bodies buried in sand.

As Jasim and Nijad rise, I say one last thing. "How are we treating Rais when we catch up to him? As a traitor…?" If so, I'm going to kill him with my bare hands.

"We wait and hear what he has to say," Nijad says firmly, still not giving up on believing the best of his friend. Taking into account everything we've discussed today, I've no conviction other than Rais has betrayed Amahad, the ruling family, and, in particular, Aiza.

Rami stands. "I'm coming too. With Rais's behaviour, all bets are off. She might believe that she wants him, unless, of course, he's shown his true colours by now. I'm going to convince her otherwise. She'll be safer with me in Alair."

No she won't. He'll have a fight on his hands. If anyone is going to snatch Aiza out of the traitor's hands, it's going to be me.

In the end we take three helicopters. Jasim and Nijad each flying the R44 four seaters, myself, Ghalib and Rami in one—I still don't trust the prince out of my sight—and in the other, Sheikhs Jibran, Sofian and Khalaf. Zaki is piloting an EC 725 Super Cougar, which will carry Dharr, twenty troops and a full medical team and equipment prepared to deal with anything thrown at them.

Gathering the right crews together takes more time than I want to waste. I try to curb my impatience making myself focus on the benefits of going in prepared. But knowing and accepting are two different things, and I'm bouncing on my feet in my desire to get moving.

At last we're in the air and heading for Aiza's last known position. I barely notice the desert rushing past beneath us, concentrating on tamping down the intuition that tells me she's in danger. She's alone with a man who my gut tells me has betrayed her. As I get out my gun and check it for the umpteenth time, I'm convinced one of these bullets has Rais's name on it. He's going to die if he's harmed one hair of my woman's head.

My eyes stare at nothing out of the window. Aiza didn't want to come to Amahad, and she was right to be cautious. If I have my way, she'll be coming home with me and never stepping foot in the motherfucking desert again. Of course, there'd need to be some adjustment. I'm a Dom, she's a Domme, we'll need to sort out our roles. I can't wait to have her under my whip in the dungeon. First her ass is going to glow red for so blithely trusting a traitor.

The sandstorm's blown itself out, which means we can take a direct route. Nijad's voice comes through my headset. "There's the helicopter straight ahead. It's half covered in sand." Then we're descending and landing close by. Even though I know she's unlikely to have stayed with the chopper, it doesn't stop me leaping down before the rotors stop turning, almost choking in the sand being blown up.

I'm not alone as I run for the stricken Apache, a wave of relief washing over me as we find no bodies inside.

"They couldn't have gone further. Intake ducts are blocked." Zaki gives his expert opinion. "Rais must have landed it safely, there's no other damage." Looking around, he must see people wandering off as he shouts an order. "Everyone stay here. There's no sign of another helicopter landing, we'll assume they've gone on by foot. If there's a trail to be found, I don't want anyone spoiling it."

He makes sense, though it's hard to stop myself just wanting to blindly charge off in any direction.

The sun might be dropping in the sky, but the heat is still almost unbearable, and sweat drips from my brow. Taking water out of my pack, I gulp down the welcome liquid. Although I've worked and lived in Amahad for some time, I never get used to the climate, and my fair skin tends to burn rather than tan. Surreptitiously I take out some sun block that I always carry with me and smooth it over my face, pulling my baseball cap over my eyes to shade them and pushing my Ray-Bans back up to the bridge of my nose.

Suddenly there's a shout. "This way!"

As we turn to follow Zaki, Nijad's shaking his head. "There's nothing close in that direction."

"And you know…?"

He points. "About ten miles that way is the location of the encampment where Cara had been brought to me. The nomads have long moved on now." He thinks for a moment. "The oasis is still there, that could be where they're heading."

Cara's my best friend. While never romantic, our friendship had started when I was a teenager fresh from the States. She needed a confidant, and so did I. I'd been furious to learn she'd been kidnapped and forced into marriage with a man she'd never met. The anger I felt at the time returns. The Kassis family's crime worsened in my eyes, as instead of taking her to the palace, they'd delivered her to Nijad in a nomadic encampment out in the middle of the desert to disorientate her. How two broken people came to fall in love is beyond me. Nevertheless, they did, coming together to make a whole.

Nijad and Cara show any arrangement can be made to work. Which means there's no reason a bodyguard can't be married to a princess.

Jasim volunteers to stay with the helicopters as the rest of us get ready to search on foot. We'll radio for him if we need him. We can't take the choppers from here on in, else any signs on the ground will be obliterated.

We walk, following Zaki in a straight line, only skirting some of the larger dunes when we need to.

Rami comes up alongside. "Rais knew where he was going. They're not diverting from a course."

A little voice reminds me it might suit Rami's purpose to put the blame on Rais. While I agree with him, I can't help but contradict. "In the desert, if you don't keep to a straight path, you end up going in circles."

"The radio in the helicopter was disabled, as was the GPS," he reminds me. "Everything points to Rais's guilt, and that this was part of the plan." He's right. Though I'm still keeping the prince firmly in my sights.

Zaki holds up his hand, bringing all of us to a halt. He doesn't need to tell us why he's stopped, even I can see the hoof prints pointing in the direction we've come, and then heading off in the other way again.

Nijad swears loudly. Shielding his eyes from the sun's glare, he points up ahead. "We need to get back to the helicopters. I know where he's taken her. *Alwadi Aljameel.*"

I look at him in disbelief. All I can see is miles of sand with no distinctive features. Then I remember this was his home for three years, and he must be reading signs I can't see. Still I question him. "And how do you know that?"

He swings around to me with a look of relief. "Rais is a clever man. He's got her to a place no outsider will ever find. Only the people of the desert know that it's there."

"Or, perhaps, it's somewhere perfect for an ambush," I growl under my breath. Nothing is going to convince me of Rais's innocence.

CHAPTER 37
Aiza

This can't be happening. This man that I've trusted all my life, yearned for for so many years, gave my virginity to… He cannot be handing me over to a terrorist wanted by nearly every Westernized country in the world. The man who wants to use and abuse me as if I'm worth no more than a camel or a horse.

As Rais holds me still for Amir al-Fahri's inspection, a million thoughts race through my head, including the words he'd said to me. *Everything I do is for Amahad.* Could he really think that selling me for any amount of money is going to help his tribespeople more than waiting for the yield from the new oilfields? *Does he truly believe he's doing the right thing? Was last night nothing more than a ploy to get me to trust him? To go with him, no questions asked?*

I have to make him see sense.

While I'm terrified, I force myself to speak. "Kadar won't be persuaded to halt oil production. I'm not that important to him."

Al-Fahri looks surprised that I've spoken, and briefly it seems like he's going to ignore me. Then he laughs.

"Twafiq wasn't the only buyer I had lined up who was happy to follow my instructions. Kadar might be able to live with the thought you are dead, but not with the thought that every day you're going through hell. At some point he'll break and do exactly what I say. He'll destroy the pipeline and halt all production on the oilfield." He steps closer, and while Rais holds me immobile, wipes his disgusting hand down my face, making me flinch to evade the touch. *He even smells evil.* "I'll send him a tape every week of you suffering abuse, of you begging him to save you. He'll give in when he sees you broken and knows the only way to stop your torture is to do what I say. I might even give you back, when not even being back in the arms of your family will stop you longing for death."

"I'll never beg." I made the same promise I'd made to Twafiq.

He chuckles. "I might even take a turn at you myself." He moves closer, ripping off my headscarf and painfully twisting my hair in his fingers. "You can't imagine what will be done to you, even in your worst nightmare. You feel like a woman now, you won't when you've been mutilated."

I shudder in Rais's arms. As al-Fahri loosens his grip and steps away, I twist to try pleading my case with the sheikh. "Rais, you can't let him take me. Not after what we just did." As I remember what happened in the pool, I cry out, "I might already be carrying your baby."

Al-Fahri barks another laugh. "Rais knew his reward was in sight, and he knew he could be careless. If you're carrying a child, we'll rip out of you. Or let you keep it to term. I'd have plenty of buyers lined up for a royal brat."

I search for a reaction, some disgust on Rais's face. It's completely emotionless. Not even the thought that a child of his could be killed or sold seems to affect him.

He's the next to speak. "Can we get on with this?" he asks, sounding bored. "Make the exchange. The money my people need in trade for the princess."

"Rais…" I'm still watching his face. "You can't do this. You can't trust al-Fahri. Kadar will kill you when he knows the part that you've played."

Now he looks down at me. "I've covered my tracks well. There'll be nothing pointing back to me."

"The money…"

"Will be carefully spent. The desert sheikhs will be pleased and will support me. Ask yourself, here in the desert where life is so cheap, what will anyone care about the loss of one woman?"

Al-Fahri nods. "We have an agreement, Sheikh. I will honour it."

I suspect an arrangement with a terrorist is the last thing that will be adhered to. I never took Rais for being stupid, yet there's so many holes in his plan, he can't be firing on all cylinders. How can he trust al-Fahri to respect his part of the bargain? Oh, I don't doubt he'll use me to try to influence Kadar, but coughing up the payment? Somehow

I doubt he'll do that. Even if he does, my brothers will fast put two and two together and realise Rais had to be behind it.

"You're a dead man walking, Rais." I try once again to reason with him. "Amir al-Fahri won't leave you alive, and if he does, my brothers will find out and kill you."

As I turn back and throw my best look of disdain at al-Fahri, Rais lowers his head and his gruff voice speaks into my ear. "I told you everything I do is for Amahad. Even sacrificing my life. As long as the money's paid, I'll happily die for the benefits it will bring to my people, the desert tribes who Kadar has neglected for so long. If you want to blame anyone, blame your brothers. They sit in their palaces while the people of the desert die for lack of medical attention. Where they can do no more than herd their meagre flocks due to lack of education. Where they die from starvation. Nothing I can do will ever be enough for my country."

His words, so full of passion, show me there's no reasoning with him. He's so wrong, I can't believe it. I know my brothers are doing everything they can for Amahad. I don't know what I can say to convince him.

"Enough. You're right. It's time to move this on." Amir reaches for my arm. I cringe back against Rais. The sheikh might now be my enemy, even so, I prefer him to the terrorist.

"I'll bring her out for you," Rais suggests. Amir thinks for a moment, then nods. "My men will take her from there."

As Rais's arms imprison me, I know he's too strong for me to escape from his hold. As he backs out of the tent, dragging me with him, my feeble struggles don't loosen his grip at all.

"*Watati warubutuha*," Al-Fahri calls out as we emerge into the sunlight. Shadows are lengthening, showing day is coming to an end as the terrorist's men approach with ropes to follow his instruction. Soon I'm trussed so tightly I know I won't be able to get free. Next, they throw me across the back of a horse and secure me to it.

It's at that moment I know exactly what I'm going to do. There's only one way out of this valley, along that dangerous path with the steep drop off. Although I hate to sacrifice a horse, I'll struggle, unbalance it, and take it with me to my death. I'd rather die than go through what al-Fahri has planned for me. Kadar can focus on avenging my death rather than giving in to blackmail.

The terrorists mount up, and tears fall from my eyes as I start the journey through this beautiful valley, remembering my first impressions of it, how awestruck I was, my enjoyment when in the water with Rais. *I hate him.* Along with my appreciation of the beauty of my surroundings, any regard I had for him has been swept away.

He stands, impassively watching as our short procession starts to move down the path. I stare at him until we go around a bend and I can no longer see him, leaving him with the memory of tears running down my face, and in no doubt of my disgust and loathing. He might think he's doing the best for his country, but he's betrayed it. *He betrayed me.*

Now, I'm going to my death.

As we cross the peaceful meadow I wriggle and writhe, trying to loosen the ropes that bind me. My struggles cause me to slip over the saddle, putting the knot tying me to the horse just within reach. Apart from killing an animal who's here by no fault of its own, I know it will be easier to throw myself into the abyss if I could disengage myself. I don't see the grass or the trees. I don't hear the water flowing. My full attention is on getting loose. I'll only have one chance of this. If al-Fahri realises I prefer death to dishonour, he'll make sure I don't get another opportunity.

I'm scared, of course I am. I might not die immediately, my body may lay broken on the rocks below, death taking its time to claim me. Those kind of thoughts I push out of my head. Rais was right, I must think of my country and my family. With me dead, Amir al-Fahri will be left with nothing to bargain with.

This path seems longer than it was on the way in. The meadow seems to go on forever. Now I've got the knot loosened, I'm impatient to get to the steepest part of the path, the thought of dying only slightly less terrifying than the thought of living in the hands of whatever buyer al-Fahri has arranged.

Visions rush through my mind as though I'm delirious. I put it down to the blood rushing to my head, as I'm lying with my head hanging down. Last night, oh, last night… How could Rais so quickly turn out to be someone so completely different? I trusted him, he'd been gentle, kind. Loving. How could he turn on me?

He must have had this planned from the very beginning. Wasn't it him who suggested I went to the southern desert to be safe? I'm pretty certain Kadar had told me it was. How he had fooled me, luring me in with those false statements that he'd loved me for years, *waited for me.* Because it was exactly what I wanted to hear, I believed him. I'd been so stupid as he reeled me in like a fish on a hook. He'd made me imagine a future with him. Somehow, he must have known I'd been infatuated with him for most of my life. Though I'd been careful to hide it, things I'd done or said must have given me away.

I risk a look behind, hoping against hope that Rais will change his mind, that his love was real and that he'll realise it and come after me before it's too late. But our group of horses plod on, and there's no one following.

"*Aistamara bialtaqdum. Nahn bihajat 'iilana 'an nakhruj min huna bhlwl alwaqt aldhy yaqae fih allayla,*" Al Fahri calls out, encouraging his men to pick up their speed, not wanting to be travelling the treacherous path when night falls. As the horses move into a trot, I wrap my hand tightly to the stirrup leather. Having loosened my ties, I don't want to be bounced off. Or not too soon. They'd only catch me and tie me back on more firmly.

Should I pray? Although born Muslim, I'm not a practicing one, and don't even know if I believe in a god at all or how he could help me now. *It wouldn't hurt.* I can't think of what to say. Save me? Save my country? Kill that bloody bastard Rais? Let him get bitten by a poisonous snake? My mind churns with hatred, and not for forgiveness for the life that I've led.

It's not long before the horses are slowed back to a walk, and instead of the plods on the earth, their hoofs start to clip clop over the rocky ground. *We are on the path.* My chance will come soon.

Unheard by anyone else, a whimper escapes from my lips. I had so much to live for, so much I wanted to do. So many children I needed to help. Rais might be looking out for his tribes, but other people matter too. Especially when they can't help themselves. *Now I've no future.* Nothing to hope for. Nothing other than oblivion waiting for me.

I eye the drop, knowing it gets steeper further up. Wanting to make sure I take the best chance of being killed outright and not left to linger and die. Not wanting to give them a chance to save me....

The path ahead narrows, a sharp turn, and the drop beneath is sheer.

With tears streaming down my face, my heart beating so fast I think it could fail me before I do this. My sense of self-preservation making me hang on just a moment longer until...until... Forcing Twafiq into my mind, knowing I never want to suffer the abuse such as he had planned, I twist and throw myself sideways off the horse.

Now I'm falling, air whooshing as it rushes past me. The last thing I hear is the loud crack of a gun echoing around the canyon.

CHAPTER 38
Rais

A s the shot echoes, bouncing off the rock walls, my radio cackles. I answer brusquely, "Speak to me."

"Amir al-Fahri is dead. Clear head shot."

Good man. My nephew might only be eighteen, but he's the best sniper I've known, a natural ability to invariably hit his target, however small and far. Stationed up high in the mountain, he was well placed to take the terrorist with a single shot.

"We're moving in now," I tell him. "Take as many of them out as you can, just for fuck's sake, don't hit the princess."

"Sheikh, A*khw al'umi.*" The tone of his voice, the way it breaks, causes an icy hand to grip my heart.

"Speak to me." Dread fills me.

"The princess. She threw herself off the horse. She's… she's gone into the canyon. The men have stopped, the ones not surrounding al-Fahri are looking down. I can't see her, I don't think they can either."

"Kill them." I issue the order while knowing he won't get them all, as they'll soon be taking cover from the sniper hidden on the slopes. "Don't let them move into the canyon and go after her." I don't know how I'm still speaking, as my heart has stopped.

"It's sheer rockface, Sheikh. She wouldn't have had a chance."

A blinding rage floods through me. I want to fall to my knees, scream out loud. *Aiza. What the fuck have you done? Why didn't you have faith in me?*

I need to get to her. Calling out a battle cry, my best warriors mount the horses we tacked up as soon as Amir al-Fahri had disappeared from sight. Once seated, I pause only to shout an instruction to my lieutenant, Suhail. "Bring rope!" Then, kicking straight into a gallop, I lead the men on, only slowing a fraction when we reach the path our sure-footed horses know how to travel fast even in darkness. The light's fading now, which won't help a rescue.

She has to be dead. She can't survive that fall. It won't do any good thinking like that. Only the thought of her being my wife and by my side keeps me moving. *Why did she take matters into her own handst? Why didn't she trust that I would save her?*

Because I acted my part too well. I gave her no reason to believe in me. In persuading al-Fahri of my treachery, I'd convinced her. All she had to rely on was herself. When it came to it, she chose death over the diabolical fate the terrorist had spelt out for her.

She can't be dead. If she's gone, I'll die too. If not by my own hand, then by those of her brothers, and I won't lift a finger to defend myself, knowing I'll deserve everything that's heading my way. A painful death, and every minute I'll relish the torture to my body. *If it wasn't for me, she'd still be alive.*

I'd taken a risk, toyed with her life. While governments all over the world may thank me for ridding this earth of the terrorist scum, the result wasn't worth the loss of *my* princess.

She's not dead. Surely I'd feel the loss to the depths of my soul if she was? *I love her.* If she's gone, why is my own heart still beating?

The thunderous sound of hooves hitting the rocky path startles the horses that have appeared in front of me. Two of them rear, miss their footing, and go over the edge. Men's screams mingle with their pitiful frightened cries. *Did she scream too?*

I dismount, keeping the wall of the path to my rear, and manage to take another man out. Some still mounted take panic and flee, and another one goes over as a loose horse takes off down the path, uncaring what it knocks into. A panicked horse rears, managing to keep a grip on the stones, though the man it kicks as it's front legs land falls over the cliff. The remaining men and horses are fleeing. I get off another few shots, seeing men drop, as unlike myself and my highly trained men, they have difficulty shooting accurately while they ride.

Those thinking they're escaping don't know they're heading straight for another group of my best warriors waiting to head them off at the bottom of the track. Not one of al-Fahri's men will be leaving this valley alive.

There, I hear it. Rapid fire shooting, men's screams quickly cut off. I pull my horse up, knowing my work here is done. Wheeling my horse on the narrow track, I weave back up the path with just one thought in my mind, finding Aiza, even if it's only her body I'll bring home.

In the distance from beneath me, the firing stops and I allow myself a quick moment of relief that my plan, in all respects but one, has been successful. As I near the place where Aiza went over, my radio crackles again.

"Sheikh. We're under fire."

"More terrorists?"

"No. Helicopters are landing, troops pouring out. They're attacking us."

Fuck. It has to be Nijad. He's the only one who could find us.

"Hold your fire. Do not fire back." I think quickly. "Sheikh Nijad should be there. Try to make contact with him. Tell him to get the fuck up here quick. No, on second thought, get him to search at the bottom of the ravine."

I might not need to wait to die. If Aiza hasn't survived, Nijad will run a blade through me as soon as he sees me. I'll deserve to join her. *If she's dead... I couldn't live without her.*

"Sheikh!" My lieutenant comes to meet me, carrying a coil of rope. "I don't know if this will be long enough. It's all we've got."

Cautiously I approach the edge and peer over. The light's going now, and it's hard to see anything below the sheer rock face. Or any handholds to climb down. Grimly I take the rope from him and start tying it around my waist.

At his look of concern, I shake my head. No one else is doing this but me. I owe her. Even if it's only to recover her broken body.

I pass my radio over. At the same moment it bursts into live.

"What the fuck have you done, Rais? Where's Aiza?"

"Nijad. You can shout at me all you want later. Now we need to get to the princess. She went over the cliff edge at the spot where the path twists."

His intake of breath is audible. He knows this place as well as myself. "What do you need me to do?"

"I can't see fuck all. I'm roped up and going over the top. Can you make your way along the old river bed? See if you can spot where she is?"

"She better fucking be alive, Rais, or you'll wish for death every second of every remaining day of your miserable life."

"I understand. I'm going now."

My lieutenant clips my radio onto my belt. "You better take it. Stay in contact. I'll belay you, call out when you find her."

I give him a quick nod, knowing he's trying to stay positive, when no one could survive that fall.

Another of my men comes running up. "Torch," he pants as he passes me a slim Maglite.

Switching it on, then grasping it in my teeth, I go to the edge, give a nod to Suhail, who calls a couple of other men to take hold of the rope, and as he starts giving me some slack, go backwards off the ledge. I bounce with my feet, then pull up with a jolt, and I start to progress more smoothly as the men let the rope out.

As I descend, the hopelessness of my situation becomes clear. There's no way she could have survived such a long drop, and it's more likely Nijad will find his sister down below, her limbs shattered and twisted. I try to quell the trembling in my hands, knowing this is no time to give in to grief.

I'm let down a little further. *They're letting out the rope too slow.* I'm a heavy man, and if they went faster it's more likely I'd drop. *And be with her.*

An overhang comes up. Full darkness has descended now, so I move my head so the torchlight can guide me. *There's red… That's blood.* Is it hers? Or is it from one of the men or the horses that went over?

I push out and away, swinging over the rock, the rope having the stretch as I land underneath. Another section of sheer cliff is beneath me. Carefully I abseil down, moving my head left to right, searching through the night, trying to find her.

Then I reach the end of the rope that's far too short. My feet are tottering on a tiny piece of rock jutting out from the bluff. It's an easy decision to make. With one hand gripping onto a tiny handhold, I undo the knot around my waist with my other hand, letting the rope fall free. Now I'm all on my own, on a suicide mission.

Taking care now, wishing I was a rock climber properly equipped, I descend slowly and carefully. If by any chance she is alive, I won't be any use to her dead. My torch now trained on the wall, I'm seeking out every tiny indent that I can get my toes, then fingers into.

I start to slide. *This is it.* But although I rip a finger nail off, my hand catches onto a slight crevice. I take a couple of seconds to catch my breath, then start to move again. A larger ledge. I pause, looking around me, and down as far as the torchlight shines.

What the fuck is that? My eyes land on a tree growing horizontally out from the rock face. And there, caught on a branch, is Aiza.

She's not moving. I try to play the torchlight over her face, but all I can see is the back of her head, as she's hanging face down, the ropes they bound her with trapping her. I can't tell if she's alive or dead.

"Nijad," I speak into the radio. "She's here."

"Is she alright?"

"I can't tell. I'm about five metres above her." I turn my head outwards. "Can you see my light?"

"Yeah. I got you. But I can't see her. Can you get to her?"

I look down. There's no handholds that I can see. *There'll have to be.* "I'm going to try."

I hear him speaking. "There's no way fucking way up. We can't help her from here. Is she conscious?"

"Negative." She's not moving at all.

"If you can get to her, I'll get the helicopter up. We can hoist her up, but she'll need you to help her."

It's her only chance of getting out of here. She'll need my help. "I'll get to her," I tell him. Though fuck knows how.

The short ledge extends a little way to my right. Inching along carefully, I position myself over the tree. Moving my hands lower to a tiny crack, I make myself lift my feet. Now I'm hanging by just one hand, and though my feet scramble, I can't find anything that gives me purchase. The crack's too small to take my weight. My fingers start slipping. Desperately I move my toes left then back to the right, scrabbling to find anything to support me. I'm hanging by my fingertips now, slowly losing purchase...

Unable to keep my hold, I drop, sliding down the face of the rock, powerless to do anything other than let gravity take its course. It only takes a split second, while it feels like eternity before my free fall is halted. By the very tree that Aiza's hanging from.

The tree bounces under my heavy weight, and I hold my breath as Aiza's dislodged and shaken further down the branch. She's slipping downwards, the branch bends, and I watch in horror as she's about to slide off.

Then is caught at the last minute, her progress halted by the flimsiest of twigs.

Very slowly I let out the breath I was holding, hardly daring to breath in again, frozen in position. When the tree stops shaking, gingerly, and oh so carefully, I take out the radio that somehow survived the fall and is still clipped to my belt. The torch had flown away as I'd slid down the rock.

"Nijad," I speak quietly, afraid even the vibration of a louder voice would shake Aiza off her perch. "I'm close to Aiza, but stuck. If I try to reach her, she's going to fall."

I hear a sharp intake of breath, then, "Flash your torch, show us where you are."

"I've lost it. Flash yours." He does. "You're about fifty metres down from me. Keep moving up the canyon. I'll tell you when you're close." I can see Nijad's torch flashing, and it's not long before he's right underneath us.

When he shines his light up, he sees the problem. "Fuck."

Yeah, right. Fuck.

"Is she alive, Rais?"

"I don't know. She's unconscious." *Or dead.* I pray it's the former, and that she stays that way. If she came too and moved... By Allah it doesn't bear even thinking about it.

"Zaki's going to fly the Cougar in. He's picking his best man to come down and winch her to safety."

"Tell him to keep high. Any downdraft might dislodge her. If I could get to her, Nijad…"

"Don't you fucking move. Don't you think you've done damage enough?"

He blames me. And he only knows a small part of it. When he finds out the rest I won't have long to live, even if his sister survives. When Aiza's picked up I might as well fall from the tree myself and save him a job. Though I won't do that. He deserves all the shots at me he wants to deliver, and to be the one who deals the fatal blow. So I cling on to that tree, peering through the darkness, trying to see if the woman of my dreams, the woman I love, is still breathing.

If only she hadn't taken action herself. If only she had trusted me. Fuad was set up in sniper position, half of my best men at the bottom of the track, and half with me. We'd have taken al-Fahri's men in a pincer action, rescued her and set her free. I hadn't given her sufficient reason to have faith and to believe I'd come for her. I failed her.

I couldn't have told her our plan, she wouldn't have been a good enough actor. Her lack of fear or any act put on would have alerted the terrorist. Any suspicion that Aiza was faking, and we'd never have led Amir al-Fahri into our trap. No, I couldn't have let her know what was happening. Not the slightest warning, or a squeeze of her hand to offer reassurance. To make it work, she had to be totally convinced. To that end, my plan was a success. Al-Fahri suspected nothing, and as a result is no longer walking this earth. Amahad, and Aiza, are free.

Unless she's already dead.

If she's not, she's never going to forgive me.

The sound of the helicopter overhead. Even though he's keeping high, there's still turbulence caused by the blades, and I stare at the branch, willing it not to bend. Aiza's so precariously held by that overgrown twig, the slightest disturbance could knock her off.

My radio channel's still open.

"Careful, Zaki. Keep it there. Get your man out fast. Tell him to come down slowly. That's it." The whole area's floodlit courtesy of the helicopter's search light. I can see Nijad a long way below looking up, dead horses and men around him. Clearly, he's giving no thought to the carnage. I don't need to make out his features, as I hear the tension in his voice.

"Up, up. He's got too much of a swing. He'll knock her… There, that's it. Try again. Slowly. *Slowly.*"

On the second pass the winch lets out gradually bit by bit, and Zaki's man drops in a vertical line.

"He's lined up. Move him over about two metres. *Slowly goddamnit!* That's right. He's almost there."

"On target." Another voice joins in. "Got my hands on her. Just securing her now." I watch as he tries to get a harness around her and fails. I can see him judder as he's forced to take her weight as she slips into his arms, and again hold my breath. "I've got her, pull us up."

"Shall I send him back down for Sheikh Rais?" Zaki asks.

There's a moment of silence, and I'm half expecting Nijad to say no and to leave me to my fate. If our positions were reversed I'd certainly be considering leaving me to die.

"Yes. Bring him up. There are many questions he needs to answer."

Reading between the lines, my death is certain, but he means to interrogate me first.

CHAPTER 39
Aiza

I 'm not dead." I blink rapidly as I open my eyes, seeing a bright light overhead, and hearing a machine beeping at my side. I didn't realise I'd spoken aloud until a deep voice, full of emotion, answers.

"No, you're most certainly not. Though you deserve to be. What were you thinking, Aiza?"

"Kadar?" I turn my head in the direction of his voice, soaking in his austere autocratic features. My eyes start to water. I never expected to see him again.

I certainly didn't anticipate the tears I'm seeing in his eyes. "Aiza, dearest sister." His hand reaches out and covers mine. "You should have trusted that I would have come for you. Whatever happened, wherever you'd been taken, no stone would have been left unturned."

Yes, he would have come. Except, by the time I'd been rescued, what state would I have been in? It was bad enough the first time, and then I'd barely been touched.

"I couldn't see I could do anything else, Kadar."

"You could. You just made the wrong choice. You're a stupid, but incredibly brave woman." His tone changes, and his rough hand now touches my face as if confirming

I'm really there. His touch makes me aware of my body. *Everything* hurts.

"How badly am I injured?" *What damage did I do to myself?*

As he strokes my cheek, he tells me. "You hit your head pretty hard, so you've got concussion. You've got bruises and contusions all over your body. Your left shoulder was dislocated, probably when the tree stopped your fall."

"Tree?"

"You don't remember?"

I go to shake my head, then wince and settle for the word instead. "No."

"You were fucking lucky, Aiza. A tree broke your fall. Rais climbed down and found you."

The machine by my side starts bleeping faster, and my hands start to sweat. "Rais?" I ask, almost in terror. "Rais, he…"

Kadar slashes his hand through the air. "Rais is a fool. He should never have put you at risk."

Tears start to leak from my eyes, and Kadar notices. "Hey, no thinking about that now. You're in hospital in Zalmā, you're safe. Amir al-Fahri is dead."

My eyes start to droop, and my mind goes fuzzy.

"You'll never have to worry about him again."

Does he mean al-Fahri or Rais? Knowing my brother, I wouldn't be surprised if they were both dead. They deserve it. What Rais had done? If I live to be a hundred, I'll never forgive him.

I awake sometime later to find someone else by my side, holding my hand, his thumb massaging the back of it, and as my eyes open he squeezes his fingers. It's Rami.

Locking his eyes with mine, he leans forwards and places a soft kiss to my cheek. "Never, ever, do anything like that again, Aiza. I nearly died from worry."

"You were there?"

"I was there," he confirms, his jaw set. "I saw you hanging from that tree, knowing a breath of wind could dislodge you."

I bite my lip and shudder. Kadar hadn't shared all the details with me.

"I'm not backing away this time, Aiza. When you're well, we will start planning a wedding. I'm never going to let you out of my sight again."

One thing Rais, the traitorous bastard, had shown me, was Rami and I together would be a disaster. "Rami, I'm sorry I worried you. Sorry I caused anyone concern. I thought taking matters into my own hands was the only way to escape what al-Fahri had planned." I pause and swallow. Though my mouth feels dry, I've got to finish talking to him. "I know you want to marry me, I know you want to protect me. I'm free now. Al-Fahri is dead. I can go back to my own life." And having found, then lost the man who I'd thought had been unobtainable, I don't want another in my life. The pain I feel at his treachery hurting worse than any injury I received in the fall. It's going to take me a long time to get over it, if I ever do. I was such a

fool to think he reciprocated my feelings, jumping in with
both feet when I thought all my dreams had materialised,
finding instead I'd stepped straight into a nightmare. "I'm
going back to London, starting my charity work again. I'm
going alone, Rami. I've nothing I can offer you."

"You're feeling weak, Aiza. You're not thinking straight.
I'll give you whatever time you need." His mouth purses
into a stubborn line.

I raise my hand that's not in a sling and touch the soft
skin of his face. "Rami, you'll always be a good friend to
me, that's all we can ever be. I can't marry you. I don't
want to marry anyone." Not when the dependable, reli-
able, protective Rais let me down so badly. The man who'd
gained the trust of the whole royal family, yet betrayed us
all. I don't know how I'll ever be able to trust anyone again.

Rami sits up straighter. "Time, habiti. Time's what you
need."

I close my eyes then open them. "A day, a week, a year,
a lifetime. It won't make any difference, Rami. I'm not the
same woman I used to be." Not when I've been let down
so badly. "I've got much to come to terms with. For that, I
need to be away from here. From Amahad, from Alair." I
pause, and firm my voice. "And from you, Rami."

While I don't want to hurt him, leaving him hoping
would be worse. While his face works as he tries to come to
terms with my pronouncement, a knock sounds on the
door. Without waiting for permission, it opens to reveal

Hunter. He gives Rami a sharp look, as if expecting me to have been alone.

Then Hunter steps closer to the bed, his eyes examining me. "How are you feeling, Princess?"

I try a smile, even my face hurts. "Like I got run over by a bus."

A quick nod of sympathy comes my way. "You're lucky to be here. Why the fuck did you try to kill yourself?"

"I've already had the lecture from Kadar." I pre-empt what I'm sure he was going to say. "Al-Fahri was going to break me, Hunter, was going to use me against Kadar. There was nothing else I could do to prevent it."

"Because of that motherfucker Rais."

At least Hunter knows Rais was guilty, even if Kadar couldn't bring himself to say the words. Even now his treachery seems hard to believe. I must still be delirious, as there's part of me that still cares for the man I'd admired from afar for so many years. I'd thought I'd hit the jackpot when he told me he loved me.

Punishing myself, as I really don't want to know, nevertheless needing the answer to the question before I can start to move on. "Is Rais dead?" I'm certain he is. All I'm asking for is confirmation.

"Dead? No. Fucker's still breathing air." Hunter's gone red. "If I had my way, he wouldn't be."

So they haven't killed him yet. But for the state crimes he's committed, it can only be a matter of time. I wonder what jail he's languishing in. One here in Zalmā, or the one in Al Qur'ah.

"He's sitting outside waiting to see you," Hunter continues. "I've told him he's the last person you'd want to see."

Wait. What? Hunter's right, there's no way I want to see his duplicitous face ever again. *How come he's here? He must have tricked them. Concocted some story...* The blood drains from my face, and my voice sounds hoarse. "Tell him to go away."

Hunter's there, his hand giving a comforting squeeze to my sheet-covered thigh. "Of course you don't want to see him, Princess. There's no need for you too. Once you're well you can leave Amahad for good." His face twists. "I should never have fallen in with the plans to bring you here. You can come back to London, I'll take good care of you."

"She's going nowhere with you." The loudness of Rami's voice as he contradicts Hunter makes my head pound.

When they start arguing I quickly have enough, but haven't the strength to admonish them. Tuning them out, my mind focuses on the man I'm refusing to see. Why couldn't things be different? Why did he send me off to die? Whether I'd have taken fate into my own hand as I had, or if al-Fahri had killed me further down the line, the result would have been the same. My death would have lain at his door.

448

Hunter and Rami are still arguing, fighting over me like dogs with a bone. Luckily the noise attracts the attention of a nurse who comes in and shoos them out with a hissed, "She's supposed to be resting."

My sleep isn't restful, dreams and nightmares get mangled together. I'm on the ship, Rais is selling me, Rais is loving me, he's putting a dog collar on me. I toss, turn, and then at last wake. My body must have rested, even if my mind was overactive. I feel stronger and able to pull myself up. I press the buzzer for a nurse to take me to the bathroom. When I come back out, Nijad and Jasim are waiting. I'm feeling a bit dizzy, so wait until the nurse helps me back into bed before speaking.

"Well, hello, brothers." I make a determined effort to be cheerful, even though I'm still dying inside.

Both of them stare at me as though they're seeing an apparition.

"What?" My hand goes to my face as if I've got a splodge of toothpaste around my mouth or something.

Nijad takes off his headdress and throws it down, closely followed by Jasim doing the same thing. It still surprises me to see my middle brother in Arab dress, as for years I'd only known him to dress in Western attire.

Nijad sits himself in the chair, unable to take his eyes off me. When I'm just about to open my mouth to prompt him again, he speaks. "Never, ever, Aiza, do that to me again. You took years off my life."

449

"That goes for me as well." Jasim rests his hand on the back of Nijad's seat, his voice breaking. "We thought you were dead."

Me too.

"If Rais hadn't have found you, we might have been searching all night. The branch you were on could have broken…"

Rais would probably have preferred me dead. "It's lucky you found me when you did." *Else Rais might have erased the evidence of his wrongdoing. I put it down to be the blow to my head, as I feel tears roll down my cheeks again.* "How did you kill al-Fahri?" *Thank goodness they got there in time. And that my grand gesture deciding my own fate failed.*

Nijad's eyes snap open. "We didn't. The actual bullet came from Fuad. Apparently the young lad's an excellent sniper."

That makes sense. I hadn't seen Fuad at the camp. At least the promising young man was not caught up in Rais's conspiracy. Idly I wonder whether he'll take over from Rais. He'll have his work cut out if he does. He's very young to take his place as his heir.

"You realise you cocked things up, don't you?" Jasim's face has a wry grin. "You should have hung tight. Fuad was waiting to take al-Fahri out, and then Rais's men were going to kill the rest. All of the plan went like clockwork. Apart from your heroic gesture when you lost your nerve."

Lost my nerve? I sit up straight, ignoring the banging in my head. "Lost my fucking nerve?" I spit. "Rais gave me to al-Fahri. Whatever story he's told you is wrong. He's a traitor. He took a huge payment in return for me. You have no idea what al-Fahri threatened me with. He was going to break Kadar, and I couldn't let him." The main reason I hadn't wanted to see Rais was I hadn't wanted to hear any more lies, falsehoods he's clearly been spouting to everyone else, *and getting them to believe him.* "Why's Rais walking around free? He needs locking up."

"Aiza, it was a set-up. Al-Fahri wanted you so badly he fell into Rais's trap."

"He didn't. *I* did." My temper stops my listening. "Rais must have planted the bombs in the palace. He got me out, yes. However, it wasn't a rescue. He took me to meet al-Fahri. It was a set-up from start to finish. But not for the terrorist, the trap was for *me.*" I rest my head back, tears now flowing. "He fooled me, and I believed him from the start. If you haven't arrested him, you better do so now. He's a traitor to Amahad. You can't believe a word that he says."

Jasim and Nijad exchange glances. "He saved you, Aiza. He risked his life to follow you down the cliff face. He was a hare's breath away from dying himself when he tried to rescue you. He never meant any harm to come to you. He's not been arrested." Nijad chuckles. "But he didn't get away unscathed."

"Can't you see he's fooling you? You can't trust him." I turn my head away, remembering Rais and everything he did to me that night that was so special, and which has now become tainted in my memory. I wish I could wipe it from my mind. Rais, the childhood friend of my brother who I admired from the day I was old enough to bug the hell out of Nijad. Always wanting to tag along with them when he was home from school. Then, later, when my brothers were away and Rais took pity on a young child, teaching me to ride when everyone else treated me as a nuisance. Right up to the day when I was eighteen and noticed him as a man.

I never thought he'd look twice at me. Ten years older, far more experienced. Damn, I was so naïve to believe him when he said he hadn't remarried as he was waiting for me. So stupid to accept his declaration of love was true. So gullible to let him take me for a second time. *Unprotected.* My uninjured arm touches my stomach. *What if I'm pregnant?*

"How long was I unconscious?" I suddenly ask.

Nijad looks surprised at the change of topic. "Two days."

So now this is the fourth. Is it too late for the morning after pill? I shiver, unable to understand my reluctance to even enquire, though knowing I'll have to. "Nijad, Jasim," I start, making sure I've got their attention. "You need to do something for me."

"Anything, Aiza. We'll do anything we can."

Jasim nods at his brother. "Aiza, we know we've failed you. Haven't been there for you. All that changes now. Where you go from here, whatever you want to do... We'll support you."

I take a deep breath. "I never want to see Rais again. He might have taken you in, but he'll never dupe me again. He..." I swallow, it's hard to get the words out. "He didn't use a condom. I need the morning after pill."

Nijad and Jasim look at each other, then Nijad draws in a sharp breath. "Talk to him first, Aiza."

Give him a chance to deceive me again? To feed me a pack of lies I suspect I'll have no difficulty believing.

"No." I refuse with one word. "When I've recovered I'm going back to London with Hunter."

"*With* Hunter?" Jasim raises his eyebrow.

I shrug, then regret it as it pulls on my injured shoulder. "That remains to be seen. Hunter's got my best interests at heart. I know he'd never hurt me."

Nijad barks a laugh. "You know I'm not a fan of Hunter. And Kadar would have a fit."

"You'll all get over it."

"Why not Rami?"

"Rami's a sub."

Jasim stands up straight, his face forming an expression he probably wore as owner of a BDSM club. "Sounds ideal for a Domme." He stares at me for a moment. "You're experienced enough to know that being submissive sexually doesn't mean you're weak outside the bedroom. His needs might fulfil yours. Hunter's a Dom, I can't see you'd ever be happy with him."

"I don't think you should make any decisions now, Sister," Nijad says sympathetically. "You've been through a hell of a time over the past few days. Don't do anything hasty. What I suggest is you come back to the palace in Al Qur'ah. Take some time to relax. Get to know your niece and nephew. You need time to recover mentally as well as physically. When you're stronger, you can decide what you want."

"Fuck, Aiza." Jasim's eyes soften. "I know better than most how it feels to want to run from Amahad and all it represents. Ni and I had to reform our relationship. Now we need to do the same with you. We've neglected you in the past. Please give us this opportunity to get to know you, and you us. I can relate to what you're thinking. I never wanted to come back home, expecting I was walking into a trap. If you still think this is a trick, I'll make you a vow. Anytime you want to leave, I'll help you. Just give us a chance first. Please."

"Come home with us, Aiza. Let us be your family."

CHAPTER 40
Rais

The scream awakes me. The scream that came from my own mouth as the recurring nightmare strikes again. The one where I see Aiza slowly slip off the branch and crash to her death in the ravine below.

My sheets are drenched with sweat, and my whole body shaking with fear, unable to comprehend how I could ever forget, let alone even start to deal with the memory that replays in my mind on a loop. I've never been so scared in my life as I was that night, perched in my own precarious position, unable to reach her.

She's safe. She's alive, I remind myself. *It doesn't matter that she doesn't want to see me.* She'll recover, no one's after her anymore. I can be content with knowing she's in the land of the living even if my knowledge of her is only secondhand, my glimpses of her from a distance.

I turn over and groan, every part of my body aching. I could have taken Nijad on with one hand tied behind my back. Fuck knows how often I beat him when we were boys. When he came at me, I didn't fight back, didn't raise a hand to defend myself. I deserved all I'd received. Every blow, every punch, and finally, when I could stand no longer, every kick.

At first when I was brought back to the palace they'd taken me to the dungeon, and not one anything like the playroom in the converted harem. No, this was a dark and dismal place where prisoners give up all hope, where traitors meet their end.

Being too early to rise, and not wanting to slip back into sleep and invite more bad dreams to assail me, I let my mind drift back over my interrogation. It was Nijad, my very good friend, who'd taken the lead. I close my eyes as I go through it again…

"What the fuck were you playing at Rais?"

I stare at Nijad. "I had a plan to kill Amir al-Fahri and avoid bloodshed. Well, except for his and that of his men."

Bertram steps up. "We wanted to take the jihadist alive. Get information."

I prefer terrorists dead. "He wouldn't have told you a thing. I doubt any prison would have held him. He's got too many followers. He would have corrupted other inmates, recruited them, and probably escaped with help from the outside."

"And you? Why should we trust you or one word that comes out of your mouth? You nearly got the princess killed." Hunter's looking like he's having difficulty holding himself back. "No one could accuse you of being stupid, *Sheikh*. Now you're thinking fast how to get out of this."

I can't blame them for their anger. Fuck, I'm furious with myself. I'd known Aiza would be frightened. The rewards were worth it. If it had gone to plan, not one hair of her head would have been harmed. But it hadn't. She's braver than I gave her credit for. Who could have expected she'd try to take her own life to avoid being used against her country?

"Just go through everything from the start. Then we'll see if we believe you." The emir's stern voice gives nothing away. My emir. The ruler of Amahad. My country that I've given my life in service for, and now will probably die for. His palpable disappointment cuts through me as sharply as any blade.

I thought I was acting for good. Now I'm in shackles and being interrogated like a traitor. I can do nothing less than tell the truth, and trust they believe me. Whether they do or don't, the end result will be the same. No one can deny it was me who caused harm to come to the princess. I can't see how it's possible for anyone to ever forgive me. I'll never stop blaming myself.

Chained to the wall, stripped down to my shalwar kameez, I'm deliberately exposed and vulnerable. Up to now they've not resorted to physical encouragement. They haven't needed to. I'm not afraid of pain, and in the circumstances, I'd welcome it. I deserve it.

Kadar pulls up a chair, turns it so the back is facing me, and straddles it. His arms resting on the back, he steeples his hands. "Tell us when al-Fahri first contacted you."

"I contacted him," I correct.

"Bastard!" Rami flies forwards, punching me in the stomach. He put sufficient power behind the blow to impress me.

"Continue." Kadar doesn't waste his breath reprimanding the prince.

"I wanted to make al-Fahri an offer which would be tempting enough for him to come in person. It was something only *I* could do. Any other intermediary would be suspect." After the royal family, as the leading desert sheikh, I speak for all the tribes of the desert. The tribes who invested in the oil exploration in Amahad. Kadar will know as well as I do that my word would have been taken as having half the country of Amahad behind it.

Kadar doesn't speak, just waves his hand for me to continue.

"Al Fah-ri had planned to abduct Aiza from the palace. He wouldn't have come himself, just sent his loyal troops. It would have been a bloodbath." *By Allah, the prince has a mean fist.* I'm having difficulty breathing.

"There was a bloodbath," Zaram growls. "Good men died."

I nod, accepting that, still taking shallow breaths. "Fewer than there would have been if he'd followed his original strategy. al-Fahri was planning to launch a major assault. Those bombs? Nothing to what he had planned."

"Go on." Kadar throws a look at Zaram, who's clearly fuming, but keeps quiet.

"I told al-Fahri that I could get Aiza somewhere secret. That in the confusion of an attack on the palace I would be trusted to take her away. And, in exchange for a few million dollars, he could have her." At their looks of derision, I hurriedly continue. "My excuse was that the tribes were fed up of promises of wealth in the future. That life was cheap in the desert, and the sacrifice of one had been agreed in return for real money now."

"It nearly fucking worked. Amir al-Fahri nearly escaped with Aiza…"

"He never would have done." I direct my comment to Hunter. "I had a sniper ready to take him out, my most trusted men waiting to kill the rest of them. He was trapped on a narrow path with no means of escape." I then glare at Bertram and Kentwell, the intelligence men. "All I'm guilty of is wanting him dead rather than taking him in for questioning. There was too much danger to Aiza if he continued breathing." I let my eyes rest on each of the key players in turn. "Even from behind bars he'd have found a way of hurting her."

There's silence, then Kadar speaks. "I, for one, will sleep easier knowing he's dead." He casts a glance at the intelligence men. "Oh, I've no doubt his men will regroup, but al-Fahri had a personal agenda towards Amahad. It remains to be seen whether any of his lieutenants still breathing have the same appetite." He brings his eyes back to me. I'm subjected to his stare for what seems like hours before he eventually nods his head and proclaims, "I believe Rais. And that he was, and remains, loyal to Amahad."

Hunter steps forwards, his face red. "He almost got Aiza fucking killed."

"That was not his intention." Kadar gets to his feet. "Enough. I have spoken. Free him."

"Free him?" Hunter is incredulous. "Just like that?"

Kadar moves fast. He may be the emir, but he's kept himself in shape. Taking Hunter by surprise, he grabs him by the throat and backs him up to the wall. "I have *spoken*," he thunders. "I know you have a vested interest in my sister, and you are very well aware of my feelings towards you." He takes one hand away and waves it in my direction. "Sheikh Rais's actions have freed Aiza from the shadow hanging over her. You know yourself the best plans in war can have casualties."

"But Aiza..." Hunter croaks.

"I agree with Hunter, Kadar. Rais cannot go unpunished." Rami offers the Grade A man his support.

"Oh, he won't go unpunished," Nijad growls from the back of the room. "I can assure you of that."

Kadar turns to look at his brother, something passes between them, then Kadar lets Hunter go. "I've made my decision. Rais is a hero, not a traitor. He'll be treated that way. *Understood?*"

As he snarls the last word there's a shuffling of feet, and nobody looks at either him or me. *I don't deserve the label of hero. I nearly got the woman I love killed.*

Now the emir softens his voice. "If Aiza hadn't taken things into her own hands, Rais's plan would have worked smoothly. Aiza's alive, no lasting harm has come to her. And she's been freed from the threat of Amir al-Fahri. *That's* what we need to focus on." He waits for that to sink in. "Leave now. Nijad can stay to have the *conversation* he wants with Sheikh Rais, and after that there will be no further retaliation."

Zaram's staring at me, then he nods to the emir. "You're right, Kadar. Apart from the loss of life during the attack on the palace, which I accept would have been greater had we been up against a larger and better trained army, it was a good plan. I, for one, admire the ingenuity of the sheikh."

Bertram shrugs. "For now, al-Fahri's organisation has been thrown into turmoil. We've identified the dead bodies, and from what we can tell, he had several of his most senior men with him. Rais, you did well."

I don't want praise.

Hunter and Rami still look unconvinced, yet follow as one by one everyone else leaves the room. I'm left alone with Nijad.

He prowls towards me, his face emotionless. "Your strategy was flawless. Nevertheless, it almost got Aiza killed. It was a miracle she lived."

He doesn't need to tell me that. I see Aiza hanging from that branch every time I close my fucking eyes. It continually goes round and round my head without relief.

Nijad reaches down and frees one of my legs, then the other. He stands and undoes the chains shackling my hands to the wall. Then steps back.

Rolling my shoulder to get the circulation going again, I stand tall and face him. The first punch comes quicker than I expected.

When I came around, I was lying in a comfortable bed, no longer in a dungeon.

That had been three days ago. My first waking thought had been for Aiza. Painfully making myself get up, I gingerly tested all my limbs and found all of them in working order. Working my mouth, my jaw is sore, but unbroken. Likewise, the blow to my nose had blackened my eyes, though there was no damage to the bone. My balls are something else, they throb and are swollen in direct opposite to my shrivelled cock, my stomach clenching in agony. When I piss there's blood in the water. *It's nothing more, and probably less, than I deserve.*

When he'd next seen me, Nijad greeted me, not warmly, yet without animosity.

My only concern was for the woman I love. I asked, even resorted to begging, but still they wouldn't allow me to see Aiza. At first the excuse came that her visitors were limited to only close family while she was unconscious. I couldn't presume on the basis of being her fiancé, that glorious dream is lost to me now. Instead I spent my time sat outside her room, waiting for news, thinking it was a bit of a joke to refer to her brothers as 'close'. When had they ever been there for her? They know nothing about her at all.

For two days I maintained my position, hoping to hear she was awake. Then when she'd woken, it appeared the last person she wanted to see was me. I couldn't blame her, but would have given up everything I have just for one chance to explain. I can't bear her not comprehending that everything I'd done was with her interest at heart, that I didn't lie when I told her I loved her. The thought that she hates me hurts worse than any blow Nijad delivered.

It's so fucking hard to stay away.

I'd had hopes of making Aiza mine for so long, it's hard now to give up my dream, resolving to continue my life of solitude, knowing there'll be no other woman for me. I go through the motions on autopilot, forcing myself out of bed in the mornings, weary from lack of sleep when the nightmare visits again. I shower, trim my beard and put on my robes on automatic pilot, part of me wishing Nijad had killed me, then I wouldn't be feeling this pain.

Today, I'm just about to leave my suite when I have a visitor.

"Sheikh Nijad." I greet him formally with a small bow, his appearance at my door unexpected. I can't presume on our previous friendship. After I caused his sister so much distress, I'm surprised he even wants to talk to me again.

Nijad doesn't stand on formality. He enters, brushing past me, taking off his headdress and throwing it down, then turns to me and frowns. "She still won't see you."

I nod. She'd made that quite clear via her messages. I'm surprised Nijad feels he needs to tell me yet again.

Making himself comfortable on the couch, he stares at me before speaking, and then gives me his next piece of news. "Aiza says she'll be coming back to Al Qur'ah when she's no longer under medical attention."

"When will that be?" I ask through gritted teeth, knowing that my presence won't be welcome in the capital for some time. Much water has to flow under the bridge before I can return. Maybe it's better to put distance between us.

"Tomorrow."

That's so soon. Once she's gone I'll no longer have a chance to correct her assumption that I'd deceived her.

Then the intonation in his voice breaks through the fog in my mind, and I look at him expectantly, realising he has more to say.

His eyes meet mine. "You took her virginity." My brow creases as I wait for censor again, noting he seems resigned rather than upset. He lifts his hands. "We all thought she was no longer pure, so I know you didn't expect to find her that way. That doesn't change the fact that you took it. She believes that was all part of your plan."

She thinks I defiled her on purpose? Fuck, how did this become such a mess? I struggle for the words, then admit to my long-time friend, "I love her, Nijad. I think I've loved her forever. Yes, for my plan to work I had to be the one she trusted and turned to, though that was only an excuse. I'd have taken any chance to bed her and make her mine." Uncomfortable with his eyes on me after my admission, I turn away, walking to the windows. "There will never be another woman for me if I can't have her."

"You think I don't know that? I've seen the way you've always looked at her. And Rais, my friend, I couldn't wish for a better man for her."

What?

It's the last thing I expected him to say. I'd been anticipating him asking me to step away so she could marry someone more suitable. I close my eyes in relief, then go to face him, sinking down on the couch opposite, grimacing as my balls still throb with any sharp movement.

Nijad notices and smirks. Then grows serious. "She says you didn't use a condom."

I sit forwards, trying to ease the pressure and the ache. Aiza seems to have told him everything. I admit it. "That last time, I didn't. I always intended to wait until we — she — was ready. When we got to the valley, I wasn't prepared. I got carried away."

"You swam?" He grins. "That's a magical place." His smile slides away. "That was the place where I decided I wasn't going to trap Cara. If she got pregnant, it was to be her choice. Not that it mattered in the end." He frowns as he remembers. "Fuck it, Rais. Maybe I'm as bad as you. Or worse, as I all but forced her."

I doubt he'd ever be able to make Cara do something she didn't want to, but now's not the time for me to give him absolution. Now I've got to deal with the mess I might have made.

"Is Aiza pregnant?" I suspect it's too soon to tell.

He confirms my thoughts. "It's far too early to know one way or the other. She just wants to make certain she isn't."

That kicks me like another blow to my balls. Easing myself up, I start to pace, just to keep moving, trying to analyse my feelings. At the time I'd had no intention of making love to Aiza again, had been unable to resist once she said she'd wanted to swim in that pool. The thought that I could pull out hadn't occurred to me. Yes, I'd taken advantage of her, my mind so preoccupied with what I knew was ahead. It had been a way of reaffirming that, in that moment, we were both alive.

If a child came out of that union… I try to think how I'd feel. When my first wife got pregnant it was just how it should be. An arranged marriage between tribes, I hadn't even known her when I took her to my bed. She seemed content enough, happy that she'd fulfilled her duties by carrying my child. I was as good a husband as I could be to her, being barely more than a child myself. We got on well enough, although there was no spark. When she and my son died in childbirth, I was disappointed, distraught, then simply growing to accept fate hadn't meant it to be. Coming to realise the pressure had been removed from me, no one could push me into another arranged marriage.

But Aiza? Seeing her stomach swell as my seed grows inside her. I close my eyes as a swathe of emotion washes over me.

"I don't want her to do anything she doesn't want to, Nijad. Neither do I want her to make a decision she might regret while she's thinking wrong of me. I need to talk to her. I need to get her to understand the truth, why I took the actions I had." My eyes are wet as I turn to him. "It's killing me, Nijad, that she's left believing I failed her, and worse, betrayed her."

I hear his robes swish, then a hand lands on my shoulder and squeezes it. "My dearest friend," he begins, his voice catching. "I meant what I said about you being the best man for my sister. I'll do all that's in my power to help you." Again he breaks off as though considering the difficulty of what he's about to promise, then says firmly, "I'll arrange it so you can talk to her before she leaves. Whether she'll listen…"

CHAPTER 41
Aiza

"Y ou sure you want to do this?" Hunter queries as I pack the few things I want to take home. Most of the clothes here are Arabian dress, not what I'd wear in London. "Your brothers won't be happy."

"They'll get over it," I throw over my shoulder. "Once I'm out of sight I'll be out of mind all over again."

"Are you sure? Selfishly I think it's the best thing you could do, though you've only just reunited with your family. You could stay while you recover and get to know them. I know they're expecting you to go to Al Qur'ah. They've been worried sick about you, Aiza."

I swing around. "Hunter, that's only because what's happened has reminded them of my existence. Don't forget, they sent me to school, then to Switzerland. They didn't give a damn what I was doing, as long as I was out of their way. If my father was still alive he'd have remembered me only when it served him to make a convenient marriage. At least Kadar's not pushing for that." Pausing, I draw a much needed breath. "This situation has shocked them into remembering I exist. They'll forget me again soon enough, and I've survived this long on my own." I pause, knowing I'm lying, and I'll miss the chance to get to know them. I straighten my back. "I want to get back to work. That's where I can best make a contribution and feel my life is worth living. I'm returning to London. Today. If you don't help me, I'll go by myself." I need to put distance between myself and Rais. If I stay close, there's a chance I might weaken and agree to see him.

Hunter leans his arm on the doorjamb, his hand supporting his head. There's a twinkle in his eye. "They're going to hate me for this. But then, your family already do, so it's not going to make that much difference. I'll help you, Princess." He breaks off, then nods slowly and corrects, "Aiza." I give him an appreciative glance, knowing he's realising I'm leaving my royalty behind once again.

Stepping back, he leans down to pick up my carry-on, all the luggage I'm taking, his actions showing he's accepted my decision confirmed by his next words. "I've organised a private jet to take us to Dubai. From there we travel commercial."

Taking one last look around the royal suite where I stayed last night after leaving the hospital, accepting I couldn't bear to sleep here again, knowing grasping my future, taking control of my life is the only way I can move past everything that's happened to me. A surprising wave of regret washes over me as I pick up the letter that had been so hard to write, and leave it on the desk where it will be in plain sight. It contains my apologies to my brothers for leaving without saying goodbye, and the explanation that the best way for me to make a full recovery is to get back to my old life. With the assurance I'll organise proper security and take up residence in a more secure location. Hunter will be able to help me with that.

He's standing at the open door, waiting. With a strange reluctance I make my feet move and precede him out of the suite. Dharr stands to attention. I wave down to the baggage that Hunter's pulling behind him. "I'm just going to see Hunter off," I explain. I don't add I'm going with him. As Dharr starts to follow, I say, "There's no danger now, Dharr. I don't need an escort."

"Princess…"

Hoping that's the last time anyone calls me by my title, I hold up my hand and say imperiously, "That's a direct order, Dharr. I no longer need protection in my own palace."

He shakes his head, clearly reluctant, but as I walk down the corridor, he and the other guards stay in position.

Hunter grins when we're out of ear shot. "Being royalty comes with perks. Just to let you know, an order won't stop me. You won't be getting rid of me that easily."

"When I get back home," I tell him as we walk down the stairs, "I know I'll need protection."

"Grade A won't be letting the ball drop again. And I'll be the one guarding you."

We'll see about that. Hunter's still hoping that we have a future together and is taking my choice of location as a sign he's still got hope. As I don't see myself with any man, not even him, I've got to make him understand he's going to have to give me some space. I don't want to be forced into a relationship by any machinations of his to stay close. I'll soon have to find a way of telling him my plans to talk to his boss and request a different close protection officer to be assigned. Even though that will disappoint him.

As we walk through the palace Hunter explains our travel arrangements. "There'll be a taxi waiting. It will take us to the airport. I'm sorry I couldn't even get first class from Dubai," he warns me. "Will you be okay travelling economy?"

"I don't care if we fly with the freight. The sooner I get away from here the better." If I don't get away I might weaken and allow Rais to trick me again.

As I walk through the corridors, skirting the areas where repairs have already commenced, I wonder whether this is the last time I'll be in this palace. Or, even whether I'll ever feel I can return to Amahad. This country holds nothing for me, relations who I share blood but nothing else with, and only bad memories should I stay. It was hard enough to sleep in the master suite alone, unable to think of anything other than how Rais had made me feel when he held me. *I'll find it easier to forget when I'm back in England.*

The palace is quiet this early in the morning. There's no one around, no one to notice or witness my escape. My fear of being stopped begins to dissipate, and I start to breathe easier as the main doors come into sight. The only sounds are those coming from the kitchens as the early rising staff are up preparing breakfast, and the rattling of the wheels of the suitcase as it rolls over the marble floor.

The doors are straight ahead now. Freedom is in sight.

Two men step out of the shadows.

"That will be all, Hunter," Nijad commands. "I suggest you take the taxi and catch the plane you chartered."

My mouth drops open as Hunter pulls himself up tall. "I'm staying with the princess." He puts himself in front of me and widens his stance.

Nijad's unperturbed. "Your services are no longer required, Hunter. I've spoken to Ben Carter, he's expecting you back in London today."

A flummoxed look on his face, Hunter glances at me, then at Nijad. It will be hard for him to ignore a direct instruction.

It's time I step up. I refuse to be cowed. "I'm going with him," I say haughtily.

My brother shakes his head. "You're running away," he accuses. "Otherwise you wouldn't be leaving like a thief in the night."

The second man speaks for the first time, his voice deep and low. "Aiza, I can understand you wanting to leave Amahad. I'd do nothing to stop you if I thought you were leaving for the right reasons."

"I want to get home, to London." It seems increasingly likely they're going to force me to stay. Though force is probably the wrong word. Even though I still hate him, it's proving hard to walk away from Rais. *This is why I couldn't trust myself to see him.* "Let me leave, please." I find myself begging, pleading. "I don't want to stay."

"And I don't blame you. But," Rais points to my sling, "you've hardly recovered. And leaving without a word to your family suggests you know this is wrong."

"I left a note to explain." I cast a glare at my brother. "I knew if I told you my plans, you'd try to stop me."

"The only reason for preventing you leaving is that we care." Nijad's face looks drawn, and I wonder how long both men have been waiting for me. The bags under his eyes suggest it could have been all night. That he knew I'd be enacting an escape shows perhaps, after all, he does know something about me.

For the first time I look properly at Rais, and as I do, wince. It's hard to miss he must have taken a severe beating. Nijad sees my face fall, and looks guilty.

Rais shrugs off my reaction. "If I thought you be better off in London, I wouldn't stand in your way. But I don't think you will be. I don't want anything else laid at my door."

My emotions entangled, now temper rises to the fore as I remember the last time I saw this man he was selling me to a terrorist. I take a step towards him. "You don't want anything else laid at your bloody door? Huh! I can well believe that. There's so much there already, you probably can't step over it to get inside." Lifting my good arm, I poke him in the chest. "You tricked me into sleeping with you, made me think you cared about me. Deceived me into thinking you were helping me escape. Conveniently forgot to use a condom when you persuaded me to have sex with you again. Sold me to a fucking lunatic who spelt out very carefully exactly what he intended to do with me, and were complicit in making me listen as he told me his plans in great detail." I prod him again and must have touched a bruise hidden under his clothing, as he flinches, though utters no verbal complaint. "His plans on how he was going to break Kadar and ultimately destroy Amahad."

I grab a breath, and my voice hitches as I continue. "*I had no choice.* You put me in the position that I preferred death rather than risk causing my brother any more distress. I had to take matters into my own hands. Taking myself out of the equation. Thwarting al-Fahri's plans, seemed the only thing I could do."

As I feel something on my face, I raise my hand to find tears streaming. Before I know it, I'm sobbing. Nijad's arms come around as he pulls me into his chest, smoothing my hair in a rhythmic motion. I can't remember ever having received anything more than a quick hug from any of my brothers before, and for the first time in my life I feel a connection to my family as he comforts me.

"Shush, sweetheart."

"And this is exactly why she shouldn't be anywhere near him." The way Hunter sneers, it's clear exactly who he's talking about. "She needs to get away from this place. Only then can she start moving forwards…"

"Just go, Hunter," Nijad tells him again.

Hunter's standing his ground. "I'm not leaving her with you. She needs someone…"

"She's got her family." And standing, being held in my brother's arms, hearing the concern in his voice as he tightens his hold around me, it dawns on me he's not trying to trap me, just doing what he thinks is best. For me.

The chill in Nijad's voice is a direct contrast to the warmth of his hug. "If you don't leave voluntarily, Hunter, I *will* have you escorted out. You need to go back to London, to Grade A and your job. When Aiza is stronger, if she chooses to go to the UK, if she decides she wants *you*, then she can travel when she's stronger. Hell, I'll even bring her over myself."

My head turned against Nijad's chest, I don't see Hunter leave. As I'm swept up into my brother's strong arms I presume that he has. To my surprise, if I'm honest about my emotions, I don't feel too much of a loss.

Still quietly sobbing, I let Nijad carry me through the palace, belatedly realising he's taking me back to the royal suite. It's only when he puts me down in the bedroom and I see Rais has come with us and has opened the door that leads to the dungeon do I come to my senses.

"No." My panicked tone leaves them in no doubt as to what I mean.

Nijad looks at me, wiping the few remaining tears away with his thumb. His dark eyes with gold flecks in them, so similar to the ones I see each day in the mirror, stare into mine. "Rais, leave us please."

I feel him obey, as the air suddenly seems easier to breathe. Pushing me towards the bed, Nijad presses on my shoulders and I sit down. He seats himself beside me. "I know we haven't had a close brother/sister relationship, and that's something I have every desire to rectify."

"I'd like that," I tell him shyly. Part of me had been expecting my family to feel relieved to be rid of the burden I am to them.

He gives me a brief hug, then sits forwards, his hands clasped between his knees, his head twisting to look at me. "Kadar, Jasim, myself and you, we're all very similar, though you've not been around us enough to see just how much. Rushdi left us a legacy, and try as we might, we can't shake it."

I tilt my head to one side, wondering what the point of this is.

"You're a strong, independent person. It's no wonder you see yourself as a Domme. You don't want to concede control in any situation."

"If you're talking about what happened with Rais…"

"That's part of it." He pauses to sigh. "Look, I've had a long discussion with Rais."

"With your fists," I butt in.

Nijad raises an eyebrow, then barks a short laugh. "He hurt you. He almost caused your death. I wasn't going to let him get away scot free. Aiza, I know Rais as well as I know myself. I believe to the very depths of my soul that at no time did he knowingly put you in danger. I also understand why he couldn't tell you his plans. You'd have to be an Oscar winner to act surprised when al-Fahri appeared. Your fear had to appear genuine."

"Rais didn't give me the choice."

"And that's at the heart of the matter, isn't it? You think he betrayed you. As a result, you've got no faith in him."

I jerk my head in a nod. "I'd never be able to trust him again, Nijad." Seeing him has broken my heart all over again, bringing back thoughts of what might have been had he not taken the actions he had.

Nijad unclasps his hands and wraps one around mine. "What would you do, dear sister, if a sub didn't trust you?"

I shrug. "I'd work to earn it. Or try to win it back if I lost it."

"So why won't you give Rais a chance? I don't have to tell you about safewords and who really holds the power in a Dom/sub relationship."

"Rais is no Dom."

Nijad laughs, a full belly chuckle that makes his body shake. "Sister, if it helps to give it a label, while I'm a Dom, in our friendship, when we work together, he's the Top in our relationship. Always has been. He doesn't have to play in clubs to prove it or learn how to use the power at his command." As I open my mouth to protest he continues, "He's in control in every situation, whether he consciously takes it or not. Don't forget how long Rais and I have been friends. I know what I'm talking about."

I look at Nijad curiously, surprised by his admission. And the implications for me. Should I decide to give Rais another chance? *I'm not really considering it, am I?* "What if I don't want to give up control?"

Taking my hand, he squeezes it. "That's the benefit of Rais rejecting any label. He can be dominant when he needs to be, he doesn't have to prove himself to anyone. He defers to me not because of my rank, but instead because he can see my worth. At other times, yeah, he'll naturally assume the lead role, and I'm happy with that. Because he's right, and I'm content to follow."

"He scares me."

Nijad huffs a laugh. "Me too, at times."

I think for a moment. Speaking to my brother has calmed me, and at last, all my tears have dried. It was cathartic to let them escape. I'm in a better frame of mind to listen. "What are you suggesting, Ni?" As he squeezes my fingers again, I realise I've never used his shortened name before.

"I'm suggesting you give him a chance." Nijad gets to his feet and opens the door, and without giving me a chance to protest, ushers Rais inside. "My proposal is that Rais takes you to the dungeon…"

"No," I repeat, as adamantly as before.

"Hear me out?" my brother pleads. When I give a hesitant nod, he looks at Rais. "I'll come down too. Not only will you have a safeword, but the assurance that should you need to use it, I'll be within earshot."

"I'm not letting my brother see me naked in a dungeon." My face fills with horror.

"Certainly not," both Rais and Nijad exclaim together.

Nijad gives a quick grin. "I said within earshot, nothing about within sight."

I look up at the man who's dressed casually in jeans and a t-shirt which hugs him as though the sight of his body will tempt me. *And it certainly does… Well, that part of me that isn't thinking straight.* The other part reminds me how much I hurt. "I don't think this will work, Rais." Even to me, my voice lacks fortitude.

Seeing an opening and snatching it, Rais comes and kneels on the floor in front of me. His hands move as if to touch mine, then he lets them drop back down at his sides. "Give me a chance. I need this, and I think you do too. One chance. If that doesn't work," his voice catches, "you can be on the next plane to London."

His dark eyes shine with earnestness, the bruises doing nothing to mar the rugged beauty of his face. Sitting back on his haunches at my feet, it's only his hands clasping and unclasping that betray how worried he is that I'll refuse.

Nijad will be there. I have a safeword. I can stop at any time.

Not at all sure I'm doing the right thing, I stand. "I correct my previous statement. I *know* this won't work. If you promise after this you'll never try to see me again, *Sheikh*, then I'll come with you and give you one last chance."

CHAPTER 42
Rais

She'll give me this. Yet she's convinced there's nothing I can do to make her trust me again, her words making it clear I've only got one stab to put things right, and if I fail she'll leave Amahad, possibly never to return. I've hurt her too much, and maybe I'll have to accept in doing so I've lost her forever. I exchange a pained glance with Nijad, he gives me a confident nod. He's given me the best advice he can. I can only hope what he suggested, along with the ideas I have of my own, will bring her back to me.

I'm not surprised when she pulls back her shoulders and leads the way down to the dungeon, stepping aside to let Nijad put his spare key into the lock. The original I had had, of course, but somewhere along the way, mislaid.

Stepping into the darkened area, Nijad flicks on the lights, then crosses to the same wingback chair I'd used to spank her, turning it so it faces the wall, and sits down. He's immediately hidden from view.

Aiza stands rigid, her back towards me. Pulling my t-shirt over my head, I decide my first instruction might be easier for her to obey without having to face me. In fact, I debate whether to put my shirt back on, my torso a mass of purpling bruises, then decide if there's a chance of once again feeling her skin against mine, I'm going to take it. Even if it might be for the last time.

"Take your clothes off, Aiza." My voice has lowered a tone.

She hesitates, and I'm not certain what she's going to do until she says snidely, "It's not as if you haven't seen it before, I suppose."

As I see her take her arm out of her sling to awkwardly undo her buttons, I think to myself, *brat*, remembering the term Nijad's used to describe wayward subs in the past. Often, and fondly, in reference to his wife. As she struggles, I offer to help. "Do you need a hand?"

"No."

The snapped word shows she doesn't want me anywhere near her. Does she not trust me even to touch her? *Or does she not trust herself?*

"No isn't your safeword, Aiza," I remind her as I move forwards and reach my arms around her to undo the buttons she's having a problem with. "How sore is your arm?"

"It feels a little stiff, not too painful. The sling's only a precaution to give it support."

My hands untie the ribbon holding her trousers up, and once released they fall to the floor. I start pushing down her pants.

"No."

"Do I have to remind you again?" My voice is low, gravelly. Now, when I undo the clasp of her bra she allows the garment to fall. She's naked before me, and while my eyes can only feast on that perfect heart-shaped arse, my recently abused cock twitches and starts to lengthen. Internally I sigh with relief, having feared Nijad had done permanent damage.

Willing my dick to behave, I remove a silk blindfold from the rear pocket of my jeans. "I'm going to blindfold you now, Aiza."

"Shouldn't we be having a negotiation? You need to explain what you're going to do, and I need to agree," she huffs, as if I don't know what I'm doing.

I inch closer, not enough to touch her, she's not ready for that, just so she'll feel the heat of my body against her back. "I'm going to use the bondage table," I begin.

"I don't want to be bound." Her body stiffens, probably in memory of how she'd been tied up by al-Fahri's men.

"I understand. I'm not going to tie you down, Aiza. I do want to take one of your senses away."

I give her a moment to decide, and when she nods. I place the blindfold around her head, making sure it's not too tight, and that she will be unable to see anything. Now, I want her to get used to obeying me. With her ability to see eliminated, she has no alternative.

"Take two steps forwards. That's right. Now one to the left. Move forwards again. Now, stop. Put out your right hand. Can you feel the table in front of you?"

Her fingers move and explore. It's a padded bench which will support her torso, and an inverted V which will support her legs.

"Can you get onto it, or do you need help?"

For an answer, she pulls herself up, and I take it she's familiar with this piece of equipment.

"I don't know why we're even doing this, Rais. It won't work."

Ignoring her statement, I tell her what I want her to do. "Lie on your back. Put your arms beside you and lay your legs flat." For the moment I've pushed the leg rests together. I can open them when, hopefully, she becomes more relaxed.

I deepen my voice. "As I said, Aiza, I'm not going to physically bind you. You *will* be bound by my voice. Keep still and do not move."

Watching, I see goosebumps appear on her skin, a physical display that she's not unaffected. Crouching, I delve into the box which Nijad had placed here for me. All brand-new toys, still in their wrappings. As I break the plastic on one, she shivers.

"Remember your safeword, Aiza."

She nods. "I'm not usually on the receiving end."

"Today you are. Relax, habiti." I lift the flogger with very soft leather strands, trailing it over her stomach. Her mouth opens and closes, her brow lined. I reckon I'm very close to her calling the whole thing off.

Lifting the flogger away, I then bring it down on her skin, so softly it's like a caress. Then I do it again, and again, getting into a rhythm, too gently for it to do more than give a slight sting, just sufficient to start to give her skin a pinkish tinge. Unlike my darker skin, hers is comparably light, and I can easily see it beginning to glow.

A stroke to her stomach and then to her thighs, and then further down her legs. As she's holding them tightly together, I can do both at once. When I reach her feet, I let the leather strand bounce off her soles, causing her to jump. Then I start moving upwards again, keeping a regular beat, as I move her soft tummy, then up to her breasts. She starts to relax, then tenses as the leather strands touch her nipples. As they start becoming erect, I surmise it's from pleasure, not fear.

Methodically striking her, keeping to a regular tempo, I continue to use the flogger. Gradually her face muscles, which had been drawn into a frown, start to lose their stiffness, and the lines start to recede from her forehead. Continuing the tender onslaught up and down her body, I only stop when she's totally loosened up, and unwittingly her legs fall open, allowing me a glorious view of her pink pussy. A sight I'd almost given up hope of ever seeing again.

When I step away from the bench, she doesn't move. Taking two more items from the toy box, I run a soft paintbrush over her erect nipples. She strains up into my touch. Then I carefully use the other implement I'm holding, this one with harsh metal teeth. She lies flat down again. Alternating between them, I gradually make my way back down her body, then return to her nipples again.

She doesn't know which I'll use. A gently stroke, or a scratch with the coarse metal.

When I widen the V, opening her more, she doesn't protest, seemingly unaware of what I'm doing. Her clit's now exposed, as well as her pussy, which has started to glisten. Using the soft brush, I paint her own arousal over her clit, and then touch it lightly with the metal prongs.

Then repeat.

She moans.

While running the metal brush over her nipples, I use the other to circle that bunch of nerves. When she tenses, I move it away. "Aiza," I start, keeping my voice calm. "Everything I said to you was the truth."

She stiffens. "You said everything you did was for Amahad."

I go back to stroking. Gradually raising her level of arousal again, her tension turns into something else, and I chance speaking once more. "Amahad is you, and you are Amahad. I wanted to free you from that bastard once and for all."

Another moan, and her mouth works as she struggles to speak, not knowing whether her head should respond to my words or her body to my touch. My aim is to get both on the same page.

"You could have killed him in that tent."

In a conversational tone, I explain why I couldn't. "Al-Fahri's men outnumbered mine. He could have killed me, and then where would you have been? I couldn't take that risk. We had to get him on the path so he was trapped."

"Ah, uh, oh…" I stop what I'm doing and move the flexible bristles to her nipples. "The things he said to me. How could you stand there and let him threaten me like that? If you cared…"

"I cared." It's hard to keep my voice even. "I fucking cared, Aiza. I had to focus on the thought of Fuad's bullet going into this head, seeing in my mind his blood and brains scattered. And Fuad wasn't going to miss. There was no chance of that. *That's* what I was thinking about."

"You…oh!" I'm torturing her clit once again. "You could have warned me."

"I thought about it. I didn't think you could pull it off. It was your genuine reaction that made him careless. He didn't expect an ambush. He thought he had me exactly where he wanted me. It fucking killed me to let you go off with him. I consoled myself knowing he wouldn't have you for long, and that soon you'd be safe."

Touching her for the first time, I lower my head, using my tongue to lick her slit then circle her clit. As the bud stiffens, I close my lips and suck that tender bundle of nerves sharply into my mouth, then I can't resist having a taste of that pussy I had feared never to touch again. Her body is trembling, her legs twitch. I put a finger inside her, then my mouth returns to her clit. Her thighs move of their own volition, her muscles tightening and trapping my head. Having teased her mercilessly for so long, she goes off like a rocket, her scream of release echoing around the dungeon. I cast a quick glance to the wingback chair. If I hadn't known he was there, he could be invisible. Nijad gives no sign of his presence.

It's not as if it isn't like any other dungeon he's been in.

My hands move to her tits, desperate to feel them. As my fingers pinch her nipples, she presses up rather than evading me. Widening her legs once again, I can't resist lowering my head. As I do, I tense, a flashback hitting me as I hear Fuad's voice echoing in my mind telling me she's thrown herself into the canyon.

As the memory of my horror and fear come back to me, trembling as I rear up, my plans flying out of the window, unable to do anything except cover my body with hers, to feel her warm skin next to mine. My mouth almost touches her lips, and I've lost control of my voice, which breaks as I go off script and I tell her, "Aiza, habiti. I thought you were fucking dead. All I wanted to do was die with you. Aiza, my love. When I knew, when Fuad said he'd watched you fall to your death… Aiza, oh, Aiza."

Disobeying my instruction, she moves her arms, bringing both around me, her hands smoothing my back, giving me the comfort I was supposed to be giving to her. Her fingers move to the back of my skull, pushing my head down on her chest.

"I love you, Aiza. I'll spend the rest of my life loving you. There's never been, or will be, another woman for me. If you can't trust me to be beside you, I'll leave you alone, but never doubt wherever you are, whatever you're doing, I'll always love you."

She's holding me tight as she processes my words, and I hope, fuck it, my whole life depends on her giving me the right answer.

I don't give a damn she's topping from the bottom when she suddenly calls out. "Brother, leave us. Unless you want to see your sister get screwed."

Nijad barks a laugh. I'm lying, covering her body as he walks past, close enough to pat me on the shoulder. The door to the dungeon opens and shuts, and we're alone. *She trusts me enough to lose her safety net.* Though she's given no commitment yet. *It's a start.*

Raising my head, I bring my mouth to hers, knowing she can taste herself on me, plunging my tongue into her mouth, relishing the chance to do something I never thought I'd do again. The kiss starts soft, both of us hesitant, me not wanting to rush this, her uncertain she's doing the right thing. She smells heavenly, that beautiful natural perfume which fills my nostrils, inciting me, making my cock feel like steel. Her hand on my head trying to hold me closer, and I swear sparks fly between us as we deepen the kiss until our lips meet with almost punishing pressure, her mouth bruising mine as our tongues twist and slide, our flavours combing until it's hard to tell one from the other. The dungeon is silent around us, no sound filters down here. All we hear are the harsh gasps for breath when we come up for air before putting our mouths together again. So many emotions go through me, the memory of my anguish when I thought I had lost her, the love that I feel that I'm trying to convey, an embryonic hope that she'll forgive me.

The more I kiss her, the more I know it isn't enough. Regaining some semblance of control, I pull away with a strangled cry, growling my next instruction. "Keep still." Then I move down her body, sucking her nipples, using my tongue to press them one by one to the roof of my mouth, biting down gently, seeing her jump and enjoy the bite of pain. Continuing downwards, kissing my way across her stomach until I reach my personal utopia, my own slice of heaven.

My fingers enter her tight sheath as I lick her most sensitive nub. She moans as I suck, then gently use my teeth, then repeat the process, all the time curling my fingers up inside her. When her muscles start clenching I pull away, undo my zip and shrug my jeans down and quickly sheave myself with a condom, knowing she'd given me permission when she dismissed her brother. Pushing her legs further apart so she's wide open to me, I can't wait any longer. Lining myself up and thrusting in, filling her completely. Then pause. *I thought I'd lost her, would never feel her like this ever again.*

Tears come to my eyes as I start thrusting. Again she disobeys me, though I'm not going to complain as her legs come up and around me, allowing me to go deeper. I watch, entranced as my cock appears and disappears into her sweet cunt. The one only I have been in.

"I've dreamt of this, habiti. I never want to lose you again," I growl, my voice deep with emotion.

"I want you so much," she confirms between gasps for breath. "Make me yours."

I thrust in deep, then lean over, pressing my lips against her cheek. "Do you mean it?"

"Rais, oh Rais. Yes."

Those glorious words. I'll make her mine so she'll never want another. When I start moving again I could no longer stop even if I wanted to. The tingling that runs down my spine, making my balls tighten, threatens to break my control. The way she's moving with me, pushing back against me, those little groans and sighs coming out of her mouth. I know I won't be able to last much longer. Any control I had has been lost.

"Come for me, Aiza," I command…or plead. It's hard to tell which at this moment.

As my fingers work her clit, her legs go tight around me and her internal muscles clench down. She cries out as my cock swells, reaching the point of no return, and I shout, "Fuck, Aiza, habiti… I'm coming."

I never expected to have the chance to do this again, to feel her perfect cunt strangling my dick, to feel my seed flooding the barrier between us.

"You're mine, fucking mine. You don't have a choice, Aiza. I'm never letting you leave me."

My cock's still pumping, emptying everything I've got into her. Both of us are panting as at last I collapse over her. "Fucking mine, Aiza."

CHAPTER 43
Aiza

As my breathing returns to normal I realise my hands are running up and down the smooth skin of Rais's back, while knowing this is where I'm meant to be. He'd been right, using my own Dominant skills against me, getting me into a place where I would listen rather than letting my fears rule me. Deep down I always knew that Rais wouldn't have wanted to hurt me. I find it hard to trust anyone. Up to now, I've only been able to rely on myself.

My family hadn't been there for me, I couldn't depend on them, I had no one to lean on. Of necessity, my Domme side never relaxed or turned off completely, always wanting, needing, to take charge. When I thought Rais had let me down, it was easier to retreat and hide in my natural inclination to count on no one but myself. *People make mistakes. Nobody's perfect.* Rais was at fault. I understand the argument that if forewarned I might have given everything away to al-Fahri just shows he had no confidence in my acting skills, or my love for my country. If he had warned me, I'd never have gone over that cliff edge.

He's lying, carefully keeping his weight off of me as I start to say my thoughts aloud. "It's not easy for me to trust," I start. He doesn't speak, automatically giving me time. "No one's ever been there for me. That's why it was easier to think you'd turned traitor. Why I took my fate into my own hands."

One of his hands moves to my face, and the blindfold falls away. I open my eyes. Only a few centimetres separate us. His pupils are dilated, his expression as gentle as any I've ever seen. "Habiti. I cocked up. If I could go back in time, I'd do everything differently. I'd tell you everything and trust you to play your part…"

"Shush. I appreciate the reasons why you hadn't told me. I do understand. I can't even argue it wasn't the right way to play it. The prize was enormous."

"But the price too high." An expression of such pain crosses his face that I want to comfort him.

"It could have been. It wasn't. I'm here. I'm alive."

His hands cup my face. "I'll never put you in danger again. I promise you that. Never keep anything from you. If you'll let me, I'll spend the rest of my life showing you that you can always depend on me. I'll be so careful. I'll never knowingly give you the opportunity to distrust me again." He breathes in deeply. "We can go as slow as you like, I'll give you all the time that you need. I want you to be mine, habiti. Nothing has changed. I never stopped loving you, and I never will."

I never stopped loving him. Deep down I always knew it. That was why I'd been so desperate to put space between us. It seems natural for the words to come out of my mouth. "I love you, Rais."

His face loses some tension. "I love you, Aiza. Fuck, how I love you."

We kiss, this time more gently, only a few seconds before our mouths part. I realise, though I didn't expect it, I liked him taking charge. "Rais," I start, tentatively, "can we do this again?"

He takes a second to work out what I'm asking. "Fuck? Oh yeah. If I had my way, you'd always be naked."

Bunching my fist, I thump him lightly on his back. "That too, though I meant play this way." I feel my face flush as I add almost shyly, "I've never been on the receiving end before."

"Yes, you have," he murmurs against my skin as he contradicts and reminds me. "When I spanked you."

Oh yeah. If I'm honest, I even enjoyed that.

"But, Aiza, I'm warning you, I'll never let you tie me up and whip me."

No, he probably wouldn't. Nijad was right. While Rais might not use the word to describe himself, he's a Dom to the core. *And that excites me.* Oh, I can see obstacles ahead as we go head to head, but I doubt there'll ever be a dull moment in our marriage. But... "Do you still want to marry me?"

His voice vibrates against me. "Marry you, keep you pregnant. Keep you safe. Love you forever."

"Barefoot in the kitchen, eh?"

"Works for me." I hit him again. This time harder.

"Ouch." He lifts his torso off me, holding his weight on his strong arms. "Careful, habiti. You'll be paying for that."

I'm sure he'll make any toll he demands worth it.

I look up to see his beautiful expressive eyes are staring intently into mine. "I love you," he tells me again, in such a tone I can do nothing but believe him.

"I think I loved you since I was eighteen." I never believed he would ever be mine. He'd seemed so unobtainable, far out of my reach. I bite my lip and make my admission. "I was worried I could be pregnant. I nearly took the morning after pill."

"Hush, Aiza. Nijad told me. It doesn't matter what you did."

I offer him a small smile. "I didn't. Couldn't do it."

He inhales deeply, his face so full of emotion as he touches my stomach. He doesn't need to say anything, his expression saying it all. My muscles clench at the thought that I might already have his baby growing inside me. When it came to it, even though at that point I'd thought I hated him, I couldn't bring myself to do anything to prevent a possible pregnancy.

Moving one hand down, he touches his fingers to my slit. "Fuck, Aiza, I didn't think it was possible to love someone as much as I do you. I promise you this. No one, *no one* except me, will ever touch you here again."

Knowing he's referring to me playing in clubs, and finding I don't mind his possessiveness at all, I glance around and smile cheekily. "Do you think Nijad will let us use his dungeon sometimes?"

His eyes follow mine, and notes what I'm seeing in the corner. "Well, I'd certainly like to try out that sex swing."

I giggle. "Perhaps Kadar will give you Shibari lessons." Yes, I've heard all the rumours about my brother being a master rigger.

Rais's eyes open wide. "I am not, I repeat, *not*, going to ask the emir how to tie up his sister."

His shock provokes a full laugh from me.

I'm still chuckling, privately imagining how that discussion would go in my head when I decide to tease him. I pout. "Well, maybe I'll ask Kadar to teach *me*."

Jaw dropping, his mouth opens wide, snaps shut, then he announces, "I don't mind having you in my knots, habiti, but a man has limits. And being bound by his wife is one of them."

I giggle. Somehow I hadn't thought he would go for that.

He grins, leans over and kisses me, then pulls away from me and stands, tucking his hardening cock back into his jeans. My eyes fix on his body, finding particular interest in what he's doing with his hands. As he sees where I'm looking at, he smirks. "You can deal with this later for me."

It will be my pleasure.

Going back across the room, he picks up his shirt and my clothes. "Here," he tosses mine to me, "get up. Nijad's probably impatiently waiting for us."

I'd forgotten about my brother.

"He's a Dom, Rais. He'll know to give us time." Nonetheless, I start dressing as he hands me my clothes, helping me into my blouse and my arm back into the sling. My shoulder only aches slightly now, yet I haven't regained full movement.

Having made ourselves presentable, we leave the converted harem and return to the suite to find Nijad is indeed anxiously waiting for us, having made himself comfortable in the living room. Well, it is *his* suite after all. He stands as we enter, and seeing us smiling and holding hands, gives a sigh of relief then smirks. "Well, it looks like you two have made up." There's no need to confirm it in words, so Nijad resumes. "You took so long, I've had time to do some thinking, and have run my ideas past Kadar and got his agreement. Come, sit. I've things to tell you."

Rais raises an eyebrow and glances at me. I shrug, not having a clue what he could be talking about. Then we go and join my brother, who's sitting at the table. The fact he's not lounging on a couch suggests this will be a serious discussion.

As if he doesn't want to let me go for a moment, Rais kicks out a chair, then pulls me down onto his lap. Nijad nods in approval, then drums his fingers on the table.

"Kadar wants Cara in Al Qur'ah permanently. While she can work remotely, he likes her close. Particularly with planning how we're going to manage the investment of the new money when it starts coming in from oil exports. She prefers living there and being with her sisters-in-law. It makes sense for the children to be together."

I can see that.

"I must admit, I like working alongside my brothers. The commute is getting tedious."

His commute is nothing like mine was in London — he pilots his own helicopter. I'm curious to where he's going with this.

"Rais, you've been the unofficial leader of the desert tribes for a number of years now. Kadar agrees we should put that on a more formal basis. He, *we*, believe the title of Sheikh of the Southern Desert should be transferred from me to yourself."

There's complete silence. Then, "Nijad, Prince... No, I'm..." Rais's stutter shows how stunned he is.

"It's the command of the emir, Rais. It's been decided. And, of course, along with that title goes the official residence. The palace of Zalmā."

This beautiful palace? This is where we'll live? Amazed and pleased, I lean so I can whisper quietly into his ear. "That will include the dungeon."

"I heard that, Aiza." Nijad chuckles.

I redden.

"Kadar suggests we have a ceremony transferring the title to you at the same time as your wedding. I take it you will be getting married soon?"

Rais and I look at each other. He raises an eyebrow, I nod. Guess that's the proposal sorted and accepted. Looking at us, Nijad smirks.

I hadn't thought as far ahead as planning a wedding. Nijad's suggestion makes sense. Making it a celebration of Rais's new role would work. My mind begins racing about how I can set up an outpost of the charity here. Work with the specialists at the hospital. Get the children we identify here to receive the treatment they need.

As if he's read my mind, Rais at last finds his voice. "Nijad, I can't thank you enough. I really don't deserve it. Nonetheless, there's so much I can achieve with Kadar's sanction. I believe I'll have no problem getting the desert sheikhs on board."

"They trust you more than me, Rais. You're one of them."

"And," Rais continues as though he wasn't interrupted, "Aiza can get started setting up a base here to serve her charity."

"Indeed, she can."

How much things can change in a short span of time. As Rais and Nijad begin thrashing out the details and what officially being the Desert Sheikh would mean for Rais, I think back over the past couple of weeks. Leaning back against Rais's shoulder, feeling his arm come around to hold me, I realise it's here where I was meant to be all along. With the man I never dared dream would want me. The idea of staying in Amahad is no longer scary. I feel myself relax, as though at last, with him, I've found a place to really call home. I move my hand, Rais's fingers entwine with mine.

"Aiza. Aiza?" Rais's amused voice gets through to me.

"Sorry, what?" I come out of my reverie.

"We were just discussing whether you wanted to convert a part of the palace for your offices or take over a disused building in Zٖalmā." Nijad looks amused that I'd been lost in my thoughts.

"I was thinking we could go to London so you can thrash out the details with your charity," Rais says. "Start getting the ball rolling as soon as we can."

I squeeze Rais's hand, realising with him beside me, that all my dreams could come true. As if he can read my mind, Rais turns my head to face him. "Habiti. Anything you want, I'll make happen for you."

EPILOGUE 1
Rais

I watch my *wife*. She's sitting behind the desk in the room we've converted into an office for her. She's got a phone lodged between her ear and her shoulder, her brow is scrunched as she types on the keyboard. Leaning back against the door, I wait for her to finish what is apparently a difficult conversation.

At last the call ends. "Problems?"

"Frustrations." She pushes her hair back behind her ears, and then shrugs. "It's nothing that money can't solve. But this problem should never arise."

Pushing away from the door, I move closer, kicking out the chair in front of the desk and sitting on it. "Want to talk about it?"

Her beautiful eyes stare at me. "There's a baby, two months old. Has been diagnosed with a hole in his heart, perfectly treatable. It wasn't diagnosed during pregnancy."

"So where's the issue?"

"His parents don't have insurance covering pre-existing conditions. His heart problem is congenital. They can't afford the treatment. We caught the Gofundme account they set up."

Frowning, I catch on to the reason why she's annoyed. This isn't a difficult case of getting a baby to the right country to have treatment, this is simply a case of money. In a third world country it would be expected. I rise, walking around the desk, pulling her to her feet, then sit with my arms around her. "You can't solve all the world's problems by yourself."

"I know." She leans her head on my shoulder. "I've authorised the full amount for treatment, yet there'll be many more cases like his. And we won't catch them all." Her hand rubs her slightly rounded stomach, and again, my face creases. With the work that she does, she comes across sick children far too often, and worries about ours being healthy.

Covering her hand with mine, I try to reassure her. "He'll be fine."

"He?" She lifts her head and looks straight at me.

I smile. "I was right that the first time I took you unprotected I'd put my baby inside you."

"You can't control everything. Even you can't determine the sex." She laughs.

"You're right, I can't." An image of a mini replica of her comes into my mind. "But, fuck me, Aiza, the thought of another one of you?" I pretend to be shocked.

As she goes to put her fist to my arm, I grab hold of it, pulling it to my lips and kissing each of her fingers instead. Our marriage was a month to the day after she agreed to give me another chance, and every day I give thanks that I

persuaded her to give me another chance. That was eight
weeks ago now, which means in about five months I'll
meet my child. The first of many it seems, if Aiza gets her
way. Me? I'm terrified of what she'll have to go through,
and unsure whether even once is too much. If Aiza asked
for the moon, I'd go hang it.

"How's your day been?" she enquires, relaxing back
against me again.

"Trying." At her cocked eyebrow, I continue. "Just the
usual, sorting out tribal problems."

"Any more goats gone missing?"

"No." My eyes narrow. "Jibran's tribe has set up
watchers so they can catch whoever's responsible in the
act. He's still blaming Sofian's men. It's hard keeping
peace between them."

"They can't say for certain. The branded goats haven't
been found, have they?"

"They've probably been eaten."

"Rais!" she admonishes.

She listens to me every evening, just as I like to hear
about her day. I never realised how amazing it was to have
someone to share things with. Every little detail she
remembers. As I try to remember hers.

"Oh, I almost forgot."

"What, habiti?"

"Jasim and Janna are coming to visit."

I bark a laugh. "Good thing we've moved out of that
suite." We've joined two others together, making a fairly

large apartment in preparation for the number of kids Aiza wants. It's light and airy, we both much prefer something that's been built to our requirements. Which means the old royal suite can be used for guests. Guests who regularly visit due to certain amenities. Nijad and Cara were here last week, and even Kadar's got a visit planned in the near future.

"I'd be honoured if I didn't know it wasn't us they're coming to see," I mumble into her ear, taking the opportunity to nibble on the lobe.

"What do you mean? They certainly are," She protests in mock horror. "My brothers want to get to know me."

"Dual purpose visit then," I appease her. "Though I suspect the dungeon's a major attraction."

"You can't blame them for that."

No, I can't. We've spent many an hour putting various items of equipment to use. To the satisfaction of us both. That sex swing had certainly fulfilled its promise.

She turns on my lap, unwittingly swivelling on my cock, making it start to harden. "Are you happy, Rais?"

Leaning down so my forehead rests against hers, I give her the answer immediately. "Happier than I ever thought I'd be. I don't deserve you, Aiza."

The minx feels how affected I am and wriggles her hips again. "I'm happy too, Rais. I'd be even happier if we made use of the dungeon before the weekend."

"You topping from the bottom again?"

Her lips meet mine, I don't turn her away, putting my hand behind her head and taking control. When we part her face is flushed, and at last she answers my question with a challenge in her eyes. "You bet I am."

I can't help but laugh. Aiza's perfect for me, our shared past a foundation on which we're basing our future. The thought that I could have lost her still haunts me, and not a day passes when I don't blame myself and want to make it up to her.

"Rais?"

"Habiti?"

"I'm free. I'm going to have a baby. I don't need to worry that someone's waiting to kidnap me." She looks at me sharply. "Don't blame yourself when what you did freed me."

I realise that I've started to frown, giving my sombre thoughts away. "I'll go to my grave regretting it."

Her hands rest on my arms, and she gives me a shake — well, as much as she can move me. "I love you, Rais. You never wanted to hurt me. Even you aren't infallible. I forgave you a long time ago. It's time you forgive yourself."

"I'll spend my life making it up to you."

She frowns. "No you won't. Anything you do should be out of love for me. Not your guilt."

Tangling my fingers in her hair, I gently pull her head back. "I love you, Aiza. Never, ever, doubt that."

"We all had hard choices to make, Rais. We're here now and happy because of the paths that we took."

"You're right, habiti." She is. I wrap the strands I'm holding more tightly in my fist. "The decisions we made brought us here."

As I bring her face to mine, she gives me that smile which looks like the sun coming out. "We shouldn't regret any of them."

Our lips meet, gently at first, then with more urgency. My cock hardens again. And, not for the first time, I end up fucking my *wife* over her desk.

EPILOGUE 2
Hunter

Rais fucking won. The motherfucker stole her away from me. That morning in the palace I was dismissed as if I was of no significance. Maybe I hadn't been all along. Perhaps I was just a diversion for her.

I hadn't seen Aiza since then. Ben had assigned me to a new case in the UK as soon as I returned. But I had heard her voice. Even as she was apologising for not speaking to me in person, it had been hard for her to keep her excitement and happiness out of her voice. I didn't need her to spell it out, the call leaving me in no doubt she's ended up with the man she really wants. The man she says she loves.

It had only taken my masochistic enquiry about the reasons for her choosing Rais over what Rami and I had to offer, to hear how she'd been secretly lusting after the desert sheikh from the time she became a woman and had first appreciated him as a man. I'd never had a chance, not when Rais had made his interest known.

If I'd possessed that knowledge at the time, would I still have tried to win her? I grin as I lean forwards, pick up my beer and take a few gulps. Of course I would. I'd have taken the challenge under any circumstances. And now I'm just being a sore loser. Hell, I'd even refused to go to the wedding, had torn up the invitation when it arrived. Now she's wed, pregnant and sickening happy. With him. Without me.

Did I really love her? Of that I'm not so sure. I lusted after her, that's a given. But love? In a rare moment of honesty I try to be truthful. I think I could have loved her. Would I have allowed her to be herself? Or tried to dominate her? One thing for sure, I'd never have allowed her to dominate me. The suggestion of a four-way relation- ship had appealed to me — what I was unable to give her, the others would have done. I had no doubts on my ability to share. But if I'm being straight with myself here, me and her, one on one… Well, the distance and time have made me accept we would probably have been a disaster.

Replacing the can on the table, I glance at the clock. *Is it too late to go to Club Tiacapan tonight?* Find a sub, maybe two, reserve one of the private rooms…

My phone rings, interrupting my thoughts. Picking it up I see *No Caller Id.* I accept the call, my finger hovering over the disconnect key suspecting I'm going to be sold life insurance or a new boiler.

"Hunter? It's Rami."

"Prince." My eyes open wide, for some strange reason, looking at the phone in disbelief. Why the fuck is he ringing me? I'd only reluctantly dropped the suspicions I'd had about him, even when we knew Rais was to blame.

There was something that made me uneasy about him. I just couldn't put my finger on what. That doesn't mean I can't do polite. "What can I do for you?"

"I'm glad you're still up."

Glancing at the clock I do a quick calculation. "It must be early where you are."

My comment elicits a strained laugh. "It's four am. I couldn't sleep."

Pulling the phone away from my ear, I stare at it again. *What's with the small talk? Does he think I've got a cure for his insomnia?*

Returning the device back into position, I ask, settling back on the couch, "What can I do for you, Rami?" I start to give up thoughts of going to Club Tiacapan tonight.

I hear an indrawn breath, then, "Have you heard from Aiza?"

"Not since before the wedding. You?"

Now he sighs. "I went to the wedding. I couldn't get out of it. Rais and Aiza, well... They're so happy together, Hunter. I might regret she's not with me, but I can't begrudge what they've found with each other."

I'm silent. His feelings are similar to mine, bringing forth compassion I've not really acknowledged before. His hurt is worse than my own, I hadn't lived years with the thought she was mine for the taking.

"I need to get away." He says so quickly it takes a moment to process the subject change.

"She wasn't right for you, Rami," I say wearily, while realising that statement equally applies to me.

"I know, Hunter. That morning when I left the suite, it," he pauses, and I know the next thing he says is going to be significant, "it wasn't just her I knew I'd lost."

Well I'll be fucked. Is he saying what I think he is?

"Rami…"

"Hunter, let me say this, please?" He cuts in fast before I can voice a dismissal. "I'm planning to come to London. And I'd like to go to Jasim's old club. I know you're a member."

"You've talked to Jasim." I'm not sure I like someone spilling my secrets.

"He thought I already knew. He didn't give you away, or only, by what he didn't deny."

I breathe in. Like Jasim must have done, listening to what he isn't saying. "You want to come to Club Tiacapan? With me? That won't work, Rami." I have to shut him down fast.

If he was here in person I think his nerve would have given out. But there's three thousand miles between us, and it surprises me when he laughs. "Not necessarily you, Hunter." There's a pause while he draws his thoughts together, and I wonder where he's going with this. "I wanted Aiza. Was happy when I thought we'd be together. But the arrangement we came up with, that changed my views. Gave me more possibilities to think about. I'm no stranger to clubs, but never a threesome. That's what I want to explore."

"You gay?" It wouldn't bother me if he was.

"No." But there's uncertainty in his answer, explained when he continues. "But, I might be…"

"Bi-sexual," I suggest for him.

He seems relieved. "Yes. I wouldn't have considered the arrangement if I wasn't. And I think you always knew that."

He's got me there. I stay silent.

"I wondered if at Club Tiacapan, we could find… someone to play with."

"A woman, as a third?"

"That's what I was thinking."

As he gives me time I sip my beer. Until his phone call I hadn't given Rami a thought since I'd left Amahad. While my brain insists I don't trust him, my body doesn't care. It seems to find the idea has some appeal, as my thickening cock tells me. "I'm making no promises, Rami. But if you come to England, I'll take you to the club and we'll take it from there." His bravery at making the call starts me re-evaluating him.

"That's all I can ask, Hunter."

"I'm not saying I'll do anything more than make intro-ductions. If I play, it will only be that. Nothing serious. No strings." It will be a long time before I consider having a relationship, and never with a man I'm not even sure that I like or respect.

"I understand." He sounds eager, not disappointed.

"Tell me when you're coming over. I'll get hold of the membership papers for you."

He thanks me, then I'm replacing the phone while thoughts race around my head. Memories of topping Rami come into my mind, the arousal when he followed my every instruction…

Rami, me, and the right woman…? Me topping them both?

I open my zip and tighten my hand around my cock, stroking from the root to the head. While my head scoffs at the idea of me topping the prince, my fingers keep working my cock that's quickly becoming rock hard as that visual comes into my mind.

OTHER WORKS BY MANDA MELLETT

Blood Brothers

- *Stolen Lives* (#1 – Nijad & Cara)
- *Close Protection* (#2 – Jon & Mia)
- *Second Chances* (#3 – Kadar & Zoe)
- *Identity Crisis* (#4 – Sean & Vanessa)
- *Dark Horses* (#5 – Jasim & Janna)
- *Hard Choices* (#6 – Aiza)

SATAN'S DEVILS MC

- *Turning Wheels* (Blood Brothers #3.5, Satan's Devils #1 – Wraith & Sophie)
- *Drummer's Beat* (#2 – Drummer & Sam)
- *Slick Running* (#3 – Slick & Ella)
- *Targeting Dart* (#4 – Dart & Alex)
- *Heart Broken* (#5 – Heart & Marc)
- *Peg's Stand* (#6 – Peg & Darcy)

Coming soon:
- *Rock Bottom* (#7 – Rock & Becca)

Sign up for my newsletter to hear about new releases:
http://eepurl.com/b1PXO5

ROCK
Bottom
SATAN'S DEVILS #7

Rock

*I've committed the ultimate crime, I've stolen from my MC.
Now, I'm out in bad standing.*

*Cast adrift from all men I called Brother, I join a rival MC.
They have welcomed me and want me to help them take out
the Satan's Devils.*

*Having to start from the bottom as a prospect is a shit job,
but I'm grateful they've given me a new home in exchange
for information about my old club.*

*The Chaos Riders are a completely different type of club,
and as I betray the Devils, I slowly learn the Riders' secrets.
Including what they keep in the basement.*

Becca

I've been kidnapped. Kept chained in this filthy place which reeks of blood. I can't remember the last time I showered or had a change of clothes, and I'm fed only enough to keep me alive.

As time passes, my hope of rescue fades. But then a new man appears bringing me my food and emptying that disgusting bucket I'm forced to use. Could he be my ticket to escape? Or is being a member of this hateful motorcycle club more important than saving me?

SATAN'S DEVILS #7: Rock Bottom

Brothers protecting their own

ACKNOWLEDGEMENTS

I've had so much support and encouragement for this series, reviews and messages letting me know that my readers are as in love with the Kassis brothers and the men from Grade A as I am. I thank everyone who's bought and read the Blood Brothers books, and especially those who've let me know how much they enjoy the series. You don't know how much those comments spur me on to keep writing.

My beta reading team are the absolute best! I'm so grateful for you reading a rough and ready book and giving me such excellent feedback to help me produce the final article. Thank you Mary, Danena, Terra, Sheri, Alex, Nicole and Zoe. Your help is invaluable and so much appreciated.

Once again, I must thank Lia Rees who brings my books alive with her brilliant cover designs.

Thanks again to Brian Tedesco, his first time editing a book in this series. It's been a pleasure working with you again.

Finally, thanks to my husband who as always supports me in my writing, and doesn't seem to mind when I zone out and live in a different world. And, of course, my son, who's always there to support me.

If you enjoy *Hard Choices*, or even if you don't, I'd love to hear from you. Authors love to read reviews of their books.

ABOUT THE AUTHOR

After commuting for too many years to London working in various senior management roles, Manda Mellett left the rat race and now fulfils her dream and writes full time. She draws on her background in psychology, the experience of working in different disciplines and personal life experiences in her books.

Manda lives in the beautiful countryside of North Essex with her husband and two slightly nutty Irish Setters. Walking her dogs gives her the thinking time to come up with plots for her novels, and she often dictates ideas onto her phone on the move, while looking over her shoulder hoping no one is around to listen to her. Manda's other main hobby is reading, and she devours as many books as she can.

Her biggest fan is her gay son (every mother should have one!). Her favourite pastime when he is home is the late night chatting sessions they enjoy, where no topic is taboo, and usually accompanied by a bottle of wine or two.

Email: manda@mandamellett.com

Website: www.mandamellett.com

Connect with me on Facebook:

https://www.facebook.com/mandamellett

Sign up for my newsletter to hear about new releases in the Blood Brothers and Satan's Devils series: http://eepurl.com/b1PXO5

Photo by Carmel Jane Photography

Made in the USA
Middletown, DE
30 April 2022